THE
ACCIDENT

R. J. TUMLIN

ISBN: 979-8-89419-037-2 (sc)
ISBN: 979-8-89419-038-9 (hc)
ISBN: 979-8-89419-039-6 (e)

Because of the dynamic nature of the Internet, any web addresses or links contained in this book may have changed since publication and may no longer be valid. The views expressed in this work are solely those of the author and do not necessarily reflect the views of the publisher, and the publisher hereby disclaims any responsibility for them.

THE EWINGS
PUBLISHING

One Galleria Blvd., Suite 1900, Metairie, LA 70001
(504) 702-6708

Chapter
ONE

....

On Fathers day, I was super excited and getting ready to pick up my father (Lance). A little bit of time passed and I was on my way. Me and my dad made plans to go out to eat, then go to the mall. I haven't seen him in forever. He's supposed to land at the Blue Grass Airport. I thought that he had stood me up. I left the airport, sad and frustrated, but most of all I was just disappointed.

I went back to my Mother's house and saw that no one was home. I went into the kitchen after turning the television on. I poured myself a glass of milk, listening to the news. Listening to what had happened, I froze. I felt like I was dreaming, I just couldn't believe it. I dropped my glass of milk, glass shattered, leaving a puddle of cold milk on the floor. I ran into the living room after hearing the reports of a seven forty seven crashing to the ground. There were ten people dead. The crash happened over an hour and a half ago. The plane went down somewhere in the state of Ohio. I grabbed the remote and turned the volume up louder. My Mother came through the back door unheard due to the high volume. "What is all this mess?" She said in a worried way.

I collapsed to my knees on the ground and just started crying. All that was clear at the moment were the numbers of the plane. I recognized the numbers of the plane from the scene on the television. My Mother notices me crying and asks, "Breea, honey! What's wrong? Where is your….." She turns to the television. She recognizes the numbers as well. She turns to me grabbing the remote, sits to cry and holds me as I cry.

After a few hours of crying hysterically. I get up and look straight at her and say, "Mom I can't be here. I gotta go help look for all the passengers. I need to know what happened and see if dad is okay." I rushed upstairs instantly, to pack my bag. Before I know it she's on her feet, going to the phone.

"Yes, I need to book a flight. I need it for the nearest time available to Wilmington, Ohio." She waits for the other person to say something.

"Yes, mam. I'm looking and we happen to have a flight leaving from the Blue Grass Airport at five o'clock. Is that enough time for you to get there?"

"Yes! Thank you!" She hangs the phone up and hollers up the stairs. "Breea, no time to pack. Got to go!" She walks over, grabs her purse and keys. Holding the door open for me, she finally realizes that my father may not be alive. For some God awful moment she starts crying hysterically.

I walk over to her to take the keys from her and say, "We don't need to have an accident. I'll drive to the airport." Then we were off to find out what had happened to cause the crash, and to find out if he was alive, harmed in any way or worse, dead.

We finally made it to the airport with just enough time to get to our gate for our plane. We were running our way through the crowd when a security officer noticed us. He walked up to us and asked, "What is the hurry ladies? We can't be running." He looks around to make sure no one else is going against the rules of the airport, then looks back at his Superior watching him. "Sorry, but it's the rules. We break them for you two, then everyone will think we'll let them by with it too."

He pauses for a moment, looking at both our eyes. "Something must have happened because both of you are crying. Come on, I can ask my Superior if we can give you two lifts to your gate." We walk over to his Superior, Charlie.

He talks to him for a few minutes and Charlie looks at us and sees for himself that his coworker isn't lying. "You ladies need to get to your gate?" Holding his hand out to support my Mother and me to get on the golf cart. "Hold on, Chris and I will get you two there." He hops on the front of the golf cart.

We get to the gate and Chris says smiling vigorously, "Here take my hand!"

As I was getting off, he took my hand and kissed the back side smiling. "Thank you so much for the lift to the gate," I say. "It means so much to us."

After getting off and walking over to the counter where we have to turn our tickets in before boarding the airplane, Chris runs up behind me. "I would really like it if we had the chance to be able to talk sometime." He reaches into his pocket and draws out a notepad. "Here's my number. Call or text me sometime, please." Then he gets back on the golf cart, and drives away with his Superior.

"We finally made it to the airplane!" My Mom, Quinn says.

I look down at my hands, rubbing the spot where Chris kissed my hand almost breaking out into tears and say, "Yea, finally. Now I just can't wait to get to Wilmington, Ohio to see if Dad is alive, badly injured and or dead." The rest of the flight was non-existent. We didn't know what time we had landed, because we fell asleep from all the crying that we had done earlier. We just remember the stewardess waking us up telling us that we had just landed and that people were unboarding. We both get up and grab our purses from the compartment overhead and walk out with the rest of the group.

We walk into the airport looking for a way to get through security without getting the special treatment. Much to my surprise, we got through without turning their heads. We were walking to the main entrance of this airport when we were spotted by a security guard. He runs over to us. "Hey, my name is Devin. I'm here to escort you ladies to wherever you may need to go." Smiling so big, he continues. "Chris from the Blue Grass Airport called me, wanted me to do him a favor. He knew that I had taken a two week vacation. He asked me to look out for you two while you were here. He said something about the plane crashing over in Wilmington and wanted to trust that you two were taken care of." He keeps walking alongside us and says, "Here we are. The main entrance to the airport. If you guys stay right here, I'll be right back with my car." He takes off running.

My Mom and I just look at each other. Smiling, my Mom says, "I guess you just stole a man's heart right out from under his nose."

I looked at her and rolled my eyes. What do I know of the Chris guy? Why would I want to steal someone's heart that I don't even know right from under him. Yes, it was nice of him to treat us the way he did! I won't forget that, but that isn't a reason to want the guy's phone number. I just reach into my purse and pull out the number that Chris wrote down, I wad it up and throw it into the nearest trash can. When I do I hear Devin ask, "What are you doing?" He pulls the trash can lid off and head dives into it to retrieve the paper that he saw me throw away. "He just doesn't give his number out to anyone! Keep it and put it in your phone. He wanted you to have it." He walks up to his passenger door and lets my Mom in. He walks around to the driver's side door, lifts the front seat up and says, "Here you go!" Pointing for me to climb in the back seat behind him.

I climb into the backseat, get my seatbelt on and look at my Mom. She's crying again, I can't even begin to make myself cry. So, I think of something to say. "Mom, I know you may not be thinking about food right now, but I'm hungry. Could we please stop to get something to eat?" I look into my purse and see that Chris not only gave me one piece of paper but three. I take them all three out and look at them. As I'm looking at all three of them I notice that on the third one there's a note on the back of it. It reads:

I don't know what your name is, but I would really like to

Get to know you. Who are you? Where have you been? If

You date? Just in case you try to throw my number away in

A trash can, I want you to know that my thoughts are with you.
I wouldn't do this for anyone else that I might happen to run
into at the airport. I hope that my friend Devin at the Columbus
Airport will help you and your mother out in this difficult time.
Hope to hear from you soon!!

;)

Chris

As I put the note back into my purse I noticed that we were stopping to get a bite to eat at Wendy's. I didn't even notice my Mom asking me, "Bree, honey. What would you like to eat?"

"I don't even know yet." I stuffed the notes back into my purse and got out with my Mom and Devin. He looked at me real funny like and smiled real big. I looked at him and asked, "What? What's so funny?"

"Nothing!" Devin answers while he's texting away on his phone. "Just texted Chris." Smiling, he turns around and types away on his phone again. So I decided to get the notes out of my purse while my Mom was up ordering the food for us to eat. I text, "hey, my name is breea. Yes, I am allowed to date. I have been living in lexington, kentucky all my life. Where have u been;)" Then I punch in his number and hit send.

A few minutes later a text came through. "Hey breea! That's a pretty name. I've lived in lexington, kentucky all my life also. I'm 21 yrs old. I live in and own a house now by myself. How old r u? It's great that you decided to text me. I'm so happy that u did. ;)"

I replied back. "Yea, i may seem like i didnt want to at first, but now im kind of glad that i did. Im 18 yrs old."

As I was eating my food Devin gets up and says, "Hey, I have to make a visit to the restroom. You ladies might want to too, before we head out on the road again." He walks away.

My Mom gets up and says that she's got to go to the bathroom and asks me, "Are you going to be okay out here all by yourself?"

"Yea, Mom." I look up at her and she seems like she's about to cry again. "Mom, just because we're doing this doesn't mean that he didn't survive. There were a number of bodies that weren't found so far. He could be passed out and hear anyone holler for him. Don't cry until we know for sure that he's gone." I looked back down at my cell phone to see if there was a text. There was!

"So you're about to go to college then? Maybe i could come by when you all get back, meet the parents and maybe we could go out on a date. Go see a movie or something. What is your favorite kind of movie?"

I text him back. "My fav (favorite) kind of movie is comedy or romance. It's a tie breaker between those 2 (two). I think u (you) may have already figured that 1 (one) out tho (though)."

As I got done sending that message, Devin comes back out and says, "Just talked to Chris. He says you've been texting him. How did you two meet?"

"We met at the airport on my way up here." I go and dump mine and Mom's tray into the trash can. Then I sat down beside him. "So how do you know Chris?"

"We grew up together." Devin smiles real big. "I moved up here after getting a job at the airport here. I had to leave all of my friends back in Lexington. I never thought that for one second that I would regret it one day."

"Why do you regret it?"

"Well, for the most part people up here are a lot different than people in Lexington. I just miss being with my friends and family. When I want to get away from it all up here, something always comes up." He looks down at his hands and sighs. "You know I'm glad Chris has finally met someone that he's interested in. I'm happy for him."

I look at him with concern written on my face and ask, "Why haven't you met someone?"

He looks down at his hands again and answers, "Girls up here are a lot different than girls down in Lexington. I had a girlfriend when I first started up here." He pauses to catch his breath. "But, she didn't want to stay with someone who was just a security guard. She wanted someone who could be there at her beck and call. She basically didn't know what she wanted until it was too late for her and I to realize that we were about to screw things up too much with each other."

"Oh, that sounds complicated." I looked toward the bathrooms to see if my Mom was coming out yet. "Why haven't you and this girl ever talked about what happened with the both of you? My parents always say that the key to any relationship is communication. Why didn't you all try to talk it over with each other?"

"Well, for one she was so concerned with what her friends had with their boyfriends. She wanted someone to be there with her twenty four seven. I couldn't be that guy. I need my space." He pauses for a few seconds. "Sure it was different in the beginning. Something new and exciting, but after a while we got to know each other well. I found myself disgusted with her. The way she dressed, the way she acted and most importantly the way she thought that I should be there with her on my time off."

"Oh, that sounds like it got serious pretty quickly. What has happened to her since the last time you saw her?"

"For one, she works at the airport in one of the restaurants. She gives me the evil eye everytime I see her now. She resents me for being the way that I am. I can't be with someone like that for the rest of my life." He pauses and crosses his arms across his chest. "She wanted us to get married and have children. I didn't realize how bad it was until she had said she was pregnant with my child."

"Wow, sounds like a soap opera here." I said smiling. "What happened to the child?"

He looks at me and answers, "Well it turns out that she wasn't really pregnant. She was just telling me that so that I wouldn't break things off with her."

"How did you know that she was lying about the pregnancy?"

"I noticed one day out of the blue that her birth control pills were in the bathroom on the counter. I looked in the pouch and saw that all of them had been taken. I'm not that smart, but I do know when a woman is pregnant, that she shouldn't be taking her birth control. So, I said that was it. I had enough of her trying to manipulate me into marrying her, when all along our relationship was based on nothing but a lie." He looks down at his feet and says, "I found out two weeks later she was seeing another guy behind my back."

"Oh, that seems to be the most God awful story that I've ever heard." I put my hand up to my heart and ask, "Well, why not move back home?"

Devin thought about that question for a while. He looks up at me smiling, "I didn't think of that. I want to go back, but I'm afraid that I won't be able to get a job down there." He looks at his phone and realizes that my Mom hasn't come out of the bathroom yet. "Hey, where is your Mom?"

I look up and say, "I don't know. Let me go check on her!" I get up and walk toward the bathroom. I open the door and go in. "Mom? Are you still here?"

She sniffs and says, "Yea, I'm still in here. Sorry honey, just trying to get myself together." She flushes the toilet and comes out. "Sorry if I scared you." She washes her hands and asks, "Is Devin ready to go?"

"Yea, I think he is." My cell phone vibrates. It's three text messages from Chris. "Yea, i already fig (figured) that 1 (one) out. Haha! U doin (doing) good so far?" The next one I open up. "U (you) there? Jw" (meaning just wondering) The last one I open up. "Hey i got to go back to work txt (text) me when u get service or some spare time. Whatever u do dont bring up devin's ex. It puts a spell on him, and u and ur (your) mom need to be around someone who is goin (going) to b (be) positive.

Ttyl (talk to you later) baby!" As I read that last text I get to thinking, already too late for that one. I open my phone and text him back. "Yea, it's too late for that! He brought it up tho. Y (why) r (are) u calling me baby? Jw. hes (he is) wanting to move back to lexington. Maybe if u could help him get on at the airport there, that he might go ahead with his plan to come back home. Have fun at work ;) ttyl tonight."

We head out onto the road once again. We were listening to the reports of the crash on the radio when Devin turned it down and said, "Hey, you know what you all need?"

My Mom and I both just look at him, with amused looks on our faces. We both ask at the same time, "What?"

He looks across to my Mother, then to me and answers smiling. "You all need to listen to some of this music." Putting a compact disc in he turns it up. "We don't need to listen to any more reports about the crash. We'll find out what it's all about when we get there." So the rest of the ride to Wilmington we listened to his compact disc.

My Mom asks, "Devin, no offense to you or anyone else, but what kind of music is this?"

Devin laughs out loud and answers, "It's punk rock. It would do you some good to listen to something like this, at a time like this. I don't want to get into the subject of talking about the crash, so I thought that this might make you two laugh a little." He kept his eyes on the road. "We'll be pulling into Wilmington around ten thirty tonight. Where would you like to stay the night?" He asks, looking over at my Mom.

She looks toward the back at me, and says, "I don't know. Where do you suggest we stay? We've never been up here before. We don't know what our options are." She looks down at her left hand. "We do have to go get some clothes and things. Would you mind taking us to a store in the morning? We need you to be with us through this difficult time. I'll pay for your hotel room and whatever else you may need." She looks over at him.

Devin looks in the rear view mirror and answers, "Yes, I can do that. I took a two week vacation anyways. I can surely help you two through this tough time. I mean it's the least I can do." He looks straight ahead. My Mom looks back toward me and says, "Breea, honey. I want to know if you would like to ride up front for a while? I'm really wanting to take a nap."

I look at her and shake my head. "If you can get Devin to pull over, I wouldn't mind sitting up front with him." I look over to a sign on the side of the highway. "There's a rest stop there. Pull into it, Devin."

He pulled into the rest stop to let me out. My Mom got out of the passenger side and lifted the seat up. She climbed in the back and layed down. I got into the front seat, putting my seatbelt on and I noticed Devin smiling. I look over at him and ask, "What are you smiling about now?"

"Nothing, just remembering some good memories. I'm really glad you agreed to get up front to let your Mother rest in the back seat." He looks in his rear view mirror to check for traffic or pedestrians before backing out of the spot. "Look at her, already asleep. You two must get along great."

I look back and see her sleeping already. "Yea, I guess we do pretty good. She's everything to me and my Father. If it wasn't for her, my Father's Mother wouldn't have the care that she deserves to this day. She would have already passed away." I look back at my Mom and remember the day that she asked me if she could adopt me. I look at Devin and say, "I remember the day that she asked me if it was okay with me if she adopted me. I had this look on my face, wondering what I do to deserve this woman for my Mother. For my Father, it was his happiest day ever. His two girls are under the same roof, getting along."

Devin looks at me and asks, "What? She's not your birth mother?"

"No, she adopted me when I was seven. I was living with my Father when my birth mother passed on giving birth to her ninth child. Complications during childbirth. I didn't know her that well, so it didn't really bother me too much."

"Oh, I didn't know that. I'm sorry that you lost your birth mom." Devin says, staring straight ahead. "You said your birth mother passed on giving birth to her ninth child?"

"Yes, why?"

"Well, just wondering if she's my birth mother. I was adopted by my Parents as well, who are Darrin and Dianna DeAtley. When my Mother was found unfit and she was pregnant with her ninth child. What year were you born?"

"I was born on September eleventh nineteen ninety four. That's the reason I was with my father, because they found my birth mother unfit. What year were you born?"

"I was born on November twenty fourth nineteen ninety one." He looked into his left side mirror then and flipped his turn signal on. "What was your birth mother's name?"

I got to thinking of what my Dad used to say, but it was so long ago that I can't remember. "I think he used to say her name was Billie Dawn Stevens." I get to thinking back into the past and remember now it was Billie Dawn. "She was named after her biological father."

"Yea, that's my mom's name too. When did you find out about her passing away?"

"I found out when I was seven. She came by the house and asked my Father if she could see me. He agreed because he was in love with her. I saw her alright. I remember her being pregnant. I asked her how many children this makes her and she said it was her ninth one. She told me that I had other brothers and sisters out there somewhere. She couldn't afford to take care of us like she should have been able to, so she gave us up. She looked at my Father and told him that she loved him but not enough to marry him and take care of the kids she had at the time. Come to think of it, I think she said their names were Darion, Cara, Daimon, Callie, Devin, Camerin, Chelsea and Dalton and of course then there was me. That I was the youngest, the eighth child, and now she was going to have the ninth." I pause to take a break from talking, then I start telling the story. "She said she and my Father met at a bar one night. They hit it off and started a relationship. It didn't last of course. She broke my Father's heart. I can forgive her for breaking his heart like she did. After she had me, she ran off and found another man that didn't treat her too well."

"Yea, I remember that time. She came by my adoptive parents house while she was pregnant with the ninth one. She wanted to tell me that she loved me and that she wanted me to forgive her for giving me up. I did, I forgave her. That was the last time that I ever saw her. I knew I had other sisters and brothers out there somewhere, but I would never dream of taking one of my youngest sisters to a plane crash site with her adoptive Mother." He looks over at me and says, "It's a small world huh? Wait til we tell Chris about this."

I look over at him and laugh along with him. "Have you ever met any of our birth mother's boyfriends before?"

"No, but I guess I'm about to though." Then it was silent for about an hour. He looks over and sees that I fell asleep. He hears his phone ringing so he pulls his cell phone out and sees that it's Chris. He pushes a button and answers, "Chris, what's up buddy?"

"Not much dude. Where are you guys at?"

"Oh, we're just about to pull into the hotel parking lot. We're all staying for a couple of days. What's up?"

"Not much. Just took a two week vacation. I was wondering, how long of a drive is it to Wilmington from Lexington?"

"Oh, I'd say it's about three hours at least. Why, you coming up?"

"Yes, I was thinking about it. I figured why not, right? How is Breea doing?"

"She's fine. She fell asleep about an hour ago. Guess what we discovered tonight."

"What's that?"

"You know how I told you that I was adopted?"

"Yea, don't tell me that Breea's Mom and Dad are your biological parents!"

"No, nothing like that." He looks over at me and smiles. "Um, her Mother isn't her real Mother. She adopted Breea when she was seven years old. Breea lived with her Father, which is her biological Father, when he met the woman that you saw at the airport. Breea and I discovered that we are brother and sister. We discussed this on the way up here. She told me the birthdate of her biological Mother and I told her that it was the same as mine. It turns out that we are brother and sister."

"Well, dude, that's nice to hear. At least now I don't have to worry about you hitting on my girl." Laughing he continues. "I know she's not mine yet, but I'm going to try to get her to date me. I mean, is that okay by her big brother?"

"Hey, man, no worries. Even if we weren't brother and sister, I wouldn't even dare dream about trying to hit on her. You mean more to me than that dude." He pulls into the hotel parking lot. "Hey, man. Can you hold on a minute? I gotta get Breea's Mom, Quinn up from her nap. We're at the hotel." He reaches back with his right arm and shakes Quinn awake. "We're here." He's pointing up to the sign and says, "Go on in. I'll wait here with Breea while you get the rooms." She gets up and gets out on the driver's side since he was already out waiting on her. "Hey, you there Chris?"

"Yes, I'm here. Are you all okay?"

"Yea, man. Just got to the hotel parking lot. Had to wake Quinn up. She's walking inside the office now to get us rooms tonight." He looks in on me to see if I'm still asleep and I am. "Hey, I'm going to ask this real quick while someone is still asleep. Are you coming up or not, man?"

"Yea, what hotel are you all staying at? You can give me the room numbers later while I'm driving there."

"We're staying at the Hampton Inn in Wilmington, off of US23. I guess I'll see you in a few hours then? Be careful. Talk to you later dude." They hang the phone up and Devin sees that Quinn is walking out toward the vehicle. He looks at her and asks, "So, we got rooms here?"

"Yea, we do. Thank you for doing this for us. I will have to thank Chris for sending you." She opens the door and says, "Breea, honey. We're at the hotel now. Come on sweetie, get up." She looks over at Devin and says, "I heard the conversation between you and Breea

13

tonight. I'm glad that she's actually found one of her siblings. It means so much to her right now."

They all climb the steps to the rooms of the hotel. My Mother, Quinn and I are sharing room two forty eight, and Devin is in room two forty nine. He gets to our door and helps us both in. He grabs the key to his room and walks on over. Quinn, and I both get into the bed and don't even think of getting anything to drink from the mini bar or turning the television on. We just climb into the bed and sleep.

Devin is in his room enjoying cold water and a candy bar. He pulls his phone out and dials up Chris' number. "Hey, dude. What's up?"

Chris answers, "Nothing much. Watching these stupid idiots on I74. They're crazy out tonight aren't they?"

"Yea, man they sure are. Be careful. I was just calling to let you know that we are in our rooms and I'm going to stay up and wait on you. My room number is two forty nine and Quinn and Breea's room number is two forty eight, right next to ours."

"Okay, dude. Thanks so much for doing this for me. I have something that I want to tell you as soon as I get there. I'm not telling you until I get there either. Do you know how Breea's Mom is paying for the rooms?"

"No, I sure don't, but if I know a woman pretty well, I'd say it's with a credit card. Why?"

"Just wondering. I thought I might pick the tab up. So, I'm coming up on the exit of Columbus, I need to get off here so that I can concentrate on driving. Talk to you when I get to the hotel. Bye!" He goes on driving listening to the radio. He hears something about a report of the passengers on the plane that crashed. "The latest update on the plane crash in Wilmington, is they have found four more people dead on the scene. There are sixty two that are in critical condition, and only three were taken to the emergency room at Clinton Memorial Hospital. No injuries but overnight observations. They are trying everything they can to contact the families of the victims. They have said what caused the plane to crash was a mechanical error. We'll have more on the next update time. Thank you for listening to Walh."

"Man, I only hope, wish and pray that Breea's Father is one of the luckier ones that didn't get badly injured or passed on." Chris says. It's only twelve fifteen when he reaches his exit. He texted a co-worker that had stayed at the Hampton Inn in Wilmington to get the address, earlier that day before leaving to head this way. "Man, I can't wait to get there. I want to see Breea's face when I show up to take her and her Mother to the store to get a few things. I can't wait to see her Mother's face when I tell her that I'm going to pay for their stay at the hotel and whatever else they may need while we're all here." He notices that he's starting to get close because he can see the sign. He slows down and turns right into the parking lot. He parks right beside Devin's car. He gets his cell out and calls Devin.

"Hello?" Devin answers on the first ring.

"Hey, man. It's me Chris. Did you fall asleep? I'm walking into the office now."

"No, I was awake. I told you I was going to be waiting on you. Why are you going to the office right now, for?"

"So, I can get the rooms put into my name and pay for them. I'll be up in a minute. Our room does have double beds right?"

"Yes dude, it does. See you in a little bit then." Devin hangs the phone up and walks out onto the balcony to see if the lights are on in our room. They were off and surprisingly so dark. "Breea will be so surprised when she wakes up and finds that Chris is here to take them to the store in the morning." Chuckling to himself he goes back to his door and waits on Chris. He notices that someone is walking up the steps now. He looks harder and notices the build on the guy. "That's definitely Chris." He starts running toward the man. "Hey, man! Good to see you!"

"Good to see you too, buddy. I don't know about you but I'm beat. Let's go in." They went into their room and found their beds. Neither one of them went to the mini bar to get anything, nor did neither one of them wanted to talk to catch up. They were too tired and went right to sleep.

Chapter
TWO

The next morning, I was up before my Mother. So, she decides that she's going to go see if Devin is up also. She gets a piece of paper and writes her Mother a note.

> Mom,
>
> Don't worry. I just went to see what Devin is into. When you wake up, you can come to his room.
>
> Love,
>
> Breea

I open the door without waking my Mother up. I shut it as quietly as I could and walked next door. I knock on the door quietly. I wait for a few minutes then knock a little harder. "Devin, you up?" After a few minutes he hadn't answered so I figured he was still asleep. I start to walk back toward my room when the door opens and Devin steps out. "I thought you were still asleep. I didn't wake you, did I?"

"No, you didn't wake me. I was already up. I hate hotel beds. They aren't anything like your own." He stretches. "So, what's up?"

"Not much, just got so much going on in my head right now it isn't funny. I'm just ready to get this day started. I want to find him and make sure that if he is passed on, that he gets to come home with us and gets the proper burial that he deserves." Rubbing my hands absently.

"Yea, I know what you mean. I have a feeling that everything is going to be alright and you'll have your Father with you for the rest of your life." He looks back to his room, noticing that Chris is up. "Hey, I'll be right back. Got to go to the restroom." He opens his door and walks in, shutting the door quickly behind him. "Hey, I was wondering when you were going to get up. She's up and she's outside waiting for me to use the restroom. If you want to, go outside and talk to her. I'll come to the window and let you know when it's safe to bring her in." He walks to the bathroom.

"Okay." Chris says smiling. He opens the door quietly and tiptoes up behind me. He puts his arms around my midsection and asks, "Guess who?"

I turn around smiling and answer, "You scared me. I thought….. wait a minute. What are you doing here?"

"I thought I would come to help you. I know that you have your brother and all to help but, nothing helps more than having a guy here that's interested in you to help." Chris says smiling. "Besides, I took a two week vacation. I couldn't stand that you would be up here going stir crazy. I wanted to come up and help you, be here for you. Is that okay with you?"

"Yea, thank you." I put both of my arms around him, hugging him and thanking him.

"You're very welcome, baby! I'm glad to be here." We stayed like that for more than five minutes. Embraced in each other's arms and enjoying the time we have together. Chris turned me around to see if he could see Devin giving him the signal and sure enough, Devin was right there. "Hey, you want to go into the room?"

"Yea." I grab his hand and walk to the door with him. Devin opens it up from the inside of the room. "Thank you, bub." I sit down on the bed that's nearest the door. Chris sits down right beside me. "I sure wish that my Mom would wake up. I'm ready to get this day over with and hopefully won't have to find my Father in that wreckage. I'm ready to make sure he's okay." I look up and smile at both of them.

"Okay, on that note. Let me go grab some breakfast. It's on me. I'll bring it back here and if Quinn isn't up before I get back, I'll wake her up on my way back to the room." Devin says. He grabs his keys and walks out, leaving Chris and I in the room by ourselves.

"I'm sure glad that I made this trip!" Chris says happily. "When I ran into you and your Mom yesterday at the airport I couldn't get a handle on my job. I couldn't think of anything but you and what you must be going through. I wanted so badly to hop on the plane with you yesterday."

"Really?" I pause for a few seconds. "That is really nice of you. I wouldn't want to. Not for two strangers I just met." I looked down at the hand that he kissed, smiling and said, "Thank you for calling your friend. Mom and I wouldn't know what to do or how to get to the site if it weren't for you. I'm forever indebted to you for it. You're one of the sweetest guys that I have ever met." I hugged and gave him a kiss on the cheek.

"Awh, it's okay. It'll be okay. I'm here for you no matter what from now on." He took my face into his hands and kissed me lightly on the lips. We sat there hugging each other until Devin got back.

"Is Quinn up yet?"

"No, not that we know of." Chris answers.

"Okay, I'll go get her." Devin closes the door and walks over to mine and Mom's room. He knocks on the door and asks, "Quinn, it's me Devin, are you up?"

The door opens and she's standing there. "Yea, I'm up. I was just heading over to your room. Is my daughter over there?"

"Yes, she is. Come on, I got us some breakfast, it's in my room." He walks in front of Quinn guiding her to his room that she thinks she paid for. When she reaches his room she doesn't expect to see Chris there.

Quinn walks into the room and gasps. "Chris, what are you doing here?" She asks him while walking over to give him a hug.

"I got some time off to help you all out here." He reaches up to her and hugs her back. "I hope that's not a problem with you?"

"No, no! You're more than welcome to join us. I'll have to let the office know about you being here though." She walks over to where Devin is getting himself an egg mcmuffin and reaches into the bag for herself to have one. "Bree, have you eaten?"

"No, mom. I haven't. I'm getting something right now though." I walk over to her and stick my hand in the bag to get myself an egg mcmuffin and open the wrapper. I take a big bite of it and walk back over to Chris and sit down beside him.

Chris gets up and walks over to where Quinn is sitting and gets himself an egg mcmuffin and says, "I have already let the office know that I'm here in this room with Devin. I have taken care of the expenses on both rooms too. I want you to know that I'm here to help in any way possible." He walks back over to me and sits down. He smiles real big at me and my Mother. "Did I hear right ladies? Did I hear that you all needed to go to the store to get some things?"

My Mom looks at him with a smile and answers, "Yes, we sure do. Would you be so kind as to let us take your vehicle and go?"

He looked over at his friend Devin and smiled real big. "I'll make you all a deal. Why don't we all go? That way we can all get some things. Then after we get done at the store and bring the things back to our rooms, we'll go to the crash site or surrounding hospitals."

Quinn looks at me and says, "All right. That sounds good, but I'm the one that will buy the things that we all will need." She looks down at her hands and says, "Besides, we're the ones that needed to come up here, not you two. We appreciate what you two are doing for us, but you don't need to pay for everything."

Chris and Devin look at each other and Chris says, "Okay, you got yourself a deal, besides I don't need anything. I have everything that I need with me." He winks at me smiling with his arms crossed over his chest.

So we all get ready to go to the store. We all get into Chris' truck and go to the nearest Wal-Mart. It's Chris driving, me in the passenger seat, Mom in the back behind me and Devin also in the back behind Chris. She notices that we went right by Wal-Mart the night before. So she looks over at Devin and asks, "Why didn't you stop last night? We went right by here, didn't we?"

Devin looks over at her and answers, "Yes we did, but I didn't think you'd want me to wake you or your daughter though. Sorry, I would have if I'd known you would have wanted that."

"That's okay. I was just wondering about it." She looks at the parking lot. She wonders if they will have everything that we'll need right now. She looks up front and asks Chris, "Do you think that we should start at the crash site first or look at the surrounding hospitals?"

He looks in his rear view mirror, smiles and answers. "It's whatever you feel would be best." He looks over at me and asks, "Which one do you think would be best to do first? On the way up here I heard over the radio about the reports from the crash site. Four more people have been found and were presumed to be passed on, sixty four more have been taken to the nearest hospital in critical condition, and three have been sent to the nearest hospital for x-rays and observations overnight, then sent on home." He looks back and continues. "It's entirely up to you two." Looking at both me and my Mom. "Remember, Devin and I are here to serve you two. Whatever you feel is best to do first, then that's what we'll do. No expense expected from either of you." He looks at me smiling and says, "Just that Breea here would agree to go out on a date with me when we're done with all of this. That would be enough." He pauses looking at both me and my Mother, and says. "I'm doing this for you all because I really would like to get to know Breea a little better. I really want to spend time with her."

Quinn studies him for a minute or two before she answers for me, "I think that could be arranged." She squeezes my shoulder and smiles. She remembers when her husband, my Father used to look at her like that. She sighs and just looks out the window while Chris is parking his truck. We all get out and walk into Wal-Mart.

Quinn and I go in our own direction to shop for some clothes for the duration of our stay. Chris and Devin both go to the health and beauty section. Chris is following Devin and tells him his big news that he's got for Devin. "Hey, man. There's something that I have to tell you." He pauses for a few seconds looking around and continues. "You remember our phone conversation, when I was on my way up to meet you all?" He looks over at Devin and sees that he's shaking his head up and down. "Well, I put in a request for you to be transferred to the airport back home." He puts his hands in his shorts pockets.

"You did what?" Devin looks at him.

"I put in a request for you to be transferred to the airport back home. So that you can be closer to your friends and family again. I hope that was okay with you?" Chris answers.

Devin looks down at the things that he has put in the cart. He brings his arms up and hugs Chris in the middle of Wal-Mart. "I can't believe that you did that." He lets go of the hug and asks, "How did you know that I wanted that to happen? What did they say?"

Chris chuckles a little and answers. "If it wasn't for Breea texting me and telling me that, then it wouldn't have happened. I haven't heard their answer from them yet. They're supposed to call you first and then call me to let me know what they said. If it does happen I hope you know that you can live with me in my house."

"Okay, cool. Thanks so much for doing that for me. I was going to put in for a transfer, but never did. I kept thinking that me and my ex were going to get back together until last week. She's already engaged."

Chris just looks at him and says, "Hey, man. No disrespect to you or to her, but from what I do know about her, why would you want to stay just because of her?"

"I don't know. Sometimes I think that it's going to work out with the two of us, then I get to work and see her with the other guy that she was cheating on me with and think that it won't. I guess I was just hoping man. She was my first love." Devin looks down at his feet. Then when he looks up he sees my Mom and I walking toward them with a cart full of things smiling at each other talking. He says, "That's enough about me though. How do you think that this relationship with my little sister is going to last? I know I haven't known her all my life, but she's still my little sister all the same. I've got to look after her feelings."

Chris looks behind him, smiles and answers Devin. "Dev, man. You know me better than that. You know I wouldn't do anything to hurt her in any way humanly possible. I'm not talking about marriage with her just yet. Just to let you know, that's where I hope it goes with her though." He turns to us ladies approaching them and smiles real big. "You two got everything you needed?"

My Mom answers smiling, "Yes, Chris. We sure have but not all of it yet. There are still some things that we still need though. Would you mind going with Bree to the makeup? She needs some new makeup, a hair brush and hair scrunchies."

He looks over at Devin smiling and says, "Sure will! I don't mind at all. It would be my pleasure." Chris and I walk toward the makeup section smiling at each other and just talking up a storm. Chris grabs my hand and holds it while we're walking.

Mom looks over at Devin and asks, "You know what his story is with my Daughter?"

Devin just looks at her and answers, "Mrs. Anderson, I wouldn't worry about him breaking her heart if that's what you are asking."

She looks back at the two of us walking and says, "Okay, I just got to make sure that he won't break her heart. I have a feeling that her heart is going to be broken when we find out what happened to her Father, Lance." She looks down at her cart full of things, sighs while a tear slides down her cheek. Looking back up at Devin, she continues. "I'm glad that she has found you though. You'll look after her right, no matter what happens? Because if we find him there at the sight and he's passed on, I don't know if I could carry on without him."

Devin just looks at her. Confused and says, "I'll tell you what. I'll look out for her if you can promise me that you will take the time, if he is passed on, and find yourself again. I know it's going to be hard to do so, but you have Breea to think of first and foremost. Then you have me and Chris here to help with anything that you may need help with. Anytime, anyplace and anywhere. Okay?"

"Okay, thank you for what you just said." She starts sniffling and trying to cover up her tears before Chris and I get back. "So, is this what you need, or do you need some clothes too?"

Devin looks at her and smiles, shaking his head from side to side. "I have to get an outfit or two, that is if you don't mind?"

"I don't mind. It's whatever we all may need. I know Bree and I didn't even have time to pack anything. So that's why we're here. Get what you need and we'll all meet up front by the cash registers. I've got to get a few more things and then I'll be ready." She pushes the cart to the makeup section herself and Devin follows her. He doesn't want to be by himself right now and doesn't want to be the third wheel with Chris and I. So he just stays with Mom.

Chris picks up a color of eyeshadow that he thinks that would look good with my hazel eyes and says. "I think this would look good with your eyes."

I look at it and ask, "You think so?" I take it from him and put it up next to my eye and say. "I think it does." Laughing with Chris. I turn around and see my Mom and brother are walking towards us. "Hey, Mom! Chris says that this color looks good with my eyes." I hold it up for her to see and giggle.

"I think it does too!" She looks for herself with some foundation and blush. Then she turns to the guys and says, "You all want to watch us pick our makeup out or do you want to go and get some other things?"

Chris and Devin both look at each other. Smiling Devin says, "I have to go get a few outfits."

Chris looks at my Mother and I and says, "I don't need anything, but I'll go with Devin and help him out."

Quinn says, "Okay, you two want to meet us up front at the cash registers when we're all done?"

Devin says, "Yea, that'll be fine." Chris and Devin both take off walking toward the men's clothing section. Devin looks over at Chris and notices something different about his friend. He looks at him real carefully and says, "Hey, I got questioned by Quinn earlier."

Chris looks at Devin and asks, "Oh, yea? What about?"

"Well, she was wanting to know what the deal is with you and Breea?"

"What do you mean by, "What the deal is?""

"Well, she was wanting to know if you only want one thing and break her heart or do you truly want to be there for her, have a committed relationship with her?"

"Oh!" Chris sighs, and continues. "I don't know buddy. Don't get me wrong, I like her. I like her enough to even think about settling down with her." He sighs and says, "I just want to take my time with her. I don't know what's going to happen between us, but I do know one thing."

"Oh, yea! What's that?" Devin asks.

"I know that if it doesn't work out between Breea and I that we'll still be friends. I'll still be here for her when I'm not even with her. No matter if I even find Mrs. Right."

"Good answer!" Devin says smiling. "I want it to work out between you and Breea. I've never seen you look at another girl like you look at Breea before. It's like you both belong to each other. Like you two were made for each other." Devin finds a couple of shorts that he likes and heads in the direction of socks.

Chris notices some bathing suits that are on clearance. He picks up two pairs of trunks, one blue for Devin and a pair of black ones for him. Then he notices that women's suits are even on sale. He goes over to the rack and picks out a white bikini suit with pink polka dots for me and finds a pink full bodysuit for Quinn. He picks them up and puts them in the cart and looks at Devin. He says, "I hope that we will have some time to swim while we're here."

Devin looks at him smiling and says, "Yea, that's what we'll all need when things calm down a bit." He looks at the suits and says, "Hopefully they'll fit the girls."

Chris looks down at them and says, "They will. I'm going to buy them for all of us."

Devin looks at him and says, "You know you don't have to buy mine. I do have a bank card that I do happen to have money on. I can get my own things."

"I know that, bub. I just want to make sure that it's not going to be hard on you when you move back to Lexington." Chris says smiling.

Devin looks at him with concern on his face. "What do you mean, "When i move back?", have you heard from them?"

Chris smiles and says, "All I can say is that you should be expecting your phone to be ringing any minute now." Just then Devin's phone starts ringing.

He looks down at it and sees that it's his airport. He answers it. "Hello?"

"Is this Devin DeAtley?"

"Yes, this is me. Who may I ask, is calling?"

"This is Steve Wallingford. I'm your supervisor at Columbus Airport. I saw that you were requested for a transfer. When did you need the transfer to take place?"

"Anytime, sir. Anytime would be greatly appreciated."

"Okay, I see here that you are on a two week vacation right now. Is that correct?"

"Yes, sir, that is correct."

"Okay, if you could stop by the airport tomorrow and sign the transfer papers, then it would be processed by the time you get there to work. You could use your vacation time as a packing up, and traveling time."

"Alright, thank you sir. Thank you so much for this opportunity for me to get back home. I'll be there tomorrow around twelve pm to sign the paperwork." He hangs the phone up and continues with his shopping, smiling.

The men finally get done with their shopping and run into us women looking at the pajamas. Chris sneaks behind me, puts his arms around me and hugs me. I look back and smile. "Hey!"

Chris answers, "Hey, baby!"

I notice that Devin is standing there all by himself. I look at him and walk over to him and give him a hug. "Hi, bub." Smiling, I walk over to Chris and hug him. "I want you to know that I'm really excited about our date when we get back." I walk over to the pajama shorts and look at them some more. I notice that in Devin's cart that there are two bathing suits and two pairs of swim trunks. I look at Devin and Chris and ask. "What are these?"

Chris looks down to what I'm pointing at and answers, "Well the hotel has a pool. I love to swim as well as Devin does. So, I figured that we would all go swimming sometime after we found your Father. Just an activity to wash all the bad things away and give us something else to do if we have to wait for anything and can't do any more at the crash site or help the other families."

Mom and I both look at each other smiling. Mom says, "Thank you boys for the thought. We really appreciate you both. I'm glad that we ran into you at the airport in Lexington and again at the airport in Columbus." She lifts the one piece up and looks at it. "This one is mine and I sure hope that the bikini is for my Daughter. I don't look good in bikinis." We go on shopping for pajamas not really worried about the bathing suits fitting us. We know that they will because we saw the sizes on them. My Mom looks at the guys and asks, "Do you boys need any pajamas?"

The boys look at her and smile. Chris answers, "No, I don't. I packed some, but I think that Dev here may need some."

Dev standing over in the pajama section for the guys and waves, smiling. "I got it taken care of, Mrs. A."

We all four laugh and keep looking for our pajamas, in the styles that we prefer. Chris sees that I'm getting a pair of white shorts with pink polka dots on it. He walks over to me and wraps his arms around me and says. "Anything will look good on you." He kisses my cheek from behind. I turn around and our lips lock.

We stood there for more than five minutes because when we came up for air, my Mother and Brother were waiting for us by the carts. My Mother says, "Okay you two love birds. That's enough for now." She starts walking away with the cart that she has for me and herself.

Chris runs to catch up to her and makes sure that Dev is in front of her with the second cart. He takes the suits out of her cart and starts running for the cash register. "I told you no expense spared for you two ladies." Then he laughs and jogs on.

Chris pays for both carts. We finally got out of Wal-Mart and loaded the truck bed up with things that we all needed. We didn't realize that it would take the whole bed of Chris' truck up. We get in and head back to the hotel before the hospital or crash site.

Chapter
THREE

....

W e finally get everything put up, hung up, folded and put away in our rooms. We were all going to meet in the hotel's restaurant before heading to the hospitals or crash site.

My Mom and I were the first one's down there. We were sitting at the table and looking at the menu when we noticed that the men were dressed up. Mom stands up trying to find her composure for their coming in, smiles and says, "It's good that you two finally decided to join us. We're ready for lunch aren't we Bree?"

I just shake my head and look over to Chris smiling. "Yes, I sure am." I noticed that Dev could dress up real nicely too. I smiled at him and stood up with my Mother. The guys came over to our seats and waited for us to sit down. Then they scooted our seats in for us. Chris found his seat, which was right next to me and sat down. Dev finds his seat facing the hostess and sits down smiling.

We were all looking at the menu when a nice skinny looking blonde walked up to the table to take our orders. She smiles real big at Chris and notices that he doesn't pay attention to her. She notices Dev sitting there basically drooling over her. She smiles at him real big and asks, "I'm Ashley. I'll be your waitress tonight. May I take your drink orders?"

Chris orders his first, without looking up at her. "I'll have a sweet tea please."

Mom orders hers second. "I'll have a non sweetened tea, with lemon please. Thank you."

I order for myself. "I'll have a sweet tea with a lemon."

Dev orders for himself last and says, "I'll have a sweet tea, and an order of you on the side." Just jokingly though, so everyone at the table including the waitress laughs. "No, I'll have a sweet tea, please. With lemon." He writes his number on his napkin, winking at her smiling while handing her the napkin, mouthing the words, "My number."

She looks down at them and winks back at him. She walks off to put the order in and walks back to the table with the food menu. She stands over by Dev and hands them out saying, "These are the menus for the food. I must recommend the Chicken Alfredo. It's to die for." She winks back at Dev and hands him a piece of paper and walks off.

Dev looks down at the piece of paper that the waitress just handed to him and reads it. He sees that it's her phone number. He gets up smiling and says. "I've got to go to the restroom." We all look around at one another and then the waitress comes back with our drinks.

Ashley hands the drinks out and says, "May I take your orders?" She looks over her shoulder and grabs her mouth. She takes off in a run toward the restrooms.

Another waitress came over to take our orders because she saw Ashley running for the restroom. "Hello, I'm Amy. May I take your orders?"

Chris is the first one to order his food again. Then it was myself, my Mother and Dev.

As soon as the food is ordered Dev gets up and says. "I'll be right back." He walks to the front of the restaurant and notices that Ashley is walking to her car. He jogs out to her and asks. "What's wrong? You don't look good!"

Ashley turns around and smiles. "I'm not feeling very well. I just got back home from Chicago about three months ago. I was at a med camp for people who want to become doctors. I went to this party with a couple of friends of mine and saw this good looking guy. Well one thing led to another, and he raped me." She just started crying hysterically and said gasping between her words. "I think I may be pregnant."

Dev looks at her then and just wraps her into a hug saying. "Okay, it's going to be alright. You need to go home and have a talk with your Parents and go to the hospital to get some tests done. You didn't know who he was right?"

Ashley looks at him and says. "No, I didn't know who he was at the time, but my friend Andrea says he's a friend of her boyfriends."

"Alright, go home and talk to both of your Parents and tell them what you just told me. You have my number, call me if you need anything." He gives her a hug and walks her to her car. He walks back to the restaurant and sees that the manager is standing at the door watching.

The manager says, "May I ask what you were doing talking to my Daughter out in the parking lot? She's sick, that's why she had to go home. I don't need her here if she can't do her job at full service."

"Yes, sir. I'm sorry, I didn't get your name?"

"My name is Eric Hampton, the owner of this fabulous restaurant and hotel. What's your business with my Daughter, Ashley?"

"Sir, I just met her at my table with my friends and sister. I'm sorry, but I can't discuss what she told me with you because it has to come from her. I think she's a beautiful girl and would like to get to know your Daughter better. I also think that maybe you need to take the rest of the day off and go have a family meeting of some sort. Your Daughter really needs you at a time like this."

"Oh, how so?" Eric asks Dev, studying him.

"Well, she's been going through something tough. I don't want to be the one to tell you what's going on though. I think you should hear it from her."

"Okay, thank you." He walks over toward the hostess Emma and says. "Emma, I have a little problem at home. I have to leave to take care of it. Call if you need anything."

Dev gets back to the table and sits down smiling real big. He looks over at Chris and says. "Hey, man when we get back to the hotel, I need to talk to you about something."

Chris looks over at him and says, "Okay." He continues his conversation with my Mom and I. Our food finally comes out and Chris says. "Thank you. Could we please get some refills on our drinks?" While getting our glasses refilled Chris looks over at Dev and asks. "What took you so long?"

Dev looks up with a mouth full of food and smiles real big. "That's what I need to talk to you about later."

"Oh, okay. It's that serious where you can't or don't want to talk about it in front of the ladies here."

"Yea." That's all Dev would say and kept eating his food.

We finally got done with our food and paid. Then we took off to the crash site.

FOUR

E ric finally pulls into his driveway and gets out of his car to discover that Ashley's car is in the driveway. He hurries up the walkway and opens the door to see what is going on with his only Daughter. He walks in to see his wife Emily crying with her hands up against her face. He looks at her and asks, "What's wrong Emily?"

His Wife Emily looks over at him and answers. "Ash is throwing up in the bathroom right now. I don't know what's wrong with her though. She doesn't have a fever or a cough. I think we're going to have to take her to the emergency room. I'm really worried about her. Every time that I have cooked something to eat here lately, I've noticed her getting up and running toward the bathroom or she pushes it away, and it's most generally her favorite food when she does this." She gets up and walks over to her Husband and hugs him.

"Okay, okay. Just calm down. We'll take her as soon as she gets out of the bathroom." He holds his Wife in his arms praying and hoping that God will provide them with an answer concerning their Daughter Ash.

Ash walks out of the bathroom just a few minutes after Eric arrives home. She's crying with something in her hands walking toward them. She looks at both of her Parents and says. "Mom, Daddy! I'm pregnant!" She hands the test over to her Mother.

Emily looks at the test and looks up to her Husband and starts bawling. Eric takes the test and sighs. He asks, "How and when did this happen?"

"It was at the party I went to in Chicago with Andrea and her boyfriend. When I went to med camp three months ago. One of his friends named Mark went with us all. He's the one that told us about it. We were just going to get something to eat and return back to the camp. I wouldn't have went if I'd known that Mark had planned that he was going to rape me." Ash starts crying hysterically. "I'm so sorry, I didn't mean to disobey anyone by going with them. I just didn't want to look like a loser." She starts running toward her bedroom, leaving her Parents shocked and standing there staring after her.

Emily tries to get up and run after her, but Eric sits her back down. He tells her, "Honey, listen to me. We need to get her to the hospital. We need to get her tested for any kind of sexually transmitted diseases and a lot of other tests. Another pregnancy test. Even though she did take one here at the house, this way we'll know for sure. The hospital's pregnancy tests are always accurate." He grabs his Wife's purse while she walks back to Ash's bedroom.

Emily knocks on Ash's door, hearing her still crying. "Baby, we just want to make sure the test isn't giving a false reading. We need to get you tested for any diseases that the creep might have given you. We're going to take you to the emergency room." She opens the door and walks on in. She sees Ash sitting on the edge of her bed. She walks over to her only Daughter and starts crying with her. She sits beside her and helps her up off the bed. "Now, we're going to go do this and then, we're going to talk about our options of either having the baby or giving the baby up for adoption. It's your choice, whether or not you want to make those kinds of decisions. Your Father and I will support whatever you decide no matter what." She hugs her Daughter sniffling, smiles and says. "Come on."

They both walk out together and finally make it out to the car. Eric is in the driver seat waiting on them. He smiles when he sees them. He waits for them to get into the car and says calmly. "Everyone put your seatbelts on please." He looks behind himself, smiles at Ash and puts the car into reverse. They back up out of the driveway and he puts the car into drive and starts on their way to the hospital. His cell phone rings and he sees that it's Austin calling him. He smiles and answers. "Hello, Son."

"Hi, Dad. Just wanted to call you and say that Bailey and I are in the hospital. She just started bleeding badly. I don't know what's going on with her. Could you, Mom and Sis come down here and wait with me?"

"Yea, sure Son. We'll be there in a few minutes." He hangs the phone up and looks over to his Wife. He grabs her hand and squeezes it giving her a worried look. He says, "That was Austin, he and Bailey are at the hospital right now. She started bleeding. He doesn't have any news about what's going on with her. We need to get there." He starts stepping down on the gas feed.

They finally arrive at the hospital and walk in. They see Austin sitting in the waiting room. Eric walks over to sit down by his Son. He talks to him trying to keep his Son occupied from not thinking about his Wife in the emergency room with the doctors doing only God knows what. He sees that Ash and Emily are getting her typed into the system. He tries to keep Austin occupied until he notices that Emily and Ash are both walking into the back department of the emergency room. Now he's worried about what kinds of tests the doctors will do to his baby girl, and if she's pregnant or not for sure. They both sit and wait to hear any news at all about either one of their loved ones.

Back in the emergency room where Bailey is, the doctors are racing against the clock trying to control her bleeding. Their attention fully on her. Emily notices that it's her in that room and stands in the door with her hand up to her mouth crying. She is pulled away from the doorway.

"Mamm, I'm sorry. You can't be here, if you're not her Mother, Father or Husband." Emily looks up to see Barbara standing on the side of the bed next to Bailey's head worrying. She nods her head toward Barbara and then walks off. She walks into the room where they took Ash and waits for the doctor to come in and see her.

Finally after an hour of waiting the doctor walks in and looks over Ash's complaint. She says, "Miss. I'm going to need you to step out of the room and wait in the waiting room for your Daughter."

Emily gets up and says, "I'll be out in the waiting room with your Brother and Father. I'll let you know any news as soon as we hear from the doctor about Bailey." She bends down over Ash's head and kisses her forehead. She walks out of the room and back into the waiting room.

After Emily sits down by her Husband and Son, she keeps her attention on the double doors for the Doctor. After another hour, she notices her Daughter coming out crying. Ash walks over to her Mother, Father and Brother and says. "I'm pregnant." She starts crying hysterically.

Emily grabs a hold of her and hugs her tight, saying. "Sorry, honey. In any other situation I'd be happy for you, because then you would be happy with yourself. Just take it one day at a time." She sits down and lets her Husband and Son hug Ash. Then they all sit down and wait to hear any news on Bailey and the unborn baby boy.

FIVE

"Oh, my goodness!" Mom gasps looking around not believing the sight in front of her. "I can't believe that it's all cleaned up. I guess we should have gone to the nearest hospital first." She starts to worry even more because she hasn't gotten a phone call from the airline about her Husband. She pulls her phone out and calls her Mother in-law. "Lena? It's Quinn."

"Oh, how are you dear? Everything okay?" Lena asks.

"No, Lena. I'm afraid it's not okay. Has anyone called from the airline or a hospital from Ohio?"

"I don't think so. Let me ask Eva." She puts her hand on the bottom of the phone and asks. "Eva? Have any hospitals from Ohio or the airline called here?"

Eva walks in and answers. "No, Mrs. Lena. I would have remembered that. Uh, but there was a call from an odd area code when I was on the phone with my Daughter in-law earlier. I didn't think anything of it until now. Is everything going okay with your Daughter in-law and Granddaughter?"

"Yes, Eva, they're fine. I don't know what's going on." She takes her hand off the mouth of the receiver and continues. "Quinn, honey! Eva says we haven't gotten a phone call from any hospitals in Ohio, but when she was on the phone with her Daughter in-law a strange area code showed up on the phone and she didn't think anything of it to answer it. If I hear anything I will call you immediately."

"Okay, thanks Lena. I guess we're going to check with the hospitals up here. The site of the crash has all been cleaned up and nothing is left out here. I'll call you if I have any news. Love you!"

"Love you both too dear." Lena hangs the phone up and looks at her caller id. She spots the number and hits send on her cordless.

"Clinton Memorial Hospital. This is Meg, how may I help you?"

"Yes, Meg. This is Lena Anderson, I was wondering why I would get a phone call from your hospital?"

"Uh, hold on mamm. I've got to look into the computer to check." She pushes a button that puts the caller on hold and she looks into the computer. She types in the last name Anderson and something pops up. She reads the issue and gets back to the phone right away. "Yes mamm, Lena?"

"Yes? I'm still here dear."

"We have a man by the name of Leelum Lance Anderson. He was brought in by an ambulance the day of the plane crash. He's stable now and we have been trying to contact his family. Would you happen to know where they might be? This was the only number we had to go by, it came out of his wallet, which was in his back pocket at the time of the crash."

"Yes, I know where they are. I can get a hold of them if you can give me the address of the hospital."

"Okay, mamm. The address is 610 West Main Street, Wilmington, Ohio. Everything is okay with Mr. Anderson."

"Okay, thank you Meg. I'll be sure to call your supervisor and tell them to give you a big raise. Thank you!"

"Thank you, mamm. Have a good day."

"I sure will now." Lena hangs the phone up and hollers for Eva. "Eva?"

Eva walks in with her hair all disheveled and asks, "Yes?"

"I need you to dial Quinn's cell phone number for me, and I want you to explain to her why you didn't answer the call from that strange area code. It was the hospital in Ohio, they have my Son and he is in stable condition." She walks out smiling and hoping that Quinn will fire Eva right there on the spot. Just, so she can have her house back to herself again. Maybe then she might be able to pass away in peace.

Eva picks the receiver up and dials Quinn's cell phone number.

"Hello?" Quinn answers.

"Is this Mrs. Quinn?:

"Yes, this is her. Who may I ask, is calling?"

"Yes, mamm. This is Eva. I was on the phone with my Daughter in-law when that strange area code came up on the caller id. I swear I didn't mean to ignore it. My Daughter in-law was having trouble with getting her little one to sleep and I was singing to her, that does the trick every time. I didn't know it was the hospital from Wilmington, Ohio."

"Okay, do you have any more information?"

"No, mamm. I don't, but I think Mrs. Lena does though. Hold on while I go find her." She puts the phone down on the stand and goes off to find Mrs. Lena. "Mrs. Lena? Quinn is on the phone for you." Eva found her in the library having tea.

"Oh, okay dear." She puts her tea down and answers the phone in the library. "Hello, dear. How are you?"

"I'm fine Lena, I need some more information about this hospital."

"Yes, dear. Let me get my paper here." She reaches over the stand to get the piece of paper that she dropped as she was trying to get to the phone. She picks it up and reads it off. "I took this information down because I know that Eva is incapable of taking messages as important as this one. Okay, here we are. The hospital is called Clinton Memorial Hospital. The address is 610 West Main Street, Wilmington, Ohio.

They only called me because they found his wallet on him and he had one of those cards filled out with my address and phone number on it. I guess he filled it out before he had Bree, met you and got married. I'm so sorry dear. I should have been here to answer the phone that day. Let me know how he's doing and how Bree is doing. Love you three. Bye." She hangs the phone up and continues sipping her tea.

Quinn gets off of her cell phone and looks at the two guys and me. She starts crying, saying. Clinton Memorial Hospital called your Grandmother, Bree. Your Father is there. I hope we can get there as soon as possible." We all four jog back to the truck and get in as fast as possible. "We need to get there now!"

We were finally on our way to the hospital. Going by the address that Grandma Lena gave us typed into Chris' GPS. We were right across the street from the hospital when we spotted our hotel. Quinn looks up and says, "You mean to tell me that we were right across the street from it and didn't even know it? I hate Ohio now." Grabbing at her stomach and almost vomiting right there on the floorboard of Chris' truck.

Chris looks back at her and tells Dev, "Hurry, get her an empty bag. Have her blow in and out of it slowly." He whips his truck into the parking lot of the hospital. I'll let you three out here, I'm going to go park the truck and meet you three inside." We all get out and walk inside to wait for Chris. Finally we see him and head straight for the information desk in the lobby. Chris walks on ahead of us three and asks the receptionist at the desk. "Yes, we need to know what room Leelum Lance Anderson is in. He was brought in a few days ago from the plane crash."

"Okay!" The woman hurriedly types in the name Leelum Lance Anderson and finds his room number right away. She looks up at Chris and says, "He's in room number 1400. Go straight through those doors and make a left. Take the elevator up to the fourth floor."

"Thank you, mamm." We all started walking in the direction the woman told us to go in and get to the elevator.

As soon as we get into the elevator Mom looks at all three of us. "I would like to talk to the doctor and the nurses first. I would also like to go in and see him by myself first. You all can sit and wait in the waiting room if you want." She turns around and gets ready to get off the elevator when I say something.

"No, I want to go with you. I want to make sure he's still alive."

"Okay, you can. I just wanted to make sure he'll be up to having company before we all go in." The elevator finally dings and we all four get off. Mom finds a doctor and stops him. "Hi, my name is Quinn Anderson. My Husband, Leelum Lance Anderson is here. I'd like to ask you a few questions."

"Okay, my name is Dr. Clark, I'm the head Doctor on this floor. How may I help you?"

"Okay, can he have visitors?"

"Yes, he can have as many as he wants in his room during visiting hours."

"Okay, how bad of shape is he in?"

"When he first got here, he was pretty badly banged up. We treated him for amnesia, because he didn't remember who he was. We had to dig through his wallet to pull out emergency contacts to get a hold of someone. We saw that he had pictures in his wallet and we used them as part of his treatment. He remembers you, his Wife and his little girl. That's as far as we've gotten. He's been in a coma since we showed him the picture of her." Pointing to me.

"Okay, has he shown any signs of waking up anytime soon?"

"He's shown signs of waking up, but all we can do now is wait for him to do so." He starts walking in the direction of Dad's room and stops in front of a door. He peeks his head in and back out. "He's right in there. Go on in."

My Mom and I go on in and adjust our eyes to the dimness of the room. Mom pulls a chair up to the side of the bed and sits down. She finds his hand and grabs a hold of it. "Hey, honey. It's me. Bree and I came all the way up here to look for you. You sure did give us a scare."

She finishes off by giving me a look and shaking her head toward the other side of the bed. "Bree is on the other side of you. She's going to hold your other hand. Can you please wake up?"

I just started crying hard and let go of his hand, but his hand clamps down. I jerk back a bit, shocked at his touch.

The guys wait just outside his door. Chris looks over at Dev. "I can't believe this. Bree and Quinn are going to be devastated if he doesn't pull through. What am I going to do?"

"I don't know. Just be here, I guess." Dev looks down at his feet and clears his throat. "I have something that I need to tell you."

"Okay, what is it about?"

"It's about me having to head back to Columbus tomorrow. I have to sign papers and take care of some things to get the transfer to go through before I arrive back home. I don't want to leave my little Sister like this though."

"Okay, I'll go get her and you can tell her that you have to go. Just tell her what you just told me. She'll understand. You are coming back to Wilmington aren't you?"

"Yea!"

Chris just looked at him and shook his head. "Okay, dude. I'll be right back." He walks into the room and gets my attention.

I walk over to him and Chris says, "Dev needs to speak to you." I look over my shoulder and make sure my Mom is okay by herself for a few minutes.

I take Chris' hand and walk out with him to where Dev is. I walk up to him and give him a big hug. "Thank you, for all that you have done. What is it that you need to talk to me about?"

Dev looks into my eyes and can tell that I'm not going to be mad at him. So, he starts off by saying. "Sis, I'm glad I was here for this. I hope everything turns out okay with your Father. I want you to know that I will be back, but I have to go back to Columbus to sign some papers. I'm getting transferred back home, the week after next. I need to get some things from my apartment and have a moving company to pack my stuff up for me. I hope you don't mind. I didn't know we were going to find him today, or else I wouldn't have said that I'd be there tomorrow to sign the papers. I hope you understand?"

"Yes Bub, I understand that. As long as you are coming back. Go, do what you have to do to get your butt back to Lexington." I hug him, whispering in his ear at the same time, "I love you, Bub." I unwrap my arms away from him and go stand by Chris. We both stand there watching him walk to the elevator waving and smiling at him when he turns around. He pushes the button to take him back down to the lobby and just disappears for the rest of the day.

"Bree, hurry up! Get in here! I think your Dad's waking up." Mom screams out the door.

Chris and I both turn around and head straight for his room. We get in there and see that my Dad is awake and talking with Mom. Smiling at her and just holding her hand. They both look up at me and he smiles. He holds out his arms and says, "Bree Bree, come here honey!" I go over to him and start crying. I lean down and give my Dad a big hug. We stay like that forever and he lets go of me. He looks toward Chris and looks at Mom and I asking. "Who is this good looking fellow?"

I look over my shoulder smiling. "Daddy, this is Chris. He took care of Mom and I at the airport in Lexington, when Mom and I were on our way up here to find you. He's a real good guy." I grab his hand and notice that my Dad doesn't like it. So I let go real quick.

"Oh, Chris. Thank you so much for taking care of my girls for me." He shakes his hand and looks at us. "Can Chris and I have a moment alone?"

Mom and I both look at each other and smile. We both answer, "Yes!" At the same time. Mom gets up and gives her Husband a hug and I do the same thing, I squeeze Chris' hand. We both walk out together and sit in the hallway until Chris opens the door for us smiling.

"I know you may think that I'm not Bree's type sir. I was the one who wanted them two to be taken care of while they were up here. I was working the day that they came to the airport. I noticed that Bree was there by herself when your flight was supposed to touch down at the airport and she left by herself. I never thought that she would be back with her Mother only an hour later. When I saw her again at the airport that day I knew something was wrong. So, I immediately offered them a ride to their gate and gave Bree my number. I wanted them to know that I was there emotionally and physically for them. I would do anything to help them, that's why I'm here now."

Lance looks long and hard at Chris and says, "Okay. You can relax. All I want to know is what do you want to happen between you and my Daughter?"

"I'm not quite sure yet, Sir. I want to take it slowly and see where this all goes. I like her enough to consider settling down, but only when she's ready to do so on her own. I'm not going to pressure her into doing anything she doesn't want to do."

"Okay, you are a good guy. You can bring them back in." He lays there waiting to hear the sound of his girls coming back into his room once again.

Chris walks over to the door and says, "You two can come back in." He waits for the both of us to walk back in and smiles. I look at him questionly and shake my head. He shakes his head to answer me back and smiles at me. I grab his hand and we both walk in together like that. We sat there for a while just talking with Dad. We talked to his doctor and the doctor told us that if he does fine through tonight and no more going into comas that he could be released tomorrow afternoon. Then Chris and I head back to the hotel leaving my Mother behind at the hospital.

Chapter
SIX

As Dev is walking out of the lobby, he notices that Ashley and her family are in the ER Department. He walks over to them and smiles at her. She immediately gets up and starts running toward him crying. He holds his arms out for her. She lands in his arms and he asks, "What's wrong?"

Ash answers, "My Sister in-law is in the emergency room. They don't know what's going on with her, but she could lose her baby. She just started bleeding when we were on our way to the emergency room ourselves. Also, I found out for sure tonight that I am pregnant." She lets go of him and notices that her Dad is behind them. She walks over to sit down by her Mother.

Dev turns around and sees that Ash's Father, Eric is standing right behind him. "What's going on, Sir? Anything I can help with?"

Eric answers, "No, I don't think so." He gives Devin the overall look and asks. "Could I please ask you a question?"

Devin looks at him questioningly and answers. "Sure!"

Eric asks, smiling. "What is your interest in my Daughter?"

Devin answers, smiling. "Well, Sir. I think that she's beautiful, smart and intelligent. I would like to get to know her better." He asks, Eric. "Why?"

"Well, there is something that you should know before trying to get to know her better." He shakes his index finger for him to follow. He bends down and says. "Have a seat Devin. We'd like to talk to you."

Dev takes a seat and looks at Ash. He notices that she's not in the best of moods. He grabs her hand smiling, pulls her up and asks, "What's this?"

She gets up, smiles real big, looking straight into his eyes and answers. "I have already told you the day we met at the restaurant."

Dev looks straight at her and says. "Okay, so why is your Father wanting me to talk to you before getting to know you better?"

"He thinks that I haven't told you yet. I haven't told them that you already know."

"Okay, don't you think that you may want to let them know that I already know."

Ash looks at Dev smiling and says, "You're right. I do need to let them know." She gets up and walks over to where her Parents are sitting. She explains to them what Dev already knows. They were stunned of course, but couldn't be happier. They now accept Dev as part of their family.

Dev has an idea to get her Parents to trust him a bit more and he moves over to ask Eric and Emily. "May I ask you both a question?"

Eric looks at him, smiling and says. "You already have." He chuckles and looks serious again. "Yes?"

"I was wondering if I could have Ash spend the night with my Sister at the hotel tonight? I would like for her to get to know me better and I to know her better, but I have to move back home to Kentucky this coming week. My job is transferring me to the airport in Lexington, and I would very much like for her to move with me."

Eric and Emily both smile at each other and Eric answers. "I don't mind if she spends the night with your Sister at the hotel. What I do mind is that you want her, my only Daughter to move with you to Kentucky?" He huffs and finishes. "I just don't know about that one yet Devin. We only just met you!"

Dev thinks for a minute and explains it like this. "Okay, say you just met Emily and she's the only woman in this world that you can't get out of your head. Only reason why you two met was because of a family member needing help and that's your number one priority. Only to come to a conclusion that you can't help but think about Emily all day long. Wouldn't you want to do anything in your power to try and keep that relationship going?"

Eric looks at Dev, then at Emily and answers. "Yes, I would want to do that." He sits there thinking for a few more minutes and finally answers Dev's real question. "I think it would be okay for Ash to move in with you. She was going to be moving to Lexington in the Fall anyhow. That's where she was going to go to college before this all happened."

Eric walks over to Ash and tells her that it's okay for her to move to Kentucky. She has to live with Dev's Sister and her Parents for the deal to work. She jumps up and down ecstatic about the move.

Ash smiles and says hugging her Parents. "Thank you, I love you both so much." She walks over to Dev and says, smiling. "I can move to Kentucky with you. I was moving there anyway, for college in August." She grabs his hand and sits down with him.

Dev notices Chris and I walking out of the elevator. He waves over at us smiling. We both look at each other and Chris says. "What does he want us to do? Walk over there?"

I look over to where Dev is and say. "I think he does."

We walk over to him smiling and are wondering who this girl is. Chris looks at her and then whispers to me. "That's the waitress we had at the hotel restaurant." I start looking and see that Chris is right. I shrug my shoulders and start walking even faster toward Ash and Dev.

"Hey, Bub. What's going on?"

"Nothing, just ran into Ash here. How is your Dad?"

I answered him. "He's groggy but awake. Mom is going to spend the night with him tonight. We're going back to the rooms now. We want to turn in early tonight, so that we can be in here early tomorrow. He may get to go home tomorrow!"

"Good! That's good news!" He looks at Ash and introduces her. "Ash, this is my Sister Bree." Pointing to me and then to Chris. "This is Chris. My best friend and roommate when I get back to Kentucky." He smiles and says. "I have a question for you, Bree and Chris. I was wondering, as you both know that I have to go to Columbus tomorrow to sign the papers for my transfer. I was wanting to know if Ash could spend the night tonight at the hotel?"

I look at my Brother, then at Chris and answer. "It's okay with me if it's okay with Chris. After all, he is paying for the rooms."

Chris looks down at her and smiles. Then he answers Dev's question. "Yes, that would be fine. We'll be right next door anyway. We'll listen for anything suspicious."

We all start giggling softly and Ash says. "Come on and meet my family. I want them to meet the girl that I'm spending the night with." We all four walk toward Ash's family and stand there while Ash explains to them what's going on. "Daddy, Mom and Austin, this is Bree and Chris. I'm going to be spending the night with Bree in her hotel room tonight. I'm going to take a day trip with Dev to Columbus tomorrow. He has to sign papers at the airport for his transfer to Kentucky." She looks down at her feet and says. "I wanted you to meet them before I go."

Chris says. "We could wait to see what's going on with your Sister in-law."

She looks back at him and says. "Thank you. I wouldn't know what to do without you guys." She sits down beside her Brother with Dev on the other side of her. Chris and I both sit down in two chairs across from Ash, Dev and her family.

After sitting there in the waiting room for another half hour, the Doctor that was called in for Ash's Sister in-law walks out of the double doors with a woman in a wheelchair being pushed behind him. Austin stands up immediately and walks over to the Doctor. So does Eric, Emily, Ash, Barbara and Bentley. Barbara and Bentley are Bailey's Parents. They are all over there talking to the Doctor looking dumbfounded. Dev gets up and walks over to stand behind Ash. He hears a little of what the Doctor is saying. "She needs a lot of bed rest. No work! She doesn't need the stress. I would recommend to follow up with her regular OBGYN Doctor and go from there. This condition is serious. Don't let her up for anything but going to the restroom."

Austin looks at the Doctor and asks, "When I'm at work should I have someone come to sit with her?"

"If you'd like, Sir."

"How long does she have to do this for?"

"For as long as her OBGYN says to."

"What does this mean for the outcome of her and the baby?"

"Sir, I know you are confused right now and there is nothing that we can do for her, but to keep her off of her feet for a little while. It may be a week or it may be until the baby arrives. The outcome of her and the baby is serious. If she doesn't follow the Doctor's orders, she and the baby could die. I'm sorry to be so blunt, but I do have other patients to see." He walks toward the double doors and pushes a button. "Have a good night you all."

Everyone walks over to where Bailey is and swarms around her. Austin jumps in and says, "I need to get her home and in bed. Talk to you all in the morning." He pushes her out to the entrance.

Ash, Dev, Chris and I all walk to his truck in the parking garage and head to Ash's Parents house and back to the hotel. We finally arrive at the hotel and walk into the guys room. At first none of us feel like talking and then Chris and Dev have the idea to go swimming in the pool. Dev gets up and walks over to Ash and asks. "Did you bring a bathing suit with you?"

She looks at him and starts laughing. "Yea, I did. You do know who owns this hotel and restaurant right?"

Dev looks at her smiling and answers. "Yes, I guess you could say that I just had a blond moment."

Shaking her head, Ash walks into the bathroom and shuts the door behind her. Dev walks over to the door and turns to tell Chris and I what is going on with him and Ash. "Hey, guys. I need to tell you both something real quick. Could you two stop making out and listen?"

We both stop and look at him and answer at the same time. "Yes, sorry."

"Okay, what I'm about to tell you two is going to come as a shock." He looks toward the bathroom door and just comes right out and says. "Ash is pregnant."

We both look at him and are stunned at the news. Chris stands up and asks. "You sure?"

"Yea, I'm sure." Dev stands up and starts rubbing his hands through his hair and says. "The baby isn't mine. She told me that she was at med camp and some guy took her and a friend of hers to a party. Her friend's boyfriend was friends with this guy that told them about the party. She said that they were there for over four hours just talking and all of a sudden he got rough with her and raped her. She just found out tonight in the ER. She just came out of there when she saw me walking through the lobby and we ran into each other."

"Okay," I say. "Just because she's pregnant and interested in you doesn't mean that she's going to hold you responsible for the baby, right" I sat back down along with Chris and said. "When did she tell you this?"

"At the restaurant earlier today, before she went home sick."

"Okay, but at least she told you before going to Kentucky." Chris says, sighing. Then he looks up at his friend and says. "I know you don't feel comfortable with the situation yet. Give it time, she's really into you dude. You can always tell her that now is not the best time for her to move to Kentucky."

"Yea, I know that. I want her to though. I don't know what to do. I keep thinking that she's going to put this on me and move to Kentucky with us and then she's going to realize that I'm not the right guy for her and break my heart like my ex did."

That's when I interrupt them. "Well, this is what I would do. I'd tell her that I'm scared. I'm scared of getting my heart broken again. I want us to happen, but you're going to have to understand that I will help with anything that I can, but I can't keep wondering after we move to Kentucky that you'll leave me when you figure out that I may not be the one." I sigh, catching my breath while sitting back down. I turn around and see that the two guys are looking at me in astonishment. I ask, "What?"

Chris and Dev are just shocked. Then Dev says, "Okay, so what you're saying is that I should confess to her that I've been in this same situation with an ex of mine and I don't want my heart broken again?"

"Yea, pretty much!" I answer, smiling at him and Chris both. "Just tell her what you're feeling when you're with her and then tell her what you're feeling when you both are away from each other. Remember what I said at Wendy's?"

"Yea, I remember what you said." Dev answers.

"What was it that I said then?"

"That the key to any relationship is communication." He sighs and looks up because he heard the door open. He looks back toward the restroom and is awestruck at her belly and the way she looks. He walks over to her and takes her into his arms. He says, "We have to talk before we go swimming." He pushes back from her and sees that she's worried. "It's nothing to be worried about." He chuckles and sits back down on the bed. "You two want to go ahead and go to the pool?"

"Bree is already in the bathroom. You want me to go to the room to get changed?" Chris asks.

"Yes, sure. Thanks buddy." He sits there waiting for his best friend to get dressed in the other room and me to get my suit on before going to change his clothes and talk to Ash.

I come out of the bathroom right when Chris gets back to the room. He grabs us two towels and Chris and I head on down to the pool, leaving Ash and Dev in the room alone.

Dev walks into the bathroom and gets his trunks on. Then he walks out and sees that Ash is sitting, waiting patiently on him to talk. She stands up and sees that he's ready. "Are you ready to talk?"

"Yea!" He grabs her hand and sits her down on the bed along with himself. "I'm feeling all kinds of emotions and feelings right now. In my heart, I know that you are what I want out of a girlfriend. In my head I'm a little scared."

Ash looks at him and cups his face. Kisses his cheek and asks. "Why are you scared?"

He thinks long and hard before answering this question. "I'm scared that I'm going to move you down to Kentucky with me and you wake up one morning and know in your heart that I'm not what you want. You'll leave me heart broken."

"No, I wouldn't do that to you." She rubs the side of his face and says smiling. "I would rather talk things over with you before making a rational decision like that." She takes her hands away from his face and says, "I heard what you were talking to Chris and Bree about. You have to know that my Parents say the same things as Bree's Parents. They know that the key to any relationship is communication. I want you to share those feelings that you have with me. Just to let you know, I'm scared too. I'm scared that the guy that did this to me is going to find out and come looking for me someday. Wanting rights to this baby that I don't think he should have."

"Oh, baby. As long as you're with me that will never happen. I'll take care of you both." Dev says and kisses her tenderly. "I want you to know that you can come to me about anything that is bothering you and tell me anytime, anyplace and anywhere. I'm here for you." He pulls her into a hug and sits there for five minutes before letting her go. "I want you to move with me to Kentucky and be my Girlfriend. Will you do that for me? I don't care that you're carrying another guy's baby. I just want to be with you. I think about you every time we're apart. When we're together I feel like I have my reason for being alive."

She looks into his eyes and sees that he really means what he's saying. She says, "I want you to know that I will get a job to help with this baby. I don't want you to feel responsible for it if you don't want to." She rubs her stomach. "When the time is right for us, we'll get married and then we'll have our own babies. Right now what's right is that we get to know each other better and not worry about what is going to happen with anything. Just be with each other. I don't want to move things too fast. That's the reason why I asked if I could move in with Bree, and her Parents, before we move in together."

"Okay, I just felt like I had to get that off of my chest. I will tell you tomorrow what happened to me, to make me feel like this." He gets up, goes to the door and asks, "Are you ready to go to the pool?" Smiling, he opens it and waits for her to walk out. "Okay, here is a towel for you and one for me." They hold hands walking down the steps to the pool. They see Chris and I just hanging out by the side of the pool. "Hey, is the water cold?" Dev asks.

Chris looks at him smiling and says. "You'll find out." He dives underneath and goes to the other end. I follow him and almost lose my focus, but then recover. "You okay?" Chris asks while holding one of his hands out to me for support.

I look at him smiling, saying, "Yes, just a little more deeper than what I thought it was going to be." I go underneath and tug on his shorts. He looks underneath to try to find me and decides that he should do the same. He swims, chasing after me when he feels my hair hit his leg.

Dev and Ash are working on getting in and watching Chris and I. Ash gets in first and goes under. Dev just watches her with her bikini on and thinks to himself that he's the luckiest man in the world. He dives underneath and swims after her.

We swam for about an hour and a half before getting out. We were getting ready to walk to our rooms when we spotted a figure coming toward the pool area. Dev and Chris both stand in front of Ash and I, blocking us from being seen by a stranger. They both keep their eyes on him, while walking to our rooms. Keeping Ash and I in front of them. Dev and Chris look to their left and see that there are more guys following us. Chris whispers to Dev. "What are these guys wanting?"

Dev whispers back. "I don't know, but the sooner we get the girls up to their room the better." They both grab us and start walking a little faster. We got by the first hallway without anyone surprising us, but when Chris and Dev both look back they see there are more guys joining the group and watching us really, really closely. They keep pushing us girls toward the door the closer they get to our room. We go into the room because it's the closest. Dev got my key from me and got the door open before the gang of guys got to us. Chris pushes us girls into the room real quick, pulling Dev in with him when us girls are sitting on the bed safely. They manage to get the door shut just before the guys could get their hands on it. Dev looks at our faces and sees that we are scared. He walks over and sits between us. "Hey, it's okay. Nothing is going to happen." We all hear a knock at the door. Dev looks at Chris, Ash and I whispering. "Just be quiet, maybe they'll go away." So we just ignored the knocks on the door and the next thing we knew it was morning.

Chapter
SEVEN

....

Ash and I were the first ones up. We couldn't believe what was going on last night after we got out of the pool. None of us knew what those guys wanted or what they were doing following us all to our room. Us girls go ahead and order room service. We weren't thinking about the guys that were following us all four last night. We didn't think anything of ordering room service because we haven't heard any commotion outside the door since we went to sleep last night scared out of our wits. I looked over to where Chris was sleeping. I smile and think, I'm so glad that those guys were here last night. Then I heard a noise in the room next to the room where we all were. I listen and know that it isn't room service. I shake Chris and Dev both at the same time and say. "I think there is someone in yours and Chris' room next door. Listen!" I put my finger up to my mouth, and we all listened.

Chris and Dev both listened and they heard the noises that I heard. They both get up and walk outside on the terrace. They look toward the window to see if any of the curtains are moving back and forth. There aren't any curtains moving, so they walk over to the window and put their ears up to it. They still hear the sounds. So they walk back into

54

my room and lock the door. They call down to the office. "Yes, I'd like to report some strange noises in a room that shouldn't have anyone in it right now." Chris says.

"Okay, Sir. Are you in the room next to it?" The clerk asks.

"Yes, I'm the one that paid for both rooms. The room numbers are two forty eight and two forty nine."

"Okay, I'll send someone up to investigate it. Did you happen to walk outside on the terrace to see if there is a cart out there?"

"Yes, there isn't a cart outside the room. It's not housekeeping."

"Okay, we'll get someone up there right away." He hangs the phone up and gets the extra key for room two forty nine. He walks out of the office and locks it up. He walks up to room two forty nine and listens to see if he can hear any noises. He does, so he gets his key out and swipes it down the slot. He opens the door and sees that there definitely has been someone in here, because they're still in the bed. He walks over to them and says. "I'm the manager of this hotel. I have to ask that you leave the premises or I will be forced to call the law." He stands there waiting for them all to get up.

The people that were in the room get up and look straight at the manager. "We paid for this room last night. I don't know what the problem is, but it's in the log book."

"Okay, if you would follow me and we'll check this out." He turns to walk out the door and walks down to the office. He unlocks the door and walks in. He grabs a book and starts flipping through the log book until last night comes up. "Okay, I see that there was someone that booked the same room you claim to have paid for, two nights ago." He continues flipping in the other direction. He finds the mistake. "May I ask you a question?" He looks to the five males that supposedly booked the room last night.

"Yea, sure go ahead. Ask away!" Mark says with his arms folded across his chest. Clearly getting angrier by the minute.

"Are you sure that the clerk on duty last night booked you in room two forty nine?"

"Yes, I'm pretty positive. The key opened the door. If it wasn't the right room, then the key wouldn't have opened it, right?"

"Yes, that is true." Carter says continuing to scratch his goatee. "Well, I guess.......wait a minute. May I ask you another question?"

"Yes, you may." Mark answers with sarcasm.

"Were there any clothes or anything in that room when you all went to it last night?"

"Yes, there were. We threw them out on the terrace. We didn't know who they belonged to." Mark answers him smiling, knowing good and well who the clothes belonged to. They didn't book the room at all. They saw four kids last night at the pool and went by, stole the key that was on the lawn chair. Mark knows whose room it was because he's been following us.

"Okay, sorry about the mistake. We will have to book another room for you all to stay tonight if you're going to. Whoever booked you last night didn't put down how long you were going to stay." He types a few keys on the computer and sees who was working last night. He makes a mental note to call this employee and ask him some questions when they leave. "Okay, we have room two twenty eight, two twenty nine, and two thirty available. Which one would you like?"

"We wouldn't like any of them. We're not staying another night. Thanks anyways though." Then the five guys walk out of the office and walk back to the pool area and drop the key that they stole next to the lawn chair. Then they went upstairs to sit and wait for Ash to walk out of the room.

Chris looks inside his towel and starts to panic. He looked in the bed that he and Dev slept in last night together and looked up at Dev, Ash and I. "Did you all see where I put my key to my room?"

Dev, Ash and I look at him and I answer. "You sure you had it on you when we went to the pool?"

"Yes, I'm sure. We walked down to the pool and I remember sticking the key into my towel. It was folded up and I laid it on that lawn chair that was sitting next to the cabana."

Dev, Ash and I all look at each other and Dev says. "I think it would be smart to see if it's still there or not. I didn't see anything lying on the ground when we went to the office earlier. Maybe you dropped it on the way back up to the room last night." So Chris walks out to look for it while Ash, Dev and I look for it on the terrace and steps.

Mark sees Ash step out and grins. "There's my girl, guys." Pointing up to Ash. Smiling, he waits until she's alone, but he won't get that chance.

"Okay, calm down, it'll be okay." Dev tells Chris. Then he notices out of the corner of his eye that there are five guys watching us. He stops and looks real good and then says to Ash and I. "We've got to get back into the room." He pushes on the small of our backs. He texts Chris. "Hey we have a prob (short for problem) 5 guys watching us." He hits send and waits for Chris' reply.

Almost immediately his phone vibrates. "In office now found key, be back up to the room in a few."

He shuts his phone and asks us girls. "Do either of you two know any of those guys standing down the hall?"

Ash and I both walk over to the window and look out toward where Dev was pointing. I answer, "No, I don't!" Then I look over to Ash and see her face go pale white. "What's wrong Ash?"

"I can't believe he found me. Oh, God. What am I going to do?" Ash runs back over to the bed and starts crying.

Dev and I both walk over to her and sit down beside her. Dev puts his arms around her and says. "It'll be okay. Who is that guy?"

Ash looks up at him and starts crying even more. She catches her breath and says. "Remember me telling you about how I got pregnant?"

Dev answers, "Yea, what about it?"

"Well, he's the guy that did this to me. I can't believe he's here. I don't know how he found me. I didn't tell him where I was from." She pauses for a few minutes and sighs. "It was at the party I went to in Chicago with Andrea and her Boyfriend. When I went to med camp three months ago. One of his friends named Mark went with us. He's the one that told us about the party. We were just going to get something to eat and return back to camp. I wouldn't have went if I'd known that Mark planned on raping me." Ash starts crying hysterically. "I'm so sorry." She got up and walked over to where Dev was and gave him a hug. She looked over toward me and saw that Chris was standing there, looking like he was disgusted with her.

He cleared his throat, smiled real big and said. "I guess we know the real story of how it happened. Now, what I need to know is why did that Mark guy ask me about you. He said that you are his girl and if he finds out that you are dating anyone else then he would have to hurt that guy." He stood with his arms crossed and watched her intensely.

Ash looked back at him and answered. "No, I swear. If I was dating him don't you think that I would be in this room right now? I wouldn't want to date a guy who raped me. He must have found out from Andrea where I was from. He had to have heard it from her." She went over and sat down on the bed and started crying even harder.

I went over to her, hugged her and said. "Everything is going to be okay. I promise." I got up and walked over to Chris. "May I please speak to you outside?" I took his hand and watched his head shake up and down. "What's the matter with you?"

He looks at me shocked and answers. "I just don't want my best friend getting into anything that could break his heart or him winding up dead. I know what that psycho said to me was just plain out stupid, and that I shouldn't believe anything he says, but Bree I don't think he was kidding when he said it."

"Okay, we'll deal with that when the time comes. Right now, the best thing that you can do is help them out. Don't interrogate her. She's been through enough already." I put my arms around his neck and kissed him tenderly. "Now, we need to get back in there and see what they want to do."

Chapter
EIGHT

W e walk back into the room and see that Ash and Dev are discussing what happened to him when he first moved to Columbus. We just walk in and sit down on the bed waiting for him to finish his story.

".....that's why I said what I said to you in the ER last night." Dev hugs her and says. "Everything will be okay. You know why?"

"No! Why?" Ash asked.

"Because we're together and I'm not going to let anything bad happen to you." He kisses her forehead and looks over at Chris. "Could I please talk to you outside?"

"Okay." Chris gets up and checks outside before walking out of the room. He doesn't see the gang of guys anywhere, so he follows Dev out onto the terrace of the hotel room. "What's up?"

"I need you to do me a favor."

"What's that?"

"I need you to drive Ash to Columbus for me. Bree can come too. It's only an hour and a half drive from here."

"How would this keep them from following you in your vehicle?"

"I just want her to be safe. I don't care if they follow me. I just don't want her to feel like she won't be safe anywhere, especially with me."

"Let me see what Bree says, then I'll let you know." Chris follows Dev back into the room and looks at me. He points at me and motions his finger for me to follow him. "Can I please talk to you outside?"

I look at him and answer. "Yes!" I get up and follow him. "What's up?"

"I don't want to do this to you, but Dev needs me to take Ash up to Columbus for him. He's going to drive his vehicle but he wants me to drive mine and follow him there to make sure the trip goes okay. He doesn't want Ash to feel like she can't feel safe with him by himself, giving everything going on."

I look around and say. "Okay, but what about my Parents? My Father is supposed to be getting out today. I want to go see him."

"Okay, this is what we'll do then. We'll go see your Father and let them know what's going on. Let them meet Ash and then we'll go to Columbus. Ash, You and I will follow Dev. We'll spend the night at his place and drive down to Kentucky tomorrow. Is that okay?" He puts his arms around me and kisses me lightly on my neck.

I look up at his eyes and say. "How did I get so lucky to have a guy like you? That plan sounds perfect to me. Let's go in and tell them." I walk into the room smiling and excited.

"What's with you little Sis?" Dev asks.

"Oh, Chris just formed a plan." I answer looking up to him still smiling. "We want Ash to go to the hospital with us in Chris' truck. You can drive over there and meet us. We want my Parents to meet Ash and see what is going on with my Father. Then we'll leave for the whole night to go to Columbus, then tomorrow we'll drive to Kentucky."

Dev looks at his watch and answers. "Okay, we'll leave my car in the parking garage at the hospital. We'll all ride over to your Parents house to get your things. Then we'll drive back over to the hospital to get my car, visit with Bree's Parents and head out to Columbus." He looks over at Chris and asks. "Does that sound good to you?"

"Sounds good to me buddy. Let's get going." We all walk out of the room and check out at the office. I have my Mom's bags, mine and Ash's with me, just in case Mark and his gang are still watching us. Chris and Dev both have their bags with them.

Chris walks into the office and checks us out while Ash, Dev and I all go to Chris' truck to wait for him. "It was so good to meet you, Ash. Hope we can still be friends. Here, this is my number. You'll call me sometime won't you? I'm so glad that I'm going to be having a responsible roommate to bunk with during my college days. Could my Boyfriend Chris, my Brother and I give you a ride back to your house? I would love to meet them." I ask her while Dev is packing our things into the back of Chris' truck.

"Okay, Sis. You can stop bugging the poor girl. Let's get your things up into the bed of the truck." He says smiling at me. "If she gets on your nerves just say so." He says to Ash. "Chris, Bree and I are going to take you home. It was nice to meet you. Too bad you're my little Sister's friend. I won't date any of her friends. It hurts the Sister, Brother code." He climbs in the front of the truck and waits for Chris to walk out, while Ash and I climb in the back.

Mark and his gang hear the conversation about Ash getting taken home. He looks back at his friend Curtis in the back seat and asks. "I thought you said that Ash is pregnant?"

"That's what I heard dude." Curtis says.

"Well, call your Girlfriend and see if it's true or not. She'll know." He keeps on watching us. He sees Chris walking out of the office carrying his bag. He puts his bag in the bed of the truck, climbs in and takes off after putting his seatbelt on. Mark follows us to see if that's where we are heading, he says to his buddies. "Just in case they're trying to pull a fast one on us."

Chris is driving and looks in the rear view mirror. He sighs, saying. "We have company! He's behind us, don't look! Do you think that we should take Ash home or not?"

"Yea, let's do that. It's only a five minute drive." Ash says. Then she leans back and starts a conversation with me.

We finally arrive at Ash's Parents house. Still aware of Mark following us. We all get out and the guys help Ash get her things. Then the guys get back in the truck to wait for me and Ash while we go inside. Ash walks in and looks at her Parents. "Hey, Mom, Daddy. I want to talk to you all for a little bit." She looks behind her and sees that I am still behind her. Pointing at me she asks her Parents. "Remember Breea?"

Both of her Parents get up and answer smiling. "Yea, hello Breea. How are you today? How is your Father?"

"He's doing good. He may get to go home today. Considering the situation we're all in, that's the best news today."

Eric, Ash's Father looks over at Ash and asks. "What does she mean?" He looks outside and then asks. "Why are the guys waiting outside?"

I got a text from Chris. "Hey whats goin (short for going) on in there" I text back. "Nm (means not much) just getting questioned hes wantin to knw (short for know) whats goin on"

"Daddy, we're being followed by Mark. The guy from med camp. He's freaking everyone out." She looks outside and sees that the guys are walking in. "We need a favor from you and Mom."

He looks outside again and asks. "What kind of favor do you all need?"

Chris and Dev come in and answer the question. "We need you to bring the girls to the hospital across from the hotel. We checked out today because Bree's Dad is getting released. They're going to go ahead and fly out. They're supposed to ride with Dev in his car to the airport in Columbus. While Ash, Bree and I all ride in my truck. Ash wants to know if you all could bring her things and put them in the back of my truck at the hospital in the parking garage."

Eric looks over at Emily and says. "Yes, sure. We'll do that." He looks over at Ash and then back at Chris. "Mark won't leave you all alone, but he hasn't done anything to make you think he wants to hurt anyone, right?"

Dev answers his question. "Yea, as far as we know he won't try anything that stupid. This is just a precaution. We don't want anyone to get hurt, that's why we need your help. My best friend here, overheard a conversation that Mark was having with one of his buddies that is with him. Let's just say that it doesn't sound so pretty if he finds out that I'm interested in Ash. He thinks that Ash is his Girl."

Mark is still waiting outside while all four of us are inside Ash's Parents house. He looks back at Curtis and asks. "Have you gotten a hold of your Girlfriend yet?"

Curtis answers him. "Yea, just got a text from her. She doesn't have calling minutes, I had to text her."

Mark asks, "Well, what does it say dumbass?"

"It says, "yes, shes prego (short for pregnant) im sure of it" is that good enough for you?"

"I'll fucking kill you if you talk to me like that again." Mark, reaching back to slap the back of Curtis' head but couldn't reach. Then he sees Curtis pointing toward Ash's house. He looks back and sees that Chris and Dev get into the truck without the girls and leave. He sits there for a few minutes, then starts to follow the guys, cause he's not sure if Ash and I got in while he wasn't looking. He hits the dash of his rental car and says. "Dammit! I hate those trucks that have full seats in the front and in the back, especially the kind that have headrests that are the height of a person. I can't tell if the girls are in there or not."

The guys pull into the hotel parking lot and park. Dev gets out and gets into his car. He pulls out before Chris does, but Chris is right behind him. They get onto the road and go down a little bit, then turn toward the parking garage of the hospital. Mark and his buddies are right behind Chris' truck. "We'll see what they're up to now." Mark says laughing. Dev pulls into a spot on the third floor of the parking garage, then Chris pulls in next to him. It's where Chris and Dev both told Ash's Parents where Chris' truck was going to be parked. They both get out and start walking toward the elevator that takes you to the lobby area of the hospital. "Well, I guess it's safe that we can go get something to eat finally. When we get back I hope they're still here." He drives on past Chris and Dev, flipping them off. They go to Penn Station that is all the way downtown, but only five minutes away from the hospital exit of the garage. "They'll have to come right by here, if they leave before we get back."

Dev and Chris are waiting for me and Ash in the hospital lobby. They have been there for over a half hour. Chris gets his phone out and texts my phone. "Hey baby were (short for we are) jw (short for just wondering) where u (meaning you) guys r (meaning are) plz (short for please) txt (meaning text) back" Then in less than a minute his phone vibrates. "Hey sorry was helping ash's parents pack her things into the truck well (meaning we will) b (meaning be) there shortly miss u;)" He texts me back. "Miss u too <3 ;)" He looks at Dev and says, "They should be getting here shortly."

It was another fifteen minutes that passed by and the guys were starting to get worried about us. Dev looks over to Chris and says. "If we don't see them in five more minutes then we're going to look for them." He stands up pacing around the lobby area, not wanting to believe something bad has happened to us. He gets too fidgety and walks over to the gift shop to keep his mind off of Ash, me and her Parents. He sees a bracelet that reads believe. He grabs one for me, both of my Parents. He walks up to the counter to pay for it when he sees this necklace. It was a cross and it had pink roses on it. He picked it up for Ash and one for her Mother. He keeps walking up to the counter and sees something that Chris and Eric would love to have, it's a thermos with the hospital's logo on it. He purchases said items and walks out into the lobby area to see that Chris is with me, Ash and her Parents. He walks over to us and says, smiling. "It's so good to see you all."

"Yea, it's so good to see you too." Ash says smiling. "Were you worried?"

"Yea, I was. I know those guys followed Chris and I but we didn't know where they went after they sped off giving us the bird. I was worried that they went back to your Parents' house." He kisses Ash's forehead. All six of us walk up to my Dad's room.

While we were in the elevator, Chris looked over at Eric. "Hey Eric, would you like to help me unload your truck of Ash's things? I would feel safer if Dev would go out with us but I know that he's going to refuse to do it." He looks down at his hands and continues. "We can get a security guard to help us. That way if Mark and his gang come back, we'll have a witness, plus safety."

Eric looks over at him and answers. "Yes, I would be more than happy to help you unload my truck. Just can't it wait until Emily and I have met Bree's Parents?"

"Sure can." Chris answers Eric's question smiling. We finally got to the floor that we needed to get off and go straight toward my Father's room.

I stop before getting to the door and ask. "Mr. and Mrs. Hampton, could you two please stand out here and wait until we all have a chance to explain our situation to my Parents? I'll come get you two when we're done."

"Sure, Breea." Eric answers. "Where is the waiting room?"

I point toward the waiting room and say. "It's straight ahead."

Then we all walked into the room with my Parents. I walk over to the side of my Father's bed and say. "Hey guys! How are you? Are you going to get out today?"

Daddy looks up and sees me. He smiles and answers. "Yes, baby girl. I am getting out today." He notices that Chris and Dev are with me. He looks at them and says. "Thanks for making sure she got through last night. I appreciate everything you two have done for my Wife and Daughter in the past three days." He looked over at Ash and asked, "Who is this?"

I look at her and smile, answering. "Daddy, this is Ashley. Mom, you remember her don't you?"

"Yes, I sure do. How are you Ashley?"

"I'm doing good. How are you?"

"Better now that I know that my Husband is here with us." She looks down at him in the bed and says, smiling. "How is the relationship with our Daughter's Brother?"

"It's going well, but a small problem has aroused." Ash says frowning.

"Oh, what kind of problem?" Mom asks looking at her Husband to watch his reaction to her comment about Dev being my Brother.

"We'll explain that to you later, Mom." I answer.

Daddy then straightens the back of his bed up and asks. "What do you mean with your Daughter's Brother? Who is her Brother?"

Mom smiles at her Husband while answering. "Dev is Bree's half Brother by her birth Mother. We didn't find that out until the ride on the way here to look for you."

Daddy looks over at Dev and says. "Oh, okay. I can see the resemblance of his and Bree's Mother, Billie Dawn. It's like I'm looking at her Brother, Don William." He looks a little closer and asks Chris. "You sure you're not Bree's Brother, right?"

Chris looks at him and smiles real big. "I'm sure, Sir. I was raised by my birth Parents" He looked down at me and tried to get the ball rolling.

I shake my head up and down and say. "Guys, I have a question to ask you two?"

"Okay, what is it?" My Parents asked in unison.

"Well, we were wondering if you all wouldn't mind if Ash stays with us at our house, while she waits for Dev to get an apartment or a house to rent or if she gets her dorm room at the University of Kentucky this August? He's going to be living with Chris when we get back to Lexington. He needs time to find something available."

Mom and Daddy both look at Dev and at Ash. They think about it for about three seconds and Mom asks. "I thought Dev worked in Columbus?"

"Mom, Dev has requested for a transfer back home. He got the transfer and has to go to the airport in Columbus today when we leave here. That's the reason why we're trying to get this all straightened out now." I answer.

My Parents are still having trouble understanding the situation. Then my Dad asks, "What situation are you all in?"

Chris jumps in and answers. "Sir, what Bree is trying to say is that Ash is pregnant and Dev doesn't want her to travel with him alone. He wants her to ride with Bree and I to Columbus so that he can sign the transfer papers in order to move back home. He's going to be working and living with me until he can find a place of his own. He wants Ash to move in with you all because he knows that you two could keep her safe. Just until he can get his own place. Ash's Parents are here to meet you two. They want to know that she'll be taken care of and safe from the guy who raped her at med camp in Chicago three months ago." He lets his breath out and sits down.

"Oh, okay." Daddy looks at Mom and agrees with her. "That's fine with us. I agree that she needs to be taken away from here, so that guy can't ever find her." My Father looks at Ash and says. "I hope that we can help with this, I wouldn't want him finding you down there." He looks at his watch and says. "I'm a police detective and I'll do my best to watch out for you. Bring your Parents in."

Ash walks out with a smile and finds her Parents in the waiting room. She looks inside still smiling and says, "Mom, Daddy! You all can come in now." She guides them to Lance's room and blows her breath out.

They all three walk in together and look at the condition that my Father is in. Eric and Emily both gasp. "We're sorry to hear about your accident. We hope that you have a speedy recovery."

"Thank you, that means a lot to us." My Father looks over to my Mother and says. "I'm Lance, this is Quinn. We're Breea's Parents. We agreed to let your Daughter come live with us." He looks down at his watch again and says. "We know the situation the kids are in. Just to let you two know that I am a police detective in Lexington. I'll help them through this ordeal. We'll make Mark and his gang think that Ash is leaving with you all. I should be getting discharged soon. It was so nice to meet you two. I hope you two know that you can come down and see your Daughter, also you can call her anytime, day or night." He pauses and gets a drink of his water out of his cup that the hospital gave him. "I think that's the Doctor now."

My Father was right, it was the Doctor. "Hello!" Dr. Schneider says, looking at all of us. "I see that you have a very good support group here for your homegoing." He puts his papers down on the table and slides them to my Mom. "Sign here, here and here. This is just telling you the instructions that he has to go by when he gets home. He's not allowed to go back to work until he gets the okay from his primary physician." He looks down at the paperwork and gives my Parents a copy of the papers smiling, saying. "Good luck. I'm glad that there were some survivors from that awful crash." His look turns sad and he continues. "My five year old Daughter and Wife were on that flight, they weren't so lucky. Now I'm burying myself in my work to try not to think about them so much."

He starts to walk out the door when Chris says. "Hey, at least they don't have to worry about going through this cruel world. They are happy and whole again in Heaven right now. Smiling down on you because you helped a bunch of others and their families out." He squeezes the Doctor's shoulder.

The Doctor looks back, smiles and says. "Thanks, it doesn't make it any better though, but I do know that that's exactly where they both are. I find comfort in knowing that too." He exits the room with no more sad looks.

Chapter
NINE

My Father looks at Chris and asks. "So, who is going to drive me and my beautiful Wife to the airport? I'm ready for some real food too!"

Everyone laughs and starts helping my Mom and I clear my Dad's belongings out of the room. Chris looks at him and answers. "Mr. Anderson, Sir. You and your beautiful Wife are going to be riding with Dev. He has a car so it would be easier for you to get in and out of. Bree, Ash and I are going to be in my truck, right behind you all." He walks out the door and says. "I'm going to go get my truck packed with Ash's belongings. Just have Bree to text me when you all are ready to go. Dev will be going with me to help Mr. Hampton and I unload and reload her belongings. I'll be able to tell him when you all are ready." He looks at Ash's Father and asks. "You can stay here with Ash, so that you all can take your time saying goodbye."

Dev says smiling. "When you two want to come visit Ash, especially if you fly, there are a couple of names that you need to know to ask for when booking your flights. One is my supervisor, Steven Wallingford. If you tell him who you are going to visit, he'll give you a decent and better flying price. Possibly, maybe first class. The other person would be Joey Goodwin. He'll make sure your bags get to the right plane like they should." He turns around and runs off to catch up to Chris.

Chris and Dev finally get down to the main lobby and notice that there was the car again. Mark's car! He was sitting right up front acting like he was waiting on someone to come out. The guys started backing up and noticed out of the corner of their eyes that they could get a security guard to go out with them to the trucks. Chris says, "Hold on, Dev! I'm going to get a security guard for us." He walks over to the security station and rings the bell.

He hears a door open somewhere behind the counter and looks up. He sees this big guy named Henry Hawkins come out. "May I help you?"

Chris looks at the guy, then back outside to Mark's waiting car, and answers. "Yes, I can't go out to my vehicle because my friends and I have been followed by that little black Chevy Malibu. I was wanting to know if you would be so kind as to follow us to our vehicles and stay there with us while we unpack my buddies, Girlfriend's Parents truck?"

"Sir, sounds to me like you need the local authorities involved." He pauses and asks. "Have they been following you all, all day?"

"Yes, they have been. We need someone like you to ask him to leave the premises or walk us out so that we can get to our vehicles safely. We can always meet up with my buddies, Girlfriend's Parents somewhere else to unload their truck onto mine."

"Okay, does your buddy's Girlfriend's Parents know that she is going with you all?"

"Yes, they're here in the hospital also. That's why we need someone to escort us to the garage and to stay with us while we unload their truck and load it into mine. Please, Sir?" Just then another security guard comes in and hears Chris begging for this guy to help him out.

He walks over to the counter and introduces himself. "Hi, my name is AJ Horn, head of security. What seems to be the problem?"

"Yes, hi. My name is Chris and I have a problem with that little Black Chevy Malibu. They have been following me and my friends all day today. I was wondering if someone could follow us out to my truck that's parked in the garage, and stay with us while my buddy and I unload belongings to his Girlfriend into my truck. This is just in case that car spots my buddy and I walking out and they don't drive by and cause any kind of trouble with us."

A.J. looks towards the car and points at it. "That car there?"

Chris looks at where he's pointing at and answers. "Yes, Sir!"

"We can help you with that. We've been having problems with them walking in and out of the hospital for the last two hours now. I can run them off of our premises. Would that be enough to help you out with?"

"By running them off of the premises, do you mean by telling them that they can't go into the garage?"

"Yes, it does. If they don't have a family member or friend in this hospital, then they have no right to be out there waiting like they have been."

"Okay, A.J. thanks. You've been helpful. I'll see you out there." Chris jogs over to Dev and says smiling. "Good news, A.J., head of security is going to ask them to leave and then walk out with us to the garage and stay with us until we get everything packed into the back of my truck. He's going to wait for us to get in our vehicles and head back to get Ash's Parents." He pauses and looks over to his right and notices that A.J. is walking toward the car.

A.J. walking toward the little Black Chevy Malibu saying, "Sir, I need you to leave the premises. I've already called the local authorities to back me up. You've been disruptive to our patients and their families. Please, leave?"

Mark looks at the security guard and laughs. "It's a free country, I don't have to leave. I might be waiting for my Grandmother to come out from her Doctor's appointment."

"Sir, I assure you there are no Doctor's offices inside the building. If you are waiting for your Grandmother to come out of her appointment it's not at this building." A.J. explained.

"Well, that shows how much you know." Mark laughs looking in his rear view mirror, saying. "Shit, you really did call the cops?"

"Yes, sir I did. Sorry if that is of any trouble to you." Just then the cop car pulls up behind Mark's rental car and turns the lights on. Mark does something stupid, he starts the vehicle and takes off almost running over an old woman and her Grandchild. The cop car takes off after him with sirens wailing behind.

A.J. runs over to the old woman, the Grandchild helping them up. He asks, "You two okay?"

She answers, "Yes, dear. We're fine aren't we Maddie?"

"Yes, Grandma."

"Sorry about that. If you want to leave a complaint or file charges we have the license plate number written down already."

"Okay, dear. Thank you! I'll go do that right now." She takes the hand of her Grandchild, and starts heading in the direction of the security station to file charges.

A.J. jogs over to the guys and says. "I don't think that they'll be trying to bother you all again. Looks like they'll be trying to outrun the police for a while." He pauses and looks back at the guys. "They're not from around here are they?"

Dev answers, "No, they're not. They're from Chicago, it's my Girlfriend's rapist."

A.J. stops short and looks at Dev. "Say what? Did she file a report on him?"

"No, from what I can tell she's scared to death of him and doesn't want anything to do with him. She wants him to suffer, but she doesn't want to have to see him in court."

"How long ago did this happen?"

"It happened a little over three months ago. She got pregnant from it."

"Oh my, sorry to hear that. Were you two dating at that time?"

"No, we just met a couple of days ago." Dev answers smiling. "I know that sounds kind of stupid on my part, but I'm in love with her."

A.J. looks back at the guys smiling and says. "No, it doesn't sound stupid on your part. I found my Wife after she was raped. Like your Girl, my Wife was pregnant too, but we didn't find out right away of course. She told me that she was expecting and I said it doesn't matter to me. I'll raise that baby if you marry me." He pauses, smiles and continues. "I met her on my vacation. Within the three days I was on vacation we fell in love. We haven't been apart since and we now have five kids together. Been married for more than twenty-five years."

"Wow, so I guess history does repeat." Chris reacts to that response. "How did you know when you ran into her?"

Dev answers. "You just know. Something inside you clicks and you just can't see your life without her." He chuckles and finishes. "That's how I feel about Ash."

Chris looks at his best friend and shakes his head. "I think I already know anyway." They finally reached the trucks and Dev's vehicle. They get busy unpacking Ash's Parents' truck and putting it into Chris'. They hear cop sirens go by and think about it being Mark and his gang waiting for them to come out of the exit of the hospital garage. They hear over A.J.'s radio, "Some weird and exciting news for the Ohio State Police assisting Wilmington PD. A car chase is in progress. Local authorities say the vehicle was stalking four young people all day, almost hitting an elderly woman and her Grandchild walking into the Clinton Memorial Hospital. Let's give these guys some room so that they can get this bad guy off the streets of our city." The guys go on with the task of unpacking the Hampton's truck and packing it all into Chris' truck, smiling because of the news they just heard over the radio. "Hey u (you) guys done jw (just wondering) tell dev (Devin) were (we are) at da (the) door waitin (waiting) on him" Chris looks over to Dev and says. "Bree, just texted, says they are at the door waiting for you."

Dev says excitingly! "On my way!"

Chris texts Bree back. "Hes (he is) on his way baby" He finishes up the packing and says. "A.J. you can go on ahead and get the Hampton's out here. I'll be in my truck waiting on them. Dev will wait on me at the door with the girls and Bree's Parents. Thanks so much for your help." Chris tips him a fifty dollar bill, shakes his hand and gets into his truck.

A.J. walks back to the hospital entrance and gets the Hampton's. "Are you the Hampton's?"

"Yes, we are. Are you ready to escort us to our vehicle?"

"I sure am. My name is A.J. Horn. How was your visit to the Clinton Memorial Hospital today?"

"It was splendid." Mr. Hampton answers. "You all have a great security station here. I would love to donate some money to help out with expenses."

"Sir, you don't have to do that, but it is very kind of you though." A.J. replies.

"Oh, yes I do. Who do I make the check out to?" Waiting on his Wife to draw out the checkbook from her purse.

"Just make it out to Clinton Memorial Hospital, Sir. I'll see to it that it makes it to the treasurer."

"Sure will!" Mr. Hampton finishes writing the check and hands it over to A.J. "Here you go." A.J. sees how much the check is for and just about faints.

A.J. says. "Thank you! I'll be sure to bring my Wife to your hotel and restaurant." They all three make it to the truck and see that Chris is still in his.

Chris rolls down his window and says. "It was nice meeting you two. Mr. and Mrs. Hampton. See you all soon, hopefully in Kentucky."

"It was nice meeting you too, Chris, take care now." Eric says waving to him smiling.

Chris pulls into the loading lane and gets out. "I'm here! Are you two ladies ready to go?"

I answer him smiling. "Yes, we are!" I look back to Ash and wave at her. "Let's go girlie!" Smiling, we both load up into Chris' truck.

We've been driving for about an hour since leaving the Hospital. Still following Dev, we start slowing down. We follow Dev onto an off ramp and pull in behind him at an Olive Garden. Chris gets out of the truck and walks over to help Ash out before he helps me. "How was the ride, girls?"

I look up at him, smile and kiss his cheek. "It was well!" Looking over at Ash and Dev, they were hugging and holding each other's hands. We all walk into the restaurant and sit down at a table. I look at my Parents and ask. "How was your ride?"

My Father answers for him and my Mother. "It was a fine ride, pretty scenery. How was yours?" Looking over his reading glasses with a stern look. Warning me with that look to be careful what I say.

Laughing at my Dad and his look, I answer. "Mine was good. We listened to music and talked the whole way. It went kind of fast."

"Well, that's good! Hopefully the ride back home will go by fast too. I wish your Mother and I could go back with you all but I know we can't because I have a Doctor's appointment first thing in the morning." He continues eating his roll, starting to get a little bit grumpy. We finally ordered our food and got our drinks.

Ash's phone starts ringing in the middle of us all eating our food. "Hello?"

"Ash, I have some news about Mark."

"Hold on a minute Daddy." She puts her phone on speaker for all of us to hear. "Okay, Daddy. Go ahead."

"Hey, everyone! I have some good news to share about Mark!"

"Alright, let's hear it Mr. Hampton." Dev replies excitedly.

"Here it goes. Mark and his buddies were arrested, after their tire blew out on the interstate leading from Columbus. You all probably passed them chasing him or the scene. I just got off the phone with A.J. Horn. He said they finally caught them and found out that they had warrants for their arrests. They were involved in drug trafficking and a lot of arsons. They are going to put them away for the rest of their lives. Isn't that good news?"

"Yea, it is!" Dev throws his hands up in the air smiling. He kisses Ash right on the lips. "I knew we were going to be able to get them arrested."

"Thanks for the great news Daddy! Love you and Mom!"

"We love you all too, be safe!"

"We will be Mr. Hampton." Dev answers him. "I can't believe this, it's all over baby." With her Father still on the phone, Dev gets up and pulls her up with him. He stands her up straight and gets down on one knee. "Ashley Dawn Hampton, will you marry me?"

She looks at Dev in shock and at the rest of us. She notices that her phone is still laying on the table. She answers as calmly as she could. "Yes, I'll marry you!"

Dev gets up and says. "Thank you! I promise you I'll make you happy everyday. I know that I don't have a ring yet for you, but we will pick one out later. It's got to be the right one for you though." He bends down and kisses her belly. "Hey, little person. I'm going to be your Daddy." He gets up and smiles real big. He notices that Ash's phone is still on and that Mr. and Mrs. Hampton is still there. He could hear them crying and said. "Thanks guys for having the most beautiful woman in the world for me to have as my future Wife."

They talk for a little while longer and then hang the phone up. Both of them sit down to finish their food, excited about what the future holds for them.

Chris gets up and walks over to his best friend. "Congratulations man. I knew something was up when I caught you on your phone prior to Ash getting that phone call from her Parents." They both sit down and Chris sees my eyes. He knows that I'm the right one for him, but he isn't going to propose just yet. He's going to wait for the right moment. He pulls me over to him and kisses me on my forehead, then he whispers into my ear. "I know that look. Don't be getting all excited here, cause I want to get to know you a lot better than I already do."

We finish our food and get ready for the last thirty minute drive of the trip. It went by in a blur. Ash got another phone call from her

Parents about her Brother's Wife going into labor. She was all excited about that, plus about the proposal. I don't know which one was more exciting but they were both up there to her. We listen to music and Ash talks about her relationship with her Brother.

Finally pulling into the airport parking lot. We all climbed out of the vehicles and grabbed the luggage for my Parents. Following Dev into the terminal. He turns around and asks. "Who needs to use the restroom?"

Ash raises her hand up in the air and smiles. "Sorry, the baby must be laying on my bladder." We all laugh and just the girls follow her to the restroom.

Dev walks up to a woman standing behind a counter. Smiling he says, "Sarah, my friends here need two airline tickets to Lexington, Kentucky."

She smiles back and says. "Let me see what we have." She types on her computer spotting that there are two that are leaving within the hour of each other. She looks back up at Dev and says. "We have a flight that is leaving in a half an hour from now. It's filling up fast, so I need to know if you want it within five minutes? The cost is huge though!"

Dev looks at my Parents and asks. "What do you guys want to do?"

They both look at each other and my Mom asks. "What is the second one?"

Sarah looks at her computer for a moment and says, smiling. "The second flight is leaving in an hour, they aren't as booked but it's still filling coach."

My Daddy asks, "What's the cost of the second one?" Apparently not really wanting to fly again.

"Well, Sir. The cost of the first one is more expensive than the second one. The first one is only filling up first class now. We still have two seats in first class on that one. The second one is just coach, and it's got sixteen more seats to fill before they start filling first class."

While my Parents are trying to decide which one to take, Sarah asks Dev. "Devin, did I hear right? Are you leaving us?"

Dev looks at her, smiles and replies. "Yes, Sarah it's true. I'm going back home. I'm engaged and going to be a Daddy soon. So I think it's high time I get my butt back home where all my friends and family are." He looks back at Chris and I and winks at us. He looks at my Parents and says. "I don't mean to rush you guys, but you two need to make a decision on the flights. They do go like hot cakes, especially when they start trying to fill first class. They discount the price a little."

My Parents look at each other and my Mother decides on her own. "The first flight, the one that leaves in a half hour."

Dev looks at Sarah and says. "You heard the lady. Book them!" He looks back at my Parents and says. "You know what Sarah. I need to talk to Steve, do you know where he is?"

"He's in his office."

"Can you please phone him?"

"Alright, give me a moment." While she's typing away on her computer. Sarah is waiting on Steven to answer his phone and then hands the phone to Dev.

Dev asks. "Steven?"

"Yes? Is this Devin DeAtley?"

"Yes Sir, it sure is. I need a favor please."

"What is it and I'll try my best."

"Great thanks. I need to book the first class flight to Lexington, Kentucky in a half an hour."

"Sure will do it. You at the airport right now?"

"Yes, I sure am. I'm sending my Sister's Parents home today and they want the family discount."

"Alright, how does seventy five dollars sound for both tickets?"

He looks down at my Parents and asks. "How does seventy five dollars for both tickets sound?"

My Daddy shakes his head up and down smiling excitedly. Not believing this is happening.

Dev says. "Okay, they'll take it. Could you send that copy of the price down to Sarah please?"

"Sure will. I guess I'll be seeing you in a few minutes then?"

"Yes, you sure will." He hangs the phone up and says. "Sarah, have you got that copy yet? I need you to phone Joey and tell him that they didn't have proper baggage. He needs to give them a concierge bag please. Then I need you to phone JD and let him know that we will need a ride to the gate." He picks the bags up that we brought in with us and sends them over the counter with Sarah.

Sarah is on the phone with Joey telling him about the baggage deal and then she phones JD and tells him to meet them before he gets to the security gates. "You're all set Devin. Congratulations!"

We all take off following Dev and get to the security gates. We all go through each one of the five that were there with no one waiting in line to get through. Then Dev sees JD and waves to him smiling. "JD, my man. What's up?"

"Working man! Thanks for this job. I love it." He sees how many people he is going to be escorting. "Wow, who are all these people?"

"This is my Sister, Breea." Dev says pointing to me. Pointing to Chris, "This is my best friend, Chris. This is my fiance Ashley!" Pointing to her and then to my Parents. "These two lovely people are my Sister's Parents Quinn and Lance."

"Well, your family is just getting bigger and bigger while you're on vacation. Congratulations on the engagement. How far along is your fiance'?"

"She's about three months along. We just found out last night while we were in Wilmington." He looks at JD and answers his question. "No, the baby doesn't belong to me biologically, but I'm going to be on the birth certificate." Dev looks back and smiles at Ash as she returns the smile.

"Here you all go. Here's your gate." Daddy and Mom get off the cart. They both say their goodbyes and hurry to the gate. They turn around one last time before walking through the tunnel to the plane. They wave and blow kisses at everyone, then hurry on into the tunnel.

Dev, Ash, Chris and I all stand there watching the plane take off. Then we were off to Dev's supervisor's office. We finally get there after passing all the security gates again and Dev knocks on the door. The door opens and he looks back at us. "I'll be right back. This shouldn't take but a minute." He grabs Ash's hand and takes her with him smiling.

Chris looks at me and says, "He's got it bad, doesn't he?"

I look at him and answer. "Yes, I think he does. He's proud though. He doesn't care what anyone thinks."

Chris looks back down at me and says smiling. "I know he doesn't, that's what I like most about him." He looks at me for the longest time and asks. "Are you worried about something?"

I look up at him, smiling. "You get my looks right on key, you know that?"

He looks at me grinning, "Yea, I know." He grabs me by my neck with the crook of his arm and starts walking toward the main entrance of the airport. "It would be nice if we would have met sooner. That way we could already be engaged and knew everything about one another. It's a shame that I'm not as daring as Dev though."

"How did you know what I was thinking?" I look up at him almost laughing. Then I take off running from him.

He runs after me and we get caught by the same security guard JD. "Hey, you two I'm going to have to ask that you don't run please."

We both look at each other and start laughing. We sit down near the doors and rest. Chris looks over at me and asks. "It's been a pretty busy day hasn't it?"

"Yea, first getting followed from last night to this morning, getting the news that my Father was getting released, and Dev's proposal to Ash. Oh, let's not forget the phone call from Ash's Father about her Brother and Sister in-law having their baby." I sit back against the seat and say. "Yea, a busy day indeed."

Chris looks at me and asks. "What are you worried about?"

"I don't know." I think about how it would feel just to do something on the spur of the moment. "How would it feel to just take the plunge like Dev and Ash?"

"I don't know how it would feel. If I ever had to take the plunge like that I would like for it to be with you." Chris gets down on one knee and lifts my head up to meet his.

I look at him seriously and ask. "You really would rather it be me than for it to be, let's see." I pause to look around and find Sarah. "Her?"

He looks over to where I'm pointing my finger and swats at it laughing. "Yes, I would rather it be you than her. I know your looks, your smiles, your body language. I know that when you're worried about something, you stay quiet, and when you're really happy about something you talk non stop as fast as a rabbit. I know that if I don't kiss you soon, that we'll both burst, and that we won't be happy until we do get engaged. So, how about it? Why don't we take the plunge like Dev and Ash?" He is still down on one knee, need I remind you.

I look at him seriously and answer. "We just met each other. There is a lot more to get to know about one another. I wouldn't mind being Mrs. Christopher Michael Lee. Wouldn't mind the feeling of our baby's kicks and toes in between the rib cage." I thought about it for a few minutes and answered as seriously as I could. "You're serious, aren't you?"

He looks up at me and smiles real big. "As serious as anyone can get with a Girl like you."

"Chris, you can't be doing this! Are you?"

He looks up at me and sits down. He puts his forehead against mine, saying. "Yes, Breea Leighann Anderson, I am serious. I think I knew the first time I saw you, that you were the one for me. I want to be your Husband, lover, and best friend. I want to be the one to make you happy. I want you to be my Wife and have my babies. I want to spend the rest of my life with you. Just think about it. We'll be able to ride in my truck by ourselves tomorrow to Kentucky and you can give me your answer then, and if you don't then you can give me an answer when you feel like giving me an answer. All I know is that I need you to want to be with me if we do this."

"Oh, Chris. I don't know what to say."

"Just say yes to him dear. That's the way it was in my day. The man asked and the woman said yes." A stranger sitting next to us heard the whole conversation. "It doesn't matter what you two know about each other. What matters is that you two have the love of one, and you two have that with each other. It's a gift that I wouldn't want to mess up by saying no." She smiles, then gets up with her bags and walks to the security gates.

Chris and I both watched her leave and we didn't even see a wedding set on her hand. We both look at each other and I say. "Yes, Christopher Michael Lee, I will marry you."

Chapter
TEN

....

He gets up and pulls me into his body. Then he tips my head back a little and kisses me tenderly. Then we just sit and wait on Dev and Ash. We agree not to say anything to those two because we want to tell our parents ourselves. "So, we're going to wait until I get a ring, then tell them right?"

Chris looks over at me and smiles real big. "If that's what you want to do. It doesn't matter to me, because I already know your answer." Then he tilts my mouth up to his and kisses me again. He whispers in my ear. "I can't wait to have you." After he says that he has a crooked grin that he makes when he's trying to be ornery.

While we were sitting there waiting on Dev and Ash we heard a sound. We look behind us and don't see anything, then we look up and see Dev and Ash celebrating. We got up and Chris asked. "What are you two celebrating now?"

Dev looked down at us and smiled real big. "I'll tell you when we get down there." They come running down the steps with Dev in front of Ash so he could catch her if she falls down. "We heard the whole thing. It's time to celebrate."

We all walk out to the parking garage and get into the vehicles. It's Dev and Ash in his car and then Chris and I in his truck. We're following Dev back to his place. My phone rings and it scares the hell out of me. I look at the caller id and say. "It's my Mom." I pick the phone up and put it on speaker. "Mom?"

"Bree honey. Just calling to let you know we made it to the airport. I didn't want you to worry the whole time. She didn't, did she Chris?"

Chris smiles and answers. "No, she didn't."

"Thanks for letting me know. We're finally on our way to Dev's now. He was a little bit of a slow poke at the airport. He had to stop and talk to everyone he used to work with. How was your flight?"

"Oh, your Father and I owe Dev a thank you." She pauses for a moment then asks me. "Bree, honey. You okay? You sound like you're bursting at the seems to tell me something."

"I'm fine Mom. More than just fine actually." I hold my hand over the mouthpiece of my phone and look at Chris. "Should I tell her?"

Chris shrugs his shoulders. "It's up to you baby." He reaches for my hand and holds it, while he's shifting down. Dev is slowing down, and pulling into a driveway.

I get back on the phone and answer her. "Mom, everything is fine. We'll have to have lunch when we return to Lexington tomorrow. Chris wants me to meet his Parents and I want you and Daddy to be with me when I do. It's got me nervous as all get out."

"Okay, I don't think that's what you wanted to tell me, but okay for now. Where do you want us to meet you all at and at what time?"

"I'll have to get back to you on that one. We have to discuss that with Dev and Ash. We don't know what time they will want to leave from here."

"Okay, just send me a text then. I'll be pretty busy tomorrow. I have to take the dog to the vet, your Dad has his appointment first thing in the morning, and we have to go see your Grandmother. Apparently she fired Eva today or yesterday over something stupid I'd say. We love you Bree Bree, talk to you later."

"Love you both too. Bye!" I hang the phone up with her and Chris let's go of my hand. I look at him not even paying attention that we're stopping. "What, are you mad at me for not telling her?"

He looks at me and smiles. "No, I could never be mad at you. I'm far from it." He reaches over and kisses me. "We're here."

I look up at the big building and wonder if we have the right place. "This is Dev's place?"

"Yea, it's his apartment building. Are you ready to go in?" He holds his hand out for me to slide across the seat to get out on his side.

I get out and can't get over how beautiful the building is. I look up to the top of the building and ask. "What floor do you live on?"

Dev looks over at me and smiles. "I live on the very top." He chuckles while I look at him with amazement. "No, Sis. I live on the third floor." He points to a window and I see his dog hopping up and out of sight with excitement. We all get on the elevator to get to Dev's floor and finally get to his door. "Well, here we are. Don't look at the place. It's probably messy. Misty doesn't like being left alone for long periods of time. She can make a mess as big as this building is if she doesn't get to go outside." He opens the door and a great big chocolate lab greets us with licks. She smells everyone taking a liking toward Ash.

We all sit down to rest a few minutes and Misty blocks Dev from sitting next to Ash on the sofa. She growls a little bit, hops up on the sofa and lays her head on Ash's belly. "Well, Misty, I've never seen you act like that before." Dev says sitting down next to Ash after sitting on the other side of Ash. "Chris, Bree. This is the living room. There is the dining room/kitchen, and at the back there are two doors on the left. The first door is the bathroom and the second door is my room. The only door on the right is the guest bedroom, where one of you will be sleeping tonight." He looks over toward Ash and says. "I know I won't be sleeping with Misty tonight, I've got someone else to cuddle up to!" He chuckles lightly and hugs her. "Chris, if you want Bree to have the room, the sofa does pull out into a bed." He gets up and helps Ash up.

They go to his room and shut the door. While he's shutting the door he looks back and says. "Goodnight guys." He turns the hallway light off.

Chris and I both sit in the dark for the longest time, staying silent. During that time I decided to get dressed in some pajamas. Chris gets up and pulls me up off the sofa. He starts kissing my neck and whispers in my ear. "Come with me!"

I follow him into the spare bedroom. We turn the light on to see that Dev keeps a pretty tidy house. Chris turns the light off and starts moving a lot. He asks, "You do have your pajamas on right?"

I answer. "Yes, Chris I do. I changed after the light in the hallway went off, remember?"

"Yea, I remember." I hear the sheets on the bed rustling and then a murmur. "Come on Bree. Climb in with me."

I climb in bed and snuggle up to him. The next thing I know it's morning.

Chapter
ELEVEN

....

I wake up beside Chris. I blink a couple of times and smile at him. He was lying there just watching me sleep. "You know you are even more beautiful when you're sleeping." He says with a smile.

I look at him and kiss him lightly on the lips, smiling I say. "Thank you. You're even more handsome waking up in the mornings." Then I remember where we're at. I set up in bed as quickly as I could and asked. "Is Dev and Ash up yet?"

He looks around and answers, smiling. "Yea, they have already left to go do some last minute errands that Dev needs to do before moving. Plus, they're going to a jewelry store to look at rings too." He climbs over top of me and rests there for a while smiling.

I look at him and ask. "What?"

"Nothing, I'm the luckiest man in the world right now." He brings his face down to mine and kisses me lightly on the lips. He raises back up and says, "Come here. I have a surprise for you."

We walk out into the hallway and walking into the dining area, I see this big stuffed teddy bear with a red ribbon on it. It has a card and a little box attached to it. I look over at him smiling and ask, "What's this?"

He looks at me smiling real big and says. "Go on, open the card!"

I walk over to the big stuffed teddy bear and feel it first. It's so soft that I wouldn't mind sleeping with it when I'm not sharing a bed with Chris. I touch the card and box. I open the card and it reads.

Breea,

I'm hoping that you will stay happy with me for the rest of our lives. I meant what I said last night at the airport, when I asked you to marry me. I want to spend the rest of our lives together. All you have to do is put the ring on. I'll love you always and forever.

Love You Baby,

Chris

I look over at him and smile real big. I pick the box up and open it. I see that it's a big diamond. It's one karat. I get it out, looking out the corner of my eye and watching him at the same time. His eyes just keep getting bigger and bigger. Then I look at it some more and walk over to him, and say. "You're supposed to put the ring on my finger." I hold my left hand toward him and give him the box with the ring. He takes the ring out of the box and puts it on my left ring finger. He grabs me up and starts kissing me anxiously.

"Oh, God! Bree, you don't know how happy you've made me today." Then he starts to carry me toward the bedroom. "I want to celebrate by doing something to you that I think you would love." He lays me on the bed, taking my pajama bottoms off, raises my shirt up and starts running his tongue along my mid section. I rise up and down cause this is a different feeling that I've never experienced before. He gets on top of me with my underwear still on. He starts kissing my shoulders, leaving trails of tiny kisses up to my neck. He kisses me on my lips tenderly but anxiously.

We keep doing this until Dev and Ash come back. Dev hollers, "We're back! Are you sleepy heads awake?" Walking back toward the rooms and Chris hurries to put my pajama bottoms back on me. I giggle and almost start laughing when Dev pops his head around the corner of the door. He looks at me laying there in the bed next to Chris all snuggled up to me, making me laugh by tickling me, and says. "It's about time you two got up. Come on, we want to show you the ring."

We both get up grumbling and walk into the living room with Dev. We see Ash standing there rubbing her belly with her left hand. We see the rock all the way from where we're standing and stop. Looking at it we both just walk closer.

I pick up Ash's hand and ask. "Is it heavy?" Absent minded about the ring that Chris gave to me and it being on my left ring finger.

Ash replies, "no, not really. It was a first, but now it's not. I've already taken pictures and sent them to my Parents. They're so happy and thrilled." She smiles, looking at herself, not believing that things are finally taking a turn for the better in her life for once. She sees my ring, "Oh, my gosh. Dev come look at this. It looks almost identical to mine."

I turn around toward Dev and hold up my left hand and smile. He looks at it and to Chris. He grabs a hold of Ash, kissing her lightly on the forehead, looking at Chris and asks. "Where and when did you get the ring?"

Chris answers Dev. "Dev, man. You know that ring belonged to my Dad's Mom. You've seen it before." He comes over by me and puts his arm around me smiling. "I went and got it the night that I traveled up here to help." He kisses my cheek.

Dev remembers, smiling and says. "Oh, yea!" He lets go of Ash and she hugs me first while Dev hugs Chris. Then vice versa. I see that Chris is smiling still and I start to believe that I made him happy like he says I do. I start smiling too.

We all sit down at the dining room table and just stare at each other for a while. Chris says, "I'm wondering? Dev, did you get everything taken care of?"

"Yeah, I sure did. They're supposed to be here around eleven to go through what all I need packed. Most of it is still in boxes, so it won't be that hard for them. The furniture stays here and the rest is my clothes, pots and pans. Those sorts of things. So, it shouldn't be too much on the movers." He gets up and walks out into the hallway. He gets a handful of boxes, then brings them to us smiling and says. "Here you go." He hands a folded up box to Chris and to me. "Now get to work," he says laughing while unfolding one for himself and Ash. They go to his room and get five boxes out of his room alone.

Chris hollers toward the living room and asks Dev. "Do you want to take these books that are in here? What about the bedsheets, cover and pillows? You want them packed too?"

Dev comes running back to where Chris and I were and looks in on Ash packing the restroom. "Yea, that's good babe." He looks in on Chris and I packing the spare room. "I'll take the cover, sheets and pillows. The books can stay here. They were here when I got here. I never touched them. That lamp goes with us though. The rest can stay here." He goes back with Ash behind him.

"The bedrooms, bathroom and living room are done." Ash says to Dev, while bending down to kiss him. "I got a picture text from my Parents with Bailey and Austin's baby boy. She pulls the picture up and shows him. "Isn't he cute?"

"Yea, babe he sure is." He looks at the picture a little more and smiles, saying. "I can't wait til this one is out." He rubs her stomach and kisses her forehead. "What did Austin and Bailey name him? How was Bailey and the baby after he was delivered? What about her condition, did the Doctor have any trouble?"

"His name is Bentley Austin Hampton, born on June twentieth at nine pm. He weighed nine pounds, twelve ounces, twenty one inches long. Mom said that Bailey did real great, and Bentley did real great. He doesn't have to stay in the NICU because of his weight. Bailey's condition got better once they got Bentley out, but when she was pushing him out they couldn't get her to stop bleeding." Ash says sitting down. "I'm worn out already."

Dev looks over at her and smiles. "Just rest babe. You don't need to do it anymore. That's good to hear about Bailey, Austin and Bentley." He goes on and finishes the kitchen. He gets up and moves to the living room and sits down. "I'm glad that's all done." He leans back and rests his head on the back of the couch. "Hey, Chris?"

"Yea?" Chris answers immediately.

"Are you all done there or what? We're running kind of behind on schedule. We need to get these boxes downstairs, before a downpour comes." He gets up and opens the door and starts pushing boxes out into the hallway.

"Yea, we're done here. Coming out with the two boxes." Walking out with a box each, I volunteer myself to help pack them down to Dev's new ride. He bought a truck with the money that he's been saving. He needed something that was going to be more dependable for Ash and the baby. We load his things into the back of his truck after we get all the boxes downstairs on the steps. He heads back up to get Ash. He walks into his old apartment and sees that she has fallen asleep on the sofa. He kisses her on the forehead. "Hey, babe. We're done. Are you ready to get on the road?"

She wakes up smiling and says, "Yea, just let me use the restroom before we get on the road. Don't want to have to stop if we don't have to." She gets up and kisses Dev on the lips before she goes. He waits on her while she does that and kind of says his goodbyes to his apartment that he was living in for over three years and puts the leash on Misty. "We've had some good times in the place haven't we girl?" Patting her stomach while she sits patiently waiting for Ash to come out of the bathroom.

He finally looks at her walking up the hallway and asks. "You ready milady?" He crooks his arm toward her, for her to put her arm through his and walk out of the apartment. Shutting the door, he takes the key with him and slides it under the building's office door. Leave the last month's rent and a letter stating that his job was transferred, and that he wouldn't be here anymore. Here's the last month's rent though.

Hopefully someone else will be able to use it. Then they walk out to his new truck. They get in and see that Chris and I are already in Chris' truck ready to go.

Chris looks over to me, smiles and asks. "You want to call your Parents and tell them that we should be in Kentucky around two? Ask them if they want to meet us around six for supper since we can't get there until two anyways."

I look at him smiling and answer. "Yea, as long as you call your Parents and do the same."

"Okay! I will!" He says back to me. "After you call your Parents first." He keeps on driving.

I get my phone out and go through my address book. I look for my Parents house number, but then remember that they probably aren't home. So, I look for my Mother's cell phone number. I find it, bring it up and push send. I wait for my Mother to answer.

"Hey, Bree! Are you all on the road now?"

"Yes, Mom. We just left Dev's apartment. How is Daddy? What did the Doctor say about him?"

"The Doctor said that everything looks good. He has to be off of work for two more weeks though, and continue his medication. The police department is going to pay the hospital bill for us since he was on a business trip." She takes a breath and then continues. "So, what time did you and Chris want us to meet you all and where?"

"He said around six. I don't know where yet. Hold on and I'll ask him." I put my hand over the mouthpiece of my phone, look at Chris smiling and ask. "She wants to know where you want to meet at six?"

Chris strokes his head with his left hand, smiles and answers. "How does Cheddars sound? I'll pay for it."

I looked at him and didn't realize that he knew my favorite place to eat is Cheddars. I smile at him and say. "That's my favorite place to eat. I love that place." I pick my phone back up from between my legs and give my Mom an answer. "He said at Cheddars. He'll pay for it."

My Mom replies back. "Okay, honey. We'll see you guys around six at Cheddars then. Have a safe drive and we'll meet you all there. Love you!"

"Love you too, Mom." I hang the phone up and look at Chris. I say, "Okay, now it's your turn to call your Parents."

Chris gets his phone out and starts hitting a random amount of numbers then hits send. He waits for someone to answer on the other end of the line.

"Hello, Chris!" Christine answers.

"Hey, Mom. How are you and Dad?"

"We're fine. He's at work right now. I'm bored to death. Wishing you were here with me right now. I just got some bad news about your Grandfather."

"Which Grandfather?" Chris asks with a worried look on his face. "Grandpa Lee or Grandpa Mikel?"

"Grandpa Mikel, honey. He's not doing so well. They are airlifting him here from the nursing home in Flemingsburg. He had a heart attack and passed out. He hasn't woken up yet." She sniffs and says. "Your Aunt Molly called just a few minutes ago and told me before you called."

"Okay, are you and Dad going to the hospital to meet him?"

"Probably will. Why did you need to ask something?"

"Yes, I was wondering if you and Dad would want to meet up tonight around six at Cheddars? Bree and her Parents will be there. I want you all to meet them."

"Okay, honey. We'll try to be there. We'll probably go to the hospital and then meet you all there. Does that sound okay to you?"

"Yea, Mom!" He gets a little bit excited and then remembers that his Mom is hurting. "Mom, tell Grandpa Mikel that I love him and that I'll see him soon. I love you and Dad too." He hangs the phone up and looks over to me. "Come here." He raises his arm up to make room for me to sit beside him in his truck.

I take my seat belt off and the scoot over next to him. I raise my head up a bit and kiss his cheek. I put the seat belt on and just sit there beside him and stay quiet. I know he's feeling a little sad about his Grandpa's condition. He looks at me smiling, asking. "What are you thinking?"

I look at him and answer. "Just how lucky we all are to have people in our lives that love us so much. Your Grandpa sounds like he's very loved."

He looks at me and smiles real big. He says, "Yea, he is loved very much. My Grandmother Maggie, met my Grandfather Mikel much like we met. I'll have her tell you the story when we get back. We'll have to drive up to Flemingsburg before my two week vacation is up and visit her. That is if she isn't in Lexington at the hospital with my Grandfather." He takes a hold of my hand and holds it until he sees Dev pulling off the highway. He goes in the same direction that Dev does and pulls into a gas station.

We all get out and stretch our bones. When we are doing this Chris and I both see Ash run off toward the gas station like a bat out of heck. I look over smiling and say. "Pregnancy, what is she going to do?" I walk in the gas station with the guys and look for a bottle of water. I find it and grab it out of the cooler. I start walking up to the counter and see the guys standing at the counter waiting on me. "Hey!" I say to them smiling.

Dev and Chris both smile back at me and say. "Hey!" I put the bottle of water up on the counter and stand aside. I take two dollars out of my pocket and hand the cashier my money to pay for the bottle of water. Chris looks over at me and frowns. I look up at him and ask. "What?"

"I can't pay for your water?" Chris asks.

"Yes, you can pay for my water if you want. I just don't expect you to do that."

"Well, I am and did." He hands me my bottle of water and smiles real big. He looks over to Dev and says. "We'll be waiting out in the truck." We both turn around and head back to the truck. We're in the truck now and we have our seat belts buckled and waiting on Dev and Ash still. While we're sitting there, we see a black Chevy Malibu pull in. Much like the one that Mark and his gang were driving. Chris looks over at me and says. "Hold on, let's wait to see who gets out of that car." We wait and see that it's some teenage girl that gets out and he looks over at me. He smiles, puts his hand underneath my chin and kisses me. "That was close, huh?"

I look at him and answer. "Yes, that was. I bet Dev was ready to pee his pants when he saw that car pulling in."

Chris takes his hand and rests it on my thigh, a little too close for my comfort. He stops and asks, "What's wrong?"

"I just don't feel comfortable doing things like that in public yet." I scoot his hand closer to my knee. "I don't want to make you mad, but just give me some time, please?"

He unlocks his grip that he has on me and says. "I'm sorry, I just wasn't thinking." He smiles and kisses my forehead to show me that he isn't mad at me. We watch for Ash and Dev to come out.

Chris starts his truck up and follows Dev out onto the highway.

I must have fallen asleep because I don't even remember going through Ashland on the interstate. When I woke up we were parked at a restaurant and Chris was shaking me. "Bree, are you hungry?"

I open my eyes and smile up at him. I answer, "Yea, I'm hungry." I take my seatbelt off and get out on his side of the truck. We meet up with Dev and Ash. We all four walked into McDonald's. As soon as we get inside Ash and I head to the bathroom after telling Chris and Dev what we want to eat. The guys go up to the counter and order the food we all wanted. Ash and I both come out of the bathroom giggling and see that the guys have already found us a table next to the bathrooms, just in case Ash had to pee again. Ash sits down beside Dev on the outside of the bench and I make Chris get up and scoot over next to the wall. We all are pretty quiet and just eat our food.

We finally finish with our food and Ash gets up and goes back to the bathroom again, while Dev and Chris get up to throw our trash in the trash can. We all three go and get refills for the rest of the ride back to Lexington and wait for Ash to come out.

She finally comes out and gets her drink and throws it in the trash can. She looks at Dev and asks him. "Dev, honey. Will you please buy me some water?"

He looks at her and answers. "Yes, babe." He goes back up to the counter as Ash, Chris and I are walking back to the trucks. We wait there by Dev's truck with Ash. We stand there for about five minutes when he starts running out. He looks at Chris, Ash and I and asks. "Are you all ready to go?"

Chris answers. "Yea, dude. We're all ready. Follow me. I know how to get there from here." I wait for Chris to unlock his truck and climb in, in front of him. He stands there and watches me to make sure that I make it in. I get my seatbelt on in the middle and wait for him to get in. He's finally in and puts his seatbelt on. He starts his truck up and holds my hand while he shifts his gears to get up to a higher speed. He makes sure that Dev and Ash are following us from behind and then Chris puts his turn signal on. We are finally on I64, heading toward Lexington. I sit back and relax listening to music on Sirius radio.

Chapter
TWELVE

....

W e finally reached Mt. Sterling on I64 and pull off to stretch our legs. We get out and walk around for a few minutes while waiting for Ash and Dev to come back out to their vehicle. Of course, she had to use the restroom again. Chris walks over to me smiling and says. "Hey, I got a phone call from my Mom while I was in the gas station getting us a snack and something to drink. She said that my Grandpa Mikel is going to be fine. He just needs to be kept for observation over night. If he doesn't have another heart attack then he gets to go back to the nursing home in Flemingsburg tomorrow."

I look at him, smile and kiss his cheek asking. "That's good news right?"

He looks at me smiling and says, "Yes. It is good news. We will get to travel to Flemingsburg when he gets out because I'm the one taking them home." He returns my kiss on my cheek and smiles real big, then continues. "You want to go with us when I take them? We'll spend the night, then drive back the next day."

I look at him smiling and answer. "Yea, I sure do. That way I can hear the story about how your Grandma and Grandpa met." I look over toward the entrance of the gas station and see Dev and Ash are finally walking out with a bunch of things in their arms. I run up to Dev and ask. "What is all of this?"

Dev looks at me and smiles, answering. "Bree, it's something for me and Ash to snack on. She's pregnant, you know they have weird cravings and want something every five minutes." He chuckles and looks toward Ash. "You need help with that stuff before you get in the truck?"

Ash looks at him smiling, answering. "Yea, if you wouldn't mind."

Dev walks over to the passenger side of the truck and helps her in. Then he hands the snacks and things up to her when she gets her seatbelt on. He looks at her and asks. "Are you ready to get back on the road again?" While putting Misty in the back seat.

Ash answers. "Yes, I can't wait until we're done driving. I want to be at Bree's Parents house and settle in. Then I want to hang out with you over at Chris' place. If that's okay with you?"

Dev looks at her answering her question with a smile. "I had planned to go to my Parents' house when we got done unpacking things." He looks toward me and smiles. I smile back at him and look toward Ash. "If you want to, you can go with me to meet them. I've met your Parents, but you haven't met mine yet. It would be a great opportunity for you to go." He smiles at her and kisses her forehead once he gets into his truck. "They don't know that I'm moving back yet. It'll be a big surprise to them."

Ash looks over at him and says, smiling. "Yea, I will go with you to meet them. Besides, I think Chris and Bree are wanting to do something by themselves without us tagging along." She looks over at me standing outside the truck and winks.

"Yea, Chris and I already have plans to meet both sets of Parents at Cheddars at six tonight. So, go on and have fun. I can always meet Dev's adoptive Parents later." I head back to Chris' truck and he opens his door and climbs out. He picks me up and helps me into his truck. I get into the middle of the seat and put my seatbelt on and watch him climb in.

He finally gets in and puts his seatbelt on. Then he looks over at me smiling and asks. "Are you ready to get back on the road again? It's just a straight shot to Lexington now."

I look over at him and answer. "Yea, sure am. I can't wait until six tonight. I want to meet your Parents and have supper at my favorite restaurant. Don't get me wrong, I liked the new restaurants that we tried up in Wilmington and Columbus, but they don't beat Cheddars."

"Yea, I know what you mean baby." He starts his truck up and pulls out onto the road to get to the interstate. We pull onto the interstate and speed up to seventy miles an hour with Dev and Ash behind us. "When we take my Grandparents back home, I'm going to take you to a back field and teach you how to drive my truck."

I look at him and say. "I know how to drive a stick shift. My Dad taught me on his Parents farm in Paris." I think for a minute and ask him. "Are you getting tired of driving?"

He looks over at me and answers my question. "I didn't know you already knew how to drive a stick shift. Sorry if I offended you." He grabs my hand and kisses the back of it. He lets it go and puts his right hand on my thigh. "I'm kind of getting tired of driving, but it's okay. As long as it's you that I'm driving. I won't be able to drive now without you being right beside me. It would make it feel awkward." He scoots his hand up my thigh and asks. "Is this okay that I'm keeping my hand here?" Shaking my thigh a little.

"Yea, it's okay. I don't mind it much now. I think I'm getting used to it." Looking at him, smiling. I can't think of him not being with me anymore. All I can see is me and him together for the rest of our lives. We kept on driving and finally hit Lexington.

Chris looks over to me and asks. "Where is it that you live?"

I look at him and answer. "I live in Willow Oak on Laurel Oak Lane."

"Okay, close to my house that I bought on Stone Crossing Lane. If I'd known that sooner, then we would have been together sooner." He takes an off ramp that takes you to Man O' War Boulevard. He looks at me and asks. "I can't wait for tonight either. My Parents are going to love you." He turns right on Man O' War and keeps on driving until he passes his street. The next street he takes a left and looks in his rear view mirror and sees that Dev is still behind us. He says, "They're right on our tail end. I guess it's been too long for Dev." He chuckles.

I look back and see that Chris was right. They were right on our tail. I look at him and say. "Okay, we're getting close. You might want to slow down before you pass it up." I point to my Parents house and see that they are home. "Right here." We pull in and park. We both get out with Dev and Ash pulling in right behind us.

They get out and walk up to Chris' truck. My Parents see that we finally made it and come out with Bubbles. Our English Bulldog. I run over to them and give them both big hugs. Squeezing too tight on my Dad. He says, "Easy Bree. Don't squeeze too hard." He lets go of me and walks over to Chris. "Hey, glad you could finally make it." He gives him a hug. He looks toward Ash and gives her one and says. "Welcome to our home. I hope you feel comfortable being here." He goes over to Dev, hugs him and says. "Thank you for all you did for my girls up in Wilmington." He turns around to face all of us and asks. "How was the drive?"

Ash, Dev, Chris and I all get done hugging my Mother and Chris answers, "It was good." He looks at me smiling and winks. "Well, let's get this truck unpacked!" We all pitch in and get the truck unpacked. I go ahead and show Ash where she'll be sleeping while Chris, Dev and my Dad all three pack the things up the steps for us. They get everything from the bottom floor and my Dad goes downstairs to sit on the loveseat with my Mom. They hang out while Dev, Ash, Chris and I are all upstairs trying to get things unpacked. Chris comes into my room and is awestruck by how I keep it so clean. "This is the cleanest room that I have ever seen in my life." He comes over to me and hugs me smiling. He whispers into my ear. "I wish we will get the chance to be able to make out on your bed." He looks at me smiling that smile that shows that he's about to do something ornery. He sits me down on my bed and starts making out with me. I guess he got what he wished for.

We hear Dev in Ash's room coming out into the hallway and going past my bedroom. He stops and looks in. "Hey, you two!"

We both get up and I go over and pick the bags up. I take them to my bathroom trash can and sit in my desk chair waiting for Chris and Dev to get done picking on each other. Chris says, "Yea, we were just goofing around." He looks over at me smiling that smile still. I look at him and see that he's still thinking about doing this again.

I get up and say. "It's time that we go see if Ash has everything done!" We all three go into her room and see that she's got everything put away and makes the bed with her bedspread that she brought from her Parent's house in Wilmington.

She turns around and sees us all staring at her. "What? I can move pretty fast when it comes to getting things done." She giggles and walks over to Dev and kisses him tenderly on the cheek.

We all walk downstairs and talk to my Parents for a little bit before heading over to Chris' house to help Dev unpack their things. My Mom gets up and hugs all of us and asks. "You boys will be back soon I hope?" She walks over to Ash and gives her a key to the house. "Here you go Ashley. We want you to feel that this is your home too."

Chris and Dev both look at my Mom and answer in unison. "Yes, mamm! You'll be seeing a lot of us for a while." They get up and shake my Dad's hand, hugging my Mom on the way out the door.

Ash gets up with my help and says to my Parents. "Thank you for letting me stay here until Dev gets his own place." She hugs my Mom and Dad and walks out the door with the guys.

My Dad walks over to me. He hugs me and says. "Be careful on the way to Chris' house. I'm glad you made it home safely." He pushes away and my Mom hugs me. We let go of each other and my Dad says one last thing. "We'll see you two at the restaurant tonight."

I look back at them smiling and waving. "Okay, see you all later." I walk over to Chris' truck and climb in the drivers side while Dev and

Ash are both getting into his truck. Chris slides up beside me and sees that my look is weird. He looks at me and I can tell he's about to ask me something. I go ahead and read his mind, answering. "I'm just worried that they will see my ring."

"Oh! If they did, they didn't say anything about it." He backs out of the driveway and honks his horn. He waves his arm out the window. He stays silent on the way over to his house. When we finally pull into his driveway he says. "Don't worry about it, baby. They'll see more of it tonight anyway." He kisses me on the cheek and gets out of his truck, helping me out.

Dev and Ash both get out of his truck and start walking up the driveway together holding hands. Smiling Dev looks at the house and says, "Wow, I can't believe this place. It looks good Chris!"

Chris says. "Yea, it takes a lot of work to keep it looking like this too!" He gets his keys out and walks up to the door. "It's time to show off the inside." He unlocks and opens while looking at my face to see my reaction. "I thought you would like it!" Smiling, he lets Dev, Ash and Misty go in, watching their reactions. He asks, "Well, how does it look?"

Dev answers. "I've seen pictures of this place on your facebook page, but didn't realize how big it was. It looks great man! Good job on the details. Keeping it the same way the builder built it." He was amazed at the architecture it had, all the details in the crown molding, the original wood floors, and the updating went all together. We all walk into the kitchen and see that it still needs some work, but it's livable. We all head outside to get Dev's things in the house and Chris' bag. Chris and I help pack things up the stairs for Dev. Ash brings in Chris' bag to the top of the stairs. Dev says, "You two go ahead and do what you have to do. Ash and I can get this taken care of." He and Ash start unpacking his things.

Chris and I go to his room which is the master bedroom. He shuts the door and brings his bag in. Lays it on the floor and grabs me. He puts me on the bed and starts kissing on my lips and neck. He stops and looks at me. "What?"

"Nothing!" I say and pull him closer to me smiling. I wait for him to go down to my neck and say. "I can't believe that this is your house. It's so beautiful! I can't wait to be your Wife! I want to take care of you and the house." He stops and looks at me smiling and I finish. "It's going to be exciting, you and me in this big house all alone sometimes. Imagine the possibilities!" I smile mischievously and wrap my arms around him and start kissing him. We keep making out until we hear Ash and Dev knocking on the door.

We both jump up and grab Chris' bag real fast and Chris says. "Come in."

"We just thought we would let you know that we are heading out to my Parents house now." Dev walks in with Ash right behind him. "We got everything unpacked and I think it'll pass your inspection." Smiling he starts to turn around and says. "We'll see you two later."

Chris says, "Okay man, be safe. Don't get lost dude." While walking over to him and handing him his key to the house. Smiling at him and Ash walking out of his bedroom door. He grabs me from behind looking at his watch, saying. "We still have an hour and a half before we have to meet our Parents at the restaurant. What do you want to do?"

I turn around looking at him, while wrapping my arms around his body, rubbing up and down his back. I say, "Let's take a nap, or not." Smiling mischievously.

He looks at me smiling, and says "Hold on a minute. Let me make sure the front door is locked." He bounces down the stairs and locks the front door, pets Misty and takes the stairs two at a time. He runs into his bedroom, shutting the door. Taking his shirt off, wraps his arms around me while walking us toward his bed. He says, "I can't believe that we're doing this. My dream has come true!" We keep on kissing each other until we are both worn out and just lay there.

The next thing I know I'm up unpacking his bag while he naps. I walk into his master bathroom and look for the hamper when I hear a commotion down stairs. I see that he's still in his bed and walk out into the hallway and see that Misty is laying in front of Dev's bedroom door. I hear it again and Misty does too. Her ears perk up and look straight at me. She gets up and walks over to me, waiting for me to take the lead. I head down stairs and walk through the formal dining room, not seeing anything. I turn around and walk through the hallway that leads to a bathroom. I walk toward that way and see that the basement door is cracked. Misty is right beside me and she sniffs. Her head cocked toward me, not growling. I walked toward it a little and saw a shadow that was low to the ground. I turn around and run back up the stairs to Chris' room. I see that he's awake and say. "I think you may have an intruder inside your house!"

He gets up, puts his shirt back on and says, "Stay close behind me, baby!" We go out in the hallway together, with Chris carrying a bat. We go downstairs into the hallway and he looks toward the basement door. He sees Misty still sitting there wagging her tail and not growling. It makes him curious about the way she's acting. She should be growling if it's a person that she doesn't know. He looks back at me, whispering. "I'm going to go check it out. Misty isn't growling, so I think it may be nothing." He kisses me on the cheek and finishes. "I'll be back." He walks into the hallway and opens the door. He looks down the steps, smiles and walks down them lowering the bat. He comes back up holding a little white fur ball and shuts the door. Misty, being excited, starts wagging her tail and prancing around. "Bree, honey. There isn't anything to worry about. It was this little girl." He shows me, holding the kitten up and smiling. "Isn't she cute?"

I look at her and say. "Awh, she's so cute!" I take her immediately and start loving her. We both hear her start purring and laugh. I look at him and ask. "Can we keep her?"

He looks down at the kitten and Misty. Misty is still excited and is following me around wanting to sniff the little white fur ball. He says, "I think we should! Only because Misty is so excited about the new addition."

I look down at Misty and squat a little bit. Letting her sniff the kitten and both of them getting to know each other while the kitten is still in my hands. Me comforting her might make her feel better about a dog sniffing and licking all over her. I look at Chris smiling and say. "Yes, that's what I want. What should we name her?"

He looks at her and says. "How about Snowball? She's pure white."

"Yea, Snowball is perfect for her." I get up and follow him back up the steps. We go into his room and he tries to pick up his bag that he left on the floor. He looks down and wonders where his bag went. He looks at me and asks. "What did you do while I was sleeping, unpack my bag for me?"

I answer, smiling. "Yes, I did." We both go back downstairs, sitting on his couch, letting Snowball and Misty play together. Snowball gets tired and climbs onto Misty's body and lays down. Chris and I watch a little bit of television before heading out to the restaurant for the supper meeting.

Chapter
THIRTEEN

As Dev is driving through his hometown, he remembers his way around. Things have changed, but not that much since he's been away. He gets ready to slow down in his truck to pull off onto his Parents street. He noticed that there was a man sitting on the corner of the street. He looks real hard and recognizes this guy. He pulls his truck over, gets out and walks over to him. He says, "Hi, remember me Mr. Monroe?"

Mr. Monroe looks up, smiles and says. "Devin, it's good to see you. How have you been, Son!"

Dev answers the old man. "Yea, it's good to see you too. I've been good." He looks back at his truck to Ash. He looks at Mr. Monroe and says. "Hold on, Mr. Monroe. I have someone I want you to meet." He jogs over to get Ash and walks back over holding his arm around her. "Mr. Monroe, this is my fiance Ashley Hampton." He smiles at her and him both.

"Well, it's good to meet you little lady." Then Mr. Monroe looks down toward Ash's belly. He smiles and says. "I see that you've been a busy guy, Devin. How far along?" He asks Ashley.

Ash smiles and answers, "Almost three months."

Dev squeezes her shoulder and smiles down at her. "Yea, we met just a couple of days ago." He let's go and hugs the old man. "Thank you for your story when I just moved here. I think it inspired me." He grabs Ash's hand and smiles at her. "I'll tell you all about the story in a little bit." They talk for a little longer to Mr. Monroe and head back to his truck. They climb in and put their seatbelts on. Then start off down his home street.

Ash looks over at him smiling and asks. "Why don't you tell me the story now?"

He looks at her, smiles and says. "Okay!" He gets a drink of his water and continues. "Mr. Monroe is like a Grandfather to me. He told me that I would marry someone that I met and known for just three days. Mr. Monroe and his Wife met like that, Mr. Monroe was a widower and his Wife had just lost her first Husband in World War II. He said that they met in the hospital waiting for their spouses to let go of life. His Wife's deceased Husband was a soldier that was shot in the stomach. Back then they didn't have the medicines and surgical procedures that they have now. He passed away just a day short of getting back here. She was devastated. Mr. Monroe's deceased Wife had cancer at the time they didn't know what was wrong with her, so they didn't know how to treat it. She passed away two days short of being admitted to the hospital. They had just gotten married a week before she passed on. He met his Wife now of fifty years that day her Husband passed on. Back then they didn't take their time getting to know one another. They just jumped the broom like us and Chris and Bree." He takes a breather, a drink then continues. "When I just moved here, I didn't know anyone and I was walking home from school. I ran into Mr. Monroe. He knew who my adoptive Parents were and invited me to his place after asking my Mom if I could visit him at his house. She let me go and that's when he told me that story and his Wife Amy. That story has stuck with me since then. Ten years later his Wife Amy passed away of a heart attack." Dev looks to see if they have already passed his Parents house and realizes that they are getting closer to it. He keeps on driving a little more and looks back to Ash. "When I met you I knew that you were the one for me. That's the reason why I couldn't let you go." He grabs her hand, slows down and says. "We're getting closer. Are you nervous?"

Ash looks at him smiling and replies. "No, I'm not nervous. As long as I have you near me I won't be." She leans over and gives him a kiss on the cheek. She sees that he has his turn signal on to the right and looks at his Parents house. She looks over at him smiling. "I can't believe that I would get so lucky to have a guy like you. I love you!"

He looks at her and smiles real big. "I love you too!" He gets out, walks over to her side of the truck to help her out. He asks, pointing to the house. "You like?"

She looks up at the house again and smiles. "Yes, it's a perfect house for the perfect man to grow up in. I bet you were happy here weren't you?"

Dev answers. "Yea, after I got to know Chris. He lived just up the street from my Parents with his Parents." He turns around and points to the house. "I don't know if they still live there or not though. Funny isn't it? Chris and Bree lived a street down from one another and didn't even know the other existed."

"Yea, it is!" Ash responds. "Are your Parents home?"

Dev looks and says. "Yea, they should be. If they aren't then we'll sit and wait for them to get home. If that's okay with you?"

"Yea, that's perfect for me!" Ash answers.

They both walk up to the door and Dev rings the doorbell. Then wait until the door is opened. When it does Dev turns around and smiles real big. His Mom is standing at the door and is in shock to see her Son standing on her front porch. "Dev, is that you?" She looks back inside the house and says. "Darrin, you better get out here quick!" She waits on him to come to the door and comes out all the way and hugs Dev. Then she sees Ash standing there smiling, rubbing her belly. Dev's Dad is standing at the door smiling real big. He comes out and holds onto Dev for about two minutes and lets him go because he sees Ash standing there smiling and rubbing her belly also.

Dev's Parents look back at him and his Dad asks. "Who is this pretty young lady?"

Dev looks at her smiling, answering. "Mom, Dad, this is Ashley Dawn Hampton. She's my fiance." He walks over to her and puts his arm around her midsection and holds her.

His Mom is the first one to hug her and says. "Welcome to our home. How did you get him to jump the gun?"

Ash looks at her smiling, answering. "I didn't get him to jump the gun. He did it himself."

She hugged Dev's Father laughing at her answer. "We like that in a girl. Telling us what she thinks." They all four walk into the house and visit with each other. Dev and Ash stay for supper and announce that they are indeed engaged. They let the cat out of the bag by announcing that Ash is pregnant and is due sometime in March of next year.

Dev's Mother is so surprised at that, that she stands up and says. "Oh my, we have got to get the ball rolling then. We have a wedding to plan!" She walks over to Ash and asks. "Would you like to have the wedding before you get too big? Wait a minute, we need to find them a house to get into before the wedding and the baby comes." They go on and talk about the upcoming wedding, baby shower and housewarming shower, while they spend time with each other eating supper.

All in all it was a very good homecoming for Dev. He got to see some of his old friends, found one of his little Sisters, got to spend time with his fiance and his Parents that he hadn't seen in three years.

Chapter
FOURTEEN

....

Chris and I pulled in at Cheddars and walked in together holding hands. He saw his Parents standing inside the door waiting for us. He went up to them and gave both of them a hug each. He looks back at me smiling and asks. "Are you nervous?"

I look up at him and answer. "Kind of am but, not much though. Let's just introduce each other and get it over with."

I walk up to Mike, Chris' Dad. I shake his hand when Chris says. "Dad, this is Breea. Breea this is my Dad, Mike."

When I went to shake his hand he grabbed me and pulled me into a hug. He chuckles a little saying. "We might as well break the ice right up front." I just stand there and take the hug like I think I should and smile at him.

Next was Chris' Mom, Christine. "Mom, this is Breea. Breea, this is my Mom, Christine."

I walk up to her and smile real big. I give her a hug and she says. "Ooh, what smells so good on you? I have to get some of that." I giggle a little, then we sit there waiting on my Parents. While we wait I look at both of Chris' Parents and ask. "I was wondering how Chris' Grandpa Mikel is doing? If you don't mind me asking."

Christine looks over at me and smiles. "Chris, I think this time you have a great girlfriend. She's so considerate of others." She turns to me and smiles, answering. "It's so nice of you to ask. He's doing really well. He's at our house right now with Chris' Grandma Mikel. They'll be leaving this weekend to go back home to Flemingsburg. Thank you for asking." We all continue to wait on my Parents and continue talking about Chris taking his Grandparents back home.

My Parents finally get to Cheddars and meet us inside the door. Chris and I both hug my Parents and smile real big. My Mom looks at me while walking behind my Dad and Chris. "Are his Parents talkative or are they the kind of people that think that they are better than everyone else?"

I look over at her and smile. "Mom, don't worry. I like them and they like me. They seem pretty down to Earth." Then we stop behind the guys and Chris introduces my Dad to his Parents. "Dad, this is Lance Anderson, Bree's Dad. Lance, this is my Dad, Mike."

Mike steps up and shakes my Dad's hand smiling and says. "It's nice to meet you, Lance. I heard you were in that plane crash a couple of days ago. How are you feeling?"

My Dad answers Mike smiling. "I'm doing just fine. Thank you for asking. Bree and Chris have also told us that Chris' Grandpa Mikel just recently had a heart attack. How is he doing?"

Mike answers. "He's doing great. He's making great progress." He steps a little closer and whispers. "I hope they go home tomorrow and don't wait until this weekend, you know. I want my house back to myself." Chuckling he turns to his Wife.

Chris introduces my Dad to his Mom. "Mom, this is Lance, Bree's Dad. Lance, this is my Mom, Christine."

My Dad and his Mom share a side hug smiling at each other. Christine says, looking at my Dad. "It's nice to meet you Lance. I'm sorry to hear about the plane crash. I heard what you told my Husband.

Thank you for asking about my Dad. I'm glad that everything worked out for you."

"Thank you Christine. It's my pleasure." My Dad stands to the side and lets my Mom take the spot.

Chris puts his arm on my Mom's shoulder and introduces her to his Mom first. "Mom, this is Bree's Mom, Quinn. Quinn, this is my Mom……"

My Mom cuts in and finishes his sentence. "Christine, I know." She walks over and hugs her. "How are you doing? I haven't seen you since you had to leave the firm."

I look at Chris and ask. "What? Do our Mom's know each other?"

He looks at me and smiles, shrugging his shoulders. "I guess so." Then we both look toward them.

"I'm doing fine Quinn. I can't believe our kids have started dating each other. Remember we used to tease each other about those two dating in the future." Pointing at us and smiling.

"I know, it's a small world after all. I love your Son very much and want you to know that he will be a joyful addition to our family if our kids decide to go the extra mile." My Mom starts smiling. Then she looks over to Mike and says. "It's so nice to see you again Mike. How are you?"

Mike looks over to her and smiles. "Is this Quinn Foxworthy?"

My Mom says. "Yes, it sure is. You haven't aged at all Mike." Laughing along with him.

"Yea, I know. Christine takes very good care of me and makes sure I eat right." He puts his arm over Christine and starts chuckling. "Who would have thought that our Son and your Daughter would be dating each other. It's a small world, but I'm glad that it's your Daughter this time. To be honest Chris hasn't brought any of his exes to the house that we couldn't stand." He turns to the hostess and says. "We'd like a table for six please."

The hostess, Megan says. "Sure thing." She grabs six menus and walks us over to our table and asks. "Is this fine?"

Mike looks at everyone and sees that everyone approves the table and answers. "Thank you, this is fine." He pulls a seat out and waits for his Wife to sit down, then scoots her in. He sits down.

Chris and I are sitting between Mike and Christine and my Parents Lance and Quinn. Chris pulls my chair out for me and waits for me to sit down, then scoots me in. He then sits down smiling and holding my hand.

My Dad pulls a chair out for my Mother and waits for her to sit down, then he scoots her in. He sits down by Mike on the other side of the table. Chris is sitting by his Mother and I'm sitting by my Mother. We all order our drinks and look at the menu talking about our trip to Wilmington. Chris' Dad asks. "I heard you ran into your old buddy, Devin, while you were up North in Wilmington. How is he?"

We both look at each other and smile. Chris answers his Dad. "Yea, we did run into him. I called him from the airport here and asked him to meet with Bree and Quinn. I didn't want them to be slammed with a lot of credit card bills renting a car to drive to Wilmington from Columbus. I was glad that he was up there to take care of them. I went up there and helped. Paid for everything with my own money and just tried to help out the best way I could." He looks over at me smiling and continues. "He's doing good. He met a girl named Ashley and they hit it off so well that they got engaged!"

Mike looks over at his Wife after his Son is done talking and says to her. "I knew that, that was his truck parked in their driveway today." Christine just nods her head up and down. Then Mike continues. "Yea, that's nice Son. I wish him the best. I bet his Parents are delighted that he decided to come home for the week."

Chris says. "Oh, Dad. That isn't all he's in for. He's been transferred down to this airport, so he's moving in with me until he can find a place of his own." He looks over at me and leans toward me. "Should I tell him that you and Dev are Brother and Sister? Should I also tell him about Ash being pregnant?"

I look at him with a serious look on my face and answer. "Yes, tell them both."

He clears his throat and says. "Dad, Dev is going to be a Dad in March. Ash is pregnant." He gets a look at his Father and Mother's faces and says. "Yea, Bree and Dev both discovered that they are Brother and Sister."

His Dad looks at Chris and I like we just gave him the worst news that he could have heard. "How are Devin and Breea Brother and Sister?" He looks toward my Mom with a weird look.

She looks up at Mike and Christine and smiles. She says. "Christine, Mike. Remember me telling the both of you that I was thinking of adopting my step Daughter?" They both shake their heads up and down. Then my Mom continues. "Okay, well. Breea's birth Mother is also Devin's birth Mother."

"Oh, okay. That's the reason why Breea looked so familiar to us when we first saw her. Nevermind that we've met her before tonight, but that was when she was really young." Christine turns to Chris and asks him. "Remember that little girl that had the curly cole black hair?"

Chris looks over at me and says answering his Mother. "Yea, was that Bree?"

His Mom smiles answering. "Yes, Son. You two have met before but don't remember it. Chris, I think you were ten or eleven and Breea just turned seven. It was the day that Quinn adopted Breea. Quinn and Lance invited us to the celebration after the court hearing." She looks at the waitress and orders a bottle of water with a lemon for herself and orders an unsweetened tea with a lemon for her Husband.

"Yea, I remember that now." He turns to me and says. "You were so mean to me that day. You said that it was your party and we played what you wanted to play. I had to play with you and be your pretend Husband." He chuckles and orders his drink. "I'll have a sweet tea and she'll have a sweet tea with a lemon."

I look at him and ask. "How did you know I wanted sweet tea with a lemon?"

"I paid attention to what you ordered at the restaurants up in Wilmington and Columbus." He brushes a strand of hair away from my eyes and smiles. He reaches underneath the table and puts his hand on my thigh, squeezes and winks at me smiling.

I felt him rubbing his thumb across my thigh area. I put my left hand over his and moved it closer up to the upper part of my thigh and watched his reaction. He doesn't do anything, except to continue to rub. He looks at me and winks. I keep my left hand underneath until we both feel that it's safe for us to say what we have to say.

The waitress walks over to my Parents and takes their drink orders. My Mom says, "I'll have an unsweetened tea with a lemon, and he'll have a coke." The waitress walks over and puts the drink order into the computer. We all sit there and talk a little more until the waitress brings our drinks out. She sets Chris' tea in front of him first, then mine. She walks over to his Parents and sets them down in front of them. She does the same with mine, then asks us to give her our food orders.

Christine says. "I'll have the filet mignon, six ounces. Medium well, with a loaded baked potato." She hands the menu over to the waitress.

Mike orders. "I'll have the twelve ounce filet mignon. Well done, with an order of macaroni and cheese please." He hands the menu to the waitress.

The waitress walks over to my Parents. My Mom looks up and says. "I'll have the six ounce filet mignon, medium well, with a side of mashed potatoes. Thank you." She hands the menu to the waitress and looks at my Dad.

"Okay, I'll have the baked tilapia with a side of rice. Thank you." He hands the menu to the waitress.

She walks over to Chris and I. I order my food first. "I'll have the baked tilapia with a side of rice also. Thank you." I hand her my menu and she moves on to Chris.

"I'll have the twelve ounce filet mignon, well done, with an order of steak fries please. Thank you." He hands the menu to her without looking at her and smiles at me. He still has his hand on my thigh rubbing it.

We sit there staring at each other then his Father interrupts us. "Chris! Snap out of it." Chuckling he continues. "We want to know if you would like to order dessert after we eat our supper?"

Chris doesn't look away from me and answers his Father. "Sure, Dad. Whatever you all want, is fine with me."

His Father watches the two of us and says. "That's love right there. I'm so glad that our Son has found it." He says to his Wife. He kisses her on her cheek smiling, he asks my Parents. "How long have you two been married?"

My Dad looks at him smiling and answers. "We've been married only twelve years." He looks over at my Mother saying. "It's been the best twelve years of my life too." He looks over at me and Chris whispering back and forth to each other and giggling. He says. "Now, Mike. If that isn't love I don't know what it is." Pointing at both of us smiling. Then whispers to Quinn, Mike and Christine. "I think something is up with these two."

They all look at us just sitting in our own little world. Chris and I are giggling about what has happened in the past couple of days. We turn and look at our Parents staring at us. Chris asks them. "What?" He gets a drink of his tea, without taking his hand off of my thigh and keeping my hand near his until he's ready for the right time to tell them our news.

His Father, Mike answers. "We were just admiring how you two look at each other. We think it's love, Son." He looks over to his Mother and sees her smiling and agreeing with his Dad, my Dad and my Mom.

I look at all three of them and ask. "What would you all think if Chris and I would do something crazy, like get married?"

Chris just looks at me smiling and shakes his head in agreement. Knowing what I'm thinking. He looks at them and asks. "Yea, we want to know what you all think about Dev and Ash getting married so soon."

They all look at each other and my Daddy answers. "We think that it's a good thing. No matter how long you date someone, it doesn't matter. As long as the two know that they are willing to try it and make the leap. You will end up either falling out of love or falling more in love with each other, because it's meant to be. Just plain and simple as that, it's like gambling. Some couples make it and others don't. What matters is that both try their hardest to keep each other happy." He looks over at Quinn and asks her. "Right?"

She looks at my Dad and says. "Yes, that's right. I agree with him fully on that. If Dev and Ash didn't meet when they did. They both probably would have met someone else and would have been unhappy with their choice. They met at the right time and both seem to be pretty happy with each other and the only thing that will make their marriage work is if they put the effort into it. Which to me Dev seems like he's got the right idea by already inviting Ash's Parents down anytime day or night." She pauses to take a breath, then continues. "Ash, seems like she's still a little unsure, but is still happy. I think that girl has been through some rough times and she's finally getting to see what happiness really is. On that note, I think that they'll make it because they are so into each other and every time I see them looking at each other I notice that they have that love in their eyes."

Mike looks at my Mom and says. "Yes, I fully agree with that." He looks around at some of the teenagers in the restaurant. He points to one couple and says. "Just like those two. They think they're in love with each other, but they're not. I can tell just by the way they are looking around the restaurant. They can't seem to just sit there and have a private conversation between the two of them. They can't seem to keep it going." He pauses for a minute and continues. "Oh, did you all see that? The guy looked at the waitress and when you are in love with someone, you sure as heck don't look at another person." He pauses again while watching the couple he's talking about and says. "She did the same thing when the young guy just walked by their table. She watched him walk away from the table."

Christine looks up and notices that her Husband is done talking and she finally gets her opinion revealed. "I think that when two people are in love with each other, they don't look away from the other person. They keep their attention on their partner. Yes, distractions are all around, but what keeps you watching and looking at your partner for the rest of your life is knowing that they love you back and that they are on your side for every little thing that may or may not bother you. You and your partner are there for life and though you are still you and have opinions of your own, you still have to think about your partner and their opinion. Pretty much what I'm trying to say is middle ground. There's always a bright picture and a dull one." She picks her drink up and takes a drink while watching Chris and I. She puts her drink down and asks. "Is there something you two want to tell us?"

Chris looks at me and whispers in my ear. "I think this is the right time for it." He brings my left hand up from underneath the table and says. "Mom, Dad, Mr. and Mrs. Anderson, I asked Bree to marry me at the Columbus Airport." He looks over at me still smiling and says. "You take it from here."

"And I said yes!" Holding my left hand up for all of them to see, smiling from ear to ear.

My Mom and his Mom get up and walk around to where we are sitting and look at the ring. His Mom says. "That's your Grandmother's ring. The one that your Father proposed to me with. Oh, Chris honey. I'm so excited for you." She hugs him and kisses him on the cheek. She comes over to me and smiles. "Come here sweetie. Let me hug you." She grabs me and hugs me saying, "Welcome to the family." She walks around the table to her seat and sits down bursting with joy.

My Mom hugs me and says. "Congratulations, you two. You two are going to be the most beautiful couple in Lexington. I'm happy for you two." She hugs Chris and says. "Welcome to the family." She walks to sit down by my Dad just bursting at the seams with joy also.

Chris' Father gets up and says. "Now, when you drop her off tonight at her Parents house. I think it's high time that us guys get together." He points toward my Dad and himself. "No friends or anything like that." He walks around and shakes Chris' hand and says. "Congratulations, Son." He turns around and grabs me up out of my chair and kisses my cheek. "Welcome to the family, Breea."

My Dad gets up and walks to me first smiling and says. "You have made me proud, girl. I love you." He hugs me and tries to hide his tears from everyone. We let go of each other and he wipes his hand across his face trying to get rid of the tears as quickly as he knew how. He walks over to Chris and says. "Welcome to the family. I've always wanted a Son." He hugs him, and walks to sit down because the waitress is bringing out our food.

She finally gets to the table with the food and gets everyone's orders right. She gives the right orders to the right people and walks off to refill our drinks. We all eat in conversation and then we ask the waitress for the dessert menu. We all ordered a sampler of ice cream truffles. It has a chocolate turnover, a peanut butter turnover and a strawberry turnover, all with a scoop of vanilla ice cream on the top. It has three different toppings of chocolate syrup, strawberry syrup and peanut butter syrup. It was so good that all of us ended up eating all of the dessert but took doggy bags home with our meals. We finally get ready to leave. We all walk out to our vehicles and give each other hugs. Chris and I finally climbed into his truck with me in the middle as usual and buckled up. We head to the park. We just sit there and watch the stars.

Chapter
FIFTEEN

....

C hris finally looks over at me and says. "I think we made our Parents happy tonight. Do you agree?"

I breathe in the night air and answer him smiling. "I know we did." Then I look up at the sky and ask him. "What are you thinking?"

He looks back over at me, smiles and answers. "I'm thinking that we should set a date." He sees my look and laughs. "It doesn't have to be right away. I know you want to get started in college and everything before we tie the knot." He picks up a stick and throws it into the water. "So, how about setting a date?"

I looked at him and knew that was what he was thinking about. "I know we need to set a date. I know that you know that I want to start college and become a teacher, but honestly I can't see spending more time going through school to become a teacher anymore than I just want to be with you." Smiling, I ask, "So what date did you have in mind?"

He looks over at me and answers. "I think we should wait until next year. That way you can start college to see if that's what you want, then and if only then you don't want that, you can just drop out and I won't look down on you for it." He straddles me from behind. "How does that sound?"

"What day and month next year?"

"I don't know, I don't have any specific month or day in mind." He raises one side up and pulls his phone out of his back pocket, opens his calendar app up and says, "What specific month and day do you have in mind? Would you want a summer, spring, fall or winter wedding?"

"I really don't have a specific month or day nor a specific season in mind. That's a great idea! I don't really care when we tie the knot because all I know is that I want to be with you regardless of how or when we get married." I look at him and say. "As much as I hate to leave you, because I love being with you alone. I do have to get home." So we get up and climb back into the truck. We buckle up again for the last time tonight and we leave the park.

Chris looks over at me while he's driving and asks. "Would you like to discuss this with our Mother's over a lunch sometime this week or would you like to come up with the date on our own?"

I look over at him smiling and answer. "I think it would be best if we just picked a day and month next year to set it. I was thinking that maybe we should get married on the day that you proposed to me in the same month too. This way we have exactly a year long engagement."

He looks over at me, smiles and says. "That's a great idea! So, what about June the nineteenth? According to the calendar it's on a Saturday."

I look over at him and say, smiling. "That sounds perfect to me. Now let's just hope that no one has any plans for anything that weekend."

Chris looks over at me while he's driving and asks. "Have you ever been swimming in a lake before?"

I look at him and answer. "No, I don't think I have. Why?"

"Maybe sometime this week we can go. We'll take Dev and Ash with us. A bunch of my buddies and I go up there on our days off and swim. Would you like to go? We'll make it an overnight trip and camp out at Cave Run Lake!"

I could see he was getting excited with the question so I answered. "Yea, sure. That sounds like fun."

He pulls off to the side of the street in front of my house. We get out and he walks me up to the door. He says to me, "Breea Leighann, I love you!" He brings his hand up under my chin to lift it up, kisses me tenderly and quietly. He waits for me to get the door unlocked and makes sure that I'm in the house before he leaves. He walks back to his truck and drives off until the next day.

I walk in and see Ash sitting in the living room talking on the phone with Dev. I smile at her and wave, then head on up to my room. I hear her tell Dev that I just got home and that my Parents are asleep. So scratch that idea about talking with my Mother about the wedding date. I get to my room and just about close my door when Ash pops up. "Hey, how was your supper?"

I look at her surprised and answer smiling. "It was good. It went better than I thought it would. I thought that his Parents were going to be some sort of snobs. You know how that goes? Meeting a guy's Parents for the first time, you do tend to get a little nervous. It turns out that they already knew my Mother from where she works. I guess they own the company or something." I pick my purse up off the stand and put it on my bedside table. I look up and see Ash still standing there and I ask her. "How was your supper at Dev's?"

"It was great. His Parents were surprised. They didn't even notice me until they walked out to hug Dev. They are overjoyed with us being engaged and having a baby."

"I'll bet they are. I can't wait to meet them myself. Chris and I are wanting to go camping at Cave Run Lake sometime next week. You think you and Dev would be up to going with us? Chris said that he and some of his buddies go up there every time they have the day off and it's not raining to go swimming. If they do go, I'll need at least one girl there that I can talk to."

Ash looks at me smiling and says. "I'll talk to Dev about it." She starts to walk out of my room then turns and says. "Good night Bree, thank you for having your Parents take me in. It means so much to me." She leaves my room and I hear her door shut.

I go over and shut my door and get undressed. I hear my cell phone vibrate. I go to the stand and get it out of my purse and shut the cabinet. I unlock my phone and see that it's Chris. He texted me this.

"Hey baby just got home i sure am gonna miss u (you) bein (being) with me 2night (tonight) have sweet dreams and ill see u (you) in da (the) mornin (morning) love u (you) baby"

I replied back to his text. "Good to knw (know) u (you) got home ok (okay) tell dev i said hi if he isnt asleep ill be thinkin (thinking) bout (about) u (you) in my dreams night sweet dreams 2 (to) u (you) 2 (too) love u baby"

I finish getting undressed and hear the vibration of my phone again. I pick it up and see that it's Dev. I read it and it says. "Hey sis (sister) its (it is) me dev i got ur (your) number from chris hope thats (that is) ok (okay) just wanted to let u (you) knw (know) that ash and i have a date set for the wedding my Mom is thrilled and she cant wait to meet u (you) and ur (your) parents she says she knows where 1 (one) of our sisters r (are) also let me knw (know) what u (you) wanna (want to) do bout (about) dat (that) love ya sis"

I text him back and say. "Hey bub glad u (you) 2 (two) set a date chris and I set 1 (one) also its (it is) gonna (going) to b (be) nxt (next) yr (year) that part is set in stone chris' parents and mine r (are) thrilled also and i cant (can't) wait to meet ur (your) parents either idk (i don't know) bout (about) da (the) sister thing yet its (it is) 2 (too) much 2 (to) handle right now ill let u (you) knw (know) somethin (something) tom (tomorrow) night love u (you) 2 (too) bub"

I finally got my clothes picked up and put them in the hamper. I turn my lamp on and turn the overhead light off by the chain hanging down from my ceiling fan. I climb in the bed and hear my phone vibrate against the stand again. I pick it up and see that it's Chris. I open it and read it. "Hey baby sorry to bother ya (you) again but i had to say it again i love u (you) wishin (wishing) u (you) were here wit (with) me i should come pick u (you) up and bring u (you) back to our house but i wont (won't) cause i knw (know) i wouldnt b (be) able to control myself night"

I reply back smiling. "Awh i miss u (you) 2 (too) love u (you) more im wishin (wishing) u (you) were here wit (with) me how is snowball" I get comfortable with my phone in my hand and wait for his response. Finally my phone vibrates again and I raise it up to my face.

"Snowball is good shes (she is) sleepin (sleeping) at my feet we need to train her tho (though) i stepped in a bunch of mess when i came into my room dont (don't) worry i cleaned it up and imma (im going) out tom (tomorrow) to get her a litter box, litter, food and water bowl, and a toy at pet smart u (you) can go if u (you) wanna (want) id (i would) love for u (you) 2 (to) go wit (with) us"

I reply back. "Yea, ill (i will) go wit (with) u (you) and snowball night baby love u (you) bunches" I finally plug my phone in and scoot down in bed. I feel around for Chris and toss and turn for half the night and the next thing I know it's morning and my Mom is knocking on my door.

"Bree, you awake?" She opens my door, walks in and shuts it. She turns around and comes to sit on my bed. She rubs her hand down my hair and says. "Hey, sleeping beauty. It's time to get up." She sits there watching me sleep.

I turn over and moan. I look up at her smiling and say. "Hey, good morning Mom." I sit up in bed and ask. "What's going on? Are we going somewhere?"

My Mom looks at me, smiles and answers. "No, honey. We're not going anywhere, but you are." She looks at my closed door and says. "There's someone here to see you." She brings her arm out from behind her and hands me Snowball.

I look surprised that Snowball is here and look up at my Mom and ask. "What is Snowball doing here?" I look at my shut door and ask. "Where is Chris, has something happened?" I get out of my bed without making it and make a run for my door. I open it with such force with Snowball in my arms. I start hollering. "Chris? Are you here?" Running down the steps I almost ran into him. I stood there shocked. Then I say, "I thought something happened to you. My Mom never wakes me up like she did just a few minutes ago, and she never lets a cat in the house." I put Snowball down and then hugged, squeezing him hard.

He looks at me smiling and asks. "Are you ready to go to PetSmart?"

I look at him like I didn't know what he was talking about and then he sees that I was really worried. He takes me into his arms and says. "Oh, baby. I didn't mean to scare you. I thought you would be up by now. I was just so lonesome without you by my side last night. I just wanted to see you, and be near you. I couldn't wait another minute."

I look at the clock and see that it's almost eight thirty. I look up at him, smile, and say. "I'm sorry. I just tossed and turned half the night. I didn't get much sleep without you being by my side either." I look down at his hands and grab the left. "I guess I just got used to you being by me in the bed, that's the reason I tossed and turned for half the night."

He pulls me into his arms and says. "Why don't you go get dressed and I'll wait down here with Snowball." He picks the kitten up and hugs it. "Then we'll go get some breakfast at one of my favorite restaurants and head to PetSmart."

I look up at him wanting to kiss him, but I don't want to right now because of morning breath. I say smiling. "Okay!" Then take the steps two at a time. I get to my room, make my bed, plug in my straightener, get dressed, brush my teeth and put my makeup on while my straightener is getting hot. When I'm done putting my makeup on I straighten my hair. After I'm done with my hair, I go into my closet and get my perfume off of the shelf. I shut my closet door, then walk over to my bedside table and get my purse and phone. I come out into the hallway leaving my door open to my room and run into my Mother. "Sorry Mom. I didn't mean to bump into you." I look at her and give her a hug. "Chris and I are going to go get Snowball some food and things from PetSmart. Do you need anything while we're out?"

She looks at me smiling and says. "No, I don't need anything. That's why he's here so early?" She looks to her bedroom and I realize that my Dad isn't up yet. She looks back at me giving me a hug and says. "Have fun!"

I say, "Okay!" I give her a kiss on the cheek and tell her. "Give Daddy a kiss for me when he gets up." Then I start walking down stairs toward the living room. I see Chris sitting there petting Snowball and just looking around. I stood there for a few minutes watching him smiling. When he notices me he smiles back and stands up with Snowball in his arms. I asked him, "Are you ready to go?"

"I sure am." He walks over to me with Snowball in his arms and puts one arm around me. We walk out to his truck and he gives me a kiss. He puts Snowball in her cage and helps me into the truck. He gets in beside me and says. "Yea, I can't wait til we take my Grandparents back to Flemingsburg. We're going to have a blast." He thinks of my Parents and asks. "Do you think your Parents will let you go, so we can just make a three day trip out of it? I want to take them home and spend that night with them, then go to Cave Run Lake and camp out. I don't want to have to go up there, then come back and then drive back up that way within two days of each other."

I look at him smiling and answer. "Yea, I think that my Parents would let me go with you to spend a night with your Grandparents. I also think that they would let me go with you and your friends to Cave Run Lake and camp out for two nights. That's only if Dev and Ash can go though. I think that they would trust that Dev and you would protect me if anything were to happen."

He looks over at me and smiles. "Good, we'll have to ask them sometime before we take my Grandparents home then." He keeps on driving until we get to the shopping center that PetSmart is in and he makes a left. He finds a parking spot and gets out. He helps me out then he gets Snowball out. He carries Snowball into the store while holding my hand smiling. We go to the aisle where the litter and litter boxes are and get the most expensive litter box and litter. Then we go to the toy aisle and see what kind of toy Snowball reacts to the most. After that we go into the food aisle. We both look down at Snowball playing with the two toys that we got her in the cart and smile. We picked out the bag of food for her. We check out at the cash register and the clerk looks at Chris smiling.

He doesn't pay much attention to her when she leans over the counter and asks. "Oh, what a cute kitten. What's his name?"

Chris looks down at Snowball and answers, staring at me. "Her name is Snowball. How much do we owe you?"

She stands back up and says. "You owe one hundred twenty seven dollars and sixty nine cents." She reaches her hand out to take the money and she says. "Thank you for shopping at PetSmart. Have a good day and come back."

We head out to the truck with Snowball in the cart and put the things we purchased for her in the backseat of his truck along with Snowball in her cage. We hop back into the truck and he laughs.

I look over at him and ask. "What is so funny?" Putting my seat belt on.

"Nothing, just that cashier thought that I would look at her when I answered her question about Snowball. It's funny how when you have a pet how many girls would be interested in you." He starts his truck up still laughing, then says. "Can you believe people?"

"No, sometimes you can't. It is weird that she wanted to know Snowball's name and call him without even looking. I would think that if I was working at a store like that, that I would look or ask if the pet was a he or a she before asking what the name of the pet was." We both laugh again and pull into a parking lot that holds a Bob Evans, Frisch's, Huddle House and a Waffle House. I look over at him and ask him. "Which one of these is your favorite restaurant?"

He looks over at me smiling and answers. "Why don't you guess which one it is."

I look around at all of them and say. "I don't know for sure, but I'm going to guess that it's Waffle House."

"You know what?"

"What?"

"You're right. I knew we were meant to be together for the rest of our lives." He takes my left hand and looks at my ring. He finishes what he's saying. "The only reason is because you know what I like and don't like. I think that's the only reason why I haven't remodeled my kitchen. I know you would love whatever I put in there, but to be honest. I need some help in that department." He looks over at me and asks. "Would you like to go to The Home Depot with me after we get done eating our breakfast?"

I look at him smiling and ask. "Why would you think I would say no to you?"

"I thought I would ask you first before assuming that you would want to help me remodel my kitchen with me. I didn't want to freak you out by wanting you to be a part of it. I think it needs a woman's sense and decorating touch that's all, because I can use it the way it is for the rest of time. I just want you to be happy with the way the kitchen is going to look." He stretches his head over to me and kisses me. He reaches into the back and gets Snowball's dish out and says. "Here, you go little girl. We're going to eat breakfast and I thought that maybe you might want yours." He reaches into the bags and gets the food and dish bowls out and fills it up with food and water. He puts the food and water bowl in her cage with her. Then he turns back around and opens his door. I get out on the passenger side and shut the door smiling. He walks over to me and grabs my hand. We walk into the Waffle House and get ourselves some breakfast.

After breakfast we headed over to Home Depot and were looking at the kitchen packages. An employee comes towards us smiling and asks. "Hi, my name is Andy. Is there anything that I could help you two with?" He looks down and sees the ring on my left hand and smiles real big. I know him from somewhere but I can't remember him. He watches Chris walk over to a certain display and ask another employee that was over there about it. He looks at me smiling and asks. "You don't remember me do you?"

I look at him and smile. "No, I'm sorry. I don't remember you. Did we graduate together?"

"No, you dated my Brother Jayson."

"Oh, okay. Well how is Jayson doing?"

"He's good. He's going to have a baby girl in the fall with Amber. They're getting married next month." He puts some boxes down on the floor, smiles and asks. "You're not getting married because of an unexpectant little person on the way are you?"

I look at him not believing what he's asking me and answer. "No, I'm not expecting, but if I were. What business of yours would it be?" I walk over to Chris smiling and say. "Hey, did you find something that you like?" I looked behind me and saw that he was finally walking away. I pay more attention to Chris and seeing the looks that he likes. We find something that we both like. I look at him smiling and standing in front of it. I say. "What do you think about this look?"

He looks at it and smiles real big. "You sure? It just doesn't seem like the type of kitchen you would want." He comes over behind me and hugs my waist kissing my neck.

I look up over my shoulder at him smiling and answer. I'm sure, if we can have this kind of kitchen I wouldn't mind it at all." I get to looking at the tiled backsplash and say. "But, I don't know for sure about this backsplash. It has some brown in it." I look over at him again smiling real big. "Maybe we should bring our Mothers to look at it all." I decided to just switch the colors around. "We'll have these cherry cabinets on the bottom with white cabinets on top. We'll put these countertops on them." Pointing to the white granite with brown specks in it. "We'll have the soft closing drawers, with the soft closing cabinet doors. Then we'll use these granite tiles with dark brown almost red specks in them on the floor. What do you think?"

He looks at me and takes me over to the employee that he talked to earlier and smiles. "Yes, Bryan. We need you to draw this up for us." He pulls a paper out of his pocket and hands it to Bryan. "It's the layout of our kitchen." He continues telling Bryan about what I would like to be put together. We go over and sit at a desk and sit there while Bryan types in the things that I said I would like to mix up in the style that we both like.

Bryan looks at us and asks, smiling. "Would you like to have white, black or stainless steel appliances? What appliances would you all like to have?"

We both look at each other and Chris asks Bryan, smiling. "If we used the stainless steel appliances in the kitchen, would it help it out better in the long run if we decide to sell the house?"

Bryan looks at us smiling, shaking his head up and down saying. "It most certainly would. If you get the appliances to match."

We both look at each other and smile. I say. "Okay, stainless steel appliances. We would like to have the stove, double oven, refrigerator, vented microwave over the stove, dishwasher and a stainless steel apron sink."

He puts those items in and pulls this beautiful kitchen up on the computer. "Here's your dream kitchen."

We both look at it and see that it's what I thought it was going to be. I look at Chris and ask, "Could I see you for a moment?" Pointing over to the style we like the most.

He gets up and follows me over. He puts his arms across his chest and asks. "What's wrong? I thought you liked the ideas you put together. What's the matter with the colors? I like it. Is it too dark for you?"

"I don't know. I just would like to see some pictures of some kitchens in a magazine or something to help me decide better."

Chris pulls me to the side of where some magazines are and says. "Here, look at this. I like your ideas and I know you want it to be beautiful for our one hundred year old house."

"I do, but I don't. I love the style, but not the colors. Especially with the stainless steel appliances and we want the stainless steel, because you never know if we'll have to sell the house that we both love so much." I sit down and look at the magazines that Chris pulled off the shelf. I was flipping through the pages when I saw the one that I absolutely loved and that would fit the age of the house. I got up and walked over to Chris and showed it to him. "This is the one that I absolutely love for the house!" I started getting excited and wondered if it would fit into the era of the house.

Chris looks at me smiling and says. "It's the perfect kitchen for the era of the house. I love it too, because it's making you so happy." He kisses my forehead and smiles at the employee who was helping us. He walks over to the employee and says. "Will you help us look for all the items that are in this kitchen?"

Bryan stands up and grabs a piece of paper. He grabs the magazine from Chris and smiles. "This is the classic kitchen for the style of your home." He walks us over to the appliances and tells us to pick out the ones we want. We do that and he puts a tag on them and asks. "When would you like them delivered to your house?"

Chris and I both look at each other smiling. He says. "Can we wait on them until we decide if this is what way we'll go with the remodel of the kitchen?"

"Sure it can. I was just asking about it." He puts the word hold on all the appliances we picked out. He says, "Okay, let's go over here. We need to pick out the tile for the floor, lower and upper cabinets style and color, backsplash, and finally paint." We follow him and get all the things crossed off on the list that we would like to have in our kitchen. We go sit down at his desk to see what it's going to cost us to put this new kitchen in. He gets done typing all of the items into the program and turns the computer screen around to show us what our layout looks like with the picture in the magazine.

We both gasp and Chris looks to Bryan and says. "We love it. It's beautiful! We'll take all the items." He gets his checkbook out and gets ready to write the check.

Bryan sees that Chris is doing this and says. "Hold on a minute. We don't remodel the kitchens for you. You have to hire someone to do it or do it yourselves." Chris puts his checkbook back into his back pocket and sighs. Bryan says, "With all these projects you want to do to your kitchen, they can all easily be done by yourself. We'll show you how to do it here at the store if you want to come back at eight o'clock."

We both look at each other smiling. I say, "Okay, that would save some money on not having to hire anyone to remodel it for us. We can do it ourselves and enjoy the house a little bit more."

Chris looks at me smiling and says. "You know, you're right. That's what we'll do then." He looks at Bryan and says. "Okay, where do we sign up for the classes?"

Bryan brings out a piece of paper smiling and says. "You just need to sign your name here." Pointing to where Chris has to sign and pointing to where I have to sign. "You have to sign here." We both sign our names and look at Bryan. "Okay, it starts at eight o'clock and won't let out until ten o'clock. We'll go over all the basic steps with you and let you do it yourselves when you think you got the hang of it. The best part of these classes is that it's free." Bryan puts into the computer that we are coming tonight for the class. He looks up at us, smiles and says. "Alright, you're on the computer and we'll see you both here at eight o'clock." He gets up and walks over to two other customers.

We walk out of The Home Depot and get into the truck. We both look back to Snowball in her cage and smile. She was sleeping. We both turn around and put our seatbelts on. Then we were off to go to Chris' house.

Chapter

SIXTEEN

....

Dev pulls into Bree's Parent's driveway after Ash that same day while Chris and I are at The Home Depot. Ash comes outside to meet Dev smiling. "Hey, what are you doing?"

Oh, nothing much. Just thought that you would want to hang out with Chris, Bree and I over at Chris' place." He looks up at her smiling. He sees Lance walk out of the house and smiles at him. "Hey, Mr. Anderson, what are you getting ready to do?"

"Oh, hey Dev! Just getting ready to mow the yard here. I can't do anything else without getting jumped onto. So, I figured I'd do a little mowing to get out of the house. I'm going stir crazy." He chuckles and throws his arms up in the air. He opens the garage and sees a big snake. He shuts the door real quick and hollers. "Oh, my lord! There's a big snake in our garage." He walks to get a hoe that he had sitting around the back of the house. "Here use this! I'm deathly afraid of them. Kill the sucker." He throws the hoe over to Dev.

Dev opens the garage door and sees the snake laying there with what looks to be a great big knot in it's stomach. "I sure hope he didn't eat anyone's dog around here. That would be awful." He smashes the head of the snake with the hoe. He chops it off and slings the body of the snake into the trash can. "I sure hope that he wasn't anyone's pet." He looks over to Mr. Anderson and smiles. "So, you're afraid of snakes? I thought police officers weren't supposed to be afraid of anything." Chuckling he walks over to Ash and wraps his arm around her midsection. "Are you ready to go?"

She looks back over her shoulder smiling and answers. "Yea, I just got to go ask Mr. and Mrs. Anderson if it's okay with them." She walks inside where Mr. Anderson went in after Dev killed the snake. "Mr. and Mrs. Anderson, would you care if I go hang with Chris, Bree and Dev for a little while tonight?"

They both look at her smiling and Lance answers. "Yea, you can, but you and Bree need to be back by twelve tonight. You have a doctor's appointment tomorrow and Bree has to go get her schedule from the University of Kentucky." He looks back at Mom and shakes his head, turns back to Ash. "And as long as you stop calling us Mr. and Mrs. Anderson. You can call us Quinn and Lance, okay?"

"Okay, thank you so much. We'll be back at twelve." She turns to walk away and climbs the steps to her room to retrieve her purse. She walks back down the stairs and gets a phone call on her cell. She looks at the caller id and sees that it's her Father. "Hello, Daddy? What's going on?"

"Nothing much sweetie. I have some good news for you and some bad news. Which one do you want first?"

"Uhm, the bad news first please." She looks up toward Quinn and Lance and smiles, while putting her phone on speaker. They look back at her with a questioning look. They walk over by her and stand there for a few minutes while Dev walks in the door.

"Well, Mark and his gang are out of jail. It seems that they might be planning to go down to Lexington sometime next week. Hopefully they won't be able to find you all, but if they do, please promise me that Dev, Lance, Quinn, Bree and or Chris are with you at all times. I don't want anything happening to my Ash or my Grandbaby." He pauses and sounds like he's taking a drink of something. Then he answers with the good news. "The good news is that your Mother and I are flying down tonight and staying in a hotel room. We're on our way to the airport in Columbus now. We'll be at the Lexington Airport at three thirty. Will you and Dev come pick us up?"

"That's bad about Mark being out of jail, but yea I'm sure we can come pick you two up at the airport at three thirty." She looks over at Dev and sees that he's shaking his head up and down, because she's got the phone on speaker.

Dev says, "Mr. and Mrs. Hampton, you two don't have to stay at a hotel. I'm sure Chris wouldn't mind for you two to stay with us while you're both here."

"Okay, thanks Dev. Will you please ask Chris before we get there? I want to make sure that we won't have to worry about a hotel room while we're flying down. If we do then that's fine. We'll be okay with that too. Ash, will you do your Mom and I a favor first?"

"Yea, what's the favor?"

"Make sure it's okay with Chris yourself. We don't want to intrude on anyone. We're just coming down to see where it is that you're living and where it is that you'll be living and having the baby. Make sure you bring two vehicles when you come to pick us up. We have a surprise for you." He looks toward the back seat of the vehicle and smiles at Austin, Bai and Bentley.

"Okay, is the surprise that big?"

"Yea, honey it is." Smiling he says, "We'll see you all soon. We want to meet Dev's Parents too, if that's okay?"

"Okay, Daddy! Love you both very much. We'll see you at three thirty when your plane lands." She gets off the phone with her Dad and jumps up and down. She started holding her side with a little bit of pain and then looked up at everyone standing beside her. "It's okay, I'm okay. Just a pain in my side." She walks over toward Dev while holding her right side and as soon as she gets to his side the pain stops. She looks up at Dev and says, "Are you ready to go so we can talk to Chris and Bree about my Parents coming in?"

Dev looks at her and sees that everything is fine with her and the baby and answers smiling. "Yea, let's go!" He looks back to Quinn and Lance, smiling. "Thank you all so much. If you all want we can stop to get you all on the way to the airport. We can rent a fifteen passenger van to go pick up her Parents. We would love for you two to come with us."

Quinn and Lance both look at each other smiling. "We would love to go with you all. What time will you be picking us up?"

Dev and Ash both look at each other and Dev answers. "They'll be at the airport around three thirty and it only takes five minutes from here to get to the airport, so we'll be picking you two up around, let's say three. That way if there's an accident between here and there we'll be able to get there in time for them to come off the plane." He looks over at Ash and sees that she's comfortable with that. He looks over to Mr. and Mrs. Anderson, asking, "Is that cool?"

"Yea, it's fine with us." They walk back over to the couch and sit down to rest before heading off to the airport while Dev and Ash walk out the door and head for Dev's truck.

Dev and Ash walk into Chris' house laughing and are greeted by me with my hair all pulled back and looking like I just got out of bed. "What's going on here little Sis?" Dev asks me, smiling.

"Nothing! We're just painting the hallway." I take the roller to the paint tray and get another load of paint on my roller while Chris is behind them with a brush painting around the trim. I walk back over to where I was painting and notice the looks on Dev and Ash's faces. "What's going on with you two?"

Chris gets down and walks over to the paint tray to dip his brush in. He notices what I am asking. He puts the brush down and comes over by me standing. Dev looks at us smiling and says. "We have to go to the airport at three today to pick Ash's Parents up. They're coming in to visit. Emily is going to go with us tomorrow to the appointment, while Eric makes a few business calls. We want to know if they can stay here? They were going to go to a hotel room, but I said that you wouldn't mind them staying here while they're in town."

"Okay, how are we going to fit everyone in the vehicle?" Chris asks Dev and Ash while looking down at me smiling. He's never seen me so sexy more than he has now. Especially with paint all in my hair and on my face.

"We plan on renting a fifteen passenger van to go, because Quinn, Lance, his Mom, Dianna and Dad, Darrin all want to go with us too. Dev's Parents want to meet my Parents." Ash answers.

"Okay, what time did you say we had to leave our houses?"

"Three, if you all can make it." Dev says smiling and looking at the both of us smiling. "Bree, you have paint on your face and in your hair. Chris you look cleaner than Bree does, but you do have a little on your cheek." Dev laughs! "When we first ran into Bree, I thought you all were doing something else besides painting." He wiggles his eyebrows up and down. Chris and I look at each other, then start laughing. Chris gets his brush and puts it in the sink. He also gets the roller and puts it in the sink to soak. He comes back into the hallway where we were painting and pulls the paint cloths and trays up.

He puts the paint cloth into the coat closet and puts the trays in the sink. He starts washing them out when I walk into the bathroom. "Hey, I'll get that if you want to go get cleaned up. All I have to do is wash my hair and face." I put my arms around his waist and looked up at him smiling.

"Okay, then you can get cleaned up too." He raises his arms up with a pair of pants and a t- shirt for me. "I got them when your Mom was waking you up this morning. I hope they're yours. I found them in the dryer."

I look up at him smiling and say. "Okay, thanks for doing that." I grab my clothes and then walk off toward his room. I get in the shower and get all cleaned up. I'm getting dressed when I hear someone in his room. I open the door to a crack and peek out. I see him in there rummaging through his drawers looking for a clean t-shirt and jeans. I dry the rest of the way off and get dressed. I open the door and say. "You scared me after I got out of the shower. I didn't know it was you in here."

"Oh, sorry. I didn't mean to scare you. You look beautiful!" He comes over to me and puts his arm around my lower back. He pulls me into a hug and kisses me softly. He pulls away smiling and says. "I have to go get a shower now." He walks into the bathroom and shuts the door behind him.

I walk around downstairs searching for Dev and Ash. I find them in the kitchen and notice that they see that we're getting ready to renovate the kitchen ourselves. I look at them and say. "Yea, Chris and I just went to The Home Depot earlier this morning and got some paint. While we were there we figured we would check the prices out on kitchen appliances and remodeling it. We're supposed to go back at eight o'clock tonight and take a fast course on laying tile, backsplash, putting the cabinets up and actually start the renovations while we go through with the renovation." I pause a minute and see them staring at me with their mouths wide open. I look at them smiling and ask. "What?"

"That's an awful lot to take in, in just an hour course. Are you sure you and Chris can do this?" Ash asks me.

"Yea, I mean sure it's a lot to take in. We have already watched DIY Network. We already know what we have to buy or rent to renovate our kitchen. If we have some trouble we are going to call Chris' Uncle, George."

Dev looks at me smiling and says, "Okay, and how is this going to help your and Chris' relationship? I have heard from almost every couple that I know of that tried to renovate a room in their house that they were almost ready to get a divorce." He kisses Ash on the forehead and continues smiling. "My buddy JD and his Wife started renovating their kitchen and almost got a divorce over it. I couldn't believe that they would ever, but they almost did. They had to go to counseling to save their marriage."

I look at Dev smiling and say. "Well, that's just too bad for those two, but Chris and I are taking these classes together. So if he isn't paying attention, then I am. Anyway, if we get into any kind of trouble, we have his Uncle, George, who will help." I walked over to the sink to see that Chris had already gotten the roller and brush cleaned out. I looked around for the trays and then remembered that he put them on the back porch. I went out and saw if they were still out there, and they were. I picked them up and saw that the paint was almost dried up in them. I brought them in and put hot water in them and some dawn dish liquid detergent. I start washing them, scratching them and getting the dried paint off of the trays.

I finally finished those while Dev and Ash were up in Dev's room. I look at my watch and think. "If they don't get that fifteen passenger van soon, we may not be able to get one. Then we'll be in a lot of trouble. I better go up and see if they're ready to go get it." I start walking upstairs and hear Ash giggling. I walk up to his bedroom door and knock. "It's just me, may I come in please?"

"Yea, it's open."

I open the door and peek my head through the crack. "Are you decent?"

"Yea, I'm decent. What kind of guy do you think I am?"

I answer him smiling. "I don't know what you guys think of or about when you're alone in your bedroom with your girlfriend or fiance'." I turn to shut the door and wink at Ash. "Have you two already gotten the fifteen passenger van yet, or what?"

Dev looks over at me and smiles. "Sis, I think you worry too much about the little things. We're going to go get it when we leave for the airport. I'll have you and Chris riding with Ash and I before picking my Parents and your Parents up. Then we'll all head out to the airport together."

"Okay, just wanting to check on it. I didn't know what you two were trying to get Chris and I into. I'll see you two before we leave then." I walk out of Dev's room and walk down the hall toward Chris' room. I knock on the door and don't hear anything. So, I just walk right in and see that he's almost asleep on his bed. I crawl up beside him and whisper in his ear. "Hey, you sleepy head." I kiss him on his forehead, smiling at him while he turns his head to me and peeks through his eyelids.

"Yea, baby? Did I fall asleep?"

"Yea, I think you did. You've had a very busy vacation so far."

"Yea, I know, I have! I think it's about to get even busier too." He pulls me to him and we lay there until Dev comes to Chris' room to get us to go to the airport with them.

"Hey, you two. It's a quarter till three. We need to leave." He goes into Chris' bathroom and gets a warm cup of water. He brings it back into the bedroom and sticks Chris' finger in it laughing. I get up on the other side of the bed and start shaking my head.

Chris jumps up and asks. "What's going on? He looks down at his hand and sees that it's a cup of warm water. He looks up to see who put his finger there. He sees Dev bent over laughing as hard as he could without crying. Chris gets up and pours the water over the top of Dev's head and just smiles. "I hate it when you do that to me, dude." Chris tosses the cup to where the water is going to spill out all over Dev and asks smiling. "How does it feel?"

Dev is just standing there still laughing and answers. "I don't care, my room is right down the hall. I can change my shirt and dry my hair in a few minutes. I just wanted to come in and tell you all that it's almost ten till three now." He heads toward the door and he turns around. "Sorry, that I stuck your finger in a cup of warm water. Are you all ready to go now?"

Chris and I look at each other smiling and Chris answers. "Yea, we'll be down right behind you." Dev walks on out the door and leaves it open. He walks down the hall to his room and walks in. He gets another shirt to wear and walks back out into the hall.

Ash and Dev start walking toward the steps and Dev looks back to see Chris and I walking behind them smiling. Dev looks at Ash and says. "I have a feeling that Chris is going to get me back." Ash looks behind her and sees that Chris is still halfway sleeping.

She looks over to Dev and says smiling. "I don't think he's thinking that. I think he's still sleeping." Then she points back at Chris smiling.

Dev looks behind him and sees that Ash is right. He looks at her and says. "I said that I was sorry. It's just that I missed him when I was in Columbus. It's pretty sad that my little Sister would have to have an emergency for him to come up and see me." He gets down to the bottom of the steps and starts laughing.

Chris and I both look at each other and moan. We put our heads together before getting into Dev's truck with him and Ash. We climb in the back seat while Dev helps Ash in. He gets in and looks back. Chris says, "Hey, buddy! Why don't you get your seatbelt on?" He looks over at me smiling real big. I'm thinking that Chris has done something to the seatbelt, but no he didn't do anything to Dev's seatbelt. He just pushed his seat all the way back and layed the back of the seat down a little more than the way Dev had it before. Dev puts his seatbelt on and realizes that something isn't right. He puts his foot to the brake pedal to shift his truck out of park and realizes that it's his seat that has been screwed with. He scoots his seat up a little and looks back at Chris and says. "Haha, very funny dude."

We finally get to the rental car company and Dev goes in to see what fifteen passenger van he can get on such short notice. He walks out and jogs over to a black one, looks inside it and tells the man something. Then he jogs back into the building and jogs out jangling keys and waving at us to join him. We all get out of the truck and walk over to where Dev is.

"Are you all ready to go get my Mom, my Dad, Quinn and Lance? We need to get a move on!" He walks over to where Ash is having a little bit of trouble trying to climb into the van. He lends her his shoulder and helps her in. She gets in and gets her seatbelt on and he gets in himself. "Now, it's been a long time since I've driven one of these, but I think I can do it." He puts the keys in the ignition and starts it up. He looks back at Chris and I smiling and says. "No tricks up your sleeve for me this time, huh?"

"Okay, you don't trust my driving?"

"Oh, I trust it alright. Just not in a strange vehicle though." Chris looks over at me and winks. He looks at Dev and asks. "Who are we going to pick up first?"

"My Parents, then we'll pick up Bree's Parents." Dev answers.

"Okay!" So Chris scoots over closer to me this time and puts his arm around the headrest of the seat. He starts kissing me on my neck. I start giggling because of his goatee tickling me. He looks up into my eyes and I can see that he's thinking about something more than just kissing. He smiles his crooked grin and I know what that holds in store for me later on tonight. He straightens up and sits up.

We finally got to Dev's Parents house and they were waiting. Dianna, Dev's Mom, gets in the van before Darrin, Dev's Dad does. She hops in the seat that sits right behind the driver and passenger in the front. Darrin sits next to her smiling. He looks back at me with his arm extended out. "Hi, my name is Darrin. This is my Wife, Dianna. We're so happy to meet you Breea. We've heard so much about you from Dev since he found out that you were his little Sister." He turns toward the front of the van and asks Dev. "When are we going to get to meet her Parents?" He looks at Chris and I both and says. "Hey, Chris! How are you doing?"

Chris answers Darrin. "I'm good Mr. DeAtley, how are you two?"

"We're good now that our boy is home." He turns back around toward the front of the vehicle and puts his seatbelt on.

We start out on our way to get my Parents when we come across a black Chevy Malibu. We all gasp and hold our breaths. Darrin and Dianna both look at us all and Darrin asks, "What's wrong?"

Dev looks in the rear view mirror and answers. "We had a stalker while we were in Wilmington trying to find Bree's Father from the crash. They stalked us in a car like that, so now whenever we see a car like that we kind of can't get it out of our minds." He looks straight ahead at my Parents coming out of the house smiling.

They get in, and climb into the second middle seat. Mom gets in first and puts her seatbelt on introducing herself and my Father to Dianna and Darrin. "Hi, my name is Quinn Anderson, and this is Lance Anderson my Husband, we're Bree's Parents."

Dianna and Darrin both look back and shake their hands and say. "We're Dev's Parents. I'm Dianna and this is my Husband Darrin DeAtley. We're so glad to meet you two finally. We've heard nothing but good things from Dev about you two. Thank you for helping the kids out in Wilmington. Dev just told us about it when they all saw a black Chevy Malibu parked just down the street." She turns back toward the front of the van smiling.

Mom and Daddy both look at each other and just wonder if it's Mark and his gang that are in that car. They don't know of anyone on their street that has a black Chevy Malibu. When they get back home tonight they're going door to door to find out if someone has gotten a new vehicle or bought one for one of their kids. They turn around to look at me. My Mom asks, "You sure it wasn't a rental that you all saw?"

I look at her smiling and say. "No, I think it was the Marshalls. I think their Daughter is driving now, so they bought her a car." I look up at Chris and say, "This is nuts. This situation with Mark and Ash is getting in the way of everyone having fun this summer. It isn't the way I pictured my summer break before college." I stare at him begging him to say something.

He finally looks down, smiling and says. "Yea, I know what you mean, but everyone will be fine. We'll get rid of him and be able to enjoy our lives without being stalked by that creep Mark." He kisses my forehead and just then we notice Dev's look on his face. We look back and see that the Black Chevy Malibu is behind us. Chris and I both tried to see who it was driving, but when the car got close enough, it turned left. We both looked up toward the front and saw Dev's face relax.

We all finally get to the airport and get out at the entrance while Dev and Chris both go to park the van in the garage. Dianna, Darrin,

Quinn, Lance, Ash and I all walk in to wait on Dev and Chris at the door. We wait for about six minutes and see them walking out of the garage across the crosswalk. We all meet up at the door again and start over to where they have the departures and arrivals listed. Ash says, "They'll be at gate four." She turns and looks straight at Chris and he walks over to the counter of the security station.

Matt looks up and sees Chris standing there. He asks smiling, "Chris, what are you doing here? Thought you were on vacation?"

"Yea, I am. I'm just here to pick someone up with my friends and fiance'." Pointing back toward us smiling. "We need a favor Matt."

"What kind of favor?"

"We need a ride to gate four."

Matt looks behind his shoulder and says. "Chris, you know I can't leave the desk until someone else takes my place. I would love to help you out right now, but all the rest of us security guards are all at gate one. We've had a heart attack on that plane and they needed all of us there to assist the Medical Squad. They have the biggest cart with them."

Chris looks back at us still smiling and looks at Matt. "Okay, that's fine Matt. Don't sweat it. We'll just walk there." He turns around and starts walking back towards us. He comes up to us and smiles. "Sorry, I can't get a ride to the gate. We'll just have to walk. They had some kind of emergency at gate one that they had to help with, and they do have the biggest cart with them."

We all look at each other and agree by shaking our heads up and down. We all start walking towards the gates. We finally get to gate four and sit down. We were sitting there waiting on the flight to show up when we heard this commotion. We all look behind us and see that there is a fight getting ready to break out between two men. Chris and Dev both get up and jog over there. Chris says, "Hey guys, what seems to be the trouble?"

One guy looks at Chris and says. "This doesn't concern you, so keep your nose out of it." He continues arguing with the other guy.

Chris looks at Dev and says. "I guess we'll have to do this the hard way then." They both grab each guy and hold them down on the ground. Chris says, "I believe I asked you a question. Now are you going to answer me, or do I have to take you into the security hold cell?"

The guy that Chris had held down to the floor answered. "I'll tell you everything, just let me up. I have a bad back." Chris gets up off of him and helps the guy up. Still holding onto his hands, Chris sits him down in the nearest seat to them.

He bends himself at the knees and says, "Okay, what's going on?"

The guy looks at him and answers. "This man came at me thinking that I had his woman. He said that she wasn't going to leave him and wasn't going to fly out with me today. I don't even know him."

"Bullshit! You know you have her with you. She's already on the damn plane. Don't give me your shit. She's leaving me to be with you. I saw her standing with you while you were getting the tickets." The other guy said that Dev had a hold of down on the ground.

Dev says, "Shut up! We'll get your side pretty soon." He looks toward Chris and gives him the look. Chris shakes his head up and down agreeing with Dev and then gets up.

Chris jogs over to me and says. "Will you please go get a backup? I don't have my walkie with me, so I can't call for backup over it." He jogs back over to the man he made sit down in a chair away from the other man.

I get up and walk out into the main hall to see if I could see any of the other guards on their way out from gate one. I finally spot one and start running toward him. I see that it's Charlie and I say. "Sorry, I had to run. Chris and my Brother that's getting transferred here from Columbus Airport have two guys separated and need you or someone else to help them with the two guys that were fighting each other." I finally catch my breath and wait on him.

Charlie says over his radio. "I have a situation at gate four. I'll probably need backup. I'm on my way to the gate now." He grabs my arm and asks. "Did you see what was going on?"

I look at him and answer. "No, I didn't see what was happening. Chris and my Brother Dev saw what was going on and they went over to break it up before it got any worse." We start walking back toward gate four.

Chris and Dev see that I was walking back toward the gate and sit down while Charlie jogs over to them. Chris explains what all was said to him and Dev and points back over to the two guys who were fighting. Charlie walks over with another security guard and takes care of the situation. Chris and Dev come back over to the gate just in time for Ash's Parents. Emily and Eric walking up the tunnel. Ash and Dev both get up and start walking to meet them after they get past the red line. Ash gives both her Parents a big hug and a kiss on the cheeks and aks. "How was your flight?" While her Brother and Sister in-law walk right past us not knowing that they are there.

Eric looks at her and smiles. "It was wonderful. Your Mother and I had a great flight." He turns to her and smiles, grabbing her hand and walking back toward the seats with Dev and Ash smiling. Eric and Emily look up to see all of us waiting on them. Eric holds his arms out for Quinn, Lance, Chris and I to come hug him. "It's so good to see you all again." He looks at my Dad and asks, "How's the leg?"

"Oh, it's good." He looks over to my Mother and smiles. "Thanks for asking." He walks over to my Mother and stands beside her.

Emily and Eric look at each other when they notice that there are some more people that they haven't seen before. They both look at each other smiling and Eric asks. "Who are these people?" Pointing toward Dev's Parents.

Dev steps up and answers smiling. "This is my Parents." He walks over to them and stands by them smiling, then continues. "This is my Mother Dianna and this is my Father Darrin. Mom, Dad, this is Eric and Emily, Ash's Parents!" He steps to the side and lets his Parents talk to Emily and Eric. They all finally get done talking and we all start walking out of the airport. What we didn't notice when we greeted Ash's Parents is that her Brother and Sister in-law and their Baby walked right past us and went to wait for us at the door.

Ash notices them standing there and takes off running. She finally reaches them all and says. "I can't believe you three came!" She throws her arms around Austin and Bailey. She looks down in Bai's arms and says. "Awh, he's so cute. May I hold him?"

Bailey looks at Austin and hands Ash, Bentley. Smiling, Bailey looks up to Austin and watches her Son in his Aunts arms. She sees Ash cooing and making funny faces at Bentley and smiles. She looks up to see Dev's Parents.

Dev comes up to Austin and Bailey and says. "This is my Parents. Darrin and Dianna." He points to each one while introducing Austin and Bailey to them.

We all stand there for a while and watch a family reunion rehash. We all walk over to the baggage claim and see that the bags are already coming through. Eric, Austin, Dev, Chris, Lance and Darrin all walk over to help with catching the bags. While us women sit in the seats and wait on the men to get the bags playing with Bentley. Dev finally jogs over to us and says. "Chris and I are going to get the van. We'll meet you all here." Pointing to the door. Then they were off, with Austin, Darrin, Lance and Eric walking out the door with the luggage, so that Eric and Darrin could smoke a cigarette before getting into the van.

Chris and Dev finally pull up out front and help Darrin, Eric, Lance and Austin with the luggage. They finally get that all put in and they send Austin in to get us. "We're ready to go." He heads toward Ash and takes Betnley into his arms. "Are you ready to go little man?" He puts his Son in his car seat carrier and straps him in the van next to his Parents. Dev helps Ash in and goes over to his seat. They are waiting for everyone else to get situated in the van. We all are in the van now and it's Dev in the driver's seat. Ash in the passenger seat. Eric, Emily, Betnley and Dianna are in the front middle seat. Austin, Bailey, and Darrin are in the next middle seat. Then my Dad, my Mom, Chris and I are in the very back seat. We all laugh and have a good time on the way to eat at Frisch's first, then on to my house to show Ash's Parents where she's been staying.

Chapter
SEVENTEEN

....

We all finally got to my Parents house and went in. Bentley is
in his car seat still sleeping. Ash shows her Parents, Brother
and Sister in-law her bedroom. While she's doing that the rest of us sit
down in the living room and talk among ourselves.

Ash, her Parents, Brother and Sister in-law finally get done and
walk down stairs to join the conversation. Eric sits by his Wife on the
couch while Austin and Bailey both sit beside each other. Eric looks
over and asks my Parents. "Is it alright if our Daughter Ash spends the
night with us at Chris' house tonight?"

My Father looks at him smiling and says. "Of course, but we do
have plenty of room here for all of you too. There shouldn't be any
nonsense about where everyone stays. Just don't want you all to feel like
you're not welcome to stay. We have two more spare bedrooms that are
waiting for company. If you all change your minds." He looks over at
my Mother and says. "It's time for my medication dear."

"Okay!" She looks at everyone and says. "I'll be right back." She
walks into the hall and walks up the steps to get my Father's medication.
She walks back down and gives him two pills and a glass of water that

she got from her bathroom upstairs. "So, where is everyone going to be staying tonight?"

Eric and Emily both look at each other and agree. Then Eric answers. "Emily and I will stay here tonight so that Ash doesn't have to spend the night with us over at Chris' house. We figured this would probably be more comfortable for our baby girl." He looks over to Austin and Bailey and asks them. "Where will you two be spending the night?"

Austin looks at Bailey and answers, smiling. "Wherever there is a soundproof room. We don't want to disturb anyone's sleep with Bentley getting up in the middle of the night." He joins in the laughter with everyone in the living room.

Chris looks over at me and smiles, then says. "I have a spare bedroom on the first floor right next to the kitchen. If you and Bailey want to spend the night at my place that will work out just fine for you two."

Austin looks at Bailey and sees that she's shaking her head up and down and says. "Yea, we'll be over at Chris' house."

We all visit a little while longer and Austin, Bailey, Bentley, Dev, Ash, Darrin, Dianna, Chris and I all take Darrin and Dianna home. We head to Chris' house to take Austin, Bailey and Bentley there, so they can get him settled down. Then Dev, Ash, Chris and I all visit with one another at the recreational park. We sit out there for a while looking up at the stars and just talking with one another. We finally look at our watches and head on back to the van. Chris and Dev take Ash and I to my house. They park the van for a while and we all walk in. Everyone's asleep in my house besides Emily. She stands up and says, "Oh, thank goodness you're home!" She comes over to Ash and hugs her tight. "I was worried about you ever since we got the news about Mark and his gang being out of jail. I thought for sure they would try to come down here and find you. Thank goodness they haven't found you yet."

Ash looks back at us all and rolls her eyes. Then she says smiling. "Mom, don't worry. He won't be able to find me here. I don't leave the house unless I'm with Bree, Quinn, Lance or Dev. I'm never alone." She hugs her Mother back and says. "We're home now, so don't worry so much." She sits down on the couch by Dev. Chris and I sit down on the love seat. We watch Emily walk up the steps to go to her room. We turn the television on and watch a movie on HBO.

We all fall asleep on the couch and loveseat before too long. Chris wakes up and sees that he's still at my Parents house. He gets up and wakes Dev up. "Hey, man. We must have fallen asleep. It's one o'clock, I think we need to get the girls up the stairs to their rooms. Then we'll head to the house to get a little bit of shut eye ourselves." Chris walks back over to me and says. "Bree, I'm going home now. I'm going to take you upstairs first though." He picks me up and carries me upstairs to my room.

He lays me down in my bed and kisses my forehead lightly. I wake up and say, "I love you Chris." Then I fall back to sleep.

Dev does the same thing with Ash. Then they both walk out of the house after locking the front door and drive to their house down the street and up another. They get in and see that there is a light on in the kitchen. Chris sneaks to investigate it and sees that it's just Bailey. She turns around and says, "Wow, you two are getting in late. How are the girls?" While she was filling a bottle up and warming it.

"They're good. We all fell asleep in the living room watching a movie on HBO. I guess the television woke me up when it was getting ready to shut the satellite off." Chris looks at her and smiles. "Just keep the light on if you need to and you all are more than welcome to anything in the fridge. I'm going upstairs to my room to sleep." He gets up and starts walking out of the kitchen. He turns his head and says, "Goodnight." He finally gets up to his room and lays in bed. He turns the lamp off and gets under the blankets. The next thing he knows it's morning.

Chapter

EIGHTEEN

....

C hris wakes up with a new message on his phone. It's from a
number that he doesn't recognize. He opens it up and reads it.
"Hey its me bree just thought id (i would) txt (text) u (you) 2 (to) tell
u (you) i lost my phone on my Moms phone were (we are) headed to
UK college now goin (going) 2 (to) c (see) what the campus looks like
and get my schedule txt (text) u (you) when i get back 2 (to) my parents
house love u (you) ;)" He texts me back. "Ok love u (you) 2 (too) i
missed u (you) last nite (night)"

He gets up from his bed and walks to the bathroom. He finally gets
done there and comes to see that his phone is flashing again. "Awh i
missed u (you) last nite (night) 2 (too) do u (you) knw (know) what i
did wit (with) my purse last nite (night) when we got home" He thinks
about that for a while and texts back. "No i dont (don't) sorry u (you)
sure u (you) didn (didn't) leave it n (in) devs (Dev's) rental" He walks
downstairs to see if anyone is up yet. Obviously they have been because
there are cups in the sink. He runs water while sitting his iphone down
on the table. He puts detergent in the sink and starts doing the dishes.
He hears someone stirring in the next room and he pauses.

Bailey gets up because she hears someone in the kitchen. She tiptoed into the kitchen and smiled. "Good morning. Didn't realize anyone was up." She says stretching. Walking over to the coffee maker. "Do you have any coffee?"

"Yea, it's in the cabinet above the coffee maker." Chris answers her. He gets done with the dishes and looks over at her smiling, asking. "I thought you were supposed to go to Ash's appointment with her, Dev and her Mother?" He hears his front door open. He walks over to see straight to the front door and sighs. "I thought you went to Ash's appointment Eric?"

Eric walks in talking on his phone and smiles at Chris. Waves his left hand at him and points to the phone. "Hold on a minute, please." He looks at Bailey and sees that she's under-slept and he asks. "Is Bentley up? If he is, go get him, I'll take care of him while you and Austin sleep." Then he continues talking on the phone. He finally puts the phone down when Bailey brings Bentley out and hands him to his Grandfather. "Okay, you get your butt back in bed. Sleep however long you feel like sleeping. We'll be just fine." He looks down at Bentley and lays him down on the washer. He changes his diaper and gives him a bottle, while sitting down in the recliner in the living room.

Chris walks into the living room and smiles at Eric with his Grandson. "He's a doll baby." He brushes his finger down Bentley's little head and says. "I can't wait till I have a baby. I hope Bree wants more than one though." He sits down sipping his coffee and turns the television on.

Eric looks over at him and asks. "Would you care to feed him his bottle while this old man uses the restroom?" Eric gets up and takes Bentley to Chris.

Chris gets a hold of Bentley and takes the bottle. He looks up to Eric and asks. "What do I do if the little guy starts choking?"

Eric smiles at him and says. "It won't happen, but if it does, just hold both of his arms above his head. It will help him breathe better and go get his Parents." Eric walks away to the bathroom saying. "You'll be fine!"

Chris turns the television down and stares down at Bentley while he's drinking his bottle and watching Chris. He doesn't even hear the front door open until I say something to him. I walk into the living room smiling and see Chris holding Bentley. I look at the two of them and then get a thought. "I wonder how many children he actually does want?" I walk over to him smiling and ask. "How are you?"

He jumps a little and it startles Bentley to where he starts crying. He looks up at me, smiles and asks. "How do I get him to stop crying? I'm fine by the way." He stands up and starts rocking back and forth on his heels. Bentley is still crying.

I step over to Chris and say, "Let me!" I grab Bentley out of Chris' arms and put the bottle back in his mouth swinging from side to side with him in my arms. I got Bentley to stop crying and take the bottle again. I look down at Chris sitting on the couch and ask. "Did I frighten you? I'm sorry if I did. I didn't mean to. I didn't know that you were going to have Bentley in your arms. I was shocked when I walked in the room and saw him in your arms. Where is Bailey or Austin?"

Chris just sits back and watches me with Bentley. He finally answers me after a few minutes. "They're still asleep. Eric is here, he's supposed to be watching Bentley while Austin and Bai get caught up on some sleep." He pauses for a few minutes and smiles, saying. "You do good with him. You should be a Mom someday." He gets up and walks over to me. He grabs me from behind and rocks with me and Bentley. He stares down at Bentley and asks. "What do you think about having a baby before we get married?"

I look at him and answer him smiling. "I don't want to do that. It wouldn't feel right to me. I want children, but only two or three. I don't want a whole house full." I pause for a few seconds and say. "I wouldn't mind having a baby right now, but I also want to make my Parents happy by being married first." I kiss Chris on the cheek, smile and look down at Bentley. We stay like that for a while, or at least until Eric walks out and sees us.

He walks into the room and says quietly. "Is he back to sleep?"

I look up and whisper back at Eric smiling. "I think so. He doesn't seem to be awake." I lay Bentley in the arms of his Grandfather and walk over to Chris. I look at him smiling and ask. "What do you want to do today?"

He looks at me and answers. "I don't care. Whatever you want to do." He sits down on the couch with me because he has a hold of my hand. "Why don't we just stay in today?"

"Okay, that sounds perfect to me." I sit there holding his hand and watching Eric with Bentley while smiling. I notice that Chris is watching me.

"What are you thinking?"

"I'm thinking I want a baby, but not until after we've been married for a year at least." I look at him and ask him. "What are you thinking?"

"I'm thinking about the day that we say, "I do" to each other and then we don't have to worry about having babies." Chris smiles at me and says. "You do know that if you were in Ash's shoes that I wouldn't hesitate for one second to be your Husband right?"

I look over at Eric and answer Chris. "I know you wouldn't have. I love you for that too." I kiss him on the cheeks and we sit there watching Eric with his Grandson. We were sitting there until we heard someone open the front door. I get up and walk in the hallway and hold my index finger up to my mouth and say. "Shhhh, Bentley is asleep." I walk over to the couch and say. "It's Dev, Ash, Emily and Dianna."

Chris and I both get up and Chris says. "We're going to go up to my room. We'll give you all the chance to talk amongst yourselves." We walk upstairs and shut the door. He turns around with that crooked grin on his face and locks the door. He walks over to me, stripping his shirt off. He stands by me and starts kissing me. Before I know it, we're in his bed with our shirts off. He's on top of me and he says. "It would be great to be able to practice, but I know that you don't want to be pressured into making love. So, if you can give me this one thing, I won't ask anything of you anymore until the night of our wedding."

I look at him smiling and ask. "What is this one thing you want done?"

He looks at me and says. "Oh, baby. I don't know if you would do it for me or not." He smiles and climbs off of me. He says, "It's something that would probably sound nasty to you."

I lay there thinking. I get what he's wanting me to do. I shake my head up and down and turn toward him. I asked him, "Is it this?" While running my hand down his belly and grabbing him.

He looks at me with that crooked smile and answers. "Yes, that's what I meant." He stops talking for a minute and enjoys the pleasure that he's getting from me stroking him. Then he pops his head up and says. "Oh, baby. I love you!" He stops my hand and starts shivering badly. He stops, smiles at me and says. "Thank you, baby. I promise I'll make it worth your while after we're married." We just lay there for a while before falling asleep.

We wake up to someone knocking on Chris' bedroom door. He gets up and puts my shirt back on me and gets his. He finally finds it, puts it on and walks over to his door. He cracks it open and peeks out. He doesn't see anyone and he opens it just a little more before spotting Ash. She looks at him with her eyes big and asks. "Is Bree awake? I want to show her the pictures of the baby from the ultrasound." She holds up the pictures of her baby in her womb.

Chris looks back smiling and says. "Can you give us a moment, I have to wake her up." He shuts the door and walks over to the side of the bed that I was laying on. He sits down beside me and asks. "Are you awake, baby?"

I look up at him smiling and answer. "Yes, I'm up. What are you doing?"

"Ash is at the bedroom door and she wants to show you her ultrasound pictures of her baby in her womb. They look pretty neat." He rubs my back smiling. "Thank you for, earlier baby. I know you didn't get any pleasure out of it, but I sure did. We'll have to continue doing things for each other that might give us pleasure before getting married. Just explore each other's bodies."

I look up at him and smile. "You're welcome baby. I don't care if I get any pleasure, as long as you do." I sit up in bed and kiss him lightly on the cheek. I get up and walk to the door. I open it and say. "Come on in Ash." I see Dev pop his head in and smile.

Dev walks into Chris' room looking for any kind of sign that we weren't sleeping, but rather doing something else. I look at him and smile real big. Ash walks over to me smiling and says. "I got my baby's first picture today. You want to see it?"

I reach over and grab it still looking at Dev and not believing his reaction to me being in Chris' room. I look down at the ultrasound picture and smile. "How do I tell what is what?"

Ash points at the little words and says. "This one here is the baby's head. This is the side profile of the baby's face." She scoots the pictures up in her hands so that we can see the next one very plainly. "This one is the baby's foot and this one is the baby's hand. The baby looks like he or she is sucking their thumb." I look at it real hard and smile.

I say, "You have a cutie pie growing in there." Then I walk back over to the bed and start making it. Dev looks at me weird and says smiling. "I don't know what you two done up here while we were all down there talking to Eric, Emily, Austin, Bai and my Mother, but we had an interesting discussion." He rubs his head and asks Chris and I this. "The reason you two are getting married is because, why?"

Chris and I both look at each other and say, smiling. "We just love one another."

Chris says, "I just knew when I first met your Sister that she's the one for me. That's the reason I was asking that security guard at the hospital in Wilmington about how do you know and all that." Chris looks over to me and winks. I fluffed the cover up to get him to get off of his side of the bed so that I could make it. "Why were you all discussing us?"

156

Dev looks at him and smiles. "We just thought that we would like to know the answer as to why you are engaged after only two days of knowing each other, that's all." He sits down on the sofa that Chris has in his bedroom beside Ash and Dev asks. "My Sister isn't pregnant is she?"

Chris gets up and walks over to Dev and sits down beside him. "No, you goofball. We haven't had sex or made love yet. We're not going to until the night of our wedding, which isn't for another year or so. I don't want to put that kind of pressure on her." He looks down at his fingers and starts picking at the nail of one of them.

I watch him intently and ask Dev. "Why would it be so bad if I was pregnant with Chris' child, and we wanted to get married?"

Dev and Ash both look at me. Dev scratches his head and looks over to Ash. Ash gets up and walks over to me. "It wouldn't be a bad thing for you two to get married just because you're pregnant." She starts rubbing her belly smiling and says. "I mean look at me. Dev doesn't have to marry me if he doesn't want to. I'm not forcing him to marry me. We were just asking because we care about the two of you and don't want you two rushing into things with each other." She walks over to the couch and sits down beside Dev.

I look at them both and say. "Well, for your information. Chris and I haven't even made love for one. For two, I don't think that I would be able to get married if I was pregnant before. For three, I'm just now starting to live my life without my Parents telling me what to do, how to do it, and when. I'm sorry, I'm happy for the two of you. I really am, but I don't want to wait another minute. I know that Chris is the one for me. I can't sleep anymore without him being by my side in bed. I sleep better knowing that he's right here." I motion to my side and say smiling. "He's the first person that pops up in my mind before I go to bed. He's all I think about during the day." I see Chris watching me and I smile. "Truly and honestly, it's scary to be engaged this young, but I know who I want to be by my side through any life given challenge." I put the sham back into place on Chris' bed and sat down on Chris' lap. "Why were you two asking all those questions anyway? Are either of you having second thoughts?"

Dev looks over at Ash smiling and answers. "We just wanted to know the reason you two had to get engaged. We didn't know if it was because of pregnancy or if you two are in love with the idea of each other. We now know for sure that it's real love between you two. How else could you two go this long without having unmarrital sex? It takes real love to respect one another the way you two do." He looks over at Ash and says. "I'm not having second thoughts about us babe. I know you're the one for me when I first set my eyes on you. You looked so damn sexy in that waitress uniform." He kisses her hand and pulls her into a side hug.

Ash looks at him and says smiling. "No, I'm not having second thoughts about marrying you. I wish we could have met sooner because of all the things I have put my family through, including you. I didn't want to be pregnant with a baby at eighteen. I wanted to get out and live my life the way I wanted to, but I can't now because like it or not I'm going to be a Mommy and a Wife. I love you with all my heart." She kisses Dev on the mouth and holds his hand.

Chris and I are so moved by the speech they gave to one another that we just start saying what we needed to say by looking at each other. After we're done Chris looks at Dev and Ash and asks them. "My Grandparents are from Flemingsburg. They want me to take them back, since my Father doesn't have the time to take them back and my Mother is too busy with her daycare." He looks up and smiles at me again. "We want to know if you two would be interested in riding with us to take them back, and we want to spend one night at their house with my Grandmother. My Grandfather has to go back to the nursing home, and after that one night we would like to know if you two would go camping at Cave Run Lake with us and a couple of my buddies from college. It'll give Dev the chance to get to know them, and gives you girls a chance to talk and just enjoy peace and quiet. We can go swimming and hiking. Although I think hiking might be out of the question, since Ash is pregnant."

Ash looks at Chris and asks. "When are they wanting to go back?"

"They want to go back tomorrow. I tried thinking of ways to bring the subject up, but couldn't ever find the right time to do so." He stands up and holds onto my hand. "What do you two think of that idea?"

Ash and Dev discuss while walking to his room and shutting the door. Chris and I walk downstairs to see that Eric, Emily, Dianna, Austin, Bai and Bentley have left to go somewhere. We sit on the couch and watch a little bit of tv. Chris looks over at me and asks. "Do you think they'll want to go?"

I look up at him and answer smiling. "I don't know. They are talking about it awfully hard right now." We both look upstairs and don't hear a sound. We go on watching tv and I ask Chris. "What do you want to do about supper, since the sink and the stove are already gone?"

He looks over at me and smiles. "Well, if you want we could go to my Parents house for supper. My Mom is cooking her famous egg rolls tonight. We can go if you want to?"

I look at him shaking my head up and down and ask him. "What should we bring?"

"Nothing! She's got it all prepared and ready. All we have to do is bring ourselves." He smiles rubbing my leg and watches more tv. After about a half hour we get up and start finishing the paint job in the hall and kitchen. While we were doing that Ash and Dev walked downstairs. They both walk into the kitchen where we were and Dev answers our question about going camping. "Yes, we'll go. We do have to run out and get a few things though. I don't want my lady sleeping on the hard ground. So, I told her that she doesn't have to worry about that because I'm buying us an air mattress and our own tent."

Chris looks at him and says. "You don't have to do that. I have two tents and four air mattresses, you two can just borrow one of the tents and air mattresses. Save your money for when you buy a house and have the baby." He looks down at me and winks. "Speaking of houses. Have you two found one yet?"

Dev looks at Chris like he was hurt by Chris asking that question. He smiles at us and answers. "No, we haven't been able to find one yet. We want something that doesn't need any work done to it at all. Turnkey, basically. There is one on your Parents street that is turnkey, but it's really expensive." He looks at Ash and lets her finish answering the question.

"My Parents bought my Brother and Sister in-law's house for them when we found out that they were going to have Bentley. He doesn't want any of his Grandchildren to grow up in an apartment building like his kids had to do for a while until they got enough saved up to buy their house. So, we're thinking of asking them to co-sign for us or to buy us a house."

Just then Eric, Emily, Austin, Bai and Bentley all came into the house laughing. "That man thought you were going to give him cash for it didn't he? I have never in my life seen someone so stunned. Especially when you handed him the check Dad." Austin was walking into the kitchen and looking up to see Ash and Dev. "Uh, just disregard that last comment I just said." He throws his hands up in the air and walks into the living room. Bai follows him out with Bentley in her arms.

Dev and Ash both look at us and shrug their shoulders. Then Ash asks. "What was Austin talking about?"

Her Mother Emily walks over to her and says smiling. "Let's just say that we need to go look at furniture, curtains and a few other things." She's still smiling when she turns toward her Husband to have him tell us all what was going on.

Eric clears his throat and says. "Ash, Dev! I hope you two don't mind that we did this. Your Mother and I bought that house on Chris' Parents' street. It's our wedding gift to you both. We want to pick out some furnishings to go along with it." He fishes in his pocket feeling for the key to the house. He finds it and pulls it out. "We've already gone ahead and paid for it all the way. So you can move into it anytime you want. We're staying until Monday to help with anything that you may need." He hugs his Wife and smiles. "Austin, Bai and Bentley are also staying to help."

Ash and Dev hug each other smiling. "Are you sure Mr. Hampton? We don't want you spending your money like this!"

"I'm sure Dev. Hell it's always better to have a house than an apartment. When we lived in an apartment for fifteen years, we didn't get any rest whatsoever. We want the best for our Children so we thought that since we bought Austin and Bai's house for them, then we would do the same for you and Ash." He holds the keys out to Ash and Dev.

Dev takes the keys and asks. "When do we sign the papers and get it into our name?"

Eric looks at him smiling and answers. "Don't worry about that part. You and Ash have to agree with some things first." Emily, Eric, Ash and Dev all four pull out chairs and sit down to discuss what Ash and Dev both have to agree on. Eric looks at the both of them, smiles and says. "You both have to agree that you two will stay married for at least three years. You have to agree that you don't do anything stupid to ruin your marriage also." He looks at both of them and says. "I've already talked to Dev's Parents about this, and they agree with the terms of us buying your all's first place for you."

Dev and Ash discuss this matter between themselves. Dev looks over at Eric and answers. "We accept!" He gets the key from Eric and all four of them stand up and hug each other individually. Dev looks at Chris and I and asks us. "Would you all like to come with us to our house?"

We both look at each other and shake our heads up and down. Eric, Emily, Austin, Bai, Bentley, Chris and I all get gathered in the van and head toward Ash and Dev's house.

Chapter
NINETEEN

....

W e're all at Dev and Ash's house looking around. Chris and I
      are looking at the renovated kitchen and sigh. Chris looks over
at me and says. "You know what? I think we missed our class at The
Home Depot last night."

"I know we did. I forgot all about it." I walk over and hug him
smiling and say. "That's okay, though. We do have your Uncle,
George, who could come down and stay with us to help us through
the renovation. If we have any trouble following the directions that
The Home Depot employees tell us to do, then we could call on him."

He hugs me back and smiles. "I'm so glad that we met. I can't think
of my future without you." He looks down at me and smiles even bigger.
"How would you feel if we went ahead and planned our wedding? I
don't know if I can wait until next year to be married to you."

I look up at him, smiling and answer. "We'll have to discuss it
over with our Parents. See what they think about it. I don't want to
disappoint them. I know my Mom wants to give a big wedding and that
your Mom wants to have a big celebration for us."

"Yea, I know. All that can be arranged within three or four months though." He rubs the sides of his face and smiles. "I tell you what, if they agree to us getting married and think that they can plan it the way they want it, within the three to four month time span, then we should do it." He kisses my forehead and goes on looking at the house, holding my hand.

I look up at him and think that I'm the luckiest girl on the planet. I have him to love me for the rest of my life. He wants the same things that I want and isn't afraid to be truthful with me. I say, "You know what? I agree with you. I think we should move the date earlier, rather than next year. I would love to be married to you. That way when I start college in the fall I won't be having a whole bunch of guys following me around asking me out, because I'll have my wedding set on and flash that at them, telling them no!"

He looks down at me smiling and says. "Oh, baby. That sounds wonderful to me. When we get back to my house we're going to go ask your Parents if that's okay with them and then we'll head on over to my Parents house and ask them what they think." He grabs my hand again and we wait on Dev and Ash to come downstairs.

Dev, Ash, Eric, Emily, Austin, Bai, Bentley, Dianna and Darrin all finally come down the steps smiling. Dev looks at us and says. "I can tell they have something to tell us." He looks back at Ash and all of them and asks us. "What's up with you two?"

Chris and I look at each other smiling and Chris answers. "We have to make sure that it's okay with both our Parents, but we want to move the wedding date a little closer. We don't want to wait until next year to get married. We want to do it within a four to five month time period. It will be around Christmas."

Dev and Ash hug each other and smile. "That sounds perfect. We're having a Thanksgiving wedding and you two will have a Christmas wedding." He pulls Ash in for a hug and a kiss. "I guess we just have good news all around today." We go to the van with Dev, Ash, Dianna, Darrin, Eric, Emily, Austin, Bai and Bentley. We all get in and Dev is in such a good mood he asks everyone, smiling. "How about we all go out to eat somewhere? It's my treat!"

Chris and I look at each other and I answer. "Thank you Dev, but Chris and I have somewhere that we have to be tonight for supper. We can't tell them that we're not coming after we told them yesterday that we will, but we'll take a rain check. I hope you understand?"

Dev looks back at me, smiles and says. "That's okay, I understand you all have other plans. You want us to drop you off at Chris' house?"

Chris answers smiling and says. "Yea, that will be fine." We get onto Chris' street and pull up in front of his driveway. Chris and I both get out along with Ash. Ash has to go to the bathroom again. She runs in with Chris and uses the bathroom while I'm standing outside on the porch with Dev to walk her back to the van. Chris walks out with something in his hand and walks over to his truck.

He looks over at me and asks. "Are you ready to go?" He puts whatever it was that he carried out of the house in the truck.

I look at him and at Dev. I say, "Yea, I'll be right there. I hope you'll forgive us this time for not wanting to go out to eat with you all. I'd love to spend some time with you all and celebrate the fact that you two got a house today, but we already told his Parents that we would be with them tonight." I hug him and say. "Good luck with furniture shopping." I walk over to the truck and climb in on Chris' side. We wait for them to get out of our way.

Chris looks over to me and says. "Thank you for telling Dev and Ash no tonight. I don't know if I could have done it or not. I didn't want to tell them no and put a damper on their day. I wanted to celebrate with them tonight." He kisses my forehead and looks up toward his house. He smiles and says, "It looks like we're on our way to discover how good of a cook my Mom really is with egg rolls and fried rice."

I look up and see that Ash and Dev are locking Chris' house up and walking to the van. They get in and Dev shuts her door. He walks over to the other side and gets in. He waves at us smiling and showing us that it's okay that we aren't going with them. We back out of the driveway and head toward Chris' Parents.

We finally get there and pull over to the side of the street. We get out and hold hands while walking up to the front door. We stop just outside the door and he looks over at me and smiles. He knocks on the door once and uses his key to go in. We are greeted by his Mom's side of the family when we walk in. "Oh, Chris! It's good to see you! How have you been?"

I look at him smiling. I ask, "Who is this?"

Chris looks at me smiling and answers. "This is my Uncle, George." He looks at his Uncle and answers. "Uncle George, meet Breea, my fiance'!"

Uncle George wraps his arms around me smiling and giving me a hug. He says, "It's nice to finally meet you Breea. I hope this family makes you as happy as it has me." He lets go and says. "Well, come on in. We won't bite you." He walks over and sits down on the couch with his Wife, I'm guessing. We walk into the living room and Chris stays standing up beside me holding my hand.

He looks at his Parents and smiles. "Aunt Molly, Uncle Matt, Maddison, Madeline, Mickey, Tommy, MaLeah, Tonya, Micah, Anthony, Aunt Gretta, Gabriel, Jayson, Gage, Andrew, Garrott, Bradley, Gabbi, and Coribeth. This is Breea, my fiance'!" He grabs a breath of air and smiles. He grabs my hand again and takes me over to sit.

We were sitting there for a while and were just talking with everyone before supper was done. He looks over at me smiling and asks. "Are you ready to go meet my Grandmother and Grandfather Mikel?"

I look up at him shaking my head up and down. "Yes, I'm ready." I get up along with Chris and follow him.

We get into the dining room and hear someone say, "Bullshit!" Then some cards slammed on a hard surface. I look at him and just keep smiling. We walk in and see that his Father, Mother, Grandfather, Grandmother and some of Chris' cousins are gathered around the table playing the card game, "Bullshit." His Mother gets up and says, "Come on in guys." She gets down head level with her Father and says. "Daddy, this is Breea. Chris' fiance'!"

Chris' Grandfather looks up and says. "You know you are the prettiest woman that I have ever seen?" He gets up out of his chair and walks over to me. "Let me get a hug. I'm glad you've finally made Chris settle down. I need some great Grandbabies." He chuckles and goes on. "They keep me young, you know." He sits back down saying. "Christine, why don't you tell this little pretty young lady my name here."

Christine smiles and says. "His name is Maximillion Lee Mikel. We call him Max for short." She looks to her Mother and she stands up, eyeing me discreetly.

Walking over to Chris and I giving us each a hug, she looks at me and says. "My name is Maggie Mae Mikel. I'm so glad that the two of you could make it in tonight. I can't wait until we get to spend a little more time together tomorrow while we're headed back to Flemingsburg. I'm so excited to get that man back into the nursing home. He does get on the nerves a little bit over being a little too bossy." She winks, smiles and sits back down.

Chris and I walk upstairs to his old bedroom that one of his cousins is sleeping in. We shut the door and Chris bends over to kiss my neck in the dark.

I let him for a few minutes and said, smiling. "I don't think that we should be in here."

He turns the light on and says. "This was my room when I lived here, but now my Parents use it as a guest bedroom." He shrugs his shoulders and walks over to his old bed and sits down on the mattress. We both hear someone say, "Ouch!" Chris gets up and raises the covers. He sees his cousin Mickey under the cover. He lays the cover back down real quick and says walking away from the bed. "Sorry, Mickey. We didn't mean to bother you. Didn't even know that you came up here to make out with your Sister's best friend Madeline." We open the door while turning the light off and walk out into the hall shutting the door behind us. He looks over at me and we both just burst out laughing.

Madeline walks out messing with her hair and putting it back up into a loose bun. She runs down the steps and walks over to Maddison and sits down. Mickey walks out and looks at Chris. "Could I please talk to you for a moment?"

Chris squeezes my hand and says smiling. "Yea, sure! Just give me a minute." He looks at me and says, "If you want to, you can go downstairs and sit with my cousins in the living room. If you don't want to do that then you can come with me while I talk to Mickey."

I look at him and say. "I think I'll just go downstairs and visit with your family. Take your time." We smell the delicious aroma of egg rolls cooking in the kitchen. "I take it that supper might be done in a little bit, so hurry. I don't want to eat without you." I kiss his cheek and start walking downstairs. I find Maddison and Madeline and ask. "Could I please sit down with you two?" They both look up at me smiling and answer by shaking their heads up and down.

Chris walks back into his old room and asks. "What's up dude?"

Mickey looks at him with a face that shows a frown. "I need to talk to you about something. It concerns Madeline."

Chris sits down on the bed beside him and says. "Okay, shoot."

Mickey looks at him and says, seriously. "You have to swear not to say anything to anyone about this."

"Okay, dude! You know you can trust me. What is it?"

"Madeline just told me that she thinks she's pregnant. She said that it would be mine if she was. We met up about five weeks ago and got a little too drunk. We had sex and now she hasn't gotten her period." Mickey just starts breaking down crying. "I don't know what to do. I don't have a job and my Parents will kill me if they find out. I need to know what to do about it."

Chris looks at him and says, "You're going to hate me for saying this, but you need to tell your Parents about it." Chris strokes his goatee and asks. "How old are you and Madeline?"

Mickey looks at Chris and answers. "Well, I'm nineteen years old and Madeline is only seventeen years old. That's the reason why I don't know what to do. I need someone to tell me what to do because Madeline's Parents are the type of people to put me in jail for getting their Daughter pregnant." He puts his head in his hands, pacing back and forth.

"Okay, here's what we're going to do. We are going to tell your Parents when you all get back to Flemingsburg. That way it isn't around all these people and in the solitude of your own home. If they agree to us telling Madeline's Parents after we tell them and with them at her Parents house." Chris gets up and grabs at his head. "Has she taken a pregnancy test yet?"

Mickey looks up and says. "I don't think she has. She's still waiting for her period to come. I don't want this to happen to her because I would hate to get married to her. I don't want to get married before I go to college. That would just ruin my whole life. I want to live my life and start my career before I get a girl pregnant. I want to be married and settled with a house already before I do that."

Chris looks at his cousin and smiles. "I know how you feel dude. I had a scare once like this before I went to college. I didn't know what to do about it either. I got the courage up to go to my Parents and tell them what was going on. They marched me over next door and talked to the Parents of the girl that supposedly was pregnant with my child."

"What happened?"

"Well, we found out from the girls' Parents that she didn't want me to break it off with her and she said that she claimed to be pregnant just to keep me from going away to Morehead to college."

"Oh, how awful that must have been for you. I hope that's the case with Madeline. I guess I need to talk to my Sister Maddison first before going to my Parents and telling them this. I hope that's the case." He stands up, feeling a lot better about his chances that she's not. He turns to Chris and says. "Thanks, our talk has been helpful." He walks out into the hall, leaving Chris upstairs all by himself.

I finally look up and see that Mickey is walking down the steps, into the living room and just watching Madeline. He comes over to pull his Sister off the couch and talks to her without anyone near them. They are talking in hushed tones. So, I walk upstairs and look for Chris. I walk to the door that I walked out of earlier and knock on it softly.

Chris is still sitting on the bed and hears someone knock on his old bedroom door. He gets up and walks over to crack it open. He sees that it's just me and smiles. He pulls me in. "Sorry, I was just trying to think of what I can do to help my cousin out. I don't want him or any of my cousins having to put themselves in shoes that they don't want any part of." He hugs me and sighs. "I'll tell you all about it later, but not now. I can't, I hope you understand right now?"

I look up at him and smile. I shake my head up and down. "I think I already know what it's about anyway. I overheard Madeline and Maddison talking. It doesn't sound good. I sure hope that it's just a false alarm. For her sake and Mickey's. She seems like a nice enough girl not to put herself in that kind of situation. If she is then he will do what's right by her."

"Yea, he will do that, but he doesn't want to get married." He thinks about the situation he got himself into when he was eighteen. He looks down at me and asks. "What are you thinking about?"

"Oh, just wanting to know why you would get yourself in that kind of situation your cousin is in?"

"It was a long time ago and she didn't want me going off to college. I didn't have sex again! I was so afraid of getting a girl pregnant after that little incident. I didn't want to be a Father back then."

"Now you do?"

"Yea, because I found the one person I'm meant to be with for the rest of my life. You're my girl Bree!" He kisses my forehead and squeezes me gently but yet hard enough for me to feel it.

We both walk back downstairs and sit at the table with Chris' family. Some are in the living room and some are in the dining room. We go and sit with his cousins in the living room and let the adults have the space in the dining room. We talk with his cousins and walk into the dining room and talk to his Parents, Aunts, Uncles and Grandparents about moving the wedding up.

Christine looks at us and asks, smiling. "There isn't something that we should know about Breea, is there Chris?"

Chris looks over at his Mother and answers. "No, Mom. Bree's not pregnant. We just want to spend the rest of our lives together, and we want to get married as soon as possible."

We look at each other smiling and see that they are starting to come around to the idea of us getting married sooner rather than next year. I see Christine and Mike's heads turn to us and smile. Mike stands up and walks over to us. "We agree with you two. Why wait when you two have so much love for one another now? You two have our blessing." He looks over at me and says. "Now, your Mom, Chrisitne and I have talked about this before you turned twelve. Christine and I said to her one day that we hoped that Chris would pick someone like you to be married to when he was older. Now look at where we are!" He walks over and stands between Christine and Chris.

Chris and I walk around hugging everyone and say our goodbyes until in the morning. We head out to his truck and hop in. We finally get back to his house and walk in and just enjoy the peace and quiet before Dev and Ash come back. We fall asleep on the couch watching tv when they walk in laughing.

I hear them over top of the tv and get up. I walk into the kitchen and see that Austin, Bai and Bentley are getting ready to go to sleep. I look over at Dev and Ash and ask. "How was your trip to the furniture store and how was the restaurant?"

Dev walks over to hug me and answers. "It was great, sorry you had to miss it. We got all the furniture over at our house. Austin, Bai and Bentley all got us a living room suit. Mr. and Mrs. Hampton got us a bedroom suit. My Parents got us a dining room suit. Now all we have to get is the baby's furniture and a spare bed for now. Our house is basically full. We're going to start moving some things over there tomorrow." He hugs Ash while she's talking to her Parents.

I say. "That's great that you all got all the furniture you need for now. I'm happy for you Bub."

He says to me, "Hold on a minute Sis. We have some news for you too." He grabs Ash by the waste and shakes his head at her. "Ash has something she wants to tell you." He looks over toward Chris and sees that they woke him up too, and he nods at him smiling.

Ash walks up to me with a big smile on her face and says. "Dev and I have found another one of your Sisters. Her name is Camerin Rodriquez. She's working as a waitress at Cheddars. She recognized Dev and said that she remembers seeing him somewhere but she couldn't think of where it was that she saw him before. We all got to talking with her and found out that her Mother in law takes care of your Grandmother Lena."

I look at myself and smile. "Really? Well, did you all ever figure out where Camerin remembers Dev from?"

"Yea, we did. We were at the table when she walks back with our drinks and says that she has a picture of Dev when he was four. Dianna and Darrin couldn't believe her, so they asked for the manager to come out and let her go to her car and get the picture. She said she had the picture in her car. So, the manager lets her go out to her car and she walks back in. She has the same exact picture of Dev sitting by your Birth Mother. He was such a handsome little boy. He was smiling at Camerin because she was the one who took the picture."

"Oh, did you all think to ask her where she lived all this time and where she lives now? I'd like to meet her, you know."

"Yea, we know where she's living. We also know who her adoptive Parents are too. It turns out that her adoptive Parents are some kind of relation to your's and Dev's Birth Mom. So, we asked her what their names were and it turns out that you and her have been living next door to each other while she was being raised. You could have been babysat by her a couple of times even. She said that her adoptive Parents still live there. Their names are Michael and Sherry Sweet."

I think for a minute and smile. "Yea, I know them. They did have a few adoptive Daughters that lived there when I was growing up." I got to thinking back to what their names were and when I thought of them I sat down. I looked at Dev and said smiling. "I can't believe that I was right next door to some of our half Sisters and half Brothers. I remember now that Sherry and Michael had three girls and two boys. I remember that the littlest, who is a boy, used to come over to my house and get sugar and tea sometimes. I always felt close to him and even when I would see him outside playing in the yard, I always watched him and thought that there was something that was so familiar about him, yet so far away too. I think his name is Dalton. Yea, that's it!" I remember the rest of the names of those kids that were raised by Sherry and Michael. "The rest of them were Daimon, Callie and Chelsea." I think of another question to ask Dev and Ash. "Did she say where the rest of them are now?"

Ash answers smiling. "Yea, she said that Callie is living in Wilmington, Ohio now. She's married to a Doctor that lost his Wife and five year old Daughter in that plane crash. I think she said his name is Dr. Carson William Schneider." She stops suddenly and then it clicks where she's heard that name before. "Oh, my god! Your Father's Dotcor's name was Dr. Carson William Schneider also. Wonder if that's the same guy?" She continues and says. "Dalton has a little baby, who was just born in March. He got into some big trouble while at school for fighting and met this girl at some kind of camp over last summer and got her pregnant. He didn't even know it until the girl showed up on his Parents front door step saying that the baby belonged to him and she didn't want to have to deal with him anymore. She was giving sole custody over to him and said that she didn't want anything to do with either one of them." She thinks about what else was said and smiles over at Dev and says. "I think you should tell the rest."

Dev gets up and sits by me and says smiling. "Yea, Dalton is still living with Sherry and Michael. Uhm, let's see here. Oh, yea! Chelsea is married to a guy named Justin Ray White and lives in Wilmington now too. His Father is mine and Chris' supervisor at the airport. How his Son ended up in Wilmington beats me. Anyways, that's all we know for now. She said that she's going to get a hold of them and ask them if they would like to come in for a Brother and Sister reunion. She should be calling me within the next few days to tell me their answers." He gets up and hugs Ash. "I can't believe that this day will end up bad, it's been a big day for all of us." He throws his hands up in the air and sits down by Chris who was up. He was just listening in and watching every little move I made, smiling.

I get up, look at my watch and smile. We still have three and half hours before Ash and I are due to be home. I walk into the living room with Ash, Dev, Dianna, Darrin, Eric and Emily. We all sit around talking about the good news and then Dev's phone rings.

"Hello?" Dev answers it.

"Yea, Dev? It's Camerin, I have some news to tell you."

"Okay, let's have it!" He puts his phone on speaker and whispers. "Shhhhh!"

We all get quiet and hear Camerin on the other end. "They all said that they would love to come in and meet. When would you like for it to be set up? Callie, Chelsea, Daimon, Dalton and I would like for it to take place within a week, if that fits yours and Breeas schedules?"

"Yea, a week sounds great." He looks at me and asks. "Do you want to talk to Camerin?"

I look at him and smile, shaking my head up and down. I take the phone and sit back, keeping it on speaker. "Hi, Camerin, it's Breea! A week from today sounds perfect to me. Where would you all like to meet?"

Camerin answers smiling. "We would like to meet here at Cheddars. It's all of our favorite restaurants."

"No kidding? I guess that's where I get it from then. I always thought I was crazy. Every other child wants McDonalds or Wendys. All I ever wanted was Cheddars." I laugh a little and ask her one more question. "Do you know where the other two of our siblings are?"

Camerin answers defeat. "I've been working on it. I have found one of them, but they refuse to meet with me." She starts tearing up and finishes. "It's Darion. Apparently he's married and has five kids, but his Wife is really sick and he doesn't want to put her through what he calls, "A waste of his time coming all the way here from New York" just to meet us. He said that if we were meant to be together then we would have been. I just don't think that he's forgiven Billie Dawn for all the bad things she put him and Cara through." She pauses for a minute to catch her breath and adds. "He says that Cara is up there too and is married with two children. He can't say no for her part, but for now he doesn't want to meet any of his siblings that were taken away."

"Oh, that's so sad. Do you have his number? Did he say that you could give it out to any of us if we wanted it?"

"Yea, I have his number and he said that if you all wanted to contact him that would be fine. He just doesn't want to travel too far away from his Wife because of her condition. She's been really badly ill for the past year. The Doctor's are trying to find out what's going on with her. I hope she makes it through for him. That way he can get back to Kentucky and be happy again. Cara, on the other hand, is sending her Son off to college. I think he may be the same age as you. Eighteen I think."

"Oh, really. That's weird. I have a nephew that is the same age as I am?"

"Yea, I think you have two nieces that are the same age as you too. We've been a busy family." She chuckles to herself and continues. "Yea, Darion's and Callie's oldest Daughters."

"Do you know what they're names are?"

"Yea, I sure do." We hear papers rattling around and then she gets back on the phone with us. "Okay, sorry about that. Had to get my papers with the information on it. It's hard trying to keep up with all these names and birthdates." She pauses for another minute and continues. "Yea, I'll just read them off to you, starting with our oldest sibling Darion Ray's Children. His Wife's name is Michelle Gayle Conway. His Children's names are oldest to youngest. Brooklyn Gayle, Brittany Rhae, Brionna Michelle, Blake Darion and Bryson Ray. Now for Cara LaRhae. Her Husband's name is Scott Raymond Wallingford. Their Children's names are from oldest to youngest. Kyle Raymond and Kylie LaRhae. Our third oldest sibling is Daimon Michael. His Wife's name is Zara Nicole Sweet. Their Children's names are from oldest to youngest. Zaiden Michael, Zyla Nicole, Zyra Michelle, Zarrod Daimon and their newborn Zander Terrance. Next on the list is Callie Michelle. She's the one married to the Doctor up in Wilmington. His name is Dr. Carson William Schneider. They just got married about a week ago. She was married before but he was killed in a car accident. He was the Father of the kids. Their names are from oldest to youngest. Blithe LeighAnn, Derrick Carson, Bethany Michelle and Deidrich William. The doctor adopted all of them a week before they got married. Her ex Husband was his best friend. He had promised him that if anything were to ever happen to him that the Dr. had to take care of his Wife and Children for him. He died in a motorcycle accident a year before the plane crashed and killed the Dr.'s Wife and little five year old Daughter." She pauses for a minute, getting a drink of water and continues. "Okay, next is me. Camerin LeTerra, my Husband's name is Miquel Terrance Rodriquez. Our Children's names from oldest to youngest. Jose Terrance, Jennifer Camerin and JoyAnna Eva. Our next sibling is Chelsea Annette. Her Husband's name is Justin Ray White. His Father is the supervisor over the security team at the airport here. Anyway, here are their Children oldest to youngest. Josiah Ray, JoHannah Annette, Jordan Justin; they call him JJ, and Josie Chelsea. The next one is Dev of course. You know all about him." She chuckles, then continues. "Then it's you. Then we have Dalton Terrance Sweet. He isn't married yet, but a damn good Daddy especially at the age of fifteen. His Son's name is Ian Terrance Sweet." She stops and sighs. "That's all the information I have on all of our siblings. I'm trying to contact Cara, but so far no luck. I hope and pray every night that Darion's Wife gets to feeling like she can travel so that they can come down to meet us all. I'll talk to you all sometime tomorrow, my eleven year old wants me to wash her hair. Goodnight guys." She hangs the phone up and Dev's phone goes black.

He hops up and gets it from me as quickly as possible. "I have to put this on charge. I'll be right back." Taking the stairs two at a time and almost falling over a few. We hear him in his room walking around and hear him walk back down. "Sorry, I had to put it on charge before it went completely dead." He rejoins us watching tv.

After a half an hour, his Parents get up and Darrin says. "I think it's time that we get going. I have a long day ahead of me." He looks at Dianna and smiles shaking his head. "I can't believe her, she sits down for just a few minutes and she's out like a light." He bends over her head and kisses her lightly on the forehead and asks. "Are you ready to go, Sugar?"

Dianna opens her eyes and looks up at him. "Yea, I'm ready to go." She gets up and walks over to Dev, Ash, Eric, Emily, Austin, Bai, Chris and I and gives us all hugs. "I guess I'll see you three tomorrow at the dress shop?"

Emily, Ash and Bai all smile up at her and shake their heads up and down. Emily gets up and walks them to the door. "You all be careful." She shuts the door and locks it. Walks back into the living room again. She looks at her Daughter and says, "I think it's time we head back to Bree's Parents house. What do you girls say?"

Ash and I look at each other smiling and Ash answers. "Yea, I'm beat." She grabs Dev's hand and walks out the front door with him and her Parents. Leaving Chris and I alone.

"I guess they're ready to go home. I don't want to leave you, but I guess I have to consider what we're going to ask my Parents tomorrow about the wedding idea." I get up and start walking away when I remember their answer about the campout at Cave Run Lake and the one night spent at his Grandparents house tomorrow night. I go to turn around and bump into him. "Oh, ye……" I start giggling and finish what I was about to say. "Yea, my Parents don't mind me going with you to your Grandparents house tomorrow night and on to Cave Run Lake to campout for two nights."

He strolls up to me and hugs me. "I already knew that answer. If you weren't allowed to go you would have already told me before now." He tilts my chin up to his and kisses me feverishly. "Why don't you just spend the night here with me tonight? I've already called your Parents and asked them if it was okay. They said that they didn't mind it. They trusted us not to do something that we shouldn't do before marriage anyways, they were just surprised that we haven't asked before now."

I look at him and get my phone out of my purse. I text Dev. "hey bub go on without me im spendin (spending) da (the) nite (night) here wit (with) u (you) 2 (two) tonite (tonight) dont worry my parents already knw (know) bout (about) it u (you) can ask dem (them) when u (you) get there if its true or not" Chris and I start walking up the steps after he locks the doors and windows when my cell phone vibrates. I take it out of my back pocket and see that I have a new message. It's a text from Dev. I open it and it reads. "Ok asked dem (them) dey (they) said dat (that) it was fine i guess ill b (be) spendin (spending) da (the) nite (night) here wit (with) ash her parents said it was alright wat (what) more could we do haha jk (just kidding) love ya both nite (night)" I laughed after I read it and text him back. "Ok love ya (you) 2 (too) nite (night)" Chris walks up behind me and holds out Snowball to me.

He says, "I've had to keep her in the utility room because of the baby. I didn't want to leave her outside so she could get into the room where Bai, Austin and Bentley are sleeping."

I grab her and take her from him. She curls up and sits comfortably on his bed. I say, "I don't have anything to sleep in tonight."

Chris walks over to his drawer and pulls out a shirt and throws it at me. "Here, sleep in this."

I pull it over my head and say. "It's perfect." I walk into the bathroom and get undressed. I pull the shirt over my head and come out in it. He looks up and whistles at me. I start laughing and jump in the bed with him and Snowball. We both turn our lamps off that sit on both sides of the bed and we cuddle each other. The next thing we both knew it was morning time.

Chapter
TWENTY

Chris and I get up, he gets himself dressed and heads down to the kitchen to cook breakfast. I get up and get dressed and start making his bed and putting his and my dirty clothes in the hamper. Today is the day that we are going to tell my Parents when we go over to pack my bags for us to go to his Grandparents house in Flemingsburg and to go camping for two more days. I can't help but feel excited about the day that we are about to start. I head downstairs to the kitchen and see that Austin is up with Bentley. I walk over to him smiling and ask. "May I hold him?"

Austin looks at me and says. "Yea! I have to get him a bottle anyway." He walks over to the cabinet and gets a bottle warmer and a bottle of water out of it. He measures the formula and puts it in the bottle. He measures the water and puts it in the bottle. He shakes it up and puts it in the bottle warmer. While he's waiting on the bottle to warm up he looks at Chris and asks. "When do you all leave today?"

Chris looks at him smiling and answers. "We leave in just an hour. Do you think that Dev and Ash would still want to go?"

"I don't know if they would or not." Austin answers Chris' question while getting Bentley's bottle out of the warmer and testing it on his wrist. He walks over to me and asks. "Do you want to feed him or should I?"

I look up and smile. Flattered that he asked me if I wanted to feed Bentley, I answered. "Yea, sure thanks."

Just then Ash and Dev both walk in laughing and walk into the kitchen. Ash says smiling, "It sure does smell good in here." She walks further into the kitchen and sees that it's Chris that is cooking. She looks over at me and says. "You have this man trained already!" Laughing, she sits down beside me. "Awh, my little nephew."

I look over at her and ask. "Do you want to feed him? He's scaring me a little bit, with the gulping between sucks." I hand him over to Ash and he starts crying because the bottle fell out of his mouth while I handed him off.

Ash takes him and puts the bottle to his lips. He takes it and starts sucking away again. "Awh, Bree being mean to my little nephew?" She looks up smiling, "How dare you Bree!" We all start laughing.

Dev steps up and watches Ash with her nephew and whispers to her. "I can't wait until ours comes. I will help you with the feedings and changing the diapers. Oh, by the way, I hope the baby is healthy. I don't care what sex the baby is. I'll still help you out." He kisses her forehead and kisses Bentley's head. He sits down next to her still watching her.

I get up and walk over to Chris and ask him. "Do you need any help?"

He looks over at me and grabs me by my side, pulls me over to him. "No, everything is good here. Why don't you go ahead and get the plates, silverware, and cups out. It'll be done in a few minutes." I walk over to the cabinet with the cups and get them out and sit them on the table. I walk over to the cabinet that stores the plates and get them out, take them over to the table and sit them down. I go to the drawer that's really hard to open to get the silverware out. I pull really hard and the drawer face falls off. We all start laughing and Chris looks at us. He says laughing with us. "It's okay, we're going to replace all the drawers and cabinets anyways." While I put the silverware on the table Chris turns around and asks Dev. "Are you two still going to go with us to my Grandparents tonight and camping with us at Cave Run Lake for two more days?"

Dev looks at him and answers smiling. "Sorry, I don't think we're going to go. Ash wants to get the house done while her family is still in. We'll definitely have to do it before we go back to work the week after next." He gets up and says. "Sorry, Sis. I hope you two understand?"

Chris and I shake our heads up and down. I say, smiling, "Yea, we understand that. I wouldn't want to leave my family either if they were in."

Chris looks at Austin and says. "Here's my key to my house. That way you and Bai can come and go when you want, and not have to worry about Dev being here to let you all in or wait on him." He hands his house key to him and smiles.

Austin replies, "Thank you Chris, but Bai and I will be with Dev and Ash mostly anyways. So we'll just use his key." He hands Chris' house key back to him smiling. Chris takes it back and puts it on his key chain. Then we all sit down to eat.

After breakfast we all get up and put our plates and dirty dishes into the makeshift sink. I start washing them while Chris walks upstairs to pack his clothes. After he gets done with that, he walks back to the kitchen and says. "I'm done packing up. Do you need some help with these?" He bends down and kisses my neck.

I look at him smiling. "That feels nice, and no I don't need any help. Just finished them." I turned around and started kissing him back. We get done kissing and I ask. "Are you ready to head to my Parents house?"

"Yea, I'm ready if you are." He smiles and grabs my hand, while we start walking toward the door. We get into his truck and head off toward my Parents.

We finally arrive and walk in. I head straight upstairs with Chris right behind me. We both walk into my room and I turn around and say. "So, this is what we're going to do. We're going to pack my bags. I'll give them to you to put in your truck while I talk to my Parents about the wedding being moved to December." I walk into my bathroom and get my hairbrush, comb, toothbrush, straightener, hairspray and my make up bag. I walk back out and see that Chris must have gone downstairs. I go on and pack the rest of my things. I walk downstairs with my bags and see where Chris went.

I walk into the living room where both of my Parents were and smile at them. I look over to Chris and ask, "Have you already started without me?"

Chris looks over at me, smiles and says. "Yes, I have! I thought that we would kill two birds with one stone. While you were packing I went ahead and explained to your Parents about the wedding being moved up." He stands up and says. "They do agree with my Parents. That us getting married sooner would be best. They think that we should just go ahead and move in together too. Your Parents are going to pay for the wedding, but my Parents are going to pay for the reception." He looks over to get their reactions. He asks, smiling. "If that's okay with you two?"

My Dad stands up. Walking over toward us he holds his arms out and says. "That would really be great. I just want you two to be happy. Ever since I've come home, I haven't gotten to see my baby girl as often as I did before I left. Now that you're in the picture I feel comfortable that my baby girl will be safe wherever she goes." He hugs the both of us with my Mom following behind him.

She looks at me when she gets closer to me and says. "I know this is the right thing for you two to do. You can still keep your house key, just in case you ever need to come home. You know that, right?"

I look at her with watery eyes and say. "Yea, but do you really think that it's a great thing that we move in together before the wedding?"

My Dad answers. "Yea, it would give you two the time that you both need together. That way you two can see the way each other are before going ahead with the wedding. If he isn't what you expected in a man then that would give you time to decide what you want to do about it." He looks at Chris, smiling and says. "It works the same way for you too. This way you can see what kind of person each other are." He gives us both a hug and smiles real big.

My Mom asks. "Is that okay with the two of you? We know that Ash's Brother and Sister in-law are in your house. We know that they aren't going to be there forever either. This way it would give you both the time that you need to find out how each other lives and want things." She pauses, looks over at my Dad and smiles. "We lived with each other for twelve months before getting married. We wanted to make sure it was going to work out between us. Yea, we had our rough times, not getting along, but that's what makes this so unique. You get to know the person without anyone else being around the two of you." She pats Chris' shoulder and continues. "So what's this camping expedition? We already know that Dev and Ash aren't going. Where are you two going to camp at and what are you two going to do while you're there?"

Chris looks over at me and answers. "We're camping at Cave Run Lake in Morehead. It's probably about a forty five minute drive from Flemingsburg. We're going to go swimming, have a campfire and sleep in a tent."

"Oh, sounds like fun." Rolling her eyes. She's always been a city girl. She's never been to a camp besides in her Parents back yard. "What are you two going to do if there's a wild animal that decides to come near when you're camping and takes all the food or worse, takes off with your tent?"

Chris and I both laugh at her question and Chris answers. "We would have to go buy another tent. Or, we would have to shoot whatever animal it is." He grabs my hand and says. "Come on, we're going to be late picking my Grandparents up." We walk out the front door of my house and head toward his Parents.

We finally got to his Parents to pick his Grandparents up. His Grandmother, Maggie climbs in the back seat. She looks up at Chris and asks. "Where do you want me?"

Chris looks at his Grandmother, smiling and answers. "Wherever you want to sit Mammie. It doesn't matter where." He carries on loading their bags into the back of his truck. He walks over to his Father and asks. "Dad, do you need help with Pappie?"

Mike looks at his Son and answers. "Yea, I need some help here." He looks up toward his Wife and smiles. Wipes the sweat off of his forehead and grabs a hold of Pappie. They both lift him into the passenger seat of the truck and Chris puts the seat belt around his Grandfather. Mike walks over to me wiping the sweat off of his eye brows, smiling and says. "Have fun with them. I hope this trip goes well for you two." He gives both Chris and I a hug and walks back toward his Wife on the porch of their house. They stand there waiting for Chris and I to get into the truck.

I look at Chris and say. "I'm going to sit in the back with your Grandmother. I don't want her to feel too lonely." I climb in the backseat and put my seat belt on. I shut the door as I wave at Christine and Mike. "See you all in three days." I shut the door and turn my attention to Maggie. We sit there and talk about things and how happy she is that her little Christopher has found the perfect young woman to be with for the rest of his life. By the time we got out of Lexington, Maggie was asleep. So was Max. I look at Chris, "That was quick for the two of them to fall asleep. I sure hope the trip doesn't wear them out too much." I stare out the window and watch the scenery, while Chris is driving and watching the other vehicles.

Chapter
TWENTY ONE

....

Ash and Dev are out looking at a four door Toyota Highlander, when she gets a phone call. She looks at her caller id and sees that it's a number that she doesn't know. She looks up at Dev and asks. "Do you know who this is?"

He looks at the number and answers. "No, I sure don't." He looks inside the one he's been eyeing. "Are you going to answer it or let it go to voicemail?"

"I don't know which one I should do. My Parents and Brother are all down here. Which only leaves Bai's Parents to call if there was anything going on. I know their number and it's not them. So, I think that I will let the voicemail get the call. If they leave a voicemail then I'll return the call." She looks inside the vehicle that Dev just looked into and smiles. She just felt the baby kick. She stands up straight and smiles at Dev. "Hey, babe! You want to feel?"

He looks over at her seeing what she's talking about. He looks down to where she has her hand and answers. "Yea, I sure do." He puts his hand on her stomach, smiles and says. "I think we have found the vehicle for us. He likes it so much that he wants to put his opinion in." He chuckles while looking at Ash.

Ash looks at him and asks. "What makes you so sure that the baby is going to be a boy?"

"I don't know. Maybe I'm hoping that the baby is a boy." Dev says wiggling his eyebrows up and down smiling like there isn't a care in this world to him. He feels the baby stop and looks at her. "You okay? He finally stopped kicking. Is this wearing you out? I don't want to wear you and the baby out, is this the one you like?"

Dev says smiling, "Yea, we can look at that one." They both walk hand in hand over to the car that Ash likes and look at it. Dev looks at her smiling and asks. "Is it the color you like for the outside and inside? It's just like the one over there on the inside." She looks at him smiling, shaking her head up and down. He sees that she's satisfied with this pick and they both walk inside the building of Green's Toyota of Lexington.

A man walks up to them both smiling and asks. "May I help you?"

"Yea, we would like to take a Highlander out for a test drive." Dev answers the man.

"Okay, sure. First off my name is Richard Veil. I'm a salesman here and I would be happy to help you two folks out. Let me go get the keys for the vehicle you want to take out for a test drive." He jogs into the back of the building into a little room and walks out smiling at the other customers. He jogs back to Dev and Ash and says. "Are you two ready to go?" He holds the key up in his hands jingling them. He gets a good look at Ash and her belly. He asks, "How far along are you?"

Ash looks down at her belly and rubs it. She looks at Dev and sees him smiling at her. She answers Richard, "I'm only four months long."

"Awh, well now is the best time to get something that is dependable and won't break down on you and the baby while you're out with him or her at the doctors." He walks in front of Ash and Dev and unlocks the Highlander they're wanting to test drive with the keyless entry. Dev and Ash walk up to him smiling and Richard asks. "This is the one you wanted to test drive right?"

Dev looks at him and answers. "Yea, it is. You have a good eye."

185

Richard opens the door to the driver's side and says. "I never buy a vehicle without looking at the engine." He pops the hood and walks to the front of the vehicle. He pushes a button underneath the front lid of the hood and opens the hood. "Now, this is the best motor that Toyota has ever had." He waves his left hand at the vehicle. "Have a look if you want." He walks over to the passenger side of the vehicle and waits on Dev and Ash to have a look at the motor.

Dev is done looking at the motor and he pops his head over the hood. "It looks brand new. Is this a brand new vehicle?"

"Yea, it's a two thousand twelve Highlander. We just got it the day before yesterday. It has a lifetime warranty on the motor and we can put the value guard on the inside of the vehicle and outside. It helps with the car not rusting on the outside and stains on the seats. All you have to do is sign a paper stating that you two will bring it in for service every seven thousand miles for the oil changes and maintenance. If there is a stain on the seat then, we will get our upholstery cleaning machine out and get the stain out for you while it's here." He pauses for a few minutes and asks. "Are you ready to take this baby out for a test drive?"

Dev looks at Ash smiling and answers. "Yea, we're ready." He grabs Ash's hand and they climb in. Ash is in the front passenger seat with Dev in the driver's seat. Richard is in the back seat. Dev pulls off in a parking lot after ten minutes of driving. He looks over at Ash and asks. "Do you want to drive it? That way you can tell me if you like it or not!"

Ash shakes her head up and down, gets out of her side of the vehicle. Dev does the same and they both walk around. Ash gets in and puts her seat belt on and Dev does the same. Ash puts the vehicle in gear and heads off toward the dealership.

They finally make it back to the dealership after driving for twenty minutes and walk into the building with the vehicle parked in front. They sit down at Richard's desk and they start giving information out about each other. Richard gets the paper work done and smiles at them both. He clears his throat and says. "Okay, Ashley you don't have very much credit on your record, Devin you do! You both look good to be able to get a new vehicle today. How did you want to set up the payments?"

Dev looks at Ash, smiles and answers. "Payments?"

"Yea, we have a finance company that we go through ourselves. We can give you the amount for the car, and extra for life insurance just in case something happens to either one of you. If something does end up happening to either one of you then the life insurance will pay the vehicle off and you won't have to worry about making a payment."

"Oh, okay!" Dev looks over at Ash and sees that she really wants the vehicle. He looks back at Richard and asks. "How much is the vehicle if we were paying in cash?"

Ash just looks at him with her mouth hung wide open. She looks back at Richard to witness his reaction to Dev's question. Richard looks at Dev, clears his throat. Smiling, he answers. "It's thirty three thousand nine hundred fifty nine dollars and thirty nine cents."

Dev looks at Ash, winks at her and looks back at Richard smiling. "Okay, if we were to put fifteen thousand down on it, how much would our payments be?"

Richard punches buttons on his calculator, smiling at them. "I take it you have bought a vehicle recently!" More of a statement than a question.

Dev answers smiling. "Yes, I have! I just bought that truck out there before moving down here from Columbus Ohio." He points to his truck out in the parking lot, he continues. "I figured that when she gets bigger with the baby in her stomach that she will have to have something that will be a little bit easier for her to climb in and out of. I don't want her to cause too much stress on herself or the baby by climbing in something so big. Plus, it's a used vehicle. I only paid fifteen thousand for it."

Richard looks out at the truck and shrugs his shoulders. "I wish I had your luck with finding vehicles like you do." He finally gets the results back from his boss and says smiling. "It would bring your payments down to only one hundred fourty two dollars and eight nine cents a month." He looks at the credit scores of Ash and Dev. "Wow, you two have very good credit for the ages that you two are. How do you do it?"

Dev answers, "We don't buy it if we don't need it." Ash shakes her head in agreement smiling.

"Wow, at your age I only wished I had this good of credit. You two have done outstanding for yourselves." He looks back at the report and sees that there was a house on their credit report. "You two just got done buying a house?"

"Yea, we sure did." Dev looks over at Ash and grabs a hold of her hand smiling.

"Wow, and already got it paid off within two days of owning it?"

"Yea, but if it wasn't for her Parents we wouldn't have been able to do it." Dev lifts her hand up to his lips and kisses the back of it. "They bought the house for us as a wedding present."

Richard looks and smiles at them. "Well, I hope that this will make you happy." He turns in his seat and grabs papers. "With the fifteen thousand down and your credit scores, your payments will only be one hundred fifteen dollars and eighty nine cents, for ten years."

Dev looks at him and asks. "You told us that if we put fifteen thousand down on the vehicle that we could have the payments down to one hundred fourty two dollars and eighty nine cents. Is that a discount for putting so much down on it or what?"

Richard answers. "It's the interest rate we were able to get you two at, with your credit score. My boss was figuring your payments up with the highest interest rate that we offer. Which one would you prefer?"

Dev looks over at Ash, "I like the one hundred fifteen dollars and eighty nine cents better." He looks back at Richard and asks. "Where do we sign and when can we take the vehicle home?"

Richard points at all the paperwork and says smiling. "Thank you for purchasing a vehicle from us today. You will sign and date here. Ashley, you will sign and date here." He keeps doing that with all the papers that he had printed out and stands up when Ash finally signs the final one. "Congratulations to the both of you." He hands the keys over to Ash and says. "If you two will need another key, just let us know." He walks out of his office and walks up to another customer.

Dev looks at the keychain and grabs it from Ash. He walks behind Richard and says. "Excuse me? How much would an extra key cost us?"

Richard looks back smiling and answers. "Oh, you want an extra key?"

"It would be nice to have an extra key, and I have another question for you too."

"Okay what is it?"

"For a spare, just in case if I'm at work and Ash is somewhere with the baby, if we were to get a copy of the key made, let's say at Wal-Mart. Would it unlock the doors for us to be able to get into it?"

Richard looks at him smiling and answers. "Yes, a key from Wal-Mart will do that, but it won't start the vehicle. They have these chips in them now that won't start the vehicle, but will unlock the doors. They're about a thousand dollar key." Richard looks at him and asks, "Do you still want the extra key?"

Dev answers, "Yea, we still want the extra key with an extra keyless entry please."

"Okay, let me put that order in and you can pick it up tomorrow." He types a few buttons on his computer, looks at Dev and smiles. "The order is in. I hope I've answered all your questions today."

"Yes, you have. Thank you!" After shaking Richard's hand he turns toward Ash. He sees that she's waiting on him, smiling and so patiently. He finally reaches her and asks, "Are you happy baby?"

"Yes, I'm happy!" She looks up at him smiling and they both walk out of the building and Dev helps her into the new vehicle. She looks at him and says. "I guess I'll follow you to the house. I still don't know much about the area, so go easy with me please."

Dev kisses her lightly on the lips and says. "I sure will babe." He shuts the door of the new vehicle and walks to his truck. He climbs in and puts his seatbelt on and pulls out of the parking space. Ash pulls out of hers right behind him and follows him to the house. They pull into their driveway and get out of the vehicles. They were greeted by Eric, Emily, Dianna, Darrin and Misty.

Dianna looked to see what kind of car they got and smiled. "I thought you wouldn't ever own a Toyota, Devin?"

Dev looks at her smiling and answers. "I thought that since you work there that I could give the place a little more money. They need to give you and Richard a raise though." He smiles at his Mother and Father and then at his soon to be in-laws. They all congratulate them on the vehicle. They all walk into the house including Misty wagging her tail in excitement and get it all arranged. Dev looks over at Ash and asks her. "Do you and Bailey want to drive to Breea's Parents house to get the rest of your things? We'll stay here tonight if you want? Your Parents can too, because earlier today while you were still sleeping I went out and got us another bedroom suit for the guest room."

Ash looks up at him and says. "Wow, babe. You amaze me, and yes I would love to go to Breea's Parents house to get the rest of my things with Bailey, but I don't know if I will be able to find it on my own without you with me." She sees Dev looking behind her and smiling real big. She turns around and sees that Camerin is walking up, smiling. Ash runs over to her and asks. "I know you just got here and that you want to see Dev, but could you please go with me and my Sister-in-law, Bailey to get the rest of my things from Breea's Parents house?"

Camerin looks at her smiling and answers. "Sure, as long as JoyAnna can come with us?"

"Sure!" Ash takes JoyAnna's hand into hers and starts talking with the little girl while Camerin and Dev both hug each other. Then Camerin, JoyAnna, Bailey and Ash all drive over to my Parents house to get the rest of her things.

Dev figured that this was his chance to get the nursery together before Ash, Bailey, Camerin and JoyAnna got back. He makes a mad dash into the house and up the steps to the nursery room. He starts putting the crib together with his Father and Father in-law. He puts the rest of the furniture together and manages to send his Mother and Mother in-law out to get some bedding for either sex. They get back just in time because Ash has just texted Dev saying that they were all done and were getting ready to head back. His Mother and Mother in-law get the curtains and bedding all up, they both walk downstairs and Dianna asks. "Devin, you all don't have any food in the house do you?"

Dev looks at his Mother and answers. "No, we haven't had the chance to go get groceries yet. Why would you want to do that for us?" He starts digging into his wallet and sees that he only has his bank card on him. He gets it out and starts to hand it to his Mother and Mother in-law. "Here, go get us some groceries."

"No, Dev. You need to save your money. We'll get the groceries. We'll get everything that you two will need and get you two stocked up on some formula for the baby. We already know what you're using." Emily said, looking at Dianna. "Dianna, I hope you and Darrin don't mind Eric and I doing this for them?"

Dianna looks over at her smiling and says. "No, not at all. I mean after all Devin doesn't have to know who bought the bedding, curtains and things to hang up in the nursery and the other rooms." She smiles winking at Emily. "Will you need me to take you to the grocery store to get these guys some groceries?"

Emily looks at Dianna smiling and says. "I sure do. Are you ready to go now? I want to get back before Ashley does, because I want to see her reaction to all the beautiful decorations that Bailey has suggested to us and the nursery."

"Okay, let me ask Devin if he's heard from her yet." She starts out in search of her Son and sees that he's outside with the guys sitting on the front porch in the rocking chairs and swing that they just got done putting together. She smiles at them all and looks straight at Dev. When she gets ready to ask him the question Ash, Bailey, Camerin and JoyAnna pull back into the driveway smiling. She turns on her heels and walks inside the house with Emily. She says, "Emily, they're already back. We'll take Ashley when we go to the grocery store."

So they both walk out onto the front porch and remember that they didn't put the back patio furniture together. Then Dianna whispers to her Husband Darrin. "Honey, did you all put the back patio furniture together yet?"

He looks at her and smiles. "No, dear. We haven't yet. We figured we'd do that while you girls go get groceries later. We want to see her reaction to all the decorating inside and the nursery room first."

"Okay, sweetie, just asking." She stands there watching her Son with his soon to be Wife, his Sister in-law, Sister and Niece. She smiles at him and starts to almost cry. They finally get up to the porch and Dev pauses with Ash there. He stands there watching her face as she notices the furniture on the front porch.

She turns around and hugs him. "Thank you, it's perfect." She gives him a kiss on the cheek and turns back around to go try out one of the rocking chairs. She looks up at Eric, Emily, Darrin, Dianna, Austin, Bailey, Bentley, Dev, Camerin, JoyAnna and Misty. She smiles at them and gets up. She asks Dev, "So what else have you been up to besides putting the porch furniture together?"

Dev looks at her smiling and answers. "Awh, you know. Just some more things that I thought that we may need for the house to make it a home. I wasn't the only one who stayed and put these things together either." He looks toward everyone and says smiling. "You have to thank them all too. They had a part in it." He said to her as he was pointing toward Austin, Eric, Emily, Dianna, Darrin and Bailey.

She looks at all of them, smiles and says tearing up. "Thank you guys so much for this. It takes most of my worries away. With my Parents, Dianna, Darrin and Bailey planning the wedding and baby shower, it just means so much to us." She starts sobbing and smiling at the same time. "Don't worry, these are tears of happiness."

Everyone walks up to her and hugs her and Dev. Then they take her into the house and show her the living room, kitchen, bathroom and the guest bedroom downstairs. Not only did Dev buy furniture for the guest bedroom upstairs. She was so overwhelmed with it all by the time they got to the nursery to show her what they had already done that she had to sit down in the hallway on a bench to catch up with all they had done since she's went to pack her things up at Mr. and Mrs. Anderson's house. She finally looks up at Dev smiling and tugs on his shirt sleeve to get him to notice her. When he looks at her he shakes his head up and down and says. "Why don't the women and children go get in Camerin's minivan and go to the grocery store while us men stay here and unpack the bags that Ash had brought back. "We'll show her the other room and the back patio when they get back." Dev walks over to Camerin standing in the back of the crowd and says. "Sis, we need groceries in the house, I'm not allowed to pay for any of it because of my Mother and Mother in-law." He pauses and digs into his wallet and says. "Here's my bank card. I'll pay for your gas to the grocery store and back. It's the least I can do for you to be a part of this."

Camerin shakes her head in agreement with Dev. She takes the bank card and heads on out with the rest of the women while the men stay back at the house. They finally get to the grocery store and Emily pays for all the groceries with her bank card. The groceries came to be about four hundred dollars. They had five carts full to the top with everything. Seasonings, mixes, cereal, formula, and etc. They decide that Camerin and her Husband are going to get them a set of dishes and things for the kitchen. So they go to Wal-Mart after the grocery store. They pick up all kinds of things from there and look at the things that they have in the baby section. Ash only dreams of the things that she sees and still doesn't know about the nursery. Emily, Dianna and Bailey all start to get worried about what Ash may want then and just start putting it in the cart. They were surprised that Ash didn't do anything like that though. They went to the cash register and paid for it, and started on their way back to the house.

The women make it back to Ash and Dev's house and pack all the things in and start unloading the bags when the doorbell rings. The women all looked at each other and sent Camerin to get the door. She looks through the peephole and notices that it's Mr. and Mrs. Anderson with three gift bags in their arms smiling and waiting patiently. She opens the door smiling and says. "Hi, Mr. and Mrs. Anderson. Long time no see." She gives them each a hug and asks them to come in.

Quinn and Lance both look at each other and wonder what Camerin is doing here. Then they see that Ash is walking through the hallway with her eyes so bright and bold wiping the sweat from her eyebrows. Quinn says smiling at her, "Hey, Ash! We wanted to bring our gift to you. We didn't know if you were going to have a housewarming shower or not so we decided that we should just bring it on over after we got some things for you and Dev." She looks over at Camerin and says smiling. "Sorry, I had my hands full earlier. Come here, let me look at you." Quinn gives Camerin a hug and smiles down at JoyAnna. "Who must be this pretty young lady?"

JoyAnna smiles up at her and says. "I'm JoyAnna, Camerin is my Mommy. I came to Uncle Dev's house with her." She looks up at Camerin and smiles.

"Well, I didn't know Dev had another Sister." Quinn says looking up at Camerin and almost immediately notices a little resemblance of Bree. She hugs Camerin and whispers in her ear. "Are you another one of Dev and Bree's Sisters?"

Camerin lets go of her, smiles real big. She shakes her head up and down and says. "Yes, Dev and Ash found me waitressing at Cheddars, which by the way is my favorite restaurant. I already know that Breea's favorite restaurant is Cheddars too. Anyway, while they were with their Parents, we all got to talking and we found out that we are indeed half Brothers and half Sisters to one another." She stands back smiling at Quinn and Lance. Then she says, "Yea, it's a small world." She walks into the living room and puts the gift bags down in front of Ash and Dev. "Here you two go. Open them up!" She walks over to stand beside her Daughter who is sitting on the floor, watching just as intently as everyone else who are watching Ash and Dev open their gifts from Quinn and Lance.

Dev and Ash are tearing into one of the bags and they find all kinds of things. He bends down to get everything and brings each and every little item out individually. He hands them to Ash and she looks at them and shows them to everyone there smiling. Quinn and Lance got Dev and Ash cleaning supplies, rubber gloves, toilet brushes, dish rags, dish towels, towels, wash rags, kitchen utensils, pot holders, paper towels, laundry detergent and fabric softener all in one bag. They started digging on the second bag and found a large pot with a lid, a four inch skillet with a lid, a sauce pan with a lid and a medium saucepan with a lid. They scooted that out of the way and started digging in the third bag. In it they found a tablecloth, curtains, cushions for dining room chairs, and a gift card from Wal-Mart. The gift card had two hundred and fifty dollars on it. Ash looks up at Quinn and Lance, she gets up, walks over to them and gives them a great big hug crying. "Thank you both." She lets go of them and gives Dev the chance to say thank you.

Dev gets up and walks over to Quinn and Lance and hugs them both too. He pulls away and says, smiling. "Thank you for the gifts. We greatly appreciate them." He walks over to where they put the things back in the bags and takes them to the kitchen. He starts putting them away when the doorbell rings again. He sits the things down on the counter and walks to the door while the others are visiting with Quinn and Lance. He peeks through the peephole and sees that it's Chris' Parents smiling holding five bags. He opens the door and smiles. "Come on in. Welcome to our house."

Christine and Mike come in with smiles on their faces and look around. Christine says to Dev. "What a nice looking house you have here." All while walking to him and giving him a hug. Dev grabs three bags out of Mike's hands and helps them both into the living room.

Dev sits down beside Ash and smiles. "Honey, I think we have more gifts to open up here."

Ash sees that he's right. She looks up and sees Mr. and Mrs. Lee sitting across from them. She looks at the bags and starts pulling things out. One whole big bag was nothing but towels and wash rags. The second big bag was nothing but kitchen things such as. A toaster, coffee maker, tea maker, bread box, blender, mixer, can opener, and a big box of silverware. The third big bag was nothing but soap, shampoo, conditioner, body wash, toothpaste, shaving cream, facial cleanser, robes and a loopa for the body. In the fourth big bag there was a great big box that had a microwave in it. The fifth bag was nothing but things for the baby. A pack of diapers, bottle brushes, pacifiers, bottles, a can of formula, bibs, three outfits, a box of wipes, a bottle strainer, toys, books, dishwasher nipple and rim holder, sippy cups, extra receiving blankets, infant car seat warmer, a bottle warmer for at home or on the go, extra nipples, extra rims and lids, dreft laundry detergent, downy fabric softener, and a gift card for one hundred dollars. Ash scoots all the bags out of the way and walks over to Christine and Mike. She looks at them both and they stand up. She hugs them crying even more and says. "Thank you, this all means so much." She pauses for a moment and continues. "I'm not crying because I'm sad, I'm crying because I'm happy." Then everyone gets up and walks over to her to hug her and cry happy tears with her.

Quinn looks over to Emily and asks her. "So, are you and Eric going to spend the night at our house or here with your Daughter and her Fiance' tonight?"

Emily answers the question with tears in her eyes. "Yea, I think we're going to spend the night with Ash and Dev tonight. I hope you don't mind that? We're just so happy for them both. We don't want to leave Lexington now. We have sold the house and the restaurant and are moving here to retire so that we can be near Ash, Dev and the baby." She looks over toward Austin and Bailey. "But, I don't want to leave my oldest one and his family either. I don't know if he could sell or not, and start his own practice down here in Lexington. What do you think we should do?"

Quinn looks at her and smiles. "I think that he could find something down here, if not his own practice. He could probably join a firm. I was thinking of offering him a job at the firm I just became a partner of. I just didn't know how to ask him. I was afraid of how he would react."

Emily claps her hands together and smiles. She says, "I'm so happy. Why don't you stand up and say something right now?"

"I don't know. I don't want to take away from Ash and Dev. Maybe Lance and I will invite Austin and Bailey out for supper tonight or something. You wouldn't mind watching Bentley would you?"

"No, I wouldn't mind that at all." She looks over to Bailey and says. "Oh, I don't know if she'll go for it or not though. Her Parents are from Wilmington." Just then Bailey's cell phone rings. She looks at the caller ID and sees that it's her Parents house calling. She gets up and walks into the other room.

"Hello, Mom." Bailey says smiling.

"Have you been crying dear?" Barb asks Bailey.

"Yea, but they're happy tears for Ash and Dev. What's going on?"

"I was just calling to say that we're going to be moving to Florida. Your Father has the notion of going through some hot weather during the winter. We're still keeping the house in Wilmington and letting your Uncle and Aunt live here while we're away. They like the cold weather for some odd reason."

"Oh, Mom. What are Austin and I going to do about Bentley though? I thought you said you would babysit him on the days that Emily couldn't watch him, while I go to work with Austin?"

"Oh, dear. I have forgotten all about that. I think your Aunt Beverly and Uncle Wayne would be happy to fill in for me when I'm not here. Besides, this has been your Father's dream to do. We finally came up with some extra cash to do this and we're going to do this. Family members come and go honey. You just have to get used to that fact."

"I know that Mom, but not when a family member promises that she would watch a certain Grandchild when her Daughter comes up pregnant." Bailey looks into the living room and waves to get Austin's attention. "I know that it's been Daddy's dream of going to Florida for the winters. Austin and I will figure out what to do, don't worry about it. When do you all leave?"

"We leave tomorrow. We're going to have a layover in Lexington. So, if you, Austin and Bentley can find a way to get to the airport around seven tomorrow night, we'll be able to say goodbye."

"Well, what about Ash and Dev's wedding? Will you all fly back in for that? What about Bree and Chris' wedding in December?" Austin comes in to see who it is that she's talking to.

He hears the voice and whispers to Bailey. "Let's go into the family room." They both go in there and Bailey puts her phone on speaker.

"Well, we haven't thought about that yet. We would love to be there, but honey what makes you think that they would invite us for? We're not really their family."

"They would invite you and Daddy because they care about you both as friends and because you are my Parents. They consider you both as their family also."

"I know that, bu......." Barb was cut off.

"Mom, are you there?" Bailey asks.

"Bai, is that you?" Big Bentley asks, Bailey's Father.

"Yea, Daddy it's me. What on Earth is possessing you both to move to Florida?"

"Well, Bai! You know it's always been a dream of mine to move to Florida. We were going to move when you met Austin, remember? You were all for it before that happened. You have your own family now. Honey, it's time for us to live our dreams for a while. We'll lease out a condo on the beach and if we don't like it then we'll move back up this way a little. I'm just tired of my joints aching in the winter."

"I know Daddy, but I'm going to hate to see that happen......." Austin and Bailey don't know it but Emily was eavesdropping on their conversation with her Parents. She had never felt so badly for her Daughter in-law than at that moment. Her heart was racing, yet also breaking for her. She remembered that Bailey's Mother Barb and Bentley were going to watch Little Bentley for her when she was allowed to return back to work. She promised Austin and Bailey that whenever Barb and Bentley couldn't watch Little Bentley that she would be there to fill in the spot. Now she even felt like a heavy weight has been set on her shoulders. She walks back up the hallway into the kitchen area and around the corner. She runs smack dab into Quinn. "Sorry, I need to talk to you now." She pulls Quinn into the kitchen and says frowning. "I just overheard Bailey's conversation with her Parents. They're going to be moving to Florida tomorrow. Her Father has arthritis and it's been a dream of his to move to a warmer climate. His joints can't take the cold weather anymore, so that's why they're going tomorrow. The warmer it is when they move down there the better off it is for his joints."

"Okay, this would be the best time to offer Austin the job at the firm then right?"

"Yes, if you would please. I'll tell them to go and have supper with you and Lance tonight. I'll watch Little Bentley for them. I hope you can get him to move down here. I don't want to disappoint them. Before they come over tonight though, Eric and I will talk to them. We're going to tell them our plans of moving here to help Ash also. You would be a great deal of help if you could do this." She hugs Quinn, looks down the hallway and sees that Bailey and Austin are still in the family room talking with her Parents on the phone.

Quinn says, "Okay, sounds like a plan to me. I just need to tell Lance about it. He's good at talking people into doing something that they know they don't want to do, but yet would love the chance to do it." She walks into the bathroom and Emily walks into the living room. She waves her hand toward Eric to get his attention and smiles at him. She starts walking up the steps to the other guest bedroom and waits on him to join her.

Eric notices that his Wife wants his attention and he excuses himself. He follows her up the steps to the other guest bedroom and walks into the same room as she does.

Quinn walks out of the bathroom and looks for Lance as quickly as she can. She finally finds him and gets him to follow her out to the front porch. They sit out there and she explains everything that is going on at the firm and everything that is going on with Bailey's Parents, and explains why she's wanting them to stay in Lexington for the firm.

Dianna, Darrin, Christine and Mike all go home. Ash and Dev are in the kitchen putting things away when they are interrupted by Emily and Eric. Ash turns around to see their faces and knows something is a miss. She asks, "What's wrong?"

Emily sits down looking down at her thumbs twitching with each other. She looks up at Eric and sees that he's about to answer. Eric answers, "Well, sweetie. Your Mother and I would love to move down here and help you and Dev out with the baby but, as you know Austin and Bailey would be up in Wilmington with Little Bentley. They won't have a babysitter at all when Bailey goes back to work with Austin. Your Mother kind of told them that when Barbara and Bentley couldn't watch Little Bentley that she would. This now creates a problem for your Mother and I, because we have already sold the house and the hotel together as a bundle package. We just found a house down here the other day, before we bought this for you two. Austin and Bailey aren't going to have anyone to watch Little Bentley for them when they go back to Wilmington."

Ash and Dev look at each other. Then Dev says, "Why don't Austin, Bailey and Bentley move here? I'm sure there are plenty of jobs out there for Austin to get. He's a pretty good lawyer. Bailey could stay at home with Bentley and they would have a good life. If Bailey does decide to go to work, then Ash will be here to watch Little Bentley, besides Emily."

Eric and Emily both look at him and smile. Emily gets up and explains this next part to Ash and Dev. "Now, I know that Mrs. Anderson is going to invite Austin and Bailey out for supper tonight. She's going to give them the chance of a lifetime. Well, not them. Austin is going to be offered a job at the law firm where Quinn works. She's going to give him a month and a half, then if everything goes the way she thinks it should go with him being employed where she works. She just might offer him the chance to be a partner in her firm. In order for her to do this and for Austin to take the job he has to say yes to her offer. Then they will move here after they have sold their house and the office space back in Wilmington." Emily ran out of breath and just sat down.

Ash and Dev both look at each other smiling. "That's good news. That's what Austin has always wanted." She gets up and walks over to her Mother and says. "I'm so excited for him and for you all. I'm glad that I'm going to have my Parents near. That way Dev and I can still have a date night after the baby is born." She hugs her Parents and walks off to find Austin and Bailey.

Bailey and Austin finally get off the phone with her Parents all bummed and depressed. They look up and see Mr. and Mrs. Anderson. They walk in smiling at Bentley and sit down. Mom gets up and says to Austin and Bailey both, while Daddy is down on the floor playing with Bentley. "Now, I know this may sound weird. As you know, I'm a partner in a law firm that was owned by Chris' Parents. I was made partner right before he proposed to Bree. Anyway, I was wanting to offer you something that will keep you very busy and maybe in a month and a half, we would all be proud to call you a partner in the same law firm. You will have to accept it tonight or it won't be there. We'll wait for you to sell your office and house up in Wilmington, and we'll wait for you to move down here. This way you'll be able to be near Ash and Dev. If you accept our invitation to a dinner tonight at Cheddars with some of my bosses then we would love to have you. Now, I have already gone and found a babysitter for you two to come out with us. Lance and I will pick you both up here at seven thirty and take you with us. What do you say?" Mom sits down and smiles at the both of them.

Austin stands up and answers. "I'd say it sounds interesting, but I don't know we would have to talk a little more about it between Bailey and I. Could you at least let us have until supper time to think about it?"

Mom shakes her head up and down smiling and says. "Yes! I will at least let you two have that long. We do need to know because they are looking at someone from Florida to fill the spot. We'll need to know by the end of supper tonight at the restaurant." Mom looks down at her hands and sighs. "You do know that this is a chance of a lifetime for your career. It'll pay more than you are used to making up in Wilmington. You've been here for a couple of days, so you know what the city has to offer. I hope you will think about it and let me know. I want you to be a part of the partnership at the firm." She walks out of the room and Mr. Anderson stands up.

He looks at them both smiles and says. "If I may?"

Austin and Bailey shake their heads up and down smiling.

"Okay, thank you. You do know that she makes more than what a Doctor up in Wilmington makes right?"

"Yea, that's pretty good money right there. I wish I had an answer right now. Where would we find a house in a few short weeks, turn around and sell ours and sell the practice up there?"

"I don't know but I do know of a great realtor. They sold me my house when I was dating Bree's biological Mother. She helped your Mother and Father find this house for Dev and Ash." He hands them the card and smiles at them both again. He walks out into the hallway and smiles. He whispers to his Wife and says. "It's in the bag." They both high five each other and walk back into the living room where Dev, Ash, Emily, Eric, Camerin and JoyAnna are smiling. Quinn looks over at Eric and Emily and shakes her head up and down. She says, "Well, Lance and I have to be going now. We have a meeting to get to tonight at eight at Cheddars. We'll see you all later." They both turn and walk out the door.

Emily and Eric smile at each other and get up. They both walk down the hallway that leads to the unfurnished family room for right now. They enter and Eric lays down on the floor by Bentley. Emily stands up and says smiling. "Austin, Bailey, your Father and I have something to tell you two." She sits down by the baby and Eric grunts to get up.

He finally makes it up and says smiling. "Now, you probably already know that we have sold the hotel and the house in Wilmington. We have been on the phone with a realtor up there and she said that she could have our things packed up and sent down if we wanted them to be. She could send our vehicles down by truck, but it's expensive. Anyway, the day we bought this house here for Ash and Dev, we also found a three bedroom house too. It's just down the street from here. It's not as big as our old house, but whatever furniture we don't need, we'll either give to you all or to your Sister and Dev. Now, I know that Emily promised you all that she would watch little Bentley if Bai's Parents couldn't watch him on certain days. I just want you two to know that this wasn't her doing. It was all me. I know what Mrs. Anderson has offered Austin tonight. I encourage you two to think it through as much as possible before going to Cheddars with them. This would be a chance of a lifetime for your career. We can have the same realtor to sell your house and the office that you two own. She can get it sold quickly and get the most money out of it as possible. We will help you with whatever you all need help with. We love you both and we wouldn't do this if we thought that we were abandoning anyone." He sits back down and waits on Bailey and Austin's response to his speech.

Austin gets up off the floor and says. "Dad, Mom. Bailey and I know that you two didn't do this on purpose. Whatever we choose to do, we know that you two still love us. Barbara and Bentley love us still, too. We'll manage if we decide to go home, if we don't we'll need all the help we can get." He walks over to them, hugs them smiling and says. "Besides, we can't let all three of our babysitters run off out of town." He gets up and walks back over by Bailey and sits down. He looks at his watch and sees that it's almost six thirty. He looks at his Wife of three years and the Mother of his Son and says. "We need to go ahead and get ready." He gets up and helps Bailey up.

Once Bailey is up she looks down at Emily and Eric and smiles. "Would you two mind watching the baby so that we can do this tonight?"

Emily and Eric both look up at her and smile. Emily stands up and walks over to her to give her a hug. "No, we wouldn't mind it at all. Besides, I already told Quinn that we would watch little Bentley anyways." She hugs Austin and says. "Go on now. You two don't want to be late." She sits back down on the floor by Eric and continues to play with Bentley until he gets ready for his bottle.

In the living room Ash, Dev, Camerin and JoyAnna are just sitting around talking and having a good time. They all see Bai and Austin heading upstairs where their bags are and giggling with each other. Camerin turns to Ash and asks her. "Where has Bree been all day? I'm surprised we haven't seen her here tonight."

"She won't be here until three more days. Her and Chris are taking his Grandparents home to Flemingsburg, then they're going camping at Cave Run Lake for two days. They needed to get away by themselves." Dev looks down and says. "Yea, by themselves, no I think Chris was going to have some friends meet him and Bree at the lake. Maybe we should have gone." He looks over at Ash and smiles at her. "I'm glad that we didn't in a way, but that's my little Sister and I don't like the idea of her being with I don't know how many guys, in the wilderness. I mean I know Chris will keep her safe, but it's just the fact that she's my baby Sister."

Ash and Camerin look at him and start laughing. Ash says, "That is the most ridiculous thing I have ever heard of." She gets to thinking and she says. "Hey, I have an idea."

"What is it?" Dev asks her.

"Why don't we all go up to Cave Run Lake tomorrow?" She turns to look at Camerin smiling. "It would be a great way to celebrate Brothers and Sisters being reunited, plus you'll have all the accommodations that every child of every age will enjoy. We don't have to camp out, just go up there and spend the day and drive back."

Dev starts thinking and says smiling. "Yea, why not? We'll do this." He looks at Camerin smiling and asks. "Camerin, do you think Miquel would be in for the trip, and everyone else if I call them and invite them? It's Wednesday anyway, most of them would already be traveling down for the one that is set next week. Why don't we call all of them and get them to get together at Cave Run Lake?"

Camerin starts thinking about it, smiling and she says. "I don't have to work at all this weekend. It would be a great thing to do this weekend with and for the kids. We could include all of the others to come too. I think Miquel could get some time off of working at Bree's Grandmother's house. I'll call Quinn and have her tell Lena that. I don't think Lena likes my Mother in-law and Husband very well, but oh well that's beside the point. She'll have everyone else there to work and I think it might do us all some good to get away from Lexington for a couple of days." She digs her cell phone out and calls Darion, Daimon, Dalton, Chelsea, Callie and Cara. "All of them agree but Darion, he says his Wife is still sick. I think he'll come around because he sounded so excited about it. Besides, I think I heard her walk in and say something to him in a cheerful voice." Her phone starts ringing and she looks at it, smiles and says. "It's Darion!"

She gets up and opens her phone asking. "Hello?"

"Yea, Camerin? This is Michelle. We would love to come to Cave Run Lake tomorrow. We'll be flying in on a red eye flight. We should be there around midnight tonight. Is there a place that we could stay tonight? Oh, by the way, Cara is coming too. She's going to be on the same flight as us. I'm very excited to meet you all and Darion will get over it. He thinks that I'm so sick all the time, but I have news for him. He thinks it's cancer, but it's not. We're going to have another baby. I don't know why he thought it was cancer. He's been through five of them so far."

"Oh, okay. Thanks Michelle. We'll see you later tonight then. You all can stay at my place if Dev will take Cara and her family in. Talk to him and tell him that it's not our fault our Birth Mother was the way she was with us. I can understand why he thinks it too, but we want to meet him and see him. He's the missing puzzle piece." She hangs the phone up smiling and says. "Well, JoyAnna, let's go get our bags packed. I'm going to have to rent a van or a bus to help with the trip to Cave Run Lake tomorrow. This is going to be fun." JoyAnna and her Mother get up and go out the front door. Dev follows right behind texting me. "Hey lil (little) sis were (we are) coming up and we have a surprise for u (you) well (we will) meet u (you) 2 (two) at cave run lake tom (tomorrow) around 5 (five) hope u (you) r (are) havin (having) fun but not 2 (too) much love ya (you)." Dev hits send, smiling.

Chapter
TWENTY TWO

....

Chris and I finally pull into the parking lot of the nursing home that Max is staying in. We both get out and stretch our legs before Maggie wakes up and sees that we're back in good old Flemingsburg. Chris walks to the back of the truck while waiting on a nurse's aid to walk out to get his Grandfather out of the truck. I walk back to where Chris is getting the bags out of the back of the truck and ask him, kissing his cheek. "Do you need any help?"

He looks over at me smiling and returns my kiss. He answers my question. "Sure, if you want to help." He notices that there is a nurse's aide walking out of the building to get a smoke break. He runs towards him and hands him a twenty dollar bill. He says something to him and turns back towards the truck. He opens the door for his Grandfather and helps the aid put him in the wheelchair. He walks back to me and says. "Follow that aid and my Grandmother. I'll be in in a minute."

I follow the aide and Grandma Maggie into the building. We finally walk into Grandpa Max's room and the aides help each other get him into his bed. One of the aides looks at Grandma Maggie and says. "He's still sleeping from that car ride, huh?"

She glances over at them and says. "Yea, Brent he sure is." She slips him a five dollar bill and he leaves the room.

I look at her and smile just sitting there waiting for Chris to walk in. She sits down right next to me. We both sit there until Chris shows up in the room with his Grandfather's bags. He starts putting them away, looks at us both and smiles. He asks his Grandmother. "So, Mammie. Do you want to stay for a little while or do you want to go on to your house?"

She looks at him and says. "I think we'll stay until he at least wakes up."

Chris says smiling. "Okay, it shouldn't be too much longer." He walks over by me and sits down. He reaches for the remote and turns the television on. He finds a show and starts watching it. He laughs at a couple of funny scenes and looks over at his Grandmother. She's falling asleep sitting up in the chair. He pokes my shoulder and whispers. "Look!"

I look over and see that she's fallen asleep. I smile and shake my head up and down. I say, "I know how she feels. That was a long trip. I'm ready for bed even."

He looks at me and whispers back. "Try driving it every time you want to see your Grandparents. Besides, Grandpa should be waking up at any moment now." He looks over at him smiling and points at him. "See, what did I tell you?"

I look over at Grandpa Max and see that he's waking up. I glance at Chris and whisper. "You know him real well don't you?"

"Yea, pretty much." He gets up, walks over to the bed. "How was your nap Pappie?"

"It was good, but man do I have a sore neck." He answers rubbing his neck glancing over at his Wife. "Thank goodness we all got here in one piece." He looks back at Chris and says smiling. "Thank you buddy. Thanks for making sure that we got back safely. What do I owe you for driving us back?"

"Nothin Pappie." Chris pauses for a few seconds and says. "I think I hear Aunt Gretta coming." Chris knew she was right in the hallway when she popped her head in and smiled.

"How was your trip Dad?"

"It was fine. Your Mother and I slept the whole way here. When did you all get home?"

"Dad, we got home last night. We didn't want to stay till this morning so we left last night at seven thirty."

"Oh, okay. Where is your other Sister?"

"She had to take her three oldest ones to work and get groceries."

"Oh, okay. I don't really feel up to company today honey. I think Chris, Breea, and your Mother are getting ready to leave. That is if she ever wakes up from her nap." He chuckles a little and falls back to sleep. One of the registered nurses walks in and checks his vitals and gives him a shot of some kind of medication. She looks at all of us and smiles. She walks back to the nurses station.

Chris walks over to his Grandmother shaking her and says. "Okay, Mammie. It's time to get up. We have to go now."

She wakes up and asks. "Has he already woken up and fallen back to sleep again?"

Chris answers her. "Yea, the registered nurse just came in and gave him a shot of his medication. I'm sure he's worn out from the ride. Let's get you home too, because clearly you are totally worn out from it too." He helps her up and we start walking back out to the truck.

We finally get to Maggie's house and get our stuff. Chris and I walk into the guest bedroom and he shuts the door leaving his Grandmother in her room to rest. He walks up to me and starts kissing all over my neck. He whispers with his goatee right next to my neck tickling it. "I want you so badly!" He keeps on kissing my neck and lays me down on the bed. I kiss him back anxiously and we end up taking all of our clothes off this time. He smiles at me and asks. "Are you sure you want to do this?"

I look down at our naked bodies and think for a moment. "I don't know. You feel so good kissing me and it feels right. Let's just see where it leads us." We go on making out and pleasing each other by doing things to each other that neither one of us thought would be pleasing.

We kept at it and the next thing we heard was a rooster crowing in the distance.

We wake up and smile at each other. We notice that we may have taken things a bit too far. We both jumped out of bed and got dressed as quickly as we possibly could. He looks over at me and asks. "Are you okay? I don't want to scare you off over us going a little too far last night."

"Yea, I'm okay. You okay?"

"Yea, I'm great." He gets up, walks around the bed and asks me, smiling. "Are you sure everything is okay between us?"

I get up and meet him. "Yes, I'm sure. I love you Christopher Michael Lee." I kiss him feverishly on the lips, whispering. "I can't wait until we can do that again." I walk into the bathroom and notice a little blood. I count the days and think. It can't be that time of the month already. The season hasn't changed, I wonder why I'm bleeding. Then I hear a knock at the door. "Yea?"

"Everything okay there?"

"Yea, everything is fine. I'll be out in a moment." I get my phone out and see that I have a message from Dev. I open it, read it and reply back. "Ok cant (can't) wait 2 (to) c (see) u (you) 2 (two) there," I text my Mom. "hey mom wat (what) r (are) u (you) doin (doing) jus (just) got up and were (we are) at chris' grandma house i need to knw (know) sumtin (something)," I go on with my business and stay in the bathroom until my phone vibrates. I get it out of my pocket and read it. "Hey sweetie whats (what is) goin (going) on," I text her back. "Its prob (probably) nutin (nothing) but i need to knw (know) dat (that) when u (you) lost ur (your) virginity did u (you) bleed the mornin (morning) after," I wait until I get another text from her and feel my phone vibrate in my hands again. I open it up and read. "Yea i did y (why) did u (you) n (and) chris finally do sumtin (something) if so its ok u (you) should bleed only for 30 mins (minutes) or less u (you) have a tampon wit (with) u (you)," I reply "yea i do thanks mom for not freakin (freaking) out and tellin (telling) me da (the) truth love ya ill (i will) txt (text) u (you) when we get to cave run lake," I get up off the commode and walk into the room to get my purse. I find it sitting on the end of the bed on top of a note that Chris left along with a tampon.

It reads:

Baby,

I hope you don't hate me. Last night was amazing. The most amazing night of my life. Don't hate me for it. It was very pleasing to know that you want me that way. We did go all the way. I asked you if you were sure and you said that let's just see where it leads us. I promise you that I wouldn't take advantage of you. If you don't believe me, then we'll go back home. I promise, baby. I don't want you mad at me. I love you from the bottom of my heart and soul. Please if you feel uncomfortable just talk to me.

Love You Muches,

Chris

I finally get done reading the note and walk back into the bathroom. I pull my pants down and see that I have stopped bleeding finally. I pull my pants back up and walk out of the bathroom and put my tampon back in my purse. Then I walk out into the hallway and see him standing there. He walks up to me with a frown on his face and asks. "Are you mad?"

"No, I'm not mad. I love you too Chris. I need you to know that I remember saying that last night to you." I point toward my purse and ask. "How did you know?"

"I told you that I am not a virgin. I hope it didn't scare you too badly." He grabs a hold of me and holds me in a hug.

I answered him, hugging him back. "It did a little bit, but I got through it. I texted my Mother about it."

He lets go of me and pushes back to read my face. "So, your Mother knows?"

Just then his Grandmother walks towards us and says, "Her Mother knows what? Come on you two, I have breakfast done."

Chris looks at his Grandmother smiling and says. "Nothing Mammie. She doesn't know anything." He looks back at me and smiles. "Oh, well. It's not like we're not getting married right? She should have expected it. I'd say your Parents did that before their wedding."

Just then his Grandmother pokes her head out into the hallway again and smiles. "Yea, I know too! It wasn't like you two were quiet last night." She looks at us smiling and says. "Come on, breakfast is getting cold." She disappears behind the wall again and we hear her pouring something into a cup. We both walk down the hallway holding hands into the kitchen. "Yea, honey. You can tell just by the way you look. You just have a different glow that isn't the regular glow you know. It's okay though. How do you know if he is good in bed if you follow everything by the book. Who says sex before marriage is a sin. It should be a beautiful thing between two people who love one another, and you two obviously love one another." She turns to look at us smiling and continues. "I didn't know what to expect from your Grandfather when we met. Boy, was I ever surprised by the way he liked things. I'm not going into detail, but man he was a wild one. Everyone takes someone's virginity sometime in their life, why not when you're young." She puts butter and syrup on her pancake. Then she continues. "If I hadn't gotten my wild years over before I met your Grandfather Chris, you probably wouldn't be here right now. See, back then when a girl got pregnant, she had to marry the guy that got her that way. I got pregnant with your Mother at the age of fourteen by your Grandfather. So excuse me when I say that sex isn't a sin. It's just a way that some people find their one true mate in life. How do you think your Grandfather and I have lasted all these years with one another, when all of our friends were divorced by their ninth year anniversary?"

Chris and I look at each other and smile. Chris says, "Okay, Mammie. We got the picture." He puts butter and syrup on his pancake, pours a glass of milk and takes my plate from me smiling. He gives me his plate and glass of milk. He does the same for his plate and looks over at me and winks, smiling that crooked grin.

I look at him and shake my head up and down. Agreeing with him that we should do something again tonight at the campsite. Then my cell phone vibrates. I take it out and it reads. "Hey breea its will jw (just wondering) if ure (you are) interested in goin (going) out 2nite (tonight) wit (with) me 2 (to) a movie," I look up at Chris and smile. I take a picture of my engagement ring and then send it to Will. I text these words underneath the picture. "No sorry u (you) had ur (your) chance when we were in high school im (I'm) gettin (getting) married," I hit send and smiled again. I playfully kick Chris' leg and smile at him. He returns the kick playfully back and sticks his tongue out at me. We finished eating our breakfast.

We get up and get our things packed and ready to head to Cave Run Lake. While listening to Mammie talk on the phone to one of his Aunt's. Mammie tells her to calm down and then looks out the window to see a vehicle approaching. "She's here, just calm down and I'll talk to her." She hangs the phone up and says. "I can't believe this mess. Chris you may want to stick around for a little while longer." She opens the door and meets Maddi in a hug. "It's going to be okay." They both walk in together and sit down at the table. Chris continues packing the rest of the things that we need for camping. Mammie looks at Maddi and asks. "What's really going on Maddi? When your Brother Mickey does something stupid like this, there is always something else that is bothering you and it's been bothering you for a while now. So, tell me what it is, child!"

Maddi looks at her and me and explains everything that is going on in her life. It isn't the thing with her Brother that has her so upset. It's her abusive boyfriend. The way he doesn't like her hanging with any of her friends or family. He thinks that she should be with him all the time, day or night. She keeps going into detail knowing that Chris is listening in on the conversation. Finally she tells the actual problem with her boyfriend and Chris goes off the handle. "I'm going to kill that low life scumbag piece of dirt."

Walking towards his truck, I catch up to him along with Mammie and Maddi. I yell, "Christopher Michael Lee, if you keep walking towards that truck I'm going home!"

He stops and turns around, looking at me like he's lost his life. "No, please don't do that." He walks towards me and pulls me in for a hug. "I'm sorry, I just can't stand guys like that. It makes me mad knowing that they're out there." He kisses the top of my head and looks towards his Grandmother and cousin Maddi. He asks, "Maddi, would you like to break it off with that piece of scumbag?"

Maddi looks at him with a puppy dog face and shakes her head up and down. Starts walking towards the truck and tells Mammie, "Tell Mom and Dad that I'm fine and I'll talk to them later about this, please."

Mammie stands there shaking her head up and down. Watching us all climb into Chris' truck. She watches us as we drive down the lane to the main road. She walks back into her house and calls her daughter to explain what was going on.

Chris, Maddi and I all get to her boyfriend's house and she lets him know that there is no way in hell that they are going to stay together anymore. She was tired of him treating her like she was a little child and she already gets enough of that from her Brother Mickey and her Parents. She was tired of him hitting on her and having to make up excuses for the asshole of a boyfriend that she's dating. He tried to knock her around a little bit but when he saw Chris hopping out of the truck he stopped and let her go. She hops back in the truck and puts her seatbelt on. She looks in the back of the truck and sees the camping gear and asks. "Are you two going camping?"

Chris looks at her and says. "Yes, we are. We're going to meet up with some of my friends from Morehead. We're going to hike, swim and meet Bree's Brother Dev and his Fiance' Ash tomorrow."

"Oh, sounds like fun!" She sits there with her arms crossed in front of her.

I look at Chris smiling. Ask him, whispering in his ear. "Could she go with us?"

He looks at me smiling and asks. "Maddi, would you like to go camping with us?"

"Yea, I sure would. I don't know if Mom and Dad will let me though." She sits back when we pull into her driveway. She looks at Chris and smiles real big. She asks, "Could you please ask them for me?"

Chris answers smiling back. "I will as soon as Madeline and her Parents leave." We all go back in and sit at the dining room table with Mammie, MaLeah and Micah. We were sitting there when we heard the front door shut and Molly and Matt walked into the kitchen sighing, rubbing their hair out of their faces.

Matt steps up and says. "Well, Madeline is definitely pregnant. Mickey is going to be giving her some money and things for the baby. He's going to help out the best way he can for now. She's allowed to come back over and see us all, but Mickey has to be gone in order for that to happen." He walks over to the fridge and gets a cold beer out. He looks at Chris and asks. "Would you like one?"

Chris shakes his head and says. "No, thanks Uncle Matt." He leans over the table and asks. "You and Aunt Molly wouldn't care for Maddi to go camping with us at Cave Run would you? We're going to be gone for two days."

Matt looks at his Wife and she shrugs her shoulders letting him know that it was up to him. Matt answers, "Yea, sure. Go ahead pumpkin." He kisses her on her forehead and walks over to Chris. "She has a boyfriend named Justin. Don't let him go up there with you all. I don't like him. He's mean and rude to her. I don't know why she puts up with him." He pulls a chair out and sighs.

"I don't think you have to worry about Justin anymore." Chris says smiling at him.

"Oh, really. Why is that?"

"Because Maddi broke it off with him just a few minutes ago when Bree and I took her to his house. She stayed outside the whole time around Bree and I. I had to get out of the truck for a few minutes too. He slammed her against it, so she's probably got a bruise on her back. I straighten him out though."

Matt looks over at Chris and I and smiles. "Thank you for straightening the situation out. This situation with Mickey is about to drive us over the limit." He takes a drink of his beer and continues. "Yea, life sure is throwing us some curveballs right now, but we'll get through them one way or another." He gets up and walks into the living room and sits in his recliner. He ends up falling asleep.

Chris, Maddi and I are all settled in the truck now and are headed toward Cave Run. We finally get to the camp site and see that his friends are already there. They hoot at Chris, smile and wave. They notice that Maddi and I are with him. One of them walked over to us. He walks straight up to Maddi and smiles. "Hi, my name is Chad. How do you know Chris?"

Chris sees that he's trying to get too flirty with his little cousin and says. "Chad, she's only seventeen. Lay off, will you?" Laughing he walks over and hugs him. "How have you been?"

"Good!" Chad looks over to me and smiles. He asks, "Who is this gorgeous young lady?"

"This is my Fiance', Breea!"

He looks at Chris and just stares at him. "What? You're getting married?"

"Yea, dude I am!" Chris walks to the back of the truck and gets the rest of the things that we brought out of the bed. "You want to help me set this up, or are you going to sit there staring at my girl the whole time?"

Chad looks at him smiling and answers. "Yea, I'll help you set it up." He looks back at me and at Chris and asks. "Does she have any older Sisters that are available?"

"No, she doesn't. Now get to work." He walks over to where the other tents are set up and sees Jeremy, Josh, and Zach. He says to them. "Hey, how are you all doing?"

They all answer back with a beer in their hands smiling. "Good! We heard you are getting married. Congratulations man." They get up walking towards him and Chad. "Where is she?"

He turns around and points straight at me smiling. "She's right there. That's Breea." He cups his hands around his mouth to holler at me and Maddi. We both look up at him and smile. We start walking back up to the tents and finally stop just short of Chad wrestling with the bag of the tent. We laugh a little and sit down. Jeremy, Josh, Zach and Chris all walk over to us and sit down. Chris says, "Bree, Maddi. This is Jeremy, Josh and Zach." He puts his hand on my shoulder and says smiling. "This is Breea, my Fiance'." Then points over to Maddi and says smiling. "This is my cousin Maddi." He looks over to Chad wrestling with the poles to his tent and says laughing. "I better help that big lug before he hurts himself or someone else." He gets up and walks over to help him. Maddi and I both just sit there talking with Jeremy, Josh and Zach waiting for them to get done with the tent.

Chapter
TWENTY THREE

....

W e were all laid back in our suits and just chilling when we heard this commotion behind us. Chris and I raise up together and smile. We saw Dev, Ash, Camerin, Miquel, Jose, Jennifer, JoyAnna, Darion, Michelle, Brooklyn, Brittany, Brionna, Blake, Bryson, Chelsea, Justin, JoHannah, Jordan, Josie, Carson, Callie, Blithe, Derrik, Bethany, Deidrich, Daimon, Zara, Zaiden, Zyla, Zyra, Zarrod, Zander, Cara, Scott, Kyle, Kylie, Dalton, Paige and Ian walking towards us. I get up and smile at Dev, Ash, Camerin and Miquel. I walk towards them with Chris holding my hand all the way. We finally all meet in the middle and I let go of Chris' hand looking at him and say. "Sorry, I need this time to myself. I want you to go spend some time with Jeremy, Chad, Josh and Zach. That's what you came up here for."

He looks down at me and squeezes my hand. He bends down and kisses my forehead and jogs over to his four friends. I continue on up the beach part and give Ash a hug. I ask her, "How are you doing? Did you all have a good drive?"

They all shake their heads at me smiling and Dev answers. "Yea, we sure did. We found the place easy enough." He looks back at Chris,

Josh, Jeremy, Chad and Zach. He waves at them smiling and says. "Okay Bree, this is all our Brothers and Sisters." He points to each one as he introduces me to them. "This is our Sister Camerin. Her Husband Miquel. Their children, Jose, Jennifer and JoyAnna. Of course you would know them from your Grandmother. Anyway, this is our Brother Darion. His Wife Michelle." He pauses another moment and looks down at me to see my reaction to her pregnant belly. Then he continues. "Their kids, Brooklyn, Brittany, Brionna, Blake and Bryson. This is our Sister Chelsea. Her Husband Justin. Their children, Blithe, Derrik, Bethany and Deidrich." He pauses for a moment to catch his breath and continues smiling. "This other tall guy here is our Brother Daimon. His Wife Zara. Their children Kyle and Kylie." He stops and looks for Dalton and smiles when he sees him. He grabs my hand and pulls me towards him. "This big short guy is our little Brother Dalton. His Girlfriend Paige and his Son Ian."

We all hug each other and smile. Saying how good it was to finally meet each other. The women walk into the tent area to change into their suits while the men stay out of the tent. All the boys go into the next tent to change. We all finally get changed and walk down to the beach. My nephews and nieces who are actually the same age as I am or above the age of thirteen, are all out in the water. That includes Brooklyn, Brittany, Brionna, Jose, Blithe, Derrik, Bethany, Diedrich, Kyle, Kylie, Zaiden and Zyla. The rest are in the water where we can run to snatch them up if we need to. Dev, Darion, Justin, Miquel, Carson, Daimon, Scott and Dalton are all out in the water. My Sisters, Sister in-laws and I all are sitting around just watching everyone else talking and holding Zander and Ian. We were passing them around when we heard another commotion over by the deep end.

We all stand up real quick and see that it's Brooklyn that is having trouble. Michelle starts running toward the area and before she gets there Chad jumps in and saves Brooklyn. He carries her up to where we all were standing concerned and says. "She said she was having a cramp and couldn't get her leg to move." He sits her down on a towel and bends over her. We all look at each other and just then Chris, Josh, Jeremy and Zach all run up.

Chris asks, "What's going on?"

I look at him answering, concerned. "Thank goodness for Chad here. He saved Brooklyn from drowning with a cramp in her leg."

He looks down at Brooklyn concerned and asks me. "Is this one of your Sisters or Brothers Daughters?"

"Yea, she's Darion and Michelle's Daughter." I watch what all Chad and Chris do and see that she's feeling better. We all relax and smile at them. I look down at Chad and Chris and say. "Thank you for helping her."

Chris stands back up and smiles at me. "No problem. She's soon going to be my niece too, right?" He bends down and kisses me. Chad, Jeremy, Josh and Zach all start clapping along with my Brothers, Brother in-laws, Sisters, Sister in-laws, nieces and nephews. We finally come up to get air and see that Brooklyn is awe struck by Chad. She just keeps staring and smiling at him.

Brooklyn finally walks over to us and smiles. "Thank you Uncle Chris." She sits down beside us and asks, smiling. "Uncle Chris, who are your friends?"

He looks over at them sitting there enjoying a bottle of water and says laughing. "This is Josh." He says pointing each one out to everyone. "This is Jeremy, Zach and Chad." He sees that everyone is thanking Chad for helping Brooklyn and smiles at them.

I look over at Brooklyn and can't believe how awe struck she is over Chad. She catches me watching her watch Chad. She scoots over and asks. "How old is Chad?"

I look over at him and smile. "Brooklyn, honey. I have no clue. I just met them today too. I can find out for you if you want me to." I look back to Darion and see that he's watching his Daughter, shaking his head from side to side. I turn around real quick and giggle.

Brooklyn looks back at me and asks. "What is so funny Aunt Breea?"

"Nothing, I think that you need to have your Father talk to him first. I don't think he likes the idea of you being near any guys."

She looks back and sighs. "Yea, that's my Father. He's pretty overprotective of us. Besides it's not like it would work out between Chad and I anyways. I'm going to college this fall. I need to keep myself busy with school." She gets up and walks back towards her Parents and sits there looking all down and depressed.

I get up and walk up to where she went to and ask Darion. "Darion, could I please talk to you for a moment?"

He looks up at me, smiles and answers. "Yes, you may." He gets up and follows me. "What's up?"

"I'm not trying to butt in where it concerns your kids, but I think Brooklyn is lonely. Have you let her date any boys up in New York?"

"Yea, Michelle and I have." He looks back at his oldest Daughter sitting by his Wife and he smiles. "She just hasn't had any luck with any of the boys that she's gone out with. Why are you asking that?"

"Well, she said that you wouldn't let her date that much. I was just wondering. I don't want to cause any trouble with you or your children. I'm just concerned because of the way she's acting. That's all."

"Okay, I'll talk with her and tell her that if she wants to date that Chad guy that he has to show me that he is more concerned about her and her feelings."

I look up and see Chris walking towards where we are talking and smile. "Well, I guess now is your chance to find out from Chris what kind of guy Chad really is." I point behind him, smiling I say. "Hey, babe!" I give him a kiss on the cheek and walk back towards everyone else. We were getting ready to eat and I sat down on my towel and noticed that Blithe was talking to Jeremy, and that Maddi was talking with Zach. I look over towards Josh and see that he was talking with Kylie. I grab my head and sigh. I look around myself to see if anyone is watching me and I notice that Dalton is walking towards me smiling. His Girlfriend isn't far behind him with Ian in her arms. He's carrying two plates in his arms with the diaper bag on his shoulders. I stand up and ask. "May I hold Ian?"

"Yea, you sure can." He sits the plates down and walks over to Paige and picks Ian up. He lays him in my arms and smiles. He pulls out a camera and takes a picture of Ian and I together. He says, "That's a picture that's in the photo album." He smiles real big and says. "I'm sure glad that all our Brothers and Sisters are back together again. Maybe it'll get Darion to come around more often." He sits down beside Paige and holds her hand while they eat.

I just hold onto Ian for as long as I can before someone else comes along and snatches him up out of my arms. I peek behind me and see that Chris is watching every move I make. I hear that Ian is getting fussy. I look over to Dalton and ask. "Is his feeding time getting close?"

"Yea, it sure is." He reaches into the diaper bag and pulls out a can of formula. He grabs a bottle of water, and a baby bottle out. He mixes the formula with water inside the baby bottle. He gets up and runs towards the car. He warms the bottle up in a portable bottle warmer. After he gets it warm, he jogs back and sits down. He holds the bottle over to me smiling and asks. "Would you mind feeding him while Paid and I eat?"

"No, I wouldn't mind. As long as he doesn't act like he's going to choke while he's sucking." I grab the bottle from Dalton and rub it on Ian's lips. Ian smiles and takes it. He goes to town without choking. I look up at Dalton and say. "I knew you would be a good Daddy someday. I just didn't think that it would be this early."

Dalton looks over at me smiling and replies. "I know what you mean. I didn't plan on having a baby at this age. I wanted to live my life but things happen and life gets in the way sometimes." He pauses and looks at Paige. "At least I have a good Girlfriend that loves Ian as her own.

I look at Paige and ask. "So, who are your Parents?"

Paige looks at me and answers sadly. "I live in a Foster Home. I was given up for adoption." She looks down at her plate and pushes it away. She wipes her eyes a little bit. "Anyway, I wasn't as fortunate to have Adoptive Parents like you all do. I live with the McCallisters."

I think of the McCallisters and remember that is Chloe's last name. I look at her and ask. "Is Chloe McCallister your Foster Sister?"

"Yea, she is! She's the best!" She looks at Dalton, smiling. "That's how Dalton and I met. She was going to visit you one day and she came home. She said she saw a little boy about my age watching the two of you out of a window. She said that she thought of me and she figured out what his name was and remembered that I had a big crush on him." She picks at her finger nail and continues. "We met at a function that the school was having and Chloe was involved. She introduced Dalton and I and we hit it off, haven't been apart since."

"What do your Foster Parents think of you dating a young man with a baby at the age of fifteen?"

"They don't mind it too much. They said at least he's taking responsibility for his Son, besides they said that there were a lot worse things in the world besides a fifteen year old with a baby that I could get into." She was quiet for a while. Almost a half an hour too quiet. She finally continues. "Yea, they meant drugs on that. That's what my Biological Parents were into. They were big pill heads. My Father is in a prison upstate Indianna and my Mother is actually in another rehabilitation, of course it's court ordered." She looked at Dalton and said sadly. "I'm not so hungry anymore."

Dalton looks back at her and puts his plate down. He gets up and helps her up. He looks over at me smiling and asks. "Would you mind watching Ian for us? I need to take her for a walk and calm her down."

"Yea, sure. Sorry if I made her sad. I was just trying to make conversation with her. I didn't mean to make her upset."

"It's okay Sis. She's always been like this when it comes to talking about her Biological Parents." He grabs her hand and starts walking towards the trail that leads up into the woods. I look on the other side of me and see that Chris just sat down. I smile at him and ask. "Do you want to hold him?"

He looks over at me and smiles, shaking his head up and down. "Yea, sure!" I hand Ian to him after I burp him. Ian is laying in his arms and I see how it makes Chris look. I get up and get a plate of food for myself. I walk back and sit down next to them. I see that Ian is awake, smiling and cooing at Chris. Chris is talking in a hushed tone to him smiling and cooing back. I smile, sit down and as soon as I do, Chris looks over at me smiling that crooked smile that he does so well. "Hey, baby? I was wondering, with all these people here. Who all is staying with us tonight?"

I look back and answer. "I don't know who all is staying the night. Dev knows that you have extra tents and mattresses with you." I take a bite of a hot day and wait til I get it ate and continue. "I can ask if you want me to. That way you can send Chad or someone else to help with setting the tents up."

He looks over at and says. "Don't worry about it just yet. Wait til it gets a little more later in the day." He keeps playing with Ian.

We all finally get done eating and everyone is either out in the water or on the beach just soaking up the sun. I'm still watching Ian for Dalton and Paige while they're still out on their hike. We hear a girl scream coming from the wooded area of the Lake. We all looked up and tried to shade our eyes from the glare of the sun and couldn't see anything. We all just go about our business until we spot Dalton walking out backwards with his arms up calmly saying. "Please, don't hurt her."

All the guys stand up and watch. They start hollering at Dalton and Paige. They start jogging over that way. It was Chad, Josh, Jeremy, Zach, Darion, Justin, Miquel, Carson, Daimon, Dev, Scott and Chris. They started to move in on the perpetrator that has Dalton and Paige hostage. The rest of us all stand up with the kids behind us. Brooklyn has Ian in her arms, while Blithe has Zander in hers. The rest of the kids are all standing up behind us. Camerin is the only one of our Sisters and Brothers that know that Ash is being stalked by a guy named Mark. The rest of them don't know what's going on. Dalton finally brings the person that's holding him and Paige hostage, out to where Chris, Dev, Ash and I all see. Ash takes off at a run and starts screaming and crying. I take off after her and hear the others shouting at me to get back. I didn't care, I wanted her to be safe. I got my phone out and started texting my Father's phone. "Need help here call the Morehead police quarters please no1 (no one) has been hurt yet but daltons gf (girlfriend) is being held at gunpoint," I put my phone back in the top part of my bra and finally caught up to Ash. We turn around abruptly realizing that it was stupid that we ran towards the scene. Then all of the sudden we hear Mark screaming. "Ashley, come here!"

I said to her, "Don't go. Just keep walking as if your name isn't Ashley." I look back and he's letting go of Paige. He pushes her down and starts running towards us. We know that all the guys are waiting for him to do something stupid, and that they're also waiting for him to start running after us. Which he did and they all tackle him down. We didn't notice that his gang was already back with the others until we got up to them.

Camerin hollers, "Just keep walking, don't come over here. We're all fine. They just want Ashley, Dev, you and Chris. They won't hurt us." So Ash and I just keep walking towards the parking lot. We're trying to get the perpetrators to follow us so it leaves everyone else out of this insane ordeal. Dev and Chris are right behind the others. While the other guys have Mark pinned down.

Ash and I finally get out into the parking lot and sit there behind a parked vehicle. I look over at Ash and say. "Now don't cry, I have already texted my Father and told him to call the police. He hasn't texted back about anything yet, but when he does I'll let you know. Just sit still and be quiet." At that moment, my phone vibrates. I get it out and see that it's my Dad that replied back. I open the message and read it to Ash whispering. "Ok bbg (baby girl) police r (are) on da (the) way i explained 2 (to) dem (them) da (the) situ (situation) and they should be gettin (getting) there any min (minute)." I look over at Ash and smile. "Don't worry, it'll be okay. I promise, the police are on their way." We just sit tight and wait to hear something. I get up a little bit to see if I can see anyone coming towards us when I see Chris and Dev have the rest of Mark's gang down on the ground breathing hard. I sit back down and smile. "I think they got them down. Let's go see what's going on." We get up and walk up to Dev and Chris.

Dev sees us and runs towards us. He says smiling, "The police are on their way. Allen says that he heard the commotion and called them. He didn't know what was going on, but when he called them he said that someone had already contacted them from Lexington." He looks over at us and says. "Good thinking ahead Sis." I nod my head at him and smile. We wait for the police there and check to see how everyone else is. We see that Paige and Dalton are okay and are sitting with everyone else. Dalton was walking up towards us smiling with Paige beside him. Dev sees them and also asks. "What are you two doing up here?" We also see that everyone else was walking towards us with the guys holding onto Mark and his gang with their hands tied behind their backs with a rope from a boat.

Dalton looks back smiling and says. "I got the rope from a boat that saw everything happening. They tossed us the rope in the water and Jeremy swam out to get it." He pauses for a minute and looks over at Paige. "Yea, Paige wants to file charges on Mark. He said that he knew you, Devin, Ashley and Chris. So we figured we would bring them down where you all were and he just up and pulled a gun out and grabbed Paige before I could get to him. He held the gun to her head and made us walk back towards the beach." He looks over at her and says. "She's pretty shaken up by it. I told her that she could press charges on him for putting her through that. She had nothing to do with any of this and he had to grab her so that he could get to you all." Dalton looks at everyone else and asks. "How was Ian? I'm sorry about being gone so long. I didn't know what else to do. I was thinking of leading them to a different part of the beach, but he could hear all the noise in your all's direction and said that he would shoot Paige and everyone else if I didn't bring them to you all. What does he want with Ashley and Devin?"

I look at him and back at Ash. Ash answers, "I'm pregnant with his baby. He wants me back and I don't want to go back with him. He raped me to get me this way. He's got some sick fantasy about me being his Girlfriend."

Just then the police arrive. The one gets out of his cruiser and walks up to us. "What seems to be the trouble here?"

Chris walks up to him and answers. "Yes, we've had a run in with these guys before up in Wilmington Ohio. After the plane crash, they followed us everywhere because the girl he raped and thought to be his Girlfriend was hanging out with us. We didn't know him and knew what he had done until he confronted me outside the hotel we were staying at. We were up there looking for my Fiance's Father that was in the plane crash. We met the girl that he was after at the hotel restaurant. My Fiance's Brother is engaged to the girl that he raped and got pregnant. Him and his gang followed us around trying to get to Ashley the whole time in Wilmington and now they have found us up here camping out. We figured we were safe to do this because when we left Wilmington, they were in jail. We knew that they were released, but didn't think that they would find us here."

The police officer shakes his head while Chris tells him about what happened in Wilmington Ohio and walks back to his police cruiser and runs Chris' ID. He walks back and says. "I need to talk with everyone involved and see if anyone wants to press charges on him." He starts walking towards Ash and I. He asks Chris, "Which one is Ashley?" Chris points to her and smiles. The police officer says. "Ashley, hi. My name is Pat. I would like to ask you a few questions please."

Ash steps forward and answers. "Yes officer." She walks a little ways away from us and he gets her side of the story.

He gets everyone involved on their sides of the story, including the witnesses and pulls his radio towards his mouth. "I need another unit here to help transport the offenders please." We wait for them to arrive and he gets two of them cuffed. Mark and Curtis are put in together in Officer Pat's cruiser and the others get cuffed and put into Officer Cheree's cruiser. They both get our side of the story of what happened at the beach. Then Officer Cheree walks over to her cruiser and waits for Officer Pat, so that they can transport the offenders to hold them. Officer Pat says to us all. "You all can go back to what you were doing, but I would suggest this. If you plan on spending the night to camp out. I would keep the area well lit and keep an eye out. We may not be able to hold them on this charge. We should be able to, but just in case. It's always better to be safe than sorry." He starts walking backwards towards his cruiser, saying. "Make a circle with the tents and keep Ashley and Devin in the middle of the camp and keep them hidden out of sight. We'll be in contact with you all. Have a good night." He climbs in his cruiser and smiles at Mark and Curtis. "You two know that you all have four warrants out for your arrest. The state police are going to love this. It's at least ten years in the pin for not turning yourselves in. You two have been very bad lately. I saw that you were arrested because you went on a wild goose chase with the Wilmington PD, and Ohio State Patrol. They're going to have to call in the FBI to take you all back to Wilmington for the charges that were filed on you all up here." He starts driving towards the State Police headquarters.

After the police leave the others walk up to where we are and Darion asks. "Everyone okay for now?"

We all look at them smiling and shake our heads up and down. We walk back to the beach while all the guys go to the campsite. They were trying to decide where else to put the rest of the tents without having to take them down. They all just decided to camp out with us tonight. So Darion, Miquel, Carson, Dalton, Chris, Dev, Justin, Josh, Jeremy, Zach, Chad Scott and Daimon just set up the extra tents that Chris and I brought with us and blew the air mattresses up. They set up two tents inside the circle, one tent is for Ash, Dev, Chris and I. The other tent is for all the little kids and two adults. The guys finally get the tents and air mattresses all done and walk back to the beach. We all enjoy the rest of the evening swimming and just visiting each other. Chris finds me and pulls me into his arms. He sighs and just holds onto me for twenty minutes.

I break away from his body and look into his eyes and ask. "What's wrong baby?"

He looks down at me smiling and says. "Nothing, just glad everyone is okay. I can't wait for tonight. You'll have to be quiet though. We can't make that much noise now."

I look up at him with questioning eyes and ask. "What do you mean?"

"I mean that the tents are all set up in the same spots as before, just that there are two tents in the middle and we are sharing our tent with your Brother Dev and his Fiance' Ash."

I give him a look as if to show him that I understand him and run into the water, hoping that he follows me. I didn't know that I was swimming towards Chris' private island. He swims to it every time he's here so he can think about things. He follows me and comes up for air. He looks at me and asks. "I thought that you haven't been here before?"

I look at him and answer. "I haven't been here before, but I saw the island from the beach and wanted to swim out here to it. I think it's peaceful. You don't have anyone else here talking or interrupting you." He's closer to me now then ever and he pulls me to him for a kiss.

The kiss was passionate and he wanted more. He pulls himself up on the bank of the island and helps me up. We walk around where the grass is tall enough so if other's swam by they wouldn't know we were there. We lay down in the tall grass and just relax a little bit. We start kissing and fooling around until we hear someone splashing nearby. Chris looked up and saw that it was Dalton and Paige. They were just swimming by without even knowing that we were on the island right next to them. We keep kissing and fooling around with each other. Before you knew it we were butt naked, making love to one another. He comes up for air and asks, "See what you do to me Bree? I can't get enough of you!" He reaches down and rubs the tip of his cock on my thigh. I giggle a little and open my legs a little more to receive him. He thrusts his bulging stick in me and moans out. "Oh, God! You feel so good baby!" He continues thrusting inside me and we both rock together. In sync with each other and just enjoying the time together. We keep at it for two more hours.

"Oh, Chris! You feel so good and this feels so right! I love you!" I yell out.

He lays down on top of me because we both climax and cum together. Looking deep into my eyes, he says. "I love you too Bree!" He leaves a trail of kisses until I get done convulsing.

We notice how dark it's getting and start getting our clothes back on. We kiss each other passionately before getting back in the water. We swim to shore and catch up to the rest of the family walking up to the campsite.

Darion notices that we're back from our swim, picking our towels up. He jogs over to us and says. "Everyone is worn out. We need to get them to camp before they fall asleep." He looks out towards the lake and asks. "Where did you two swim to?"

I look at him and answer. "We were on the island out there. We were just talking." I looked over at Chris and watched him pull his t-shirt over his tight muscles.

He looked back at me, smiling. "Yea, we were just talking with one another trying to figure out how we're going to fit everyone in the tents tonight. Plus trying to figure out a date for our wedding."

Darion looked back at me and smiled. "Yea, just talking my ass! I was young once too you know. I'm not that stupid." He chuckles. "So, what do you think of getting to the campsite before it turns dark?"

Chris and I shake our heads up and down and walk with him back towards the others waiting on the trail. Holding each other's hands we walk back to the campsite with everyone behind us whispering. We smile the whole way back and notice that Brooklyn, Blithe, Kylie and Maddi are all already at camp with Chad, Jeremy, Josh and Zach. We all sit down around the fire roasting marshmallows for s'mores.

In Chris' four person tent it was Ash, Dev, Chris and I. In his other four person tent there was Cara, Scott, Darion and Michelle. In Josh's four person tent there was Chad, Josh, Jeremy and Zach. In Chris' ten person tent there were Dalton, Paige, Ian, Kyle, Kylie, Brooklyn, Brittany, Blithe, Derrik, Bethany, and Maddi. In Josh's fifteen person tent there were Camerin, Miquel, Callie, Carson, Brionna, Blake, Bryson, Josiah, Jose, Jennifer, JoyAnna, Deidrich, Zyla, Zyra and Zaiden. In Josh's ten person tent there were Chelsea, Justin, JoHannah, Jordan, Josie, Daimon, Zara, Zarrod and Zander.

We finally work it out with who's going to sleep in what tent with who. Chris' tents are surrounding the one tent that Dev, Ash, Chris and I are sleeping in. It's in the very middle of the campsite. We're all just talking and having a good time together.

Callie gets up and walks over to check on the children. She checks on the little kids first and notices that they are all sound asleep. She backs off quietly smiling and checks on the older kids. She notices that Brooklyn, Blithe, Maddi and Kylie are all still up chit chatting. They look at her smiling. Blithe says, "Aunt Callie, everyone else is asleep. We're getting ready to go to sleep soon."

Callie just shakes her head up and down at Blithe. She turns around and leaves the door unzipped a little bit. She comes back to the campfire and sits down saying. "All the kids are asleep but Brooklyn, Blithe, Maddi and Kylie." She looks back towards the tent where the girls were still awake. She notices that Blithe is looking at Chad smiling real big. She turns to Jeremy, Chad, Josh and Zach and asks. "So, what kind of guys are you? You didn't bring any girls with you all. Why is that?"

They all look at her smiling and Jeremy answers. "Well, when we were in college Chris, Chad, Josh and I all came up here without any girls and camped out. During the summers we would do this too. We would actually leave our Girlfriends out of the picture because of us wanting the time together without the girls." He scoffs a little at what he's saying then turns to look at Josh, Zach and Chad, saying. "Maybe that's why we aren't married yet or don't have any Girlfriends." He falls over laughing over what he just said.

Chris gets up and says. "Sorry, he's a little too drunk." He walks over to Jeremy and picks him up and puts him in the tent. He walks out smiling and says. "Sorry about that. He can't hold his liquor very well." He sits down next to me and grabs my legs and lifts them over his. We notice that Darion and Michelle get up. Chris looks over at them and asks. "Are you two turning in?"

"Yea, I think we are. We're pretty tired from the red-eye flight we took. Plus the trip from Lexington to here." Darion answers smiling and he turns around as soon as they get to their ten and says. "Goodnight."

Callie and Carson get up and walk to their tent. We notice that they turn out their light. The rest of us keep on visiting and talking in hushed tones. Camerin and Miquel head to their tent, zip the closure up and turn their light out. Next, Chelsea and Justin turn in. Daimon and Zara finally get up and notice that Ash is falling asleep. They both pass them, Chris and I, walking to their tent. "Goodnight guys, see you all in the morning. Oh, by the way. Ash is falling asleep sitting up. She needs her rest, so take her to the tent Dev."

Chad, Josh, Zach, Dev, Chris and I all turn around to see that Zara is right. Dev gets up and smiles. He walks over to the tent and unzips the door. He turns around and walks back over to pick Ash up and carries her to the tent. He lays her down on the air mattress and turns around to zip the door up, saying. "Goodnight guys." He turns the light out.

It's just Chad, Zach, Josh, Chris and I all up now. Chad is almost passed out and leaning over a log. He gets up and says, belching. "Goodnight!" He walks over in a staggering line and falls into the tent. He's followed by Zach and then Josh.

Chris looked over at me smiling that crooked smile and asked. "Do you want to take a walk?"

I look at him smiling and answer. "Sure!" We both get up and leave the fire going. We walk a few feet into the woods and Chris has to use the bathroom. He walks over behind a tree so that he's not spotted by anyone. He whistles over to me and motions for me to join him after he gets done using the bathroom.

I reach him and he asks. "Would you like to walk over there? Pointing toward a log that has fallen down."

Pointing toward the dark spot of the woods, where the fallen down log is, I agree. We start walking hand in hand speechless at how peaceful it is out here. Even with all the campers that are camping out. We run into the log, cross over it and sit down. I look over at him and side hug him. "It's so peaceful here. I wouldn't mind this too much. It's just enough to get away from the life in Lexington." I pull him a little closer and start kissing on his neck.

He sits back a little and whispers. "I wouldn't do that if I were you. I'm already ready to take your clothes off right here and make love to you."

I stop and look at him smiling. "Oh, really?" I think a little bit, then start kissing on his neck again.

"I told you. Now you're in trouble." He gets up and picks me up over his shoulder. Smacked my ass until I begged him to stop. He lays me gently down on the ground and climbs on top of me. "I told you, you'd get into trouble doing that." He saw the look on my face when he climbed on top of me and asked. "What's wrong?"

"Nothing, I can just feel you." I rub my hand down his muscled chest and abs and down to his manhood. Grabbing his enlarged cock I said. "I'd love to make love to you right here, right now, but I'm afraid I won't be quiet."

"Oh, well. We can try it if you want. It's your choice, I won't pressure you." He starts kissing my neck and I moan. Grinding against him, he raises his head and says. "Shhhhh. You'll wake up everyone and that would be embarrassing wouldn't it?"

I lay there thinking of how I can be quiet. I ask, "Does it bother you if I bite you to try to keep quiet?"

He stops kissing me and looks deep into my eyes, answered. "I don't think that's going to distract me, baby. I like it rough sometimes too." Chris continues to kiss my neck and down to my breasts. He lifts me up to where he can pull my shirt off and lays me back down. He takes his shirt off while he's still sitting up. I see those abs and all I can do is to sit up and kiss his tight chest and abs. He laid back down on top of me and said. "Oh, I wish you would answer me. I don't want to pressure you into doing this if you don't feel comfortable with it."

"Yes, Chris. I want to." He continues on down towards my cookie. He unbuttons my shorts and very quietly slips them off. He unbuttons his shorts and pulls his hard private out. He takes control. He kisses me where he left off and starts down towards my cookie. He lifts up and runs his tongue along my mid section back up to my face. He laid a little closer to me to help with the sounds, kissing my lips and letting me bite him to keep the moans and screams from waking all of the others up. He thrusts inside of me. This continues on for another three hours. He's got me going into a state that I'm so quiet and enjoying the pleasure he's giving to me. He opens his eyes and looks at my face. He reaches for the flash light and turns it on, pointing at my face. He looked at me and whispered. "Bree, I love you!"

I whisper back at him. "I love you too, Chris." While my fingernails are scratching his back and I'm biting his shoulder, pulling him closer to me. We rock back and forth together until we both have the best orgasm ever. It was like fireworks going off inside of me. I felt everything that he did to me. Every little tongue stroke inside my mouth and every little kiss on my neck just sent shivers up my spine and across my entire body. My toes curled, and I raised my midsection up toward him, letting him know that I was on the edge again. He thrusts harder and faster, letting me know that he's about to orgasm also. He lets it go finally and rolls over to the side of me. I roll over on him and kiss him softly on the lips. I asked, "Wow, babe! That was OMG, awesome!!"

We lay there for a few more minutes before looking for our clothes. He grabs the flash light and starts looking around. He grabs my bikini top and hands it over to me. I saw his t-shirt and handed it to him. He locates my bikini bottoms and shorts. Handed the flash light over to me so that I could get dressed. He turns around and gives me the privacy I need to get them both back on. While I'm doing this Chris hears something walking towards us. We both shine the light toward the noise and see that it's just Maddi. We get up as quickly as we can and Chris asks. "Maddi? What are you doing out here?"

"Oh, Chris. I know this might sound like I'm paranoid, but I heard a noise behind our tent. I got out as quickly as I could, and headed toward the fire. I knew your tent wasn't far from the fire. So, I opened it and shined the light on your side of the tent and didn't see you. I start freaking out and wake everyone up. There wasn't anything behind my tent, but Zarrod is missing. He wasn't in the tent when we looked inside it. We don't know where he is." Just then the rest of the family walks up behind Maddi. Chris and I just look at each other and sigh. We head back towards the others.

Zara and Daimon are both hollering for Zarrod when we walk up on them. Chris says, "Hey, calm down. I put a tracker on all the kids earlier. I told them that I wanted to make sure if they got lost that we would be able to find them." He starts walking towards our tent and walks in to get the tracker receiver. He walks back out and looks at the screen. "It says he's right over there in that direction." We all start heading in that direction and find him.

Zara and Daimon rush over to him and see that he was using the restroom. They walked back laughing and said. "Sorry, you all. He was just using the restroom." They sit down, and wait for their youngest to come back through." When Zarrod walks back through the campfire. Zara stops him and sits him down. She said smiling. "You gave your Father and I a big scare. You need to wake someone up when you have to go out of the tent and let them know where you're going."

He looked at them and said, "Okay, Mommy. I didn't know. We've never been camping before. Sorry." He gets up and walks back to the tent with his Parents. They walk in the opening of the tent with everyone else finding their way inside their own tents.

Chris and I just sit outside for a little while longer and make sure everyone else is asleep before we turn in ourselves. We get inside the tent and get on our mattress. Then we cuddle with each other and fall asleep until the sun is up bright and shining.

Chapter
TWENTY FOUR

W e get up and walk out of the tent to follow the noise that is going on. We walk up to the rest of the gang packing their things up. I look over at Dev and Ash and ask. "What are you all doing?"

"We're packing up to head back home. Cara and Scott have to be in Lexington before twelve for their flight. We're all going back so that they can be there in time and visit for a few minutes before they have to leave." Ash answers.

I walk back towards Chris smiling and say. "Besides Chad, Josh, Jeremy and Zach we're going to be by ourselves for the rest of the camping trip."

He looks at me and knows that I am sad that they can't stay, but on the other hand he knows that I don't want to miss out on the chance of seeing my Sister leave. He says smiling. "Well, she'll be back down this way later on in the week right? We'll get to visit with her." He hugs me and pulls me closer to him. They all walk over to me and start saying their goodbyes. They hug and kiss me, then start walking towards the bus that they rented for the trip up here.

I notice the look on Kylie's and Josh's faces. I get to thinking about how it must feel to be away from the boy you just met and can't get out of your mind. I turn around and ask Chris in a whisper. "Would you mind if Kylie stays with us for a couple of days?"

He looks at me, smiles and says. "No, I wouldn't mind that. She's more than welcome to stay anytime she wants to. That goes for all of them." He walks over to Scott and Cara. He asks. "Scott, could I please talk to you for a few minutes before you go?"

Scott answers, "Sure!" He walks over to him and asks. "What's up Chris?"

Chris looks at him and asks. "Cara and Kyle are coming back here in the middle of the week for Kyle's tour at University of Kentucky, right?"

"Yea, they're scheduled at the campus at twelve noon on Wednesday. Why do you ask?"

"Well, Bree and I were wondering if it would be alright for Kylie to stay with us until then. She wants to get to know Kylie a little bit better and spend some time with her."

"Okay, I don't see a problem with that. I will talk it over with Cara real quick before we go." He sees that Kylie is hugging everyone goodbye, including Josh, Jeremy, Chad and Zach. He walks over to where his Wife was and says. "Honey, we need to talk."

She looks behind him and asks. "What's this about?"

"I think we could let Kylie spend a few days down here with her Aunt Breea and Uncle Chris couldn't we. They want to get to know her while they have the chance to."

Cara looks over at us smiling. "Sure, that seems fine with me." She digs through her purse and pulls her cell phone out. She texts her Daughter. "U (you) wanna (want to) stay wit (with) ur (your) aunt breea and uncle chris until i bring ur (your) bro (brother) down here for his tour and he starts college" She stands aside and waits for her reply. Her cell phone vibrates and she opens the message up. It reads, "yea that wld (would) b (be) gr8 (great) thanks (thanks) mom" She looks up at her Daughter over to her Husband hugging him goodbye and helping her Brother dig her bag out of the bags that is in the back of the bus. She walks over to her Daughter and gives her a hug, saying. "Now, just because you're down here where we can't see you doesn't mean that you have freedom without it costing you." She gives Kylie a hug and smiles.

"Awh, Mom. I'm not that stupid to ruin this. I promise I'll be good for Aunt Breea and Uncle Chris." She gives her Parents and Brother one more hug and walks to us while waiting for them all to leave.

I look over towards Brooklyn and Brittany and see that they don't really want to leave either. I walk over and talk to Darion and Michelle. I ask, "I would like to know if Brooklyn and Brittany could spend the night with Chris and I up here tonight? Maddi doesn't have to be home until tomorrow evening. She was wondering if they could stay. Cara and Scott are letting Kylie stay with us for a couple of days until Cara and Kyle travel back down here for his tour at the campus. So, she'll be here too."

Darion and Michelle look at each other and smile. "Yea, that will be fine with us. As long as they come back with you two and not Chad or Jeremy."

"Okay, they'll come back with us I promise. We won't let anything happen to them." I turn to the girls and say smiling. "Your Parents said yes!"

They start jumping up and down screaming, along with Maddi and Kylie. We all sit there in the parking lot to watch the others leave. We wave smiling at them and as soon as the bus is out of sight Chad, Brooklyn, Jeremy, Brittany, Josh, Kylie Zach, Maddi, Chris and I all walk back up to the campsite. We sit around for a while then us girls head down to the shower area. The girls and I all take a shower and get ourselves prettied up. We walked back up to the campsite to see that the guys weren't there. We sit around and wait for them to return.

The girls and I were all sitting there waiting for the guys to come back up to the campsite when my phone vibrated. "Hey come down 2 (to) the beach just u (you) tell da (the) girls that the others r (are) out on the trail waiting for them to hike with them c (see) u (you) in a bit ;)" I get up and walk over to the trail. I see Chad, Josh, Jeremy and Zach all waiting there. I walk over to them smiling and ask. "Why didn't you all just walk over to the camp when we hollered for you?"

Josh looks up smiling and answers. "Chris didn't want us to. He said to leave it to him. Tell the girls we're ready to go hiking if they want to. Chris is waiting for you down at the beach."

"Okay, I'll go get the girls. There better not be anything planned with the girls other than just hiking." I walk back to the campsite and smile. "Girls, Chris and I want to spend some time alone together for a little bit. Josh, Jeremy, Zach and Chad are all out on the trail waiting for you to take a hike with them. So go on and take a hike." I start walking toward the trail that leads to the beach and look back to check on the girls and guys. I see the girls walking over to the guys getting ready for their hike. While walking down the trail to the beach, I smile wondering what Chris has planned for us to do today. It's going to be just him and I for a little while. I finally reached the beach and it's crowded. I move through the crowd and spot him. He's standing there with a rose in his hand smiling, waiting so patiently. I take the scene in for a moment, I start running towards him. I look up at his face and ask. "What do you have up your sleeve?"

He looks at me when he puts me down on the ground, smiles. "Follow me and you'll find out." We walk towards the other side of the trail that is from the campsite. I look at him and smile. He looks at me smiling and asks. "Have you ever been on a boat?"

I look out toward the water and think for a little bit. I answer, smiling. "No, I don't think I have. Why is that what we're doing?"

He looks over at me and grabs my hand smiling. He says squeezing my hand. "Okay, that's a good thing because I want to be the first person you experience this with." He pulls my arm underneath his and he pulls me closer to his body. "It's going to be all about us for a couple of hours. Us by ourselves and no one else around besides the driver of that boat." He points towards a boat that's sitting in the water by the dock.

I look over at him smiling and ask pointing towards that boat. "That boat there?" I look up in time to see his head shaking up and down. "That's a pretty big boat. We're not going to sleep on it are we?"

"No! We have nieces and a cousin all alone with my friends that are horny. I wouldn't put them in that position. I thought we would love to have a few hours by ourselves though." He looks down towards his feet, sighs and says. "Besides, we'll be going right by the campsite anyways. I'm going to look real good to see if there is anything that is going on. If there is, I'm jumping off the boat and swimming to the shore below our campsite. I'll protect them and you." He stops and asks. "Are you ready for the boat ride around the lake?"

I look and say. "That's a big ride though. Maybe we might find a secret spot that we could camp out at sometime." I giggle a little and walk holding his hand on the dock leading towards the boat.

We finally reach the boat and Chris lets go of my hand. He steps up onto the boat and leans down towards me with his arm extended out. "Here, let me help you up."

I put my hand in his and take a big step up on the boat. We are side by side again on the boat deck and holding each other's hands. We walk around to the front of the boat and I see that there are two candles on a table and it's set. I look up at him smiling and ask. "How long have you had this planned?"

He looks over at me smiling and answers. "I've had this planned since we got to my Grandmother's house. This boat is my Uncle George's. He's got a driver and caretaker that takes care of it out here at the docks. He doesn't like having it at his house where he lives right in town. He doesn't really have the room in his driveway or garage to store it there. So it stays here for whenever someone in the family wants to use it for whatever reason." He takes a breath and continues. "This is where I had my college graduation party. It was all family of course, but I had a few friends out on it the night before. I think Uncle George and Aunt Gretta's oldest Son Gabriel had his graduation party on this boat and everyone just crashed out on it. They all didn't wake up until the next day around three and they were all sunburned from head to toe. Gabriel knows how to throw one heck of a party." He chuckles and pulls out a chair for me to sit in. "Mi lady!" He bows, smiles, holding his hand extended out towards the seat of the chair.

I sit down and smile. "Thank you kindly sir." I look back at him still smiling and watch him walk over to his side of the table and sit in his chair.

"Now, our supper should be here any moment." He looks up towards the driver and shakes his head up and down. Signalling to him to start driving. He looks over at me and says. "Hold on for a few minutes." I hold on for a few minutes while the boat starts moving backwards. I look up at him and just take this moment in. I can't believe that I have found a guy that is more than willing to spend time with me. He wants to spend time with me for the rest of his life. He's got me doing things that I never thought I would like to do. I remember wishing that I would have someone as good looking as Chris and wishing that I would find him before my nineteenth birthday. I feel like I'm the luckiest girl in the world. He looks across the table at me smiling and asks. "What are you thinking?"

I look up at him and smile. "I'm thinking about how lucky I am." I get up when I see that we are out on the water safely, and walk over to sit on his lap. I give him a peck on the lips and smile. I sit there until we both hear a noise behind us. We both look back and see that it was our food on it's way to our table. I get back up and walk over to the other side of the table. Chris gets up behind me and pulls my chair out for me. I sit down and he scoots me in towards the table.

He walks over to his side of the table and sits down. He spreads his napkin over his legs and looks over at me smiling. "I hope you enjoy your meal." The woman that brought them out takes the lid off of my plate and I see that it's egg rolls with fried rice.

I look at him and ask. "Is this your Mom's famous egg rolls?"

"Yea, it sure is! I remember how you said that you loved them. So, I called her up late last night and asked her to give the recipe to Aunt

Gretta. She wanted to know why I wanted her to give the recipe to Aunt Gretta and I told her that you loved them the night we went to her house for supper. She said that she didn't have a problem with it and she faxed it to Aunt Gretta. Aunt Gretta gave it to the Wife of the caretaker of the boat." He takes a bite of his egg roll and moans. "This is just like my Mothers. It's so good! Try it!"

I take a bite of the egg roll and look over at him smiling. "Yea, this is just like your Mother's. If I didn't know any better, I'd think she was on the boat herself." I take another bite of the egg roll and look up above him. I notice that the caretaker of the boat is his Father. I look straight back at him and smile. "I thought you said that we were going to be by ourselves?" I point up to the driver smiling and waving.

He looks behind himself, smiling as he waves at his Father. "Yea, that part of this trip is going to be tough. They promised that they would stay away from us though. We can say hi to them if you want."

I look at him smiling and say. "Yes! I want to say hi to them. I don't want to be a snob towards them, Chris." I get up and climb up the ladder to the upper level of the boat deck. I hug his Father and turn around to see Chris' Mother and Chris. I smile at her, run to her and hug her. "I can't believe this. I love your egg rolls." I hug her again and smile. I step back and watch his Parents. We walk to the side of the boat and see another campsite. I look up at him and ask. "Is this where they've been staying?"

"Yea, they have been here since the day before we got here. They had to come up and set things up for us." He smiles at me and says looking behind me. "Oh, yea! There's someone else here to see you too." He points behind me smiling.

I turn around to look at who he was talking about and see that it is my Parents walking up to the boat. I wait for them to get on the boat and run to them. I give them both a hug and a kiss on their cheek. "When did he have time for all of you to come up here without me noticing? I have been with him the whole time we've been here." I start walking back over to Chris and his Parents. Smiling I say. "I'm glad that you all could be here. I miss you all." I gave his Parents and my Parents another hug.

We all just sit around for a half an hour and my Parents have to get off the boat at the campsite. Chris' Parents have to get off there too. We all say our goodbyes and Chris and I continue with our ride. Chris is driving the boat while I'm sitting there with him on the top deck smiling and enjoying the view of the lake. We come across this location that looks like a campsite that no one has used for a while. We see eight heads pop up. We get closer and look to see what was going on and then Maddi gets up laughing. Chris and I both look over at each other and he decides to pull the boat over to the side. We get off the boat and get in the canoe. We row ourselves over to the site and get on shore. Then we notice that Zach, Josh, Jeremy, Chad, Maddi, Brooklyn, Brittany and Kylie are up there drinking a beer. We walk up quietly behind them all and start giggling. We cover our mouths. Not wanting to be heard, we sat there for a few minutes. We see that Brooklyn is sitting beside Chad making out with him. Then we look over to see that Maddi is making out with Zach, we also see that Brittany is making out with Jeremy and that Kylie is making out with Josh. We decided to walk up on them.

Chad hears something coming up behind him and stops making out with Brooklyn. "Just be quiet for a minute." They stop to listen and he asks her. "Do you hear that?"

"Yea, I hear that. Where is it coming from?" She looks behind her and Chad, behind the rest of them. She turns around to see Chad sneaking off into the woods towards the noise. She gets up and says. "Hey, Chad! Wait on me." She follows behind him and is startled to see Chris and I standing there smiling. She asks. "How long have you two been there?"

"Long enough to see that you all have something going on with each other." He looks over at Chad. He puts his arm around his back and asks. "What are your intentions with my niece?"

Chad looks up to him, smiles and says. "I don't know just yet." Chuckling he takes a drink of his beer. "I just want to see if she would date someone like me." He takes another drink of his beer and sees that Brooklyn and I are walking back to the site where they were. Chris and Chad both start walking back. Chad asks him. "How did you and Breea meet?"

"We met at the airport in Lexington." He smiles remembering the look on my face when he first met me. "Yea, I remember her looking like she was scared to death. All I wanted to do with her was just pick her up and take her away from her nightmare. I didn't want her going through what she was about to go through with her Father missing. That's when I called Dev, my friend who turned out to be her Brother. I called him to help her through the roughest time of her life. Her Mother was trying to look for her Father."

Chad asks. "Well, why didn't you just hop on the plane with them and go?"

"Well, for one I was working and two, I didn't know if she would appreciate that from me."

"And now?"

"Now, I'm glad that I sent Dev there to the Columbus Airport to wait on them to get there. I'm glad that I took the two week vacation time off to go up and help them. I'm glad that I did all of that so that we could be together. And now, I'm happy to say that we're engaged and about to get married a week before Christmas. I don't want to spend another day without her in my house. I can't see that happening. I love her man."

"So, it really did happen that quick?"

"Yea, it did. It's not just because she was in a stressful time, that made me fall in love with her. It was the way she handled herself at that time. She was surprisingly calm and beautiful." He looks over at me and smiles. I caught his look and smiled back at him, and returned my attention back to my niece Brooklyn. I have already broken the make out sessions up and we were all just sitting around talking with one another. He looks back to Chad and says. "What is with Brooklyn and you?"

"I like her dude. Enough to have a relationship with her, but I don't know if it's going to work out between us."

"Why is that? You'll never know if you don't try it."

"Well, for one she's from New York. For two, she's starting college in the fall. I live here in Morehead. I don't know how it's going to work out. I don't believe in long distance relationships." He sighs and says. "I guess I saw what it done to my Parents and I hate that it tore them apart."

"Well, you are not your Parents for one thing. Secondly you and Brooklyn have more common sense not to do what they did to each other. If you let her know that you're willing to try to make it work, then she'll give you the time of day to try it herself."

"I didn't think about it that way." He walks over to the rest of us. I stand up and see that he's walking fast back towards the rest of us.

I look at the others and say smiling. "I'll be right back." I start walking towards Chris and pass Chad. He stops me and asks. "What did she tell you?"

"She didn't tell me anything. Whatever it is that you are trying to do with my niece, I'm confident that she will let you know herself." I pat his shoulder and smile. I start walking towards Chris. I get up to him and ask him. "What did you two talk about?"

"Nothing really. Why?" Chris asks me smiling, and looks at me and says. "We just chatted about how Chad likes Brooklyn. He said that he doesn't know yet if it's true love, but he would like to have the chance to find out." He puts his arm around me smiling and asks. "Are you ready to get back on the boat, or do you want to sit here with them?"

I look back and see that Chad, Brooklyn, Josh, Kylie, Zach, Maddi, Jeremy and Brittany are all walking back towards the campsite. I look at Chris, smile and say. "Nah, I want to get back on the boat with you and spend a little more time together." We start walking back towards the boat.

We finally get on and start it up. We start heading down towards the docks and we end up finding a spot on the embankment that has its own little private beach and a nice piece of flat ground. We look at each other and smile. Chris says, "I think we just found our spot for the next time we're here camping. We won't bring anyone else up here to it. It will be just for us." He continues towards the boat docks and we pull in. He climbs down the ladder from the top deck and ties the boat to the dock with Clay.

He helps Chris tie the boat to the dock and asks. "Did you two have a great cruise around the lake?"

Chris looks at him smiling and answers. "Yea, we sure did." He looks back at me smiling and asks. "Is there any chance that we can sit on the boat for a while?"

Clay looks up at Chris smiling and answers. "Yes, you sure can. As long as the owner knows that you are on the boat."

"Okay, thank you." Chris walks back towards me in the front of the boat. He leans down towards me and kisses me passionately. He pulls me up and smiles. He asks, "Would you like to go to the bottom deck with me?"

I look at him smiling and answer. "I thought you would never ask." We walk down the steps to the bottom deck and make out. We get to the point where we're almost naked when Chris gets a text. He pulls his phone out and it reads. "Jw (just wondering) where u (you) 2 (two) r (are) B" He smiles at me and says. "I think we're being summoned back to the campsite. Brooklyn just texted me." He turns his phone around for me to see and I smile.

I say, "Let me see that." I grab his phone and text back. "Dis (this) is ur (your) aunt well (we'll) b (be) there shortly jus (just) tryin (trying) 2 (to) spend some quality time 2gether (together)" I hit send and hand Chris back his phone smiling. I grab him around his neck and pull him back towards me. We start kissing again and the phone goes off. I say whispering into his ear. "Just ignore it." We keep trying to make love and get another text message.

Chris gets up and says. "Sorry, I can't ignore it. We have to make sure everything is okay." He grabs his phone again and answers it. "Hello?"

"Yea, Chris! This is your Aunt Molly. I was wondering, when are you all going to bring Maddi back? Are you with her right now? We just saw the news! It happened just about an hour ago."

Chris gets a puzzled look on his face and asks. "What are you talking about Aunt Molly?"

"I'm talking about the holdup on the beach. There is a guy holding everyone up with a gun to a teenage girl's head. They aren't releasing any names that are involved right now. I just got to worrying about Maddi. I need to know if she's okay or not. I tried texting her, but I didn't get a response."

"Okay, Aunt Molly. I will check on her. She should be in her tent with Bree's nieces. I will call you back after I check on them." He hangs the phone up and puts his pants and shirt back on. He looks down at me laying there on the bed. Smiling, he says. "Sorry, baby. We have to get to the campsite. My Aunt Molly is worried about Maddi. There is some guy on the beach holding a teenage girl hostage with a gun to her head. We have to go! We'll finish this later." He finishes getting dressed and helps me up. I got up and put my clothes back on and we ran out of the cabin of the boat. We climb up to the main deck and down on the dock. We both start running towards the beach. We don't see anyone until we round the bend in the trail. There are a lot of people just standing with their hands over their mouths. Chris just pushes through the crowd. We got up to the front of the people who were standing there watching and saw that it wasn't anyone we know. We both sigh in relief and walk around to the parking lot. We walk up the side where there is no opening for vehicles to exit or enter. We get stopped by a police officer.

Chapter

TWENTY FIVE

....

"What's your hurry?" Officer Pat asks.
We turn around and Chris answers. "We're just trying to get up to our campsite to check on our nieces and my friends. We didn't know what was going on until my Aunt called us and she's worried sick about her teenage Daughter. I have to get to her to make sure that's not her that the hostage has a hold of."

Officer Pat looks at us a little bit harder and asks. "Weren't you the ones that needed our help here yesterday? Chris and Breea! Something about her Brother being engaged to Ashley. The guy that was after her was the one who raped her and got her pregnant."

"Yea, that was us!"

"Okay, sorry. You can go on up. I'll be up to check on everyone shortly."

"Okay, thank you!" We walk on up towards the campsite. We hear a gunshot, we both turn around and see the guy go down. So we both started running, finally arriving at the campsite and seeing that there wasn't anyone sitting by the fire. Chris gets his phone out and sees if there's any text messages on it. There isn't and he walks over to the tents and looks inside them. No luck with the first two that he looked into. The third one no one again. He started getting worried when we heard a noise coming from the wooded area behind the tents. He grabbed his flashlight from the tent we slept in. He shines it over to where the noise was coming from and sighs. "There you guys are. We were worried sick about all of you." We start walking towards them and see that the guys are all tied up to a tree. Chris takes the tape off all of their mouths and asks. "What in the world are you dorks doing? Where are the girls?"

Chad gets up and says. "I'm going to kill the bastard!" He starts running towards the tents and walks into the one that he slept in last night. He comes back out with a gun. "I'm ready for some action." He holds the gun up in the air and takes off in the woods.

Chris and I untied the other guys and Chris asked again. "Where are the girls?"

Jeremy looked up at us and said. "Maddi, Kylie and Brittany are all in their tent that they slept in last night. Brooklyn was taken by a guy that says he knows her!" Jeremy, Josh and Zach get up and follow after Chad. They all holler for Chad while chasing after him.

Chris says, "I'm going to go calm Chad down. You stay here inside the tent with the girls. Try to keep them calm and quiet." He kisses my forehead and puts me in the tent with Maddi, Brittany and Kylie.

They were all crying silently when they saw me. They all started asking questions. I hold my hands up and whisper. "We need to stay quiet. No one talks." I get in the middle of them and let them rest their bodies on me. I whisper, "We need to sit where we can see all sides of the tent. We need to look out for anyone walking up the trail. If you see anything just rub a finger on each other." We get into the position that I suggested and we sit there waiting.

Finally someone stops Chad. The guys take his gun away and all the guys walk back to the beach. They saw that the cops have the perpetrator in custody and in the back of the cruiser. They look inside and don't recognize him. Chad spots Brooklyn. He starts walking towards her and says. "Brooklyn! I thought you were gone for good!"

He picks her up, hugging her. Chris, Zach, Josh and Jeremy move in with Chad.

Chris asked. "Brooklyn, who is that?"

Brooklyn answers. "It's my ex-boyfriend. He followed my Parents and I here from New York. He's nothing but bad news." Then she's interrupted by Officer Pat and tells him the story of how her ex-boyfriend Kevin raped her best friend and made her watch. She was the key witness in the case against him but his lawyer got him only three months in jail. Chris, Zach, Josh, Jeremy and Chad all listen to the story and gasp.

Chad looked back towards them and said. "This is like deja vu, isn't it?"

All the guys looked at each other and Josh said, "Yea!"

The police finally get done talking to Brooklyn and release her into Chris' custody. They walk back up to the campsite and the girls are all scared because they see people walking up. I look at the shapes of the bodies and whisper. "It looks like the guys and Brooklyn. Just sit tight! If something happens to me, please run towards the beach and get the cops attention." I climb out of the tent and sneak around to where the people can't see me. I peek over the side of the tent and start running towards them. I ask, "Chris, Brooklyn?"

"Yea, baby. It's us." He meets me in the middle and hugs me tight. "It turns out that your niece and Sister in-law are very wanted girls around here." He kisses my forehead and I release him and grab a hold of Brooklyn. We all get the other girls out of the tent and come up with a way to keep each of them safe while we all sleep. Brooklyn is going to sleep in the tent with Chad. Maddi is going to sleep in the tent with Zach, Kylie is going to sleep in the tent with Josh and Brittany is going to sleep in the tent with Jeremy. Chris and I in another tent all surrounding each other. We leave the other tents up just in case someone tries to mess with us while we're sleeping in the middle of the night.

Chris and I were in the tent finally when his Aunt Molly called. "Chris, I was just wanting to check to make sure everyone that's with you is safe and secure before I go to bed."

"Yes, Aunt Molly. We're all okay. It was Brooklyn that was being held at gunpoint by her ex-boyfriend. The girls are all safe though. We have them sleeping in the middle of the campsite in a tent all together."

"Okay, just wanting to check. You know me. I'm a worry wart." Giggling, she says. "Thank you for doing this for Maddi. She really needed to get away. We just have way too much going on around here right now. With Mickey and Madeline. I figured she was going to be needing some, one on one time." She sighs and finishes. "Well, I'll let you get some sleep. Tell that beautiful Fiance of yours Matt and I say hello and that we love you guys. Be careful on your way back tomorrow. Goodnight."

"Goodnight!" He hangs the phone up and lays down beside me. Chuckling he says. "Aunt Molly says her and Uncle Matt say hi and that they love us."

"Okay, hi back and love them too." I roll over on top of him and smile a crooked grin.

He looks at me smiling and asks. "Really?"

I shake my head up and down smiling. We start making out. We keep doing this until we're sure that everyone else is asleep and we strip each other down. You can guess what happens next. It's morning before we're both done with making love. We got about four hours of sleep before we got woken up by Brooklyn. I lift my head up to see her head peeking through the tent door smiling, I ask. "Brooklyn, is anything wrong?"

"No, just checking to see if you all were awake or still asleep. Didn't know what time you wanted to head back. Josh, Jeremy, Zach and Chad are all out here cooking some bacon for breakfast. When you all wake up, just come on out and join us. It's almost finished." She zips the zipper back up and walks over to the fire.

I looked over towards Chris and saw that he's awake watching me. He smiled, grabbed me and said. "I wish we could stay like this forever. I'm the luckiest man in the world right now. I won't ever take you for granted." He kisses my lips softly.

I looked at him, smiled and said. "Same back at you. I love you Christopher Michael Lee!" I kissed his lips softly.

We both get up and get our clothes on. We climb out of the tent and walk to the fire where the others are sitting. We see that Chad, Josh, Jeremy, Zach, Brittany, Brooklyn Kylie and Maddi are all sitting there finishing their breakfast. They all look up and smile at us. Chad stands up and says, "It's about time you two sleepy heads." With everyone chuckling we sit down and grab some bacon.

After breakfast, we all pitch in and take the tents all down. We get them all to the truck in the beach parking lot, and we all take a hike before we leave. Chris and I go a different path holding hands while the others all walk different paths. Josh and Kylie hike up to the campsite to make sure no one didn't leave anything behind. Chad and Brooklyn walk a different trail, holding hands. Jeremy and Brittany just sit at the truck and talk while waiting on all of us. Zach and Maddi hike over to the boat docks, holding hands.

We all get back to the truck about the same time. Then Josh asked Chris. "Chris, uhm." He looks back at the other guys smiling toward him, while the girls and I are all getting into the truck. "The guys and I were wondering."

"Yes, Josh. What is it?"

"We were wondering when is it that you have to go back to work? We heard that you and Breea are remodeling your kitchen. We were wanting to come down to your house for a couple of days." He looked back at the others and smiled. "So, how about it?"

Chris stands there smiling. He answered, "That would be great. I can use all the help that I can get. Breea's going to be starting school this week. So, she'll be going to the campus to get her schedule and shopping with her Mother for things that she will need for school. This would be perfect. I want to surprise her. She thinks we're going with the first design we picked out. She doesn't like it very well as she does the second design she picked. I want her to be happy and if this is what's going to make her happy, then I want to do it for her. She deserves the best." Chuckling, he asked Josh. "When are you all showing up?"

Josh looked back at the others and back to Chris. "We figured we'd come down later tonight. We'll stay until Friday. Then we could all come camping again, but just the guys this time. No offense towards Breea, but we want to spend some time with our buddy before he gets married."

"Okay, that sounds great to me. I guess we'll be seeing you around seven tonight then?"

"Yea, that sounds good. We'll call when we're on our way."

"No, just text me. I don't want her to know about this. I want it to be a surprise."

"Okay, I'll text you then." Josh turns around and shakes his head up and down smiling towards the other guys that were waiting on him at his truck. He turns around and waves at us all pulling out of the parking space. We all wave back and smile.

Chapter
TWENTY SIX

....

We finally arrive at Maddi's Parents house and drop her off. We visited for a little bit, and we drove over to his Grandmother's house. We sat and talked to her for a while. Chris wanted me to prove to him that I could drive a stick shift if I had to, so we headed out into the pasture with an old white beat up four wheel drive pickup. Chris pulls off to the side of the dirt path a little and turns to me smiling. "Are you ready to show me how you know how to drive a stick shift?"

I looked at him, smiled and answered. "I guess I am as ready as I'll ever be." I scoot over to the driver's side of the truck and wait for him to walk around the back of the truck. He climbs in smiling and scoots over to me and says. "Okay, I'm ready!" He watches me while I start the truck up. I look over at him still smiling, then I ease off the clutch and the brake at the same time. I killed the truck because it's been such a long time since I drove a stick shift. He starts laughing a little and so do I. I start the truck back up and easily get it to move without killing it. I shift the gears just as easily as he did in his truck. I keep on driving while he's got his arms crossed behind his head just leaning back in the seat relaxing.

I see a cabin and slow down. I look over at him smiling and say. "See, I told you I knew how to drive a stick shift. Who lives in that?" I asked, pointing to the cabin.

He looked up and smiled. Then he looked over at me and said. "That's what I wanted to show you."

So I stop the truck and kill the engine. We both got out and I followed him to the porch of the cabin smiling. He reaches up to one of the rafters and grabs the key to the door. He unlocked it and said. "Before my Grandpa got sick, he and I built this. We're the only ones who know that it's back here. We used old barn wood." He walks in and shows it off with a smile and a proud look.

I look around at all the things that they found on their farmland. A set of deer horns, a cow's skull, and a snake skin. I step over him real quick, like I'm afraid that there is a snake in the cabin with us right now. I say! "Chris, I think there might be a snake in here." I point down to the floor below us and bite my bottom lip.

He looked down and said. "No, that is a snake's skiing that we found on the farm. We don't know what kind it is, but we thought that it would fit perfectly in the cabin. So we picked it up and put it in here." He bent down to pick it up and said. "I wonder how it got down here." He puts it back where he and his Grandfather put it before they locked the cabin up. He looked around and saw a big gaping hole in the floor. He walked over to it and inspected it. He saw something move and said. "Bree, walk out on the porch slowly and lightly." I did what he asked me to do onto the porch.

He stayed inside and I stood there at the door looking in. I asked, "What is it Chris?"

He looked underneath the bed and said. "Holly cow." He climbed underneath the bed and stayed under it for about five minutes.

I asked, grabbing onto the door frame. "What is it Chris?" All I saw are his legs and the lower part of his body wiggling.

I heard him answer. "Bree, can you please go to the truck and get that feed sack for me?"

I walk to the truck and get a feed sack for him and run back up to the cabin. I walked in lightly and tapped the calf of his leg. "Here!" I walked back out of the cabin lightly and onto the porch. I still saw his legs wiggling and asked. "Chris, are you okay?"

He finally answered me after five minutes. "Yea, I'm okay." He started wiggling his body out backwards and held up a snake. He said, "I caught the sucker!" He looked at it and said, "I think it might be a copperhead." He was holding the thing with one hand by it's head. He reached down to the floor with the other hand and grabbed the feed sack. He put the snake in it without getting bit to my amazement and he looked up at me. "Sorry, if I scared you! I just had to catch him." He got up and started walking towards the entrance of the cabin. I stood back because I didn't want anything to do with the snake. He tied the bag and put it on the back of the truck. He walked back up on the porch of the cabin and said. "We have to find something that will block that hole in the floor there." He held his hand out to me and smiled. "Do you want to go with me? Or do you want to stay here?"

I looked over at him and then back at the swing on the porch of the cabin. I answered, "I'll go with you." We walked down the steps of the porch and searched for something on the back of the truck first. We didn't find anything that would help block the hole in the floor. So, we started out walking behind the cabin where there's an outhouse. He walked in there and saw that there's a cinder block in it.

He grabbed it and walked back out saying. "I think this will hold them at bay until I can get back up here and patch over the hole." He walked back upon the porch and into the cabin. That's when he noticed that there was another snake in it. He shut the door and searched the cabin up and down for it. He hollers out to me, "I caught another one! Would you go get another feed sack, please?"

"Yes!" I walked back to the truck and got a different feed sack. "Here, baby. I have another feed sack for you!"

He opened the door carefully and grabbed the bag with his left hand. He said, "Thank you!" He shut the door back and put the snake in the feed sack. He walked out of the cabin and locked it. He grabbed my hand with his left hand and led me to the truck. He let me get into the cab of the truck and shut the door. He put the feed sack on his side, in the bed of the truck. He started the truck up and we pulled out of the lane. We drove all the way back up to the main house and we pulled over into the grass area by the barn. We got out and walked into his Grandmother's house. "Mammie?"

"Yea, Chris?"

"Hey, I wanted to let you know that we're done with the farm truck." He put the keys back up on the key rack by the back door.

"Okay." She walked through the hallway into the kitchen. "Did she do good?"

"Yea, she did a wonderful job Mammie." He looked back at me and smiled. "I have something that I need to tell you though."

"What is it Chris?"

"Well, I know you have already found out about the cabin that Pappie and I built last year before he got sick right?"

"Right, go on!"

"Well, Bree and I went into it today. We found a snake skin on the floor and two snakes in it."

"Oh, goodness! Did you get the snakes out for me? I go back there every once in a while and just sit."

"Yea, Mammie. I got them out for you. They're on the back of the farm truck."

"Okay, I'll call your Uncle George up. See if he can't get out here right away to kill them for me." She gets on the phone with George and smiled when she heard him answer. She hung the phone up with him and said. "He'll be on his way over with Gabriel. You two want to stay until they get here to kill them?"

"Yea, Mammie. We will stay with you until they get here." We sat down at the table and talked while waiting for George and Gabriel to show up.

It was nearly five o'clock when George and Gabriel finally showed up. They walk in through the back door and smile at Chris and I. George said, "I thought you two already headed back to Lexington." He walked over to the coffee maker and fixed him a cup of coffee and Gabriel just sat down at the table smiling. George walked over to the table and said. "Gabriel, there's no time to sit. We have work to do before the sun goes down." He walked outside with the cup of coffee in his hands. Whistling he walked over to the farm truck and looked at the bed. He saw the two feed sacks and looked back at Chris. "You caught them and put them in a feed sack?"

Chris smiled. "Yes, I did. Why?"

"Oh, just wondering. It's not often that you get to see a city man capturing a snake." He opened the bag and waited for it to climb out. He spotted it and asked shockingly. "You caught a Copperhead, using your bare hands?"

"Yea, I did."

"Well, well. Maybe you aren't a city boy like we think you are." George opened the other bag and just gasped. "Another copperhead? Where did you catch these boogers?"

"On the farm. In that field, close to the fence line." Chris answered, pointing out to the field.

"Oh, wonder what they're doing out there. There must be a nest of them somewhere close. They aren't interested in cattle fields. That's weird." He looked down at them and said. "They have babies out there somewhere. That would be the only thing that I could think of that would keep them here." He turned around and said, "Keep an eye on them, Son." He started walking towards the barn and walked out with a garden hoe. He had it over his shoulder whistling. He looked at Gabriel and shook his head down once.

Gabriel grabbed one of the snakes the same way Chris did and put it down on the ground holding the tail. George said, "Okay, you can let it go!" Gabriel lets it go and George swings the hoe over his shoulder and lets it come down in front of him, just in time before the snake tries to strike him. Mammie and I both just jump and gasp. Then George shakes his head down again at Gabriel. He picks the second snake up and watches his Father. George said, "Okay, you can let it go!" Gabriel did what he was told to do and the same thing that happened with the first snake, happened with the second one. He looked up to Chris smiling and asked. "Do you want to go with Gabriel and I to see if we can find any more of them?"

Chris looked back at me and at his watch. He answered, "Yea, I'll go with you all. There's something back there that you all need to see anyway." He ran into the barn along with Gabriel and came back out carrying another garden hoe. Just like his Uncle and cousin did. They drive out into the field and I stay with Mammie until they come back.

We were sitting at the table when we heard the truck coming back towards the house. We both get up and walk over to the window and see that they're in a big hurry. We both looked at each other puzzled and hurried up outside. We stood there waiting to see what was going on.

George gets out of the vehicle without Chris and Gabriel with him. Mammie and I both looked at each other and she started running. "What's going on George?"

George looked at the both of us and answered. "We've found the nest. There are a lot of them in it. It doesn't look so good for your favorite cow Bessy." He puts a shovel in the back of the truck and walks into the house. He came back out in five seconds, carrying a gun and some extra ammo.

Mammie looked at him almost crying and asked. "George, what's the gun for?"

"It's for Bessy, she was bitten by one of them when we were trying to get to it. She ran up on it before she noticed it and it bit her." He loaded the gun up and asked. "Do you ladies want to go with me?"

Mammie looked at him and frowned. "No, George we don't. We'll just stay here. Just make sure you bury her after you shoot her. Then bring her calf up here to the barn. Breea and I will go to Hinton Mills Farm Supply and get a bottle and formula mix." She looked over at me and smiled. She asked, "Would you please go get my purse off of the stand by the back door, grab my keys off the key rack and lock the door behind you." She looked over to George and asked. "Would you mind if I take your truck since you have the farm truck?"

"No, go right ahead. We'll try to be done with the job at hand before you ladies get back. Call Gretta and let her know what we're doing. She's expecting us to get back soon, because we were going to travel to Lexington to take Gabriel to the campus. He has to sign into his dorm room and move things in."

"Okay, I'll call her Uncle George." I said smiling and dialing the number.

He looked over at me and smiled. "I like how you just said that young lady. You two be careful." He got back into the farm truck and drove off backwards.

Mammie and I both climb into his truck and start driving down the driveway. We got to the road and saw that there were a bunch of kids riding their bikes and Mammie pulled over. She rolled her window down and said smiling. "Kids, I'm going to need you not to go down to my house today. I don't want you all there because my Grandson's and Son in-law have found a nest of copperheads in the field right behind the house. Please, promise me you all won't go down there."

They all looked at her smiling and said in unison. "Okay, Mammie. We won't!"

She asked them. "Do you all need a lift back to your houses?"

"Yea, thank you Mammie."

Mammie and I both climb out of the truck and put the bikes and kids on the back of the truck. We got back in before we heard the first shot. She put the truck into gear looking over at me, smiled and said. "Breea, have you gotten a hold of Aunt Gretta yet?"

"Yea, she said that she would wait on them at her house. She doesn't want to hear the gun go off." I put my phone back down in my purse and hold on because Mammie is jerking my body all around the truck. I looked back and saw that the kids were all holding on tight. I smiled at the one she talked to earlier and he returned my smile. He winked at me and started talking to his friends. I looked toward the front end of the truck and saw that we're almost to a house.

Mammie slammed on the brakes of the truck and got out. "Here you go boys. Have a great day!" She climbs back in and slams me against the back of the seat. She started laughing and said. "Honey, you might want to hold on. I know these roads like the back of my hand. I was raised here. So, hold on tight." She slammed the brakes on again and held her tongue out to the side of her mouth. We pulled into the parking lot and I smiled over at her. She smiled and said. "I'll be right back. It won't take me long."

I was sitting in the truck when I noticed a boy that looked familiar to me. He saw the truck and smiled real big. He started running over and said. "Hey, how is Maddi?" Then he looked and said, "Sorry, I think I got the wrong truck."

He started walking back to his truck and I said, "Hey hold on a minute." I got out of the truck and walked over to him. I smiled and said, "I'm Breea, I know I've seen you at Chris' Parents house in Lexington."

"Yea, you did. I thought you were in George's truck. I'm sorry if I startled you. I just wanted to see how Maddi is. You know with the news of her best friend and Brother going to have a baby together."

"Oh, she's fine. She just got back to her house from camping with Chris and I at Cave Run Lake."

"Oh, well I'm glad that she got to get away from life here in this small town for two days."

He started walking back to his truck and I asked. "Hey, what was your name?"

My name is Tommy. I went to school with Mickey." He looked down at his foot pushing the gravel around in the parking lot and looked up at me and said, smiling. "I've had a crush on Maddi since she was a freshman in high school. I just never let her know that before or anyone else. I didn't want her Brother knowing and it ruined our friendship."

"Yea, that can hurt it can't it?" I looked down then and thought about what Dev must think of Chris and I being together. I make a mental note to ask Dev what his thoughts are about us being together when I get back to Lexington. I looked at him, smiled and asked. "Have you ever talked to Mickey about the crush you have on his younger Sister?"

"No, I wouldn't dare! He always told any of us that hung out with him not to even think about it. He said it would be too weird and he wouldn't want to hear the details of the relationship if we did."

"Yea, that would be weird with him, and that sucks for you because if you like her, who's to say that you aren't going to be able to hold off until you and Mickey go your separate ways?"

"Yea, it does suck. I guess I could wait until he leaves then go to their house and confess my feelings to her. I know that Mickey and his Parents are going to Lexington today sometime to take him to his dorm and get his schedule at Sullivan." He smiled at me and asked. "Do you know if Mickey and Maddi's Parents are going to take anyone else with them today when they leave?"

"No, I sure don't." I looked behind me and saw that Mammie was coming out smiling and she's got a brown paper bag in her arms. She walked over to us and said, "Helly, Tommy. How are you today?"

"Im fine Mrs. Mikel. How are you?"

"Considering the fact that they are shooting my favorite cow today, not so good. I'm happy that they are getting the copperheads' nest out of my fields though. They've already taken Bessy away, leaving her poor little calf orphaned." She put the bag down on the ground and asked. "What's got you out here on this fine day?"

"Oh, nothing really. Just getting ready to go over to Mickey's house before he has to leave for college. Going to say goodbye to him."

"Oh, that sounds like fun." She looked at her watch and said. "Well, I hate to run, but we have to be back at the house before the men get back. I want to be there to feed Bessy's calf. I don't know when she was bitten or what condition the calf's in." She started walking back to the truck and hollered at Tommy. "Tommy, I hope you figure out what you're going to do about that crush you have on my Granddaughter, Maddi. It may be too late in a couple of days." She looked behind her and smiled at me, winking.

We both climbed back into the truck to head back to her house and I asked her. "How did you know about him having a crush on Maddi?"

"I just know these things dear. I knew that Chris was going to propose to you the night he did. I had a dream about it." She looked over at me taking her eyes off the road for a few seconds smiling. "Don't think that I'm crazy for saying this, but when I saw a picture of you two when you two were about ten years old, I just knew then that you were going to be in the family. Everytime Chris came here to spend the week with his Grandpa and I in the summer. Gretta, Molly, George, Matt, Pappie and I all used to tease him about his little girlfriend in that particular picture." She paused for a moment, letting the memory come to life in her head. Then she continued, "I caught him one night in the spare bedroom looking at the picture and saying. "Oh, Breea. I'm going to marry you one day. I'll make you happy." He would kiss it and put it under his pillow. The next day when he got up I asked him about it."

"You did? What did he say?"

"He said that I was crazy and I didn't know what I was talking about."

"Oh, that's so sweet. I'm going to ask him about it when we're on our way back to Lexington tonight." I sat back relaxed a little more, knowing what to expect from Mammie's driving. We went past the road she was supposed to turn down and I noticed. "Mammie, I think we just passed your road."

She looked over at me smiling and said. "Yea, I know. I have to replace the gas in George's truck for him. He and Gabriel have a long drive ahead of them and I didn't want to take their truck to get this stuff. So, I'm just going to fill it back up for them so that they won't have to." She kept on driving into town and singing along with the radio smiling.

We finally pulled into the gas station and she filled George's truck back up. She walked over to my window and asked. "Do you want something to drink?"

"No, thank you." I watched her walk into the gas station and I turned to watch people over at the Dairy Queen. I saw them all laughing and enjoying themselves with ice creams in their hands. I smiled and turned away. I didn't want them to know that they were being watched. I got a text on my phone from Chris. I smiled and read the text. It said, "hey baby we r (are) done where u (you) all at" I texted him back. "Hey babe were (we're) at da (the) gas station across from dairy queen mammie thinks she had to put gas back into georges vehicle lol (laugh out loud) ill (I will) b (be) ready as soon as we get back i have a big day ahead of me tom (tomorrow)" I hit send and waited for his reply.

Finally Mammie came back out smiling and she climbed into the truck. She looked over at me and asked. "What time are you and Chris heading back to Lexington? I was wondering if he was going to go see his Pappie before he left town."

I looked over at her smiling and answered. "I don't know what he's going to do. I do know that they're done though. He just texted me and told me before you walked out of the gas station." Just then my phone vibrates and I check to see who it is. I saw that it's a text message from Chris and I smiled. I say, "It's Chris!" I read his message. "Ok well (we'll) go after we visit my pappie at the rest home u (you) all on ur (your) way back yet" I texted him back smiling. "Yea, were (we're) on our way back now ur (your) mammie was wantin (wanting) to knw (know) if we were gonna go visit him b4 (before) we left" I hit send and put my seatbelt on as she was pulling out of the parking lot of the gas station. We were finally headed back to her house when her cell phone rings.

She looked down at the caller id and saw that it was her Daughter Gretta. She answered, smiling. "Hey baby girl. What's going on?"

"Nothing much Mom. Just got through visiting Daddy. I was wondering, are the men done with whatever it is that they had to help with?"

"Yes, baby girl. They are, they'll be leaving as soon as I get back with your truck. They had to get rid of some copperheads for me. They were invading your Dad's cabin that he and Chris had built before he got sick."

"Oh my! Are the cattle alright?"

"Yea, most of them are. I have an orphaned calf now. Bessy got bit by one of the little monsters. She had a calf on her and now it's orphaned. I had to go out and get the formula for it and a bottle."

"Oh, poor little thing. I'll send Gabbi out to help you with it when we leave. Gage and Garrott will bring her out there in about an hour. She doesn't want to go with her Dad and I, she doesn't want to stay with her Brothers either. So, I figured you wouldn't mind the company for a couple of days." She paused and said. "You wouldn't mind that would you?"

"No, of course not. I'll be expecting to see her. I can't wait." She looked over at me smiling and winked her right eye at me. "Well, baby girl. I'm gonna get off of here. Heading into Elizaville, and you know as well as I do that it's a dead zone."

"Okay, Mom. Talk to you in a few minutes. Be careful. Love you!"

Mammie finally hung the phone up and looked over at me smiling. She turned the radio up and sang along with the music. We finally pulled into her driveway and saw the men all sitting out by the barn with three feed sacks. George is pointing down to them smiling. We both climbed out and I watched Chris and Gabriel walk over to the back of the truck.

Mammie said, smiling. "That's right boys. You know what to do with it." As she pointed towards the barn with her right index finger smiling. She walked up to George and asked him. "Did you all get all of them?"

"Yea, we sure did. The more we shot, the more we saw. It was a nasty little nest they had. There were, I'd say at least ninety babies in it. The mothers were on striking mode also. Chris almost got bit and so did Gabriel. I got to them before they got to them though." He wipes his left hand over his eyebrow. "I think I would like a glass of sweet tea and just to get out of this hot weather." He started walking behind Mammie while I walked over to the barn with Chris and Gabriel.

Chris is holding my hand while he has the bottle in the other. Gabriel is carrying the formula bucket ahead of us. Chris looked over at me smiling and asked. "How do you like my Mammie's driving?"

"She scared me a couple of times in the beginning. After riding with her to the farm supply store though I got used to it. I don't ever want to ride with her again though." I answered him smiling. I whisper, "I'd like to go back to the cabin again when the snakes are all hibernating. We can spend the night back there and go four wheeling with some of your buddies if you want."

"Okay, sounds good!" He kissed my forehead and smiled at Gabriel watching us. We got the bucket of formula into the barn where the little calf was pinned and I sat there rubbing the little gal's head while Gabriel and Chris did what their Mammie told them to do for her.

We finally got done with mixing the formula for the calf, to my surprise she came walking into the barn summoning Gabriel to leave with his Father. She walked right past Chris and I and she smiled. She took the bottle of formula and put it up to the calf's mouth. The calf started sucking like it's going out of style and she smiled, saying. "That's right, little one." Petting it's head. "I bet you miss your momma don't you. I'm going to take care of you though. I'm gonna name you little Bessy. You look exactly like your momma." She looked up at Chris and I watching her and asked. "Don't you two have to get back to Lexington?"

Chris looked at her shaking his head up and down and walked over to her. He said, "Yes, we do." He gave her a hug and said, "You take care. I'm only a phone call away."

"I know. Are you going to see your Pappie before you two leave town?"

"Yea, Mammie. We are. You know I wouldn't leave town without going to see him." He gave her a hug and a kiss on the cheek and started walking back towards me. He grabbed my hand and we walked to his truck. We both climbed into the driver's side door and he looked over at me and asked. "Do you want to drive to the rest home?"

I looked down at his gear shift, then down at the clutch. I looked at him smiling and said. "Yea, sure. You probably do need a break from driving anyways right?"

"Okay, I'll help you in and walk over to the other side." He climbed in after I got in the driver's seat and put my seatbelt on. We drove towards town and pulled into the rest home. We reached Pappie's room and we sat there for a good hour before he woke up and saw us sitting there.

"I thought I heard someone come in." He looked at us smiling. He noticed that I'm there, and he said, "I thought you took her back the day we got home?" He held his arms up to me to come over and give him a hug.

I walked over to the side of his bed and bent down. I gave him a hug and a peck on the cheek smiling at him. He looked at Chris with a sheepish grin. "I just got a kiss from a beautiful young woman." He winked at Chris smiling and said, "You didn't think that you would have her to yourself for the rest of your life did you?"

"No, Pap. I didn't think that at all." Smiling, he came over to stand beside me. He took my hand and said, "You can have her anytime day or night."

I look at him with a surprised look on my face and back at Pappie. I said smiling. "Well, if I can't have Chris, I'll go with the next best man." I grabbed Pappie's hand and smiled down at him and winked at the same time towards Chris.

We sat there for about another hour and a half before heading back to Lexington. We finally got ready to leave when we both saw that he's about to go back to sleep. We got up and walked over to his bedside. Chris said, "Pap, we're going to be leaving now. I won't be back up here until next weekend. I love you." He bent down over his Grandfather and gave him a hug. He straightened back up and waited for me to say goodbye to him too.

"Pappie, we're leaving now. I'll see you the next time I come up with Chris." I bent down to give him a hug and he reached his mouth over my cheek. I looked up at him smiling and said, "I'll see you later alligator."

He said back, "After, while crocodile." He squeezed my hand and smiled at the both of us. He waved at us and fell right to sleep again. Chris and I both walked out silently and got into his truck. We put our seatbelts on and started on our long journey home.

Chris looked over at me smiling and asked. "Are you hungry?"

I looked over at him smiling back and answered. "Yes, sort of. Why? Are you?"

"Yea, I am. We'll go to this Mexican restaurant while we're here. It's pretty good, but not amazing as Cheddars is." We pulled into the parking lot and got out of the truck. We walked in together holding hands and we got seated by the host of the restaurant.

The host asked. "What would you like to drink?"

I looked at the menu and answered, smiling. "I'd like a sweet tea please, with a lemon."

Chris answered, "I'd like the same thing too please."

We both continued looking at the menu and I looked over at Chris smiling and asked him. "What do you recommend?"

He smiled at me and answered. "Knowing you, I'd say you are a taco salad person. That's what I would get. Ask for the cheese sauce." He put his menu down when he saw the waiter/host walking back to our table.

The waiter/host sat our drinks down and smiled at me. He asked, "What can I get you two?"

Chris orders for me and himself smiling. "I'd like a taco salad with cheese sauce. Another taco salad with cheese sauce and jalapenos please." He waited until the waiter/host got done writing and held the menus up for him to take. Chris looked over at me smiling.

I looked over at him smiling and asked, "What?"

"Nothing, have I ever told you how beautiful you are?"

"Yes, you have." I said smiling back at him and we held hands across the table. We just sat there staring at each other rubbing the tops of each other's hands with our thumbs. After a half an hour we're still waiting for our food. We finally saw the waiter/host walking towards our table smiling. He's carrying a tray with our taco salads. He handed me mine first and then Chris'.

The waiter/host asked us, "Do you need refills?"

Chris answered smiling. "Yes, thank you." Handing the waiter/host his glass then grabbing mine and handing it to him too. I smiled up at the waiter/host and he smiled back. He refills our glasses and brings them back.

I squeezed the lemon into my tea and pushed it to the bottom of the glass. I looked over at Chris smiling and asked. "How is your food?"

He looked up at me smiling and answered. "It's good, really. Try yours." He leaned over to my side of the table and took my fork. He got a bite of the taco salad onto the fork and guided it to my mouth. I opened my mouth and took a bite. I let the taste of the taco salad with the cheese sauce move around in my mouth.

I said smiling, "You are right. This is good!" I took another bite and waited until I got done chewing it. Then I said, "This is the first time that I've tried Mexican food at a restaurant. I've had taco salads before, but nothing can compare to this. This is good!" We kept on eating our salads in silence.

The waiter/host walked up to the table one more time and offered the check. He pushed it towards Chris and smiled at me again. He asked, "May I get you two anything else?"

Chris shook his head from side to side. "No, thank you." He handed the waiter/host his bank card and we waited for him to bring it back.

We finally got out to the truck after receiving Chris' bank card back from the waiter/host. We climbed in the truck and I'm sitting in my usual spot, right beside Chris. He started the truck up, driving towards his Aunt Molly's house to pick Brooklyn, Brittany and Kylie up.

Chapter
TWENTY SEVEN

I t's been about an hour and I'm already asleep. My head is on his shoulder and he's resting his on my head. He looked up and started to shift down. He nudged me and said. "Bree, we have a roadblock. You need to get up."

I got up and saw that there was a roadblock going on. I looked over at Brooklyn who was sitting beside me asleep. She had her seatbelt on. I looked into the back seat and saw that Brittany and Kylie also had theirs on. I quickly put mine on without moving my upper body. I finally got it on right before we got to the officer checking id's.

Chris rolls his window down and hands the officer his id. The officer looked inside the vehicle and asked, "Are these girls supposed to be with you?"

"Yes, sir. They're my Fiance's nieces." Chris said pointing at me. I waved my hand at him smiling.

The officer walked to the back of Chris' truck and came back up. "Okay, you all can go on. Just so you know we're looking for five people who have been known to stalk on young men and ladies. They were arrested in Wilmington about a week and a half ago. They were arrested in Morehead at Cave Run Lake. So, be careful. Don't pick any strangers up."

"Okay, thanks officer." Chris looked over at me and said, "I knew they wouldn't be in jail that long." He shifted his gears and we took off smoothly.

I looked over at Chris and asked. "Do you think we should have said something to the officer that checked your id at the roadblock about the people they're looking for?"

"No, I don't want to cause these girls any harm. If we do happen to run into them, then they won't know that it's us because we have different people with us."

I just shook my head up and down agreeing with him. We drove onto Lexington and the girls were finally up. They were watching the scenery and staying quiet. It really felt good to not have to hear any of them talking, just to keep my mind at ease. We finally pulled into the driveway of Brooklyn and Brittany's Grandparents, which is right next door to my Parents house. I walked them to the door and Chris and I walked over to my Parents house. I used my key to get into the front door and walk inside with Chris right behind me. He sat down on the couch and said, "Just hurry and get your things. I feel like there's something wrong at Dev and Ash's." I ran up the steps and got some of my things in my bag. I turned the light off and ran back downstairs. I found a piece of paper and a pen. I wrote a note to my Parents.

Mom & Dad,

Chris and I were here when you two were gone. I got a couple of outfits and a few of my things. I'm going to be staying at Chris' for a couple of days. At least until the first day of college. I'll call or text you all later.

Love,

Bree & Chris

I grabbed my keys and had Kylie ride with me to Chris' house. We pulled into the driveway and put our things in the foyer. We all walked out the door again and we all climbed into my orange Volkswagen Beetle. We headed straight to the hospital all the while Dev was texting Chris' phone the whole way there.

Chris looked over at the speedometer and said smiling. "Honey, if you want to get there as soon as possible I'd suggest you go the speed limit."

I looked down and saw that I'm only going forty five miles an hour, in a fifty five zone. I looked over at him smiling and punched the gas. I heard his phone go off. I looked over at him and asked, "What's he saying?"

Chris opened the message up and answered, "It says, hey at hospital they think ash has high bp (blood pressure) and high bs (blood sugar) dk (don't know) nething (anything) else yet theyre (they are) doin (doing) tests on her rn (right now) come on over if u (you) want everyone else is here includin (including) brees parents, we'll c (see) u (you) in a few!"

I looked over at him and said, "Okay, we're going to get there as soon as we can."

He texted on his phone, replying back to Dev. "k well (we'll) b (be) there asap (as soon as possible) traffic is bad" He put his phone back down on the console of my car and held my right hand. He squeezed it and smiled, "Everything is going to be alright with her. Just calm down and get there safely. I shouldn't have told you to speed up. I'm just as anxious to get there as you are." He turned the radio up a little more. He looked back at me and said, "Maybe this will help keep your mind off of the ordeal right now." He tapped his right leg and moved his head with the beat of the music on the radio. I looked into the back seat to check on my niece Kylie. I saw that she's just listening to the music just like Chris was. I smiled and shook my head. I pulled into the parking garage of the University of Kentucky Hospital. I found a parking space and we all got out of the car.

We started walking towards the entrance of the hospital and saw Dev standing at the door waiting on us. He smiled while walking over to us and gave us all a hug. He looked at Kylie and said, "You haven't changed much since the ordeal at the campsite." He pulled her beside him and kept his arm protectively over her shoulders. He said to Chris and I. "I'm so glad that you all are back home. I can't wait until this ordeal is over with. The doctors have both of us on edge." He shook his head and kept walking towards the elevators. We got on one and he pushed the fourth floor button.

We got off and followed Dev to Ash's room. Emily, Eric, Austin, Bailey, Bentley, Lance, Quinn, Camerin, Miquel, Jose, Jennifer, JoyAnna, Daimon, Zara, Zaiden, Zyra, Zyla, Zarrod, Zander, Darion, Michelle, Brooklyn, Brittany, Brionna, Blake, Bryson, Kylie, Chris and I are all there now. I looked around at everyone smiling and said. "Well, if this isn't another family reunion for us all." We all laughed and turned our attention around on Ash. I asked her, "How are you feeling now?"

"I'm feeling better, but the blood pressure and blood sugar is still spiked. They're going to keep me overnight for observation. I hate spending nights in the hospital." She sat there looking down at her feet at the foot of her bed. She looked up at her Father and said. "Daddy, will you please go get me a cheeseburger from McDonald's?"

Erick looked at her smiling and said. "No, baby. I can't! Sorry, it's the doctor's orders. I can go to the nurses station and see if they can't get something up here for you to snack on."

"Okay, do that!" She threw her arms up in the air and sighed. "I don't like being pregnant." She folds her arms up around her chest and sat there until her Father walked back with a nurse behind him.

They both walked in with smiles on their faces. Nurse Leah asked, smiling. "I heard that someone is wanting a cheeseburger from McDonald's. Now why on earth would you want to get your blood pressure to spike even higher. Are you ready for that baby to come out already?"

Ash shakes her head smiling and said, "No, I don't want him or her to come out already. That's just what I'm craving."

We all looked over at her smiling and the nurse said. "Well, honey we aren't McDonald's, but here is a cheeseburger." She handed over the cheeseburger and smiled at Ash. She takes Ash's vitals and smiles. She turned to Dev and Ash's Parents and said, "I think we have had a break in her blood pressure!" She walked out the door and walked to the nurses station. She called Ash's doctor. She hung it up smiling, walked back into the room and said. "We're still going to keep you overnight for observations. Make sure your blood pressure stays down and if it's down tomorrow morning your doctor wants to release you with some instructions and a blood sugar monitor for home." She walked back out of the room shutting the door smiling.

We all looked over at her smiling and Camerin said. "That's very good news for you." She looked at all of us and said, "I hope for Ash's sake that the next four months go by fast and easy." She sat back down beside her Husband and Children. We all visited a little more with Ash and Dev and we all left at the same time. Ash and Dev's Parents are going to get some things and bring them back for Ash and Dev for the night.

Chapter
TWENTY EIGHT

K ylie, Chris and I all leave to go to the house. It's going to be Kylie's first night at the house with Chris and I. We want her to have fun but yet safe clean fun. So we decided to order pizza and rented a movie off of the satellite.

We pulled into the driveway and got out. We all started walking up to the back door and Chris unlocked the door. Kylie walks in surprised to see that the house that Chris bought was so clean, big and not right for a bachelor. She walked upstairs with her bags and unpacked for the three days that she's going to be staying with Chris and I. Chris pulled me over to the side before I went upstairs to unpack our bags. He smiled and said, "I have something for you."

I looked up at him smiling and asked. "What is it?" He held up a set of keys then, dangling them in front of my face. I looked at them and one looked like a copy of his truck key and the other two were copies to the house. I turned to him and said, "Baby, you really didn't have to do this. I would have been able to get a copy made."

"I know, but since you are moving in slowly with me, I wanted you to have your own set, to the house and my truck. So you can be able to come and go without having to wait for me to be home." He bent down putting the keys into my hand and kissed me softly on the neck.

I returned the kiss back smiling and said, "Thank you!" I wrapped both arms around him after putting the keys on a keychain that he bought me. It reads Chris loves Breea and he bought one for himself that reads, Breea loves Chris. I said, "I appreciate the thought you put into this!" I kissed him passionately. When we pulled apart, I smiled up at him and said. "I'm going to go unpack our bags. Start a load of laundry, and wait for you and Kylie to join me in the living room."

"Okay baby!" He returned my kiss smiling his crooked smile. "Be ready tonight when we all go to bed." He finished saying that right when Kylie walked into the kitchen.

She looked around at the kitchen and looked into the living room. She looked at us both and asked, "Are you all remodeling?"

We both looked at her smiling and said. "Yes!"

"I thought so. It looked good everywhere else in the house, but here." She sat down at the table and asked. "So, what are we going to do now?"

I looked at her and smiled. "Well, Chris is going to take the tents and things into the garage and pack them away until the next time we go camping again. I'm going to go upstairs and unpack our bags. Start a load of laundry and walk back up here to visit with you and your soon to be Uncle." I started walking out the back door. I stopped and asked, "Kylie, would you like to join me?"

Kylie shook her head up and down and followed me. She said, "I need to call my Mom and let her know that we're at your house now. I hope you don't mind me using your cell phone to do it though. My battery died and I forgot my charger."

I looked at her smiling and said, "No, I don't mind. What kind of phone do you have? Maybe Chris or I have an extra charger that might fit your phone." We walked up the steps and went straight into the double doors.

"Yea!" I hand her my phone along with the charger for her phone to charge. I pointed my finger into the room where she's staying and said, "There's a plug in underneath the window. Just plug it in right there and charge your phone without turning it on. It'll help the battery life live longer."

"Okay!" She got up and walked out smiling. She finally gets her Mother's number dialed up and said, "Mom, hey!"

"Hey, baby girl! What's going on? You, Aunt Bree, Uncle Chris, Brooklyn and Brittany all have a safe trip? Did you all have fun camping out again after we left?"

"Nothing too much going on. Just going to rent a movie off of the satellite and ordered a pizza with Uncle Chris and Aunt Bree. Yes, we had a safe trip and yes we have had fun so far. I think Brooklyn and Chad are dating though."

"Oh, really? I wonder what your Uncle Darion thinks about that!" She giggled a little and said, "Are you dating that Josh guy that you just met?"

"No, Mom. I know that it wouldn't work with me living up in New York with you and Dad. It would be too hard to date him, with him living so far away."

"I would like for you to know that your Dad and I wouldn't care for you to date someone that age. It isn't the number that counts in a relationship. It's the….."

"Way he treats you! I know Mom." She shook her head from side to side, rolling her eyes and smiling. "Yea, Uncle Chris has recruited Josh, Chad, and Jeremy all to help remodel his and Aunt Bree's kitchen. So he'll be arriving to stay with them for a couple of days later on in the week." Just then she heard the doorbell ring. "Mom, hold on. Someone is at the door." She walked out to the hallway and saw me walking to answer it smiling. She heard her Mother saying something. She put the phone up to her ears and asked, "What was that Mom?"

"Who is it?"

"I don't know yet. Aunt Bree hasn't answered the door yet. I think she's halfway scared too." She looked harder and saw that it's Chad,

Jeremy and Josh. She smiled and turned around quickly. She said with a smile in her voice. "Mom, it's Josh, Jeremy and Chad. They showed up to help with the remodel of the kitchen already. I think Uncle Chris was wanting to surprise Aunt Bree with the remodel. He was wanting them to come down later in the week when she started college."

"Well, honey. Why are you still talking to me on the phone? Go, have some fun while you're still young." She whispered something to someone and said, "Kylie, your Dad and I will be seeing you in two more days. Love you!" She hangs up and doesn't even give Kylie the chance to say it back to her. She started walking back into the master bedroom and put my phone down on the stand. She sat on the bed and waited for me to come back up and finish unpacking.

I walked back up the steps and said, "Kylie, you still up here?"

"Yea, I'm in here."

"Okay!" I walked into the master bedroom smiling and said, "Josh, Jeremy, Chad, Brooklyn and Brittany are all here. They wanted to hang out a little bit with us tonight. I hope you don't mind?"

"I don't mind that." She got up and started walking towards the stairs.

I smiled and said, "Hold on, I'm done up here. I just need to get this hamper to the basement." I walked into the bathroom to get the hamper and smiled when I walked out humming to myself. We both walked down the stairs and she walked to the couch to sit beside Josh on the couch with Brooklyn and Chad holding hands. Brittany and Jeremy are on the other couch holding hands. I saw that, stopped and said, "I'll be right back. I'm going to get Chris and let him know that you all are here and put a load in the washer."

"Okay!" They all said smiling at me.

It's then that I got the feeling that they're here for more than just to hang out. Maybe to visit Chris about something. I don't know, so I shook the feeling and walked into the garage smiling.

Chris looked at me and asked. "Bree, what's wrong?"

"Nothing, just happy to be home!" I walked over to him and put my arms around him. I tip toe up to him and kissed him on the lips. I said, "Guess who's in the living room right now?"

"Who?"

"Jeremy, Brittany, Brooklyn, Chad and Josh."

He looked at me smiling with a look on his face that's almost saying. I thought I told them to wait until she started college. "Really?"

"Yea, they're in the living room waiting for you and I." I picked the hamper back up and said, turning around. "I'm just going to put these in the washer real quick."

He said smiling. "Okay, but let me help you with that." He walked over by me and took the hamper out of my hands and said. "I can't have you tripping down the stairs of the basement, and hurting yourself." We started walking towards the stairs to the basement. It's one part of the house he didn't take me to.

We got down there and I looked around smiling. I said, "I didn't realize that this was already finished. It's pretty down here." I walked over to the sectional and sat down. Blowing air out of my nose I turned to watch him load the front load washer up with the clothes. I smiled, got up, walked over and said. "Let me do this." I took the clothes from him and put them in the washer. I filled the compartments up with the detergent and fabric softener. I walked back out to see him sitting on the couch smiling and said. "I'm done! Are you ready to go back up to the living room?"

"Yea!" He walked towards me smiling and I tried to run, giggling. "Come here." He grabbed me from behind and whispered. "I love you, your butt and oh, how would I love to see you on your hands and knees naked."

I turned around and looked at him smiling. "I know you would. You will one of these days." I giggled and started running up the steps. He chased after me laughing too.

We finally made it to the kitchen and stopped. We held hands and walked into the living room to see that everyone was making out on the couches. Chris smiled and said, "What's up guys?"

Josh, Kylie, Jeremy, Brittany, Chad and Brooklyn all jumped and smiled. Chad said, "Hey, bro. What's up?"

"Nothing much. What are you all doing here?"

"Oh, we thought we would come down a little earlier than we planned. Josh, Jeremy, and myself all got a week's vacation off of work. We wanted to spend it with you. You don't mind that do you?"

Chris looked over at me asking with his look. He saw that I don't really mind it at all and turned to the guys smiling. "Okay, it's fine with me if it's fine with my soon to be Wife."

I said, smiling. "As long as we'll get a week alone after we get married. We won't even be out of the bedroom."

Chad, Josh and Jeremy all threw their fists in the air and said in unison. "Allright!"

Chris, Chad, Josh and Jeremy all finally walked into the kitchen and decided what kind of pizza to order. They all decided on Domino's and ordered five extra pizzas. One is just plain cheese, the second one is extra cheese and pepperoni. Third one is meat lovers. Fourth one is just extra cheese and sausage. Fifth one is veggie lovers pizza. They all walked back in and sat down by their girls. Chris stood up smiling and said, "The pizza will be here soon." He walks out to sit on the front porch. Chad, Josh and Jeremy all walk out and sit with him. Before Chris walked out the door with the guys he turned around and said, "Girls, it's your choice what we're going to watch tonight. Go down to the rec room, choose the movie using this, and wait for us to bring the pizza and pop down." He pulled his bank card out of his wallet and handed it to me.

I smiled up at him and shook my head from side to side and said. "No, I got it tonight." I dashed upstairs for my purse and got my bank card out. I ran back downstairs, stopped in the hallway and said smiling. "Let's go girls!" I started walking towards the basement steps and walked down the steps to the rec room. I saw the girls' reaction to the rec room and asked. "You all don't have a room like this in your houses?"

"No, we don't . We don't have a house. We all live in apartments." Brooklyn answered in awe.

I looked at all of them and said, "Oh, I didn't know that. Sorry, that you all had to be raised in a tiny apartment."

Brittany, Brooklyn and Kylie all looked at me and smiled. Brittany said, "It's okay. We're really close to our Parents that way though. It keeps us grounded and we don't do things that we're not supposed to do." She walked over to sit at one end of the sectional. While Brooklyn picked the love seat to share with Chad, and Kylie picked the other end of the sectional. Brittany asked, "So, Aunt Bree, what are we going to watch tonight?"

I looked up at her and answered, smiling. "I don't know. We have to see what is on pay per view first, then we decide." I turned the satellite on and went to the pay per view channels. We finally saw what all was playing and we decided on what we wanted to watch. I hit the select button on the remote and we are connected to the channel. I paused the flat screen and we sat around waiting for the guys to get downstairs with us.

Chris stood up and walked to the steps of the porch. He got his wallet out and took some money out of it. He handed the money over to the delivery guy and said, "Thank you!"

They all got up and followed Chris into the kitchen. Chad got the paper cups and paper plates. Jeremy grabbed the napkins and forks. Josh grabbed the liters of pop. They all started walking down the basement steps and they all sat the pizzas, paper plates, paper cups, forks, napkins and liters of pop down on the pool table. Chris walked over to me and asked, "What kind of pizza would you like? We have plain cheese, extra cheese and pepperoni, meat lovers, extra cheese and sausage and finally veggie lovers."

I answered smiling. "Veggie lovers please." I got up and started walking towards the pool table to get myself something to drink.

Chris looked at me smiling, shaking his head from side to side and said. "No, go sit down and I'll get you something to drink." He pushed me back towards the couch and I graciously walked back.

He brought me my plate smiling and asked. "What do you want to drink?"

I looked over to see what we had to drink and I answered smiling. "I would like a cup of Mt. Dew please." I turned around to see how much more time we have until the movie started and said, "Guys, we don't have that much time left. Are you sure you all don't need any help?"

They all looked over at me smiling and Jeremy said. "Thanks for asking, but no." He grabbed Brittany's plate, her cup of pop and took it to her. He walked back over to the pool table and got his. Just like Chris after he brought me my pop. Josh and Chad did the same thing for Brooklyn and Kylie. They got theirs and sat down next to their girls. I turned around and saw that Chris was unloading the washer and loading the drier.

I smiled and said, "Baby, it's about to start."

Chad looked at me and asked, "What are we watching?"

I answered, smiling. "We're watching American Reunion." I watched their reactions and saw that they're shocked. I asked, "Why? Did you all think that it was going to be something like Breaking Dawn part one? Cause if that's the case I can change it real quick?"

They all said together, "No, American Reunion is fine with us."

Chris joined me as the movie was just starting and started eating his pizza. I smiled and thought to myself. I'm going to remember this for the rest of my life. Having fun with some of my nieces and Chris' friends. I turned my attention to the movie.

We all fell asleep during the movie. Chris was the first one to wake up and noticed that we fell asleep. He looked over at me with my head resting on his shoulder. He smiled and shook me a little. "Hey, baby. We fell asleep. We need to get the girls out of here." He got up after kissing my forehead and smiling. He walked over to Brooklyn and Chad and said. "Chad, dude. You all fell asleep. The movie is over."

Chad looked up at Chris smiling and said, "Okay, dude." He got up and picked Brooklyn up. He carried her out to the vehicle and waited on the others to walk out also.

Chris walked over to Kylie and woke her up, shaking her a little bit. She looked up at him and noticed that we all fell asleep. She smiled at him and said. "I'll get Josh up." She got up and shook Josh a little. Smiling at him she said, "Josh, it's time for you to get up. You have to leave with the guys."

He woke up and looked up at her smiling and said, "I have to leave huh?" He looked towards Chris and asked. "Chris, buddy. Can the guys and I stay here after we take the girls back to their Grandparents?"

Chris looked over and said smiling. "You know you can." He got Jeremy up. "Dude everyone fell asleep!"

Jeremy got up and picked Brittany up. "Thanks man for the movie and pizza. Chad and I will be back to crash if you don't mind."

Chris watched his buddy carry his soon to be niece out the door into the cool weather. He got my phone off the stand at the end of the couch and called my Brother Darion.

"Hello?"

"Darion, it's Chris. I was wondering would you mind if Brooklyn and Brittany spent the night here tonight. We all fell asleep watching a movie on pay per view."

"Sure, that's fine. They just have to be back here before noon tomorrow. We have to show them something."

"Okay, sounds good." He hung the phone up and smiled over at me.

I looked up at him returning his smile and asked. "Well?"

"Surprisingly he said yea." Running up the steps to catch the guys walking out to their vehicle. He reached Jeremy and Brittany and said, smiling. "I just got off the phone with Darion, explained to him what happened and he said that the girls could stay here tonight. They just have to be back to their Grandparents around noon tomorrow."

Jeremy looked back to Josh and Chad. He moved his head back towards the house and the other two followed him with Brooklyn in Chad's arms. They all walked back in the house and we put the girls in one room upstairs together. We gave the guys pillows and blankets to sleep downstairs in the guest bedroom that's near the front door.

Chris and I walked up to our room and shut the double doors. We walked over to the bed and unfold the covers on the bed. I walked into the bathroom and changed into a pair of night shorts and tank top. He had already stripped his shorts off and climbed in the bed. I walked out, turning the light out in the bathroom and saw him waiting on me. I smiled at him and climbed in the bed next to him. We stayed there for a while until he started rubbing his goatee up against my neck. We started kissing each other passionately. One thing led to another and the next thing we saw was that it was morning again. We both got comfortable and fell asleep in each other's arms.

We were woken up by laughter coming from downstairs. Chris and I both looked at each other and smiled. We got up and got dressed. Chris walked downstairs while I made the bed real quick. I walked into the living room fifteen minutes later to see Chad, Brooklyn, Josh, Kylile, Jeremy, Brittany and Chris all laughing at a looney toons cartoon. I shook my head from side to side smiling and walked into the kitchen. I noticed that we didn't have anything to cook for breakfast. I waved my arm at Chris in the living room and shook my head up and down.

He walked in and asked. "What's wrong?"

"Oh, just that we don't have anything to cook for breakfast." I answered him smiling. I pulled him into a hug and said, "Thank you for last night. It was great!" I kissed him on the cheek and let go of him. I walked over to the refrigerator and was looking in it when I felt someone walk behind me and rubbed up against me. I looked over my back and saw that it was Chris. I smiled and stood up. I asked, "What are we going to do?"

"They guys and I could go to McDonalds real quick and bring back sausage biscuits."

I smiled and shook my head up and down. I said, "That sounds great to me." I followed Chris into the living room and sat down on the couch by Brooklyn, Kylie and Brittany.

Chris stood there watching everyone, smiling and said. "Guys, why don't we go out to get some breakfast from McDonalds?"

Chad, Josh and Jeremy all three looked at him smiling and Josh said. "That sounds great." All three of them stood up and walked over to my nieces. They each gave them all a kiss on the foreheads and waited on Chris.

Chris walked over to me smiling and kissed me on the lips and said. "I love you!"

"I love you!"

He turns around and walks off with the guys out the front door. The girls and I all sit down on the couch in the living room and look around at first. I stood up and said, "Come with me girls, we'll play pool while we're waiting on the guys to get back." They all got up, looked at each other and at me. I walked down the steps to the rec room and looked at the girls and smiled. I asked, "Does anyone want to play pool?"

Brooklyn, Brittany and Kylie all looked at each other smiling and Kylie answered. "No, I don't want to. I don't know how to play."

Brooklyn picks up a stick and says, smiling. "Sure Aunt Bree, I'll play." She walked over to the chalk and rubbed it on the tip of the stick. She looked over to Brittany and said. "Come on Sis. We'll show Aunt Bree and Kylie how to play pool."

Brittany shook her head up and down smiling and walked over to Brooklyn. She picked up a stick and rubbed chalk on the tip of it. She asked Brooklyn, "Do you want to break, or do I?"

Brooklyn answered her smiling. "You can, I suck at breaking."

Brittany walked down to the cue ball and hit it as hard as she could. She broke all the balls up and put two striped balls in the corner pockets. She looked up and said. "We have stripes. Aunt Bree and Kylie have solids." She stood up smiling and said, "Brooklyn it's your turn."

Brooklyn walked over to where she thought there was a shot and bent down. She lined her stick up with that particular ball and aimed it with the cue ball. She made contact with the striped ball she was aiming for. She made it into the side pocket. She stood up, smiled and said. "Brittany it's your turn!"

I looked at both of them smiling and said. "I didn't think you two would know how to play so well. Have you both been in a tournament up in New York or something?"

Brittany answered, smiling. "No, we just have a pool table at home. We play all the time." She bent down and aimed at another striped ball and got it in the corner pocket. She stood up and whispered something into Brooklyn's ear.

Brooklyn smiled and said. "Okay, we're going to take it easy on you two for now." She shot the cue ball straight up and down the table and let it come to rest right in front of a solid ball and in front of the left side pocket of the table. She stood up and shrugged her shoulders. "If only they were all that easy for everyone."

We all laughed and Kylie walked over to shoot the ball. She aims at it and it goes flying off the table. Everyone jumped and Brooklyn grabbed the ball. She walked to the other end and placed the cue ball where it should go. She looked for a shot and aimed at a striped ball that was on the other end of the table. She concentrated on it and lined it up with her eyes. She bit her tongue and struck the ball with the tip of the stick. We all watched holding our breaths and watched it fall down the pocket. She threw her arms up in the air and said. "Whew, I didn't realize how hard that shot was going to be. I didn't really think it was going to make it up there."

We looked at her in amazement. I put my pool stick down and said, smiling. "You should become a professional pool player."

Brooklyn looked at me smiling and asked. "Do you think I should?"

"Yea, I think you should. You're great at it." I walked over to the sectional and the girls followed. We all just sat around talking until we heard footsteps walking across the floor above us. I looked at the girls and smiled. I said, "I think they're back!" We all got up and ran up the steps. We ran smack dab into Chad.

He looked at us and asked. "What's the rush?" He stepped out of our way and let us all through. He shut the door behind us and walked with us into the dining room. He smiled and said to the guys. "I think they were up to something down there." He walked over to Chris and whispered. "I think we may need to walk down there to see what they were up to when we were gone."

Chris looked over at him handing out food smiling and said. "What makes you think they were up to something?" With a worried expression on his face he looked over at me. He saw that I'm laughing and having a great time with my nieces and his friends. He walked out of the dining room and walked to the basement door. He quietly opened it and started walking down the steps. He got to the bottom of the steps and saw that the pool table cover was off. He brought his hand up over his chest and coughed a little. He walked over to the door that's right by the big flat screen. He reached up on the door jam and grabbed the key. He unlocked the door and walked in shutting it behind him. He walked into the room and saw that nothing was touched. He sat down and thought. I should show Bree this before we get married. I don't want to hide anything from her, but I don't want her to know about this just yet either. It may ruin our relationship. He sat there for about an hour when he heard someone in the rec room right next to the room he was in. He walked over to the door and cracked it a tiny bit. He saw that it was me and Kylie. He listened.

"Yea, I hope that Chris won't mind us playing a game earlier." I looked around and asked, "Speaking of Chris, have you seen him since the guys got back with the food? I remember grabbing a sausage biscuit out of his hands and winking at him, but I don't ever remember him eating with us."

"No, I haven't seen Uncle Chris since they all got back." She looked around and saw the door. She smiled at me and asked. "What does that door lead to?"

I looked behind me and noticed the door. I looked back at her, smiled and said. "I don't know. He hasn't shown me that part." I walked over to it and tried to open it. I looked down at my feet and said frowning. "I guess it must be his secret room with all of his high school trophies in it or something. The door is locked." I walked back over to the pool table and grabbed the cover. I covered the pool table up and turned the light out. Kylie and I walked upstairs to clean the mess up in the dining room.

Chris saw that the light was turned out and he came out quietly looking and listening. He shuts the door real quickly behind him and locks it. He put the key back on the jam of the door and walked quickly to the steps and out the door. He opened the back door in the mud room and shut it. I looked over at him smiling and said. "Hey, what happened to you? We all missed you eating breakfast with us. Did you get anything to eat?"

"I decided I wanted to think about something, so I went out into the garage. Yes, I had something to eat. I took it out there with me." He pecked me on my cheek and I knew instantly that something was wrong.

I looked at Kylie and shrugged my shoulders. She looked at me and asked. "May I go up to my room now? I have to call Mom and see where they're at now."

"Okay, go ahead." I cleaned the mess up and walked into the living room where Chris was and stood there watching him. I walk over and sit down by him and notice that he scooted over a little. I grabbed the remote, paused the show and asked him. "What's wrong?"

He looked over at me, smiled and said. "Are you sure you want to get married?"

I looked at him and I am speechless. I don't know what to say. He said looking dead into my eyes. "Are you sure you want to get married? Especially to me?"

"What are you talking about? Yes, I'm sure I want to get married to you. You're my everything." I looked down at my ring and back up at him smiling. "Why, are you having second thoughts?"

"No, I'm not." He looked towards the stairs, sighed and said. "Do you really want to know what's wrong with me?"

"Yes, baby, I do! Please tell me."

"Okay!" He grabbed my hand and locked the front door. We walk down the basement steps. He turned the light on in the rec room and led me to the door that was shut and locked earlier. He got the key from the jam and unlocked the door. We walked into the room together and he shut the door and turned the light on.

I looked around and asked. "What is all of this?"

He sat down on the bed and sighed. "I haven't been all the way honest with you Bree. This is the old bedroom furniture I had with my first wife. We got married when she told me that she was pregnant. She said it belonged to me. I was happy with that. I married her and bought this house. We slept on this bed in the master bedroom. We were just Freshmen in college." He got up and walked over to me. I stood by the door, ready to run out because I don't want to hear the story. I turned away from him and he came around to face me. "I'm sorry I didn't tell you in the beginning. I didn't want to ruin anything between us. All I want is for you to be happy." He grabbed his head and sighed. He said, "What happened with her and I is water under the bridge now. I just wanted you to know now before we go any further with our relationship." He stood up again and walked over behind me. He tried to wrap his arms around my waist but I stepped away from him. He said, "Please, don't let this ruin our relationship. That was three years ago. She had an abortion with the baby. I couldn't forgive her for a long time for doing that. She didn't even want to talk about it with me. The day after she told me that she had the abortion, I went and filed for an annulment on our marriage. She moved out and I haven't heard anything from her since." He stepped in front of me and said. "If you want to leave, have some time to think about this engagement, I would suggest you do it now. I don't want to have to go through anything like that marriage with you. That's the reason why I've been so distant today. It's the day that we got married. Three months later on the same day we got the annulment." He stood there watching me.

I looked at him and said, "Chris, you should have said something about this sooner. I haven't kept anything from you since meeting you.

I know that this isn't right. What am I supposed to do now? Are you over her?" I noticed that Snowball was walking underneath my legs, rubbing against them. I bent down and picked her up. I looked at Chris and asked. "Why didn't you tell me about this sooner?"

"I wanted to, but my Mother told me that it would be bad for the relationship. I'm sorry I didn't tell you sooner." He walked towards me and wrapped his arms around my waist. "I love you Bree, you're the only one that I do love." He bent his head over my neck and started kissing it. He said, "I'm so sorry baby. I didn't mean to hurt you this way. If I did hurt you."

I turned around and looked at him. I smiled and wrapped my arms around his waist and said. "I know you told me that you had a scare before college, but you never told me about this. Was it with the same girl?"

"Yea, it was her. I traveled all the way from Lexington to Morehead everyday for school. When I found out that she had the abortion I got pissed and moved out for a while. I moved into a dorm room and that's how I met Chad, Josh, Jeremy and Zach. We became good friends and I returned to Lexington after graduating college and saw that she had moved out. My Parents told me that she had had different men here since the night I left. They got tired of seeing it and told her that she should take them and leave. Her name wasn't on the deed to the house, that's the reason why I got it."

I looked at him and said, "Well, that is a sad story. I'm sorry it happened to you. I just wish that you would have said something to me sooner about it, instead of leaving off in the middle of the story." I walked away from him, walked up the basement steps and turned around. "I think I'm going to go visit my Parents for a few hours." I continued walking up the steps and left him standing down in the rec room watching me walk away.

I ran up the steps crying when I ran into Kylie. I looked at her and asked. "Would you want to go with me to my Parents house? I'm going to go visit them for a little while." I walked into the master bedroom and grabbed my purse and keys.

Kylie followed me into the master bedroom and asked. "What's wrong Aunt Bree?"

"Nothing, just shocked that Chris would keep a secret from me. I don't know what to do now. I love him, I really do and I want it to work out between the two of us. I just don't know if I can trust him to tell me the truth anymore." I started walking down the steps and saw that Chris was standing there at the bottom of the steps. He smiled and handed me a rose from the neighbors yard.

"Bree, I'm sorry. I really am. I didn't mean to hurt you like this. I should have told you about it sooner. I was just enjoying the way we clicked. I never thought about finishing the story that I started telling you about. Please, come back to me tonight."

I just walked out the door and said. "I'll be back tonight, but I don't know if I'll be sleeping in the same bed as you." I turned around with Kylie right behind me, following me to my car. We both got in and I started backing out of the driveway.

Josh, Jeremy and Chad all got back to Chris' house and saw that my car wasn't there. They all walked up on the front porch and saw that Chris was sitting on the porch swing looking depressed. Chad walked over and asked. "What's up bro?"

"I told Bree about Wendy."

"Oh, okay. Where is Kylie and Bree?"

"They both went to Bree's Parents house for a few hours. She said they'll be back, but I don't know about that. She was looking like she hated me for the first time in our relationship."

Chad sat down grabbing at his hair and sighed. "Well, you do know that it's in your past. She could forgive you for it and come back. I mean it wasn't like you two were dating when it all happened."

"Yea, but it's like this too. I should have told her like I wanted to. I shouldn't have kept it a secret. Now she's probably wondering if the ring that I gave her was the one that I gave to Wendy when I proposed to her."

"No, I don't think that's the case."

Chad and Chris were both sitting on the front porch when Josh walked out. He rubbed his hand across his head and asked. "Chris, would you mind if I used your truck? Kylie just texted me and wanted me to come to Bree's Parents house. She wanted to talk to me."

Chris looked up at Josh and said, "Sure!" He dug his keys out of his pocket and handed them over to him. "Just tell her that I'm sorry. I didn't mean to keep it from her."

Josh looked at Chris and shook his head up and down. He walked off the porch and got in Chris' truck. He pulled out of the driveway and started in the direction of my Parents house.

Chris pulled his cell phone out and started typing a text message to me.

"U (you) sure ure (you are) okay i didnt (didn't) mean for dis (this) 2 (to) happen i just had to knw (know) im so sorry baby please forgive me and come back to me i still love u bree."

I finally pulled into my Parents driveway and got out of my car. I walked up to the front door and used my key to open it. I felt my phone vibrate and got it out and read the text message. It's from Cris and I cry. I texted back.

"I still love u (you) 2 (too) but i need to think"

I laid there in the dark in my bedroom waiting to hear the doorbell ring and remember that Chris has a key to my Parents house. I got up and walked downstairs, grabbed myself a cup of coffee and sat in the living room waiting for Josh to walk through the door. I heard a set of keys jangling and I got up and walked over to the front door. I saw Josh opening the door and I turned around and said. "Kylie, your boyfriend is here." I walked upstairs to my bedroom and shut the door. As soon as I shut my door, I laid on my bed. I was laying there for a few minutes when I heard a knock on my bedroom door. I got up and answered it. "Yes?"

"Aunt Bree, it's me, Kylie. Josh wanted to say something to you. Could we please come in?"

"Yea." I opened the door a little bit and let them in. I walked to my bed and sat down. I looked up at Josh and asked, "What do you have to say?"

He looked at me, smiled and said. "Sorry, I don't want to get in the middle of yours and Chris' problems. He asked me to give you a message though." He looked down at Kylie's hand and smiled at her. He said, "He wanted you to know that he didn't mean to keep it from you. It was his Mother that didn't want him to speak of that marriage ever again. He doesn't want this to ruin what you and he have. He loves you with all of his heart and soul. He wants you to come back."

I looked up at him crying and said. "I know he does. I want to go back to him, but how can I ever trust him again with the things that he needs to tell me in the beginning? I don't know if I could trust him again."

Kylie answered my question smiling. "Aunt Bree, no offense, but that's what a relationship is. You have to work on it too. It can't be just one of you working on it all the time, it has to be both of you. You've opened your heart to him and trusted him with every breath in your body. He just wants that back again. You both can have that again." She pulled out a brochure from her pants pockets. She smiled and handed it to me. "This is to let you know that my Parents almost split up once before over something like this. It was stupid and they realized that they were making a big deal out of nothing." She turned around and left Josh in the room with me. She shuts the door and doesn't come back in.

Josh walked up to me and sat down beside me. He put his arm across my shoulders, smiled and said. "Trust me when I say, Chris has had given his heart before. It got hung up and dried out. It's been a while since he's been in a relationship. He wants you to come back to him and talk this problem out. I understand his point and yours. You both have to make some sacrifices for each other though. It was in his past because I remember him showing up in the middle of the night at my dorm room. He was looking for a place to stay. He told me what had happened and I told him that we would go to the dorm office and get him a dorm. He couldn't forgive Wendy for doing what she had done. Who could blame him. She kept something from him, that was that important. He had kept something that was important from. You feel like he should have told you about it sooner and he felt the same way Wendy should have felt back then. Just think about what I said and take into consideration that he too has been hurt in almost the same way as you." He got up and walked to the door. He walked out and grabbed Kylie by the waist. They both walked down to the living room and sat and waited on me to make my mind up.

I finally thought of someone else that I could talk to about my situation with Chris. I got up off my bed and walked out my door. I ran down the steps and said to Josh and Kylie. "Hey, I'm going over to Dev and Ash's house for a few minutes. You two can come with me or stay here or go to Chris' house. I just have to talk to them real quick. I grabbed my purse and walked out the front door. I looked behind myself and saw that they were walking out the door. I got into my car and saw that they were getting into Chris' truck. They pulled out in front of me and I backed out of the driveway. I waited for traffic to clear and drove to Dev's.

I pulled up in front of Dev and Ash's house and walked to the front porch. I knocked on the door while looking at Chris' Parents house. I saw his truck there and just started bawling again.

Dev finally answered the door smiling and asked. "Bree, what's wrong?" He pulled me into the house and sat me down on the couch next to Ash.

I looked up at him smiling through my tears and said. "I'm sorry to bother you. I know you have things that you're worried about right now, but I need someone to talk to about something. I think Ash is the best person for the job."

She looked over at me and asked with concern written on her face. "What is it Bree? You can talk to us both no matter what we're going through. We're always here for you."

"Yea, I agree with Ash. Come on talk to us Sis."

"I'm sorry. Chris just told me about his past marriage." I looked up at Dev and asked. "Did you know anything about that?"

Dev looked at Ash frowning and said. "Yes, Bree. I knew about that. Sorry I didn't say anything sooner. It's in the past though. That girl, Wendy. She broke his heart when she had the abortion. She only did it because of the fact that she knew he was loaded, plus she could trap him. He knew the baby didn't even belong to him, why do you think he was so concerned about me when we found out that Ash was pregnant?"

"I never knew why it meant so much to him. I didn't think about that. He said that he got a girl pregnant when he was a senior in high school. I thought that maybe that was the reason he was so concerned with you and Ash being together. I never thought of that." I got up, stood in front of the fireplace and said. "Well, I don't know what to do. He never said those things to me before this. I just want to know why? Why did he have to keep something this important from me? Especially when we're supposed to be getting married in December." I hugged Dev and Ash both and walked out their front door. I got into my car and saw Chris driving from his Parents house. I knew he saw my car because he slowed down and shut his truck off. He came running over to my car and I sat there waiting on him.

He walked up to my car and knocked on the passenger side window. I rolled it down and heard him ask. "Could we please take a ride?"

I shook my head up and down and unlocked the door for him to get in. He smiled and said. "Baby, I didn't mean to keep something this important from you. I'm sorry that I did. I was just doing what my Mother told me to do. I didn't mean to hurt you the way I did. I know that it doesn't feel good to be hurt that way." He looked down at his hands and started crying.

I pulled out of Dev and Ash's driveway and started driving towards a park nearby. We arrived and got out. We walked beside one another not holding hands or anything and sat down next to each other on a bench. I was watching children playing soccer in a field with a bunch of Parents cheering for them. I looked over to Chris and said. "I'm sorry that I ran out like I did. I just couldn't comprehend what was happening. I didn't want to believe the story you were telling me. I'm more mad at myself than I am at you or anyone else." I fiddled with my thumbs together and just stared at my hands.

He reached over with his hand and grabbed mine. I looked up at him and smiled. He scoots closer to me and kisses me on my lips. We kissed for five minutes and he said out of breath. "I just had to see if we still have a connection." He waited for a few minutes then continued, "We do, Bree! I promise not to do anything this stupid again. I will tell you everything about my past that you don't already know." He started telling me about his past.

Chapter
TWENTY NINE

....

I t's now November, one day before Dev and Ash's wedding. I'm sitting in the dress shop waiting for Ash's appointment. I sit waiting for Ash and her pregnant seven month sidekick to show us what her wedding dress looks like. Austin, Bailey and Bentley just moved to Lexington from Wilmington. They bought the house right next to Chris and I. Everything is working out great with Chris and I and Dev and Ash now. She is considered to be free of her high blood pressure and is taking better care of herself.

"Oh, my goodness!" I look over at Ash. "She's so beautiful and glowing!" Emily says, smiling with tears coming out of her eyes. She walks over to her Daughter and gives her a hug.

I look up and smile. I stand up and walk over to her and say. "You are the most beautiful bride I have ever seen." I rub her belly and laugh. "You are the most beautiful baby of the bride ever!" Everyone laughs about it, including Ash. Chris' Mother walks in with Maddi, because Maddi is in the wedding ceremony. Maddi and Ash hit it off at the campsite at Cave Run. I look up and see them walking towards us. Christine smiles at me and embraces me, while Maddi is running towards Ash with her arms outstretched in front of her. I say smiling. "I was wondering when you two would show up." I give her a big hug and look at Ash. "Here's the blushing bride." I walk over to sit down and watch everyone with Ash. I smile and am so happy for her and Dev. I stand up and walk over to the dresses to look.

Christine spots me out of the corner of her eye and walks over to me. She says smiling. "I'm so glad that Chris took everyone else's advice and told you everything from his past. I'm sorry that I made the mistake and told him not to say anything about it to you. Mike and I both miss you coming by. We were afraid that you were mad at us."

"No, I'm not mad at you or at Mike. I have been busy with school. I haven't had time to even visit my Parents. Chris and I have been so busy with the preparations of the wedding and me going to school with him working almost non stop. Sorry, if I gave that impression to you and Mike." I hug her smiling with my ring on my left hand ring finger.

"Now, just because you and Chris are so busy doesn't mean that you can't stop by and bother us with some of the details of the wedding, even your Parents are calling us wanting to know what the deal is. We miss both of you coming by." She hugs me and walks away and watches all the bridesmaids try their dresses on.

I stand there thinking about what she said and I smile thinking to myself. I walked over to where she took a seat and smiled. "You're right. We shouldn't be staying away. I'm sorry that we haven't been visiting." I sit down beside her and wait for my turn to try on the bridesmaids dress for Ash and Dev's wedding.

She looks over at me, smiles and says. "Honey, I know that it gets a little busy sometimes, but that's what your Mother and I are here for. We want to help."

I look down at my feet and say. "Okay, again I'm so sorry for the way we may be making you and Mike and my Parents feel. We're just trying to work on our relationship a little more and make it a little more stronger. Did you know that we have a meeting tonight with the preacher that is going to marry us? You and Mike can come with us if you want!"

"Yea, okay. Mike and I will be there. What time is it? Does your Parents know about it? Are they going to be coming also?"

I look back up, smile and say. "No, not yet. I'm going to tell her right now." I get up and walk over to my Mother helping Ash's Mother, Emily help her out of the dress. I clear my throat and make them all three look behind them. I ask, "Could I please speak to my Mother real quick?"

Ash looks at me smiling and answers. "Go ahead."

I take my Mother out of the dressing room away from Ash and Emily. Smiling at her, I say. "Okay, Chris and I are going to be talking to the preacher tonight that is supposed to marry us. I was wanting to know if you and Dad would be interested in going with Christine, Mike, Chris and I?"

"Yea, your Father and I would love that! Thank you for thinking of us. How have the plans been going so far?"

"They've been coming along pretty well. We just have the flower arrangements to pick out, the wedding cake to pick, the wedding dress and tuxedos to pick out. Like I told Christine earlier, we've been pretty busy."

My Mom takes my arm and smiles. She says, "I know how it is. Your Father and I almost emptied our savings out on our wedding. It doesn't take long. How is that credit card working out for you?"

"It's working out great. We've booked a band, the chapel and the colors. It has put the deposit down on everything so far without any glitches." I stop and sit down at the chairs along with Christine and the rest of the girls that were going to be in my wedding that are in Dev and Ash's wedding. I look back up at her and say smiling. "Yea, it's been going great." I look down at my feet and say, "We haven't had any luck with the dresses or tuxedos though."

My Mom looks at me and says smiling. "Maybe the reason for that is because you haven't had me or Christine with you when you're looking." She looks around and spots the sales clerk and walks over to her. She asks, "What time does your shop close tonight?"

The sales clerk looks up at her and smiles. She answers, "We don't close until nine tonight." She continues looking in the magazine for an article to read.

"Okay, thank you. That helps us out." She walks over to the dresses and looks at them. She waves her hand over at me smiling and says. "Come on over here and help me look at the dresses."

I get up and walk over to her. I start looking alongside her and see that she's watching me. I look up at her smiling and ask. "What?"

"Nothing, I can't believe we're looking at dresses for your wedding. Your Father and I are proud of you. You know that right?"

I look down at my feet and ask. "You are?"

"Yea, why wouldn't we be?"

"Well, I don't know." I do know and I'm not going to say anything until I talk to Chris about it. I don't want to get anyone's hopes up about us expecting. I don't want to disappoint my Parents by saying that.

My Mom looks at me and asks. "Bree, what's wrong? Are you having second thoughts of marrying Chris?"

I look up at her and smile. I answer, "No, I love him. I guess it's just a little too much going on all at once. With Dev and Ash's wedding, our wedding and me going to school."

"Oh, you are feeling the pressure. It's not good to feel that pressure." She continues looking at dresses and Christine joins us. We pick out a couple of them and I go in to try them on. I walk out in the one that my soon to be Mother in-law picked out. I step up on the pedestal in the middle of the mirrors and say smiling. "I like it, but I don't like the ruffles." I get down and go back into the changing room and take that one off. I tried the one that Ash picked out for me. I walk out and stand on the pedestal again and see that it's not the one. I get down and walk back into the dressing room. I got the one that my Mother picked out for me and tried it on. I look in the mirror in the dressing room and walk out with a smile on my face. I stand up on the pedestal again and say. "I think this is the one for me." My Mother gets up smiling and goes to pick out a veil and a tiara for me. She brings that back to me and puts it on my head.

Christine gets up and says smiling, almost tearing up. "I love it, Breea! It's beautiful and it makes you beautiful too." I swing around in it and see all the others watching me and they all smile, shaking their heads up and down.

Agreeing with everyone, I say smiling. "We'll take it."

My Mother takes a picture of me in it on her phone and sends it to my Father who is at the tux fitting for Dev. He comes running into the shop after five minutes of receiving it and looks at me in it. He says with his hands over his mouth. "Oh, honey it looks beautiful on you." He looks over at the saleswoman and asks. "How much is this all going to cost me?"

She gets a catalog out and looks it up. She finds it and says. "It's two thousand seven hundred forty five dollars and sixty nine cents without tax. The veil is two hundred and the tiara is one thousand."

My Dad sits there and does the math. He says out loud. "That adds up to be three thousand nine hundred forty five dollars and sixty nine cents. Without tax. With tax it's going to be four thousand one hundred eighty two dollars and forty three cents." He looks back at the sales clerk and asks. "What's the charge on fittings?"

She looks at her sheet and says smiling. "I'll throw them in for free if you buy the dress, veil, tiara and the bridesmaid's dresses from here."

He looks at me and then at my Mother. He sees us shaking our heads and asks. "Will I get a police officer discount?"

She looks at him shaking her head up and down smiling. She says, "It'll be fifty percent off the whole purchase."

He adds that all up. He asks her one more question. "Is there a charge on the fittings for the bridesmaid's?"

"No, I don't charge a fitting fee if you buy the dresses from here. If you bring in a dress that I don't have then I will charge."

"Okay, thanks." He adds that up in his head. He says smiling. "If that's what you want the dress, veil, shoes and tiara then we'll take it."

I start crying and laughing at the same time. "Thank you Daddy!" I give him a hug.

He says, "Her dress alone will end up being two thousand ninety one dollars and thirty one cents." He asks the clerk. "How much are the shoes?"

"Depends on the style." She walks into the back and brings out six pairs of shoes in all different styles. He looks at them and says. "You ladies have fun picking the shoes out. I gotta run down here to the tux shop. I got to get fitted for a tux." He turns around and says to his Wife. "I don't care what it costs us. We have the money. Get what she wants." He kisses her and runs out the door.

Mom turns around smiling and says. "Okay, Bree. I know we've already decided on who the bridesmaids are going to be. Why don't you call them and tell them to get here as quickly as they possibly can. I'm going to call Grandma Lena." She starts calling her and walks outside before I can tell her that all the bridesmaid's are already here.

"Hello, The Anderson residence." Renee answers the telephone.

"Yea, Renee. It's Quinn. Is Lena around?"

"Yes, hold on please." She takes the phone over to my Grandmother. She says, "It's Quinn on the phone." She hands the phone to Lena.

"Hello, dear. How are we today?"

"We're doing great Lena. How are you feeling today?"

"Great, except for all these people coming in and out of my house. I'm so tired of them all being here. I'm ready to just walk out and never come back." She sighs and asks Quinn. "To what do I owe this pleasure?"

"I was calling with some great news!"

"Oh?"

"Yea, Bree and Chris are at the tuxedo and dress shop now."

"Oh, good! I can't wait to see them. I hope they plan on coming out to the house to see me sometime soon."

"Yes, we can arrange that." Mom sighs and smiles asking. "Bree and I would like for you to come to David's Bridal, to try on some dresses with us. We've already found her dress. We just have to find the bridesmaid's and Mother dresses."

"Oh, that would be so welcomed right now. I would love to come and be in on the excitement."

"Okay, I guess we'll see you in about twenty minutes then?"

"Yes, dear you all will." She hangs the phone up and smiles. She knew her Granddaughter would work things out with Chris. They just had to give me my space so that I could come to my senses. She finds Renee and says smiling. "I just got some great news about my Granddaughter. Your Daughter in-law's Sister. The wedding is happening in four weeks. They need me at David's Bridal right now. Could you please drop everything and take me?"

"Yes, Ms. Lena. Just let me get my purse and the keys." Renee walks off into the mud room to find her purse and keys. She walks back to Lena and says. "We're all set and ready to go."

"Okay, dear." She gets up and makes her way slowly out to the car. She gets in the back seat and puts her seatbelt on. She sits back and relaxes for the drive to David's Bridal.

"I thought it looked nice on you girls." Mom says to Camerin, Chelsea, Michelle, Paige, Maddi, Zara, Cara and Ashley.

They all look at her and smile. "Well, it doesn't matter what we think. It's not our day. It's Bree and Chris' day. It should matter what she thinks." Camerin says smiling.

"I don't really care what you all wear. As long as it goes with the color theme and you all are comfortable in the dresses we pick out." I look out the window of the shop and see my Grandmother fussing with Renee. I look at my Mother, smile and say. "I'll be right back." I walk outside to where my Grandmother and Renee were and say, smiling. "Grandma, it's so nice to see you!" I walk over to her and give her a big hug and a peck on the cheek.

She looks up at me smiling and says. "It's about time we get this wedding underway. You and Chris took a long time getting things in order." She grabs my arm and starts walking with me.

I look back at Renee and say smiling. "You can come in too if you want. This way you can see your Daughter in-law."

"Okay, thanks Ms. Breea." Renee says cheerfully and walks in behind us.

"Okay, Grandmother is here. Let's get her to try a dress on while you girls debate over the dresses, styles and shoes." Mom says and walks over to me and my Grandmother. She gives her a peck on the cheek and smiles. She says, "So, Lena! We were thinking that you need to wear something that is matching, in style and age appropriate. Your dress will be matching Christine's Mother's dress. Bree wants it that way."

Lena looks over to Mom and rolls her eyes. "Don't you mean you want it that way dear? It's not the bride's decision to make. It's the Mother of the Bride's decision." She put her hand on Mom's forearm, winking and smiling at her. She focuses her attention on Christine. "So, this must be Christine?" She holds her hand out, extending her arm to shake Christine's hand.

Christine looks at her and smiles. Then she said, "No, in my family we don't shake hands. We hug one another. We're going to be family soon, so we might as well start practicing for holiday get-togethers." We all laugh, besides my Grandmother. She just looks at us all like we're crazy.

We finally get the dresses picked out for the bridesmaids and matron of honor which is Ash. It is a red strapless satin gown that has a sash with it. We get the dresses picked out for the Mothers and Grandmothers also. We decided that their dresses will be the color green. The men in the wedding party are going to be dressed in black tuxedos with green and red cumberbund. Christine, my Mom and I all go to the flower shop. Christine is on the phone with Chris asking him to come down to the flower shop with us and then we're going to pick out the cake. He finally agrees to come. He'll be here in twenty minutes or so. Christine hangs the phone up, when we're passing a cafe'. My Mom looks at us both and asks, smiling. "Would you two care to stop in here? I have got to get some energy."

"Sure! I could use some energy myself." Christine says smiling. "Between the caterer and Chris, I think I'm going to go nuts."

We both look at her then and I ask. "What do you mean? Chris is doing okay with all of this isn't he?"

"Yeah, he is. He just doesn't see what the big deal is about him being involved in everything." She wipes her brow and blows out her breath. "When I got married, it was all on the bride and her Parents. Now, it's like everything that the bride wants she has to consult with the groom or his Parents. Though I don't mind because I don't have any girls. Just Chris and he's the only child that I'll ever have. I couldn't see Mike and myself not helping with the expenses a little."

My Mom looks over at her and smiles. "Yeah, I guess it's true. They say it's not just the bride's job to plan the whole thing without the input of the groom." She looks at me smiling and winks. She says, "We appreciate that you and Mike are taking care of the reception. We wouldn't want it any other way. Where is the reception going to be held?"

"It's going to be held at the ballroom inside the Hampton Inn Hotel. Eric and Emily offered it to us for free. We don't have to pay for the room. Most importantly he threw in the bar also, free of charge. He said that if it wasn't for you and Bree, that his little girl probably wouldn't have met Dev. He's very thankful for that."

Mom smiles and says. "Well, there's something for free. Glad it could be something so elegant as that ballroom inside the Hampton Inn. It's gorgeous in that room."

I looked over at my Mother and asked. "Have you been in it Mom?"

"Yes, I have. We had our company Christmas party there last year. It's a beautiful space. You'll love it Bree." She notices Chris' truck pulling into a vacant parking space. She starts running towards him and throws her arms out. "Chris, I'm so glad you could come."

"Yeah, me too." He hugs her and looks for me. Smiling, he walks over to me and my heart skips a beat. I smile back. He hugs and asks, "What kind of an opinion are you looking for from me concerning the flowers and the cake? I have an appointment tomorrow for the tuxedo

fittings. I think my Father and I have found the ones we want to wear."
He walks over to his Mother and kisses her on her cheek and does the
same with my Grandmother and Mother. He walks back to me and
whispers in my ear. "Have you told them yet?"

I smile up at him and give him a passionate kiss. Then I answered
him. "I don't know, maybe your input is more important than you think
it is. No, I haven't told anyone anything yet. I don't know how they'll
take it." We embraced each other and stayed like that for twenty minutes.

Chris is smiling and says. "Okay, I guess my input for the cake
is important." He grabs my hand. He whispers in my ear smiling. "I
think we should have dinner tonight and invite them over to tell them.
I don't want them to be in the dark on this. I want everyone to know
what we're expecting."

I look up at him smiling and say. "Okay, all that's fine and dandy,
but I thought we were going to wait until we found out for sure." I
look up at him smiling and see that he's hurt a little, and I continue. "I
mean, I wouldn't mind telling them, but I want to be sure that's why
I've been getting up in the mornings being sick."

"Okay, sounds good to me, Baby!" He pecks me on the cheek.

"I can't wait! All this shopping is making me want to get married
sooner." I grab his hand and walk to the flower shop, only to see that
it was closed already. So, we continued to walk to the cake shop. We
look around at the different pictures of wedding cakes that they have.
I look up and see his facial expression and I look into the mirror to see
mine. It was the same facial expressions we had on both of our faces.

I was smiling when we sat down still holding hands when Martha
walked out. She says smiling at us. "Now, I hear that the wedding is in
December. I can make a cake the night before, decorate it the way you
want it and deliver it the next morning. I usually wait until then anyway,
because the fresher the cake, the fresher your heart is." She sits down
smiling and asks us. "Did that make sense?"

We shake our heads up and down smiling. My Mom stands up and
says. "They're getting married on the twenty third, that's when all the

family gets together. We wanted to make sure we could kill two birds with one stone. Instead of having the family fly or drive in for dinner one week, then having to turn right back around again and heading this way for the wedding."

"Yeah, I get that. That was smart thinking of the two that are getting married." Martha says smiling. "My Husband and I had a Thanksgiving wedding. It was so beautiful too. We had all the fall colors in it. What colors are you two wanting? I just thought that maybe since it was so close to Christmas, that you all decided on the color theme of Christmas."

I look over to Chris and see that he's about to speak. "Yes, we've decided on the colors to be red, black, white and green. We never thought about incorporating the Christmas colors in it."

"Well, that's a good answer. I was just simply asking." She writes his statement down and looks up at a book. She stands up and gets it down. She hands it over to us smiling. She says, "These are all the cakes that I have done, besides what's up on the wall. Go through it while I go get us some samples to see what flavor you would like for the cake." She gets up and walks into the back of her shop. She disappears behind two stainless steel swinging doors.

Chris and I are marking all the cakes that we like with little stickers. The orange stickers mean that we like it but not the price. The green stickers mean that we love it but not the price. The pink stickers mean that we absolutely love it and the price. The red stickers mean that we hate it all together. As Chris was flipping through the cake book with me. My Mother, his Mother and both of our Grandmothers were over at a little table looking out of the window drinking coffee. They were talking in hushed tones. I turn back to him and see that he's waiting for me to put a sticker on the picture.

I put a red sticker on one that he put an orange sticker on. I look up at him and ask, smiling. "Do you really like that cake?"

He looks at me, smiles and answers. "It doesn't matter to me what kind of cake we get. What it looks like. Hell, Bree. It's taking all of my energy to sit here going through these when we can walk right down the street to the Justice of the Peace."

"Awh, I love you too." I kiss him and smile. We were almost done looking at the book when we remembered she had some up on the wall. We close the book up and sit it on the little table. We get up and look at the cakes up on the wall. I point to one and ask. "What do you think about this one?"

He looks at it and smiles. He says, "If that's the style you want." He puts an orange sticker on it. We continue looking at the pictures of the cakes on the wall and we come across this one that is square. It has five tiers to it. I stand there looking at it smiling. I look over at Chris and see his expression also. I put the pink sticker on it and the price is reasonable. The cake was only fifteen hundred dollars. Happy with the decision we just made, we show our Mothers and Grandmothers. They walk over to us and smile.

Christine says. "I love it. It's simple, elegant and just beautiful like the groom and bride are going to be." She hugs and kisses Chris' cheek. While my Mother agrees with her and is doing the same to me. They both switch and do the same thing. They walk back over and sit in the chairs.

Martha walks out into the shop with a tray full of little bites of cakes and a pot of tea. She sits it down and smiles at us. She holds her finger up to us and says smiling. "Ladies, if you would like to come over and taste these samples with us. It usually takes more than just the couple to pick out the flavors." She turns to us and asks. "What cake did you two pick out?" She grabs the book and sees that there weren't any pink stickers throughout the whole book. She puts it down and walks over to the wall. She finds the picture that I put the pink sticker on and pulls it off the wall. She smiles and says. "This is my most popular cake. With all the different tiers to it we can do a variety of flavors. You can have the bottom layer of your most favorite flavor, then with the other ones you can have the other flavors that you like, but not love. On the top layer you have again the flavor you absolutely love." She sits down and hands us each a plate, saying. "This one is the strawberry flavor."

We all take a bite of it and shake our heads up and down. Chris and I like it, but not love it. I see that he agrees with me smiling. "We like this one."

"Okay, I'll mark that one down on the list. We have to choose at least four flavors." She writes that one on the list and hands us another plate. "This one has a lemon flavor."

We all take a bite of it. It's lemon alright. It was very sour. Chris sees the looks on everyone's faces and says smiling. "No, not this one. That's for sure." Pointing over to his Mother's face. We all laugh a little and she takes our plates.

She says, "Okay, that one's out of the question, as it usually is." She picks up another flavor. She hands us the plates and says. "This one is chocolate."

We take a bite of it and like it. I say, "We like this one." I have my plate to her smiling. The others do the same thing.

"Okay, chocolate goes down." She writes it on the list and hands us all another plate. "This one is called strawberry, vanilla swirl. It's a marble cake."

We all take a bite of this one and like it. Chris loves it and I see his expression and say smiling. "The groom and I love this one. We definitely want it on the list."

She writes it on the list and hands us all another plate while taking the other ones up. She says, "This one is called chocolate, strawberry swirl."

We tried it and it's really good. I see Chris' expression and say smiling. "I think this one is definitely going on the list too. We love it also!"

"Okie dokey!" She writes it down on the list too. She hands us another plate and says smiling. "This is the last flavor we have. It's vanilla."

We all take a bite of it. I look around and see their expressions and say, smiling. "I think that we should put this on the list for people who are allergic to chocolate and strawberry."

"Okay, that one is my most picked over." She picks the plates back up and puts them on the tray. She sits down and says. "Now, you all put down strawberry, chocolate, chocolate strawberry swirl and the traditional vanilla."

Chris and I both shake our heads up and down smiling. Chris answers her. "Yes, we want all those flavors."

Martha looks at us smiling and asks. "Which ones would you prefer for each of the tiers?"

We look at each other smiling and I answer. "We would like for the chocolate strawberry swirl to be on the top layer. The bottom layer would be vanilla. The second layer would be chocolate. The third layer we would like to be strawberry, the fourth layer we would like vanilla strawberry swirl." I look over to Chris and see that he's happy with what I chose. I look back at her and ask. "With all the different flavors of the cakes, would it cost more?"

"No, honey. It will only cost fifteen hundred. I need half of it today, then you can pay the other half when we deliver it to the reception site."

"Okay!" I get up and hand Martha the credit card for the wedding. "Thank you for seeing us on such short notice." I shake her hand and let her go down the line to Chris, Christine, Grandma Lena, Mammie, Marjorie and my Mom. We are all smiling as we all walk out of the cake shop and head to our cars. I'm walking with Mom and Chris. I see what time it already is and say. "It's almost eight o'clock now. We need to get to the Chapel."

So we all just started walking to the Chapel. It's right up the street anyways. We met my Dad, Mik, Pappie, Leelum and Marvin there. We all greet each other and hug and kisses are exchanged. We all walk into the Chapel and see Pastor Kevin. He walks up to us smiling and says. "It's so nice to meet Bree and Chris' Parents and look like Grandparents."

Chris looks back at everyone smiling and answers. "Yes, mine and Bree's Parents. Christine, Mike, Lance, Quinn, Lena, Mammie, Pappie, Marjorie and Marvin." He turns back around facing Pastor Kevin. "I guess we're ready to get started."

We went in to have the last meeting with Pastor Kevin and both sets of Parents and Grandparents were involved. It was an intense meeting but a good one. Everyone got their fears out on the table and their likes about Chris and I being a couple for life. We all walk out of the doors of the Chapel and stop walking. Chris smiles and whispers in my ear. "I'll meet you at the house!" He pauses and gives me a kiss and says. "I love you, Baby!"

I grab his hand and pull him back towards me. I give him a passionate kiss and say, "I love you Babe!" We both went our seperate ways to our vehicles. I drove my Mother back home and said. "Love you Mom. Thanks for what you and Daddy are paying for."

I finally pull into mine and Chris' driveway and get out of my car. I started walking into the house and noticed that someone was watching me. I turn around to look and I don't recognize who it is. So, I quickly walked inside the house. Staring out the window, I didn't see Chris standing there waiting on me.

He walked over to me, wondering what was wrong with me. He grabbed me by my waist and asked. "What's wrong Baby?"

I jump a few feet away from him and turn around quickly. I stare at him trying to focus on who I'm seeing right now. I finally notice that it's Chris standing in front of me. I finally get my voice and say, "There was someone standing outside our house on the other side of the street watching me get out of my car and walking up to the house."

Chris walks over to the window and looks out. He stands there looking out for at least ten minutes then pulls the curtain closed. "Could you make out how tall or what color he was?"

I looked at him and shook my head from side to side. Shivering I wrapped my arms around him, holding him tightly against me. We stood there for five minutes and he asked. "How about we lock the doors and windows and climb in bed?"

I shake my head up and down afraid to speak. I follow him while he locks all the windows and doors. We climb the stairs and turn the lights off as we walk into our room. We both get ready for bed, climb in and kiss each other while holding onto each other.

Chapter
THIRTY

....

W e got up and noticed what time it was. We both look at each other and smile. We lay there just talking with one another and I finally said. "It feels so good to have almost everything done for the wedding. I think all we have to do is the flowers, then everything else is done.: I paused for a minute and continued, smiling. "I can't wait to marry you Christopher Michael Lee!" I kissed him and started feeling nauseated. I ran into the bathroom and threw up.

Chris ran in after me and asked. "Are you okay, Baby?"

I looked up at him from the floor and answered. "I feel fine, what is going on?"

He walked to the sink and got me a glass of water. He walked over to me and handed it to me smiling. "Here, Baby. I think I know what is going on with you."

I looked up at him again from the floor, afraid to move away from the commode. I asked, "What do you mean?"

"I think you may be pregnant." He looked down at his feet and continued. "Remember Cave Run Lake?"

"Yes, I do but I've been taking my birth control."

"Well, maybe we need to go to the store to get a pregnancy test." He looked at me again and said. "It's just a suggestion. I just know that women have morning sickness all day long if they're pregnant. Plus, we weren't double protecting ourselves either. I didn't wear a condom. So, it could be possible, Baby."

I sit there and think about what he's saying and I start counting the days in my head and on my fingers. Finally a light bulb started glowing in my head and I said. "No offense Babe, but I hope I'm not pregnant." I sat there hugging myself and he walked over to me and sat on the floor right next to me.

Rubbing my upper arm he asked. "So, you don't want to be pregnant anytime soon?"

I looked at him and said, "Honestly, no Babe. I want to be married to you for a year at least. I want to be able to go out and do things without having to worry about what I'm doing. If what I'm doing is hurting the baby or not."

"Yes, I see your point. I wouldn't mind you being pregnant, but at the same time I want you to have and get what you want too. I want to make you happy, but we may want to make sure that isn't what is causing you to get sick here recently. That way if the test is negative we can get you to a doctor to figure out what it is."

"I know Babe. I think you may need to go to the store to get a test. Then we'll take it from there." He really made me feel more comfortable with being pregnant that a little part of me wanted to be to make him happy. But there's another part of me that wants to take our time to have a baby together.

Chris got up and kissed my forehead, and out of the bathroom he walked. I noticed that he was walking out with his head hanging down. Like, I just gave him the worst news ever. I got up and felt a little dizzy, and walked into the bedroom. I looked over at my phone and texted Ash. "Hey its (it's) me bree i was wonderin (wondering) how did u find out u were prego (pregnant)"

I walked into our closet and got out an outfit to wear to the hotel for Ash and Dev's wedding that day. I was going to wear a button up shirt with a pair of shorts and sandals. While waiting for her to reply.

She replied, "i found out that i was expecting when my mom suggested for me to go to the er to get tested after me runnin (running) into yall (you all) + (plus) i was gettin (getting) sick every day for 3 (three) months everytime my mom would fix my fav (favorite) food i would run 2 da (the) bathroom and throw up."

"Ok, thanks (thanks) jw (just wondering) is all", That's all I sent to her. I went ahead and got dressed and waited for Chris to get back.

Finally Chris got back with the test and I took it as soon as he walked in the room. We were waiting for the results. We were just sitting there with a little distance between us. I looked over at him and saw that he was staring at the floor a little disappointed to learn what I had told him before the trip to the store. I reach over to grab his hand. He lets me for a few seconds, then let's go. I scooted closer to him and said. "I'm sorry if I hurt you by saying that I don't want a baby right now, but it's the truth Babe. I want us to have some more time together. It would be nice to be pregnant with your baby, but when we are both ready for that. I don't think that I am ready for that."

He got up and rubbed his head, pacing back and forth. Finally, he sat down next to me, grabbed my hand and started rubbing the top of it with his thumb. "I understand what you are saying, but ever since Wendy said that she was getting an abortion with my baby, that wasn't mine, I've wanted kids. It was like something clicked inside me and said that it was my time to become a Father." He shifted towards me, looked straight into my eyes and said. "I love you and nothing will ever change that. Not your opinion, not you not wanting a baby right now, and most definitely not you wanting some more time with just us." He kissed me passionately until we both heard the timer buzzing. We stopped and looked at each other. We both got up and ran to the bathroom.

I picked the test up and saw the result. Something inside me made me instantly happy. I felt like I was ready to be a Mom. I looked at him smiling and said, "Congratulations, Daddy!"

"Really?" He looked at me and asked.

I stood there by the sink shaking my head up and down smiling. He walked over to me and picked me up, kissed me softly and gently put me back on my feet on the floor. He felt my stomach and started rubbing it, then kissed it. He said, "This little guy or girl is going to be such a blessing to the both of us. I'm going to enjoy being a Father." He kissed me again for two more minutes, then realized that we had to get ready for Dev and Ash's wedding today at two o'clock. "You want to take a shower with me?"

I got up smiling and got undressed again. We fooled around while in the shower. We washed each other's bodies, we got out and he walked into our bedroom to get his tux, and got dressed. I threw my clothes back on that I had on before he returned from the store. I walked out with my hair a mess and started taking his bed sheets off. I said while looking at him smiling. "I think we may need to wash these."

He looked over at me smiling and asked. "Why is that?"

"Because of what we did last night. I think it's a no-brainer to get it done before tonight." I walked over and smacked him on his ass smiling and said. "You know you have a great looking ass!" I started running for the door and down the steps.

He ran after me saying. "I'll get you soon. Just wait and see!" He sat down on the couch and waited for me to return from the basement.

I took the sheets, blankets and pillow cases to the laundry room and put them all in the washer. I put the washing detergent in, fabric softener and started the washer up. I shut the door and walked back upstairs. I walked into the living room and saw him sitting there waiting patiently for me. I smiled and asked. "When are you going to get me again?"

"I think you'll find that out tonight at Dev and Ash's wedding. You wait and find out." He got up with his tux hanging on the door of the hall closet. He grabbed it, smiled and asked. "Are you ready to go to the hotel to meet Ash, Camerin, Cara, Michelle, Zara, Chelsea, Callie and Maddi?"

I looked at him smiling because I'm so happy and shook my head up and down. I ran up the steps to fetch my purse from the bedroom and made a mental note to vacuum the rose petals up. I headed back downstairs to where Chris was waiting for me at the foot of the steps smiling. I finally got down to him, smiling up at him and said. "I'm waiting on you now."

We got out of the house and I locked the door up. I ran over to his truck and climbed in. We drove past my Parents' house on the way to the hotel and saw that they're both outside waving at us while they're gardening. We waved back and finally arrived at the Hampton Inn. We walked in and were greeted by Dalton and Paige. Chris asked, "Where is the Groom's room?"

Dalton answered smiling. "Right this way Chris." They started walking towards the Groom's room talking.

I looked over at Paige and asked her, smiling. "Where is Ash's room?"

Paige looked at me smiling and answered. "It's on the top floor. Room six zero one. I'm headed that way now if you want to follow me."

Chris and Dalton finally got to Dev's room and knocked on the door. Darion answered the door and said smiling real big. "Come on Chris and Dalton. We've been waiting for you two." They walked in and Chris saw that Dev was already dressed in his tux. He walked into the rest of the room and sees Eric, Darion, Daimon, Dev, Scott, Kyle, Blake, Justin, Josiah, Jordan, Miquel, Jose, Carson, Derrick, Deidrich, Zaiden, Zarrod, Zander, Ian, Austin, Bentley and Zach. He smiled at all of them and said. "Hi everyone."

They all nodded their heads towards him smiling and Darion asked. "How are you?"

Chris looked at him and answered, smiling. "I'm good, very good!" He clapped Darion on the back and smiled, starting to undress and into his tux.

Paige and I walked up to the door from the elevator and knocked. Emily opened the door smiling and said. "Come on, girls. You two are

315

almost late!" She pulled us in by our shirt tails and said. "Paige you need your makeup done first while Breea gets her hair done. Then it's time to switch." She walked into the room with us and that's when I saw everyone. I saw Cara, Michelle, Brooklyn, Brittany, Brionna, Chelsea, JoHannah, Josie, Camerin, Jennifer, JoyAnna, Callie, Blithe, Bethany, Zara, Zyla, Zyra, Bailey and Maddi.

I smiled at everyone and said, "Hey girls! Sorry I'm a little late. Had trouble finding a parking spot." I sat down in the chair to let Matilda do her thing with my hair. I looked into the mirror and saw what she's done with it and smiled looking at Ash in her dress. "You look beautiful Ash. How does my hair look?"

"It looks just the way I pictured it would look, and thank you. You're going to look stunning too. As do all of my bridesmaids!" She held up a glass of milk smiling and everyone else held theirs up also. I walked over to the makeup and got my face painted by Melinda. I looked into the mirror and said. "Thank you, it's beautiful!" I got up and walked into the bathroom to change into my dress. I have a short train on the back of it because I'm the matron of honor. I walked out smiling at everyone and we started walking down to the formal room of the hotel. We all walked into a tiny room and waited while guests were being seated by Chad, Josh and Jeremy.

Ash and Dev's wedding party consisted of the following people. Father of the bride, Eric William Hampton. Mother of the bride, Emily Dawn Hampton. Mother of the groom, Dianna Brianne DeAtley. Father of the groom, Darrin Bryan DeAtley. Matron of honor, Breea Leighann Anderson. Best man, Christopher Michael Lee. First bridesmaid, Bailey Nicole Hampton. First groomsman, Austin Eric Hampton. Second bridesmaid, Michelle Gayle Conway. Second groomsman, Darion Ray Conway. Third bridesmaid, Cara LaRhae Wallingford. Third groomsman, Scott Raymond Wallingford. Fourth bridesmaid, Zara Nicole Sweet. Fourth groomsman, Daimon Michael Sweet. Fifth bridesmaid, Callie Michelle Schnieder. Fifth groomsman, Carson William Schnieder. Sixth bridesmaid, Camerin LeTerra

Rodriquez. Sixth groomsman, Miquel Terrance Rodriquez. Seventh bridesmaid, Chelsea Annette White. Seventh groomsman, Justin Ray White. Eighth bridesmaid, Paige Renee Porter. Eighth groomsman, Dalton Terrance Sweet. Ninth bridesmaid, Maddison Jane Jones. Ninth groomsman, Zachary Lane Roark. Junior bride, Brionna Michelle Conway. Junior groom, Deidrich William Schniedcr. Flower girl, Josie Chelsea White. Ring bearer, Zander Terrance Sweet. First usher, Chad Landon Manning. Second usher, Joshua David Jones. Third usher, Jeremy Wayde Roark. Fourth usher, Kyle Raymond Wallingford.

We finally got word that it's about time to line up in order. We are waiting for Kyle to come in and escort Emily down the aisle. While we're for him we hear the music start to play. That's our cue to walk on out leaving Ash and her Father in the room. We walk down the corridor in this order. Kyle and Emily walk down smiling and they are followed by Jeremy and Dianna. Zach and Maddi walk out smiling, then it's Dalton and Paige, Justin and Chelsea, Miquel and Camerin, Carson and Callie, Daimon and Zara, Scott and Cara, Darion and Michelle, Austin and Bailey. Then it's time for the junior bride and groom to walk down, which is again, Deidrich and Brionna. After them it's the flower girl and ring bearer which is again, Zarrod and Josie. Finally it's my turn to walk down the aisle. I stopped just in front of the door smiling and waiting for our cue to walk. I finally heard it in the music and started walking slowly down. I looked back and smiled at Ash, I winked at her and looked straight ahead. I got to my spot and waited until the music changed. The wedding march started to play on the organ, then Eric and Ash started walking down the aisle smiling. They finally get to the end of the aisle and I started fluffing her train of her dress to fan out before the crowd. The preacher started talking. "Dear heavenly Father we come together today to join this man Devin Bryan DeAtley and this woman Ashley Dawn Hampton in holy matrimony. Who gives the woman?"

Eric answers smiling and tearing up. "Her Mother and I." He raises her veil over her head and kisses her on the cheek. He walks off stage and sits down with his Wife and Grandson.

317

Preacher Kent starts saying. "This is a day of rejoicing in the life that is going to be shared by one new soul. Let us pray." We all bow our heads and listen to the preacher as he prays about patience and understanding. Working together in the times that life calls for and helping each other out in the times that life throws curveballs. I blocked the rest out because I felt eyes on me and I peek through my hair and see that it's Chris. He's smiling so big that I think I see some mischievousness in it. I close my eyes and wait for the prayer to be over with. When it finally is, the preacher says. "It's time for the Mothers of the bride and groom to light the candles that represent the bride and groom."

Emily hands Bentley off to his Grandfather and smooths out her skirt. She walks up to the stage and waits till Dianna is at the other side. They both walk up the steps and over to the middle of the stage where the unity candle is located. Dianna and Emily both light the two little candles on each side of the big candle. Dianna walks over to Devin and gives him a kiss on the cheek and Emily does the same to Ash. They walk back to their seats.

The preacher says. "These two candles that were just lit by the Mothers of the groom and bride represent the groom and bride's past lives. I find it amazing that everyone is doing that in their ceremonies. It represents these two becoming one. That's when they will walk over and light the unity candle in the middle, by using the two individual candles on the side." That was my cue to take Ash's bouquet from her. I take it smiling at her and see that she's been tearing up. I hand her a tissue when I grab the bouquet out of her hand. They walk over to the candle while their favorite song is sung by Blithe LeighAnn Schnieder. She sings the song, "God Gave Me You," by Blake Shelton. They finally get done and walk back over to the preacher. I bend down to fan out Ash's train once more while they're both facing each other.

The preacher says. "It's time for your vows. Repeat after me please, Devin." He turns a page in his bible and says. "I, Devin Bryan DeAtley."

"I, Devin Bryan DeAtley."

"Take you Ashley Dawn Hampton." Brother Kent says smiling.

"Take you Ashley Dawn Hampton." Devin repeats.

"To be my lawfully wedded wife." Brother Kent says, still smiling.

"To be my lawfully wedded wife." Devin repeats, smiling.

"To love, honor, cherish, and obey you." Broth Kent says smiling even bigger now.

"To love, honor, cherish and obey you." Devin repeats, smiling bigger and bigger by the minute.

"In sickness, and in health, for richer or poorer."

"In sickness, and in health, for richer or poorer."

"All the days of my life."

"All the days of my life." Devin repeats, smiling really big.

"This is my solemn vow."

"This is my solemn vow." Devin repeats, smiling as big as big could get because he's done now.

Brother Kent turns to Ashley smiling and says. "Repeat after me please. I, Ashley Dawn Hampton."

"I, Ashley Dawn Hampton."

"Take thee Devin Bryan DeAtley." Brother Kent says.

"Take thee Devin Bryan DeAtley." Ashley repeating.

"To be my lawfully wedded husband." Brother Kent says, smiling.

"To be my lawfully wedded husband." Ashley repeats, smiling while a tear is falling down her cheek.

"To love, honor, cherish and obey you." Brother Kent says, still smiling.

"To love, honor, cherish and obey you." Ashley says, still crying and smiling at the same time.

"In sickness and in health, for richer or poorer." Brother Kent says, smiling bigger.

"In sickness and in health, for richer or poorer." Ashley repeats as she's still crying silently and smiling.

"All the days of my life." Brother Kent says, still smiling bigger.

"All the days of my life." Ashley repeats, still crying silently while smiling bigger.

"This is my solemn vow." Brother Kent turns the page in his bible, still smiling.

"This is my solemn vow." Ashley repeats smiling while crying still.

Brother Kent asks. "What symbol do you two choose today?"

Ash and Dev both say together smiling. "This ring." Dev turns around to Chris holding his hand out. Chris bends down to get the wedding bands off the ring bearer's pillow which is Zaiden. Chris finally gets them and hands them over to Brother Kent. Brother Kent hands me Dev's wedding band and I hold on to it for now. He hands Chris, Ash's wedding band to hold on to.

Chris hands Dev, Ash's wedding band. He slides it on her left ring finger while saying. "I love you Ashley. I'll love you even when we won't see eye to eye. I'll love you when you seem like you're having a bad day and want it all to yourself. I'll love you till the day I die. This is my second solemn vow."

I hand Ash, Dev's wedding band. She slides it on his left ring finger and says. "I love you Devin. I'll love you even more when we won't see eye to eye. I'll love you when we get into a fight over something as stupid as a boiling pot of water on the stove. I'll love you when you seem like you're having a rough day and want your old life back. I'll love you till the day I die. This is also my second solemn vow."

Brother Kent says, smiling. "We'll have another song sung by Brooklyn Gayle Conway."

Brooklyn walks up on stage and sings, "I Wanna Make You Close Your Eyes," by Dierks Bentley. While Brooklyn is singing this song, everyone is watching Dev and Ash smiling and whispering between each other.

The song ends and Brooklyn exits the stage, walking back to the pough she was sitting in with Chad and her Sister and two Brothers. Brother Kent says smiling. "Devin, Ashley. I now pronounce you Husband and Wife. You may now kiss your bride." Dev pulls her face over to his and holds it while he kisses her softly, yet passionately. They both turn around while Brother Kent says. "I now pronounce you Mr.

and Mrs. Devin Bryan DeAtley. A reception follows right after the ceremony in the Grand BallRoom of the hotel." He exits the stage through a back door.

Ash and Dev walk out with her bouquet in her hands smiling with Dev beside her. Then Chris and I follow them smiling too. The line goes in order, Austin and Bailey, Darion and Michelle, Scott and Cara, Daimon and Zara, Carson and Callie, Miquel and Camerin, Justin and Chelsea, Dalton and Paige, Deidrich and Brionna, Zaiden and Josie, Zach and Maddi. We are all standing out in the hallway waiting for the guests to arrive into the ballroom. The guests stopped and congratulated the bride and groom before entering the ballroom.

The guests are finally into the ballroom and the DJ, Joshua David Jones walks out into the hallway and gathers everyone's names that are in the wedding party. He says, smiling. "Don't come in until you hear me over the speaker system. I'll announce your names as you enter. The bride and groom will be the last two that I'll holler for." He walks back into the ballroom, grabs himself a plate. He walks over to his stand and starts eating a little bit. Then he looks around to make sure everyone is sitting at their seats. He turns the music down and gets a CD ready to be played with each couple that he calls into the ballroom. He starts out with, "Good evening ladies and gentlemen. I'm Josh, the DJ for this wonderful occasion tonight. It's that time right now that I would love to announce the wedding party." He pauses for a few seconds and switches his cards. He says, "Alrighty first we have Zach and Maddi. Friends of the bride and groom. Let's hear it for them yall!" He claps his hands above his head with the beat of the music, and screams real loud into the microphone. "Alrighty, that was good, but I know we can do better than that. Get your voices together for Dalton and Paige. The groom's baby brother and his girlfriend. Let's hear it for them!" He claps his hands and screams. "Alright, getting better out there. Put your hands together for these two awesome people Miquel and Camerin. The groom's third oldest Sister and her Husband." He moves his card over to the next three couples. "That sounds a lot better, keep that up guys. Next is Carson and Callie. The groom's second oldest Sister and her Doctor of a Husband. Their oldest Daughter Blithe, stand up out there, sang "God Gave Me You." Put your hands together!" He waits for a few seconds and says. "Give it up for Daimon and Zara. The groom's second oldest Brother and his Wife." He waits while he switches his card to the second one and says. "Alright now crowd, we got to scream for these two lovely little people. It's the flower girl Josie and her cousin Zaiden the ring bearer. The groom's niece and nephew. Daughter of Justin and Chelsea. The son of Daimon and Zara." He finds a spot again and is laughing when he comes back over the microphone. "They're so cute aren't they? Now let's make some noise for the junior bride and junior groom. Brionna and her cousin Deidrich. Brionna is the Daughter of Darion and Michelle. Deidrich is the Son of Carson and Callie." He watches them walk to the table for the bridal party and get in their chairs with their plates already in front of them. Josh says, "Alright, let's hear a big wedding crowd noise for Scott and Cara. The groom's oldest Sister and her Husband." He waits for a few seconds and clears his throat, saying. "Okay, the crowd is starting to get tired of me. Don't be doing that guys. Let's liven this party up. Next we have Darion and Michelle. The groom's oldest Brother and his lovely Wife. Their oldest Daughter, Brooklyn sang the song "I Wanna Make You Close Your Eyes," let's hear it for them!" He turns his last card over and says smiling. "This next couple is the only Brother of the bride. Give it up for Austin and his Wife Bailey!" He sees the next couple and holds off for a few minutes. His voice speaks back into the microphone and says, smiling. "This next couple are the most important people in this room besides the bride and groom. If it weren't for them, there probably wouldn't be a wedding today. It's Chris and Breea! The groom's first youngest Sister, and her fiance." We walk in and see everyone standing up clapping and screaming for us. Chris bends me over his knee and kisses me square on the lips. He pulls me up and we get out of the way of the bride and groom. "Now, for the moment we've all waited for. Give it up for Mr. and Mrs. Devin Bryan DeAtley!"

Dev and Ash both strut in smiling real big and just scream along with the crowd. Dev dips Ash over his knee and kisses her fully. He pulls her up and smiles waving at everyone. They both walk through the tables and guests, making their way to the bridal party table. On their way through, they stop at every other table and greet their guests. They finally make it to their table and sit down. We all eat our food and after that's done we get our plates cleared off and Dev and Ash make their way out to the dance floor.

Josh's voice speaks volumes over the speaker system, saying. "Okay people, the bride and groom would love to have their first dance. Make room for them as they make their way to the dance floor." He puts the song that Brooklyn sang in the ceremony, "I Wanna Make You Close Your Eyes, by Dierks Bentley. Everyone steps onto the dance floor and crowds around to watch them dance their first dance as Husband and Wife. You see Dev and Ash both talking and laughing. When that was over we danced a few more dances and the DJ, Josh's voice announced. "It's time for the bride to have her Father come to the dance floor." Ash walks over to her Father and smiles. Grabs his hand and pulls him up out of his seat. Leading him onto the dance floor they start dancing to, "This Dance," by Scott Thomas. Every guest at the wedding sits and watches Ash and her Father dance to this song and cry with each other. That song is finally over and Josh's voice speaks. "Now, I would like for the groom to get his Mother. They have to dance to the song, "All To You," by Scott Keo. When a young man gets married, he's considered no longer his Mother's and Father's Son. He's considered as someone's Husband for the rest of his life." He pauses and sees Dianna making her way to the dance floor and announces. "Please, clear the way for the Mother of the groom." The music starts playing as soon as she reaches Devin. Being watched by everyone that's either sitting at their tables or standing on the edge of the dance floor. Ash is sitting at her Parents' and Dev's Parents' table watching her Husband and Mother in-law dance. She smiles when the song is over at Dianna and hugs her. She whispers something into Dianna's ear and hugs her even harder, wiping a tear out of her eye. She gets up and walks back to her table with her Husband.

Everyone is still at the reception at eleven thirty. That's when Josh's voice makes another announcement. "Okay, party people. You have been the greatest crowd that I have had since I started this company on the side of my real job. You all are the best. Thank you. It's time for the bride and groom to toss the bouquet. Come on out to the dance floor you two." He waits for a few minutes while Dev and Ash make their way to the dance floor. Ash has her bouquet in her hands and makes it to the dance floor and stands right in front of Josh's stand. "Now, we need to have all the single ladies to come out. Join in on the fun of catching the bride's bouquet." He waits for a few more minutes while all the single ladies walk out. He announces to Ash. "Now Ashley, we need you to throw your bouquet to all those single women out on the floor behind you. On my count though." He pauses for a few seconds and counts over the system. "One, two, three! Throw it!" She throws the bouquet and it magically appears in my hands. I shake it and smile. "Okay, we have a catcher. Her name is Breea Anderson, the matron of honor. Watch out Chris, your wedding is next." Laughing he takes a break, getting himself something to drink. He announces, "It's time for the groom to bring his lovely bride out to the dance floor. He's going to do the garter toss, so we need all the single men to come out to the dance floor." While there is a chair being set up for Ash to sit in, Dev is standing behind getting red faced at the fact that he's going to have to dig for her garter on her leg. Finally all the single men are out on the dance floor behind Dev and facing Ash. Josh's voice speaks over the system. "Okay, Dev. Let's get this done so that your lovely Wife can get to your honeymoon in time. I need you to take that garter off of her leg, hold it until I count to three and then throw it behind you." He puts on some stripping music and says, "Start!" Dev gets down on his knee and starts walking his fingers up Ash's right leg smiling at her while doing it. His fingers find it and he puts his head under her dress and drags it off with his teeth. Everyone in the crowd starts hooting and hollering real loud and laughing. His head pops out from under her dress, with the garter in his mouth, smiling. He looks at Josh and waves it around smiling. Ash gets up with the help from her Brother Austin and he helps her off the dance floor. Josh walks over to the speakers and turns the music off, he says over the speakers. "Okay, now on the count of three I want you to throw it. One, two, three!" Dev throws it into the crowd of single men and low and behold Chris walks out of the crowd holding the garter smiling. Dev walks over to stand by his Wife. Josh announces, "That was the best man ladies and gentlemen. He's also engaged to the matron of honor. They're getting married in December. Come on over here you two."

Chris and I walk over in front of the speakers and face the crowd. "Okay, Chris sit Breea down in that chair." Josh waits for a few seconds and makes sure that I'm sitting down. He says, "Okay, there is an old folklore that whoever catches the garter, that single guy has to put it on the single ladies leg that caught the bouquet. In this case I guess it's a good thing that they are getting married." Laughing, he takes a drink before continuing. "Okay, here's the one rule with this folklore. The further the single guy pushes the garter up the single lady's leg, the longer Devin and Ashley's marriage will be." He pauses and looks over at Chris, smiling Josh says. "So, I'd make sure that garter is pushed way up there Chris." Josh starts the stripping music again and he announces. "Start!"

Chris starts pushing the garter over my shoe and underneath my dress. I feel his hand rubbing the upper part of my thigh. I start giggling and beg him to stop, cause I can't stand the tickling part any longer. He keeps on pushing it until it's right up there against the line of my underwear. Josh's voice beams over the speakers and announces laughing. "Okay, Chris, Breea. Thanks for your cooperation. That is going to make Devin and Ashley have a lifetime of a marriage. Give those two a hand will you!" He starts some more music before the bride and groom cut the cake.

We all danced for about another hour, then Josh's voice booms over the system. "Okay, lovely people! It's time for the bride and groom to cut the cake. Gather around so that they can get their first slice of cake." He moves over to where he can see the bride and groom. Everyone else gathers around to watch them also. Dev and Ash get the slice cut and they take a piece from the piece they cut and hold it in their hands. Dev gives Ash a bite, neatly and easy while Ash gives Dev a bite all smashy and nasty. Everyone claps and laughs along with Dev and Ash.

Everyone danced their hearts out and just had a good time. Then it was time for the bride and groom to make their exit for their flight to their honeymoon in Cancun. Everyone lined up to say their goodbyes and blow bubbles at the newly weds. Chris and I were the first people out there and we were talking. "Yea, this night was the best night of Dev's life. I can tell you that from my past with him. He's always dreamed of having someone like Ash. I hope they do well together." Chris says, smiling.

"Yea, they will. They just can't stop believing in each other." I rub his back and see out of the corner of my eye that Dev and Ash are walking outside to their limo. I see the limo pull up, smile and say. "Well, they're coming out now." He turns around and holds me from behind. We both smile at them, blowing our bubbles at them. They both looked at us and threw us both a kiss and we threw one back at them. We stand out there watching their limo pull off into the distance. We walk back in and get our things. We walk out to the foyer and have the valet guy get Chris' truck. He drives around and holds the door open for us. I climb in first and then Chris climbs in after me. We drove back to our house.

We pulled into the driveway and ran into the house. We get inside to a warmer safe place and lock the front door. Snowball walks in meowing at us. We both look at her smiling and remember that we haven't fed or watered her today. Chris walks past her and I pick her up saying. "Sorry, baby girl. Didn't mean to be gone all day today. Daddy's going to get you some food and water." I put her down and watch her run over and rub up on Chris' legs meowing. He pours the water and food in her bowl, watching her and playing with her with his free hand. He gets done pouring it in her bowls and watches her attack the bowl. He smiles at her and looks up at me.

I'm resting my body against the frame of the kitchen door, watching him with the cat. I smile when he looks up at me and says, "I think I'm beat, I hope you have another sheet, pillow cases and cover that we could sleep with tonight. I don't feel like going to the laundry room in the basement to get them out of the dryer." He looked at me smiling and said. "Oh, don't worry about them being in the washer or dryer. I asked my Mom to come over and get them all the way done and make our bed for us." He grabbed my hand and walked me over to the living room near a CD player. The song, "Only You Can Love Me This Way," is playing. It's by Keith Urban. We dance with each other and start kissing. I kick my shoes off underneath the coffee table and keep on dancing with him. After we got done dancing we walked up to bed, exhausted from the night we just held onto each other and fell asleep.

Milton Keynes UK
Ingram Content Group UK Ltd.
UKHW020716030524
442155UK00003B/21